Island of Bewilderment

Middle East Literature in Translation
Michael Beard and Adnan Haydar, *Series Editors*

Selected Titles in Middle East Literature in Translation

Animals in Our Days: A Book of Stories
Mohamed Makhzangi; Chip Rossetti, trans.

The Ant's Gift: A Study of the Shahnameh
Shahrokh Meskoob; Dick Davis, trans.

Gaia, Queen of Ants
Hamid Ismailov; Shelley Fairweather-Vega, trans.

Hafez in Love: A Novel
Iraj Pezeshkzad; Pouneh Shabani-Jadidi and Patricia J. Higgins, trans.

Hot Maroc: A Novel
Yassin Adnan; Alexander E. Elinson, trans.

Packaged Lives: Ten Stories and a Novella
Haifa Zangana; Wen-chin Ouyang, trans.

Solitaire: A Novel
Hassouna Mosbahi; William Maynard Hutchins, trans.

Sons of the People: The Mamluk Trilogy
Reem Bassiouney; Roger Allen, trans.

For a full list of titles in this series,
visit https://press.syr.edu/supressbook-series
/middle-east-literature-in-translation/.

Island of Bewilderment

A Novel of Modern Iran

Simin Daneshvar

Translated from the Persian by
Patricia J. Higgins and Pouneh Shabani-Jadidi

Syracuse University Press

Originally published in Persian as *Jazireh-ye sargardani*
(Tehran: Kharazmi Publishers, 1993).

Syracuse University Press
Syracuse, New York 13244-5290

First Edition 2022

22 23 24 25 26 27 6 5 4 3 2 1

∞ The paper used in this publication meets the minimum requirements of the American National Standard for Information Sciences—Permanence of Paper for Printed Library Materials, ANSI Z39.48-1992.

For a listing of books published and distributed by Syracuse University Press, visit https://press.syr.edu/.

ISBN: 978-0-8156-1147-9 (paperback) 978-0-8156-5561-9 (e-book)

Library of Congress Cataloging-in-Publication Data

Names: Dānishvar, Sīmīn, 1921–2012, author. | Shabani-Jadidi, Pouneh, 1971– translator. | Higgins, Patricia J., translator.
Title: Island of bewilderment : a novel of modern Iran / Simin Daneshvar ; translated from the Persian by Patricia J. Higgins and Pouneh Shabani-Jadidi.
Other titles: Jazīrah-'i sargardānī. English
Description: First edition. | Syracuse, New York : Syracuse University Press, 2022. | Series: Middle East literature in translation | Includes bibliographical references.
Identifiers: LCCN 2022015693 (print) | LCCN 2022015694 (ebook) | ISBN 9780815611479 (paperback ; alk. paper) | ISBN 9780815655619 (ebook)
Subjects: LCSH: Iran—Fiction. | LCGFT: Novels.
Classification: LCC PK6561.D263 J3913 2022 (print) | LCC PK6561.D263 (ebook) | DDC 891/.5533—dc23/eng/20220408
LC record available at https://lccn.loc.gov/2022015693
LC ebook record available at https://lccn.loc.gov/2022015694

Manufactured in the United States of America

Contents

Translators' Introduction

Island of Bewilderment (*Jazireh-ye sargardani* in the original Persian) is a historical novel set in Tehran, Iran, in the early 1970s, just a few years before the revolution of 1977–79, which ended the fifty-year rule of the Pahlavis and led to the establishment of the Islamic Republic of Iran. It was a tumultuous period during which Iran was awash with oil money; the streets of northern Tehran, in particular, were peppered with American and European advisers, businessmen, and their families; thousands of Iranian students filled US and European universities; and Mohammad Reza Shah Pahlavi was depicted in the Western press as an enlightened monarch firmly leading his country into a golden age of economic development and cultural flowering. Yet the gap between rich and poor was widening; the rural population, squeezed out of their niche by the mechanization of agriculture and the importation of foodstuffs, was flocking to urban slums; there was growing resentment among the traditional middle and lower classes and among some intellectuals as well of the presence of so many foreigners; religious leaders railed increasingly publicly against the erosion of traditional values by Western cultural influences; and a few small groups of dissidents were preparing for and initiating armed struggle against the state. *Island of Bewilderment* vividly depicts many of these social, cultural, and economic fissures in Iran at that time and explores the roots and stirrings of political protest.

On page one we meet twenty-six-year-old Hasti Nourian, a college graduate, artist, and employee of Iran's Ministry of Art and Culture who aspires to be, in her own words, a "new woman"—independent, strong, and in control of her own destiny. Due to the early death of her father and her young mother's subsequent remarriage, Hasti and her brother have been raised by their paternal grandmother. They live in a modest, somewhat old-fashioned house near central Tehran, supported by their grandmother's retirement income from her former employment as a teacher. Meanwhile, Hasti's mother, Eshrat or Mother Eshi, lives in a large house in upscale, northern Tehran with her second husband, their young son, and half a dozen servants. Her mother's husband works with American educational experts, and the couple hobnobs with a mixed group of Americans, English-speaking Iranians, and a British expat and his Pakistani wife. Her mother's daytime life seems to revolve around a Western-style gym and spa, her hairdresser and seamstress, and party planning.

As the book opens, Hasti's mother has persuaded her to come to the spa where she plans to show her off to the mother of an eligible young man from a wealthy family. Hasti protests that she is opposed to this type of arranged marriage, but grudgingly goes along to please her mother. She herself has been in love for several years with a former college classmate, Morad Pakdel—an artistically minded architect whose radical political philosophy leads him to be exceedingly critical of Iran's Westernized bourgeois class. Hasti is torn between love for her mother and the attractiveness of some aspects of her mother's lifestyle, on the one hand, and the Marxist analyses of this and other friends, shared to some extent by her grandmother, on the other. When she meets the eligible young man, Salim Farrokhi, Hasti's life becomes even more complicated, since she is quite attracted to him, despite his religiosity and his somewhat conservative view of women's proper role in society, in contrast to her own more secular and feminist orientation.

This and several subplots become the framework through which the author explores family tensions and dynamics, neighborly relations in stable urban communities, the political thinking of students and the intelligentsia, different styles of religious belief and behavior, and the struggles of the poor "masses" concentrated in southern Tehran. A number of prominent Iranian writers and political activists are introduced to the reader by way of discussions among the main characters, as are many traditional Iranian customs, religious and secular. Political events in the years before the revolution of 1977–79 play an important part in the novel, as do several then-current social critiques, political philosophies, and activist movements, including revolutionary messianism and various versions of Marxism. An unusual feature of the book is that the author writes herself into the story. In the novel, she was one of Hasti's professors who has become a close friend and who continues to mentor Hasti as she negotiates turbulent emotional and political waters.

When *Jazireh-ye sargardani* was published in 1993, its author, Simin Daneshvar, was already well-known as a skilled and accomplished writer of prose literature, especially fiction. Her early collection of short stories, *Atash-e khamoush* (The Quenched Fire), published in 1948, was well received and widely acclaimed as the first collection of short stories by an Iranian woman. Similarly, her first novel, *Savushun*, published in 1969, is recognized as the first novel published by an Iranian woman. Moreover, *Savushun* soon became the all-time best-selling novel in Iran (Milani 1992, 183). The novel has been translated into English by M. R. Ghanoonparvar as *Savushun: A Novel about Modern Iran* (1990) and by Roxane Zand as *A Persian Requiem* (1991) and into a dozen other languages as well, including Russian, German, Dutch, French, Italian, Spanish, Chinese, and Turkish. It has also been widely praised by literary critics worldwide for its development of fully rounded characters, female as well as male; its beautifully detailed descriptions of times, places, scenes, interactions, and the inner lives of key characters; and its realistic and balanced depictions of social and cultural tensions between Iranians and World War II Allied occupying forces. A number of Daneshvar's short stories have also been translated into English and other languages, and they have enjoyed similar literary acclaim.

While *Jazireh-ye sargardani* was not as wildly successful in Iran as Daneshvar's first novel, it was "welcomed by a number of scholars and critics from a number of perspectives" (Khalifi and Moshayedi 2019, 25). As background to their own analysis of the book, Khalifi and Moshayedi cite eight other scholars who had previously published analyses and critiques of *Jazireh-ye sargardani*. These scholars highlight the book's concern with instability versus stability, identity and colonialism, relativism and philosophical uncertainty, and the component of time in human experience—all themes that transcend the book's specific locale.

Simin Daneshvar was born in Shiraz in 1921 and spent the first twenty years of her life in that southern Iranian city. Her father, Mohammad Ali

Daneshvar, was a physician, and her mother, Qamar al-Saltaneh Hekmat, was an artist and the principal of an art school for girls. Simin completed her primary and secondary education at Mehr Ain English-Persian bilingual school and then attended Tehran University to pursue her studies in Persian literature. After her father's death in 1941, Simin began writing essays for Radio Tehran and the newspaper *Iran* under the pseudonym Shirazi-ye Binam (Anonymous Shirazi) to support herself (Milani 1992, 182; Mozaffari 2005, 82).

One year after publishing her first collection of short stories (Daneshvar 1948), Daneshvar received her doctorate in Persian literature from Tehran University. In 1952 she received a Fulbright scholarship to study estheticism for two years at Stanford University, where she worked closely with the American novelist Wallace Stegner (1909–93) and made significant improvements in her writing style. Returning to Iran, Daneshvar continued to write and publish fiction and to be active in Tehran literary circles. She also translated several American and European classic novels from English into Persian, including *The Cherry Orchard* and *Enemies* by Anton Chekhov, *The Scarlet Letter* by Nathaniel Hawthorne, and *Arms and the Man* by George Bernard Shaw. In addition, she taught art history at Tehran University from 1959 until her retirement in 1979. While many intellectuals left Iran to relocate in Europe or the United States after the establishment of the Islamic Republic, Daneshvar remained in Tehran, where she continued to write and publish until her death in 2012.

During the later years of her life, Daneshvar was criticized by some for not protesting sufficiently strongly against the Islamic Republic regime, whether by choosing self-exile, by giving more support to the Iranian Writers' Association, or by making more overt anti-government statements (BBC Persian 2013). The very fact that she could continue to publish while the works of other prominent writers were banned or drastically censored, and while some writers were assassinated or died under mysterious circumstances, may have engendered the suspicions of some and the envy of others. One can interpret some passages in *Island of Bewilderment* as addressing this situation, such as the character Simin's statements concerning her strong roots and attachments to her home and surroundings and their associated memories. In her 1988 letter to the reader (published in *Daneshvar's Playhouse*), she states, "I wanted to stay home to be a witness of my own time and place, and give testimony in my writing" (Daneshvar 1988, 160).

In 1950 Simin Daneshvar married the already prominent Iranian intellectual, writer, and social critic Jalal Al-e Ahmad (1923–69). Al-e Ahmad is best known for his book *Gharbzadegi*, translated as *Gharbzadegi [Weststruckness]* by John Green and Ahmad Alizadeh (1982) and as *Plagued by the West* by Paul Sprachman (1982). Written in 1962, revised in 1964, but not openly published or distributed in Iran until 1978 (Green 1982, vii), this extended essay is bluntly critical of the impact of the West on Iranian society and culture. It was widely circulated unofficially from 1962 on and contributed to Al-e Ahmad's almost cultlike status among some sectors of Iranian youth. Al-e Ahmad also wrote short stories, novels, ethnographies, travelogues, and other essays, most similarly critical of the Westernization process in Iran.

Though the vehicles through which they chose to express themselves and their styles of writing differed substantially, Daneshvar and Al-e Ahmad shared many ideas and values and encouraged and assisted each other in their work. Their marriage was unusual for its time and place in that they acted as partners and respected and supported each other. Daneshvar was able to exercise a degree of autonomy, agency, independence, and freedom usually reserved only for men in mid-twentieth-century Iran. Daneshvar and Al-e Ahmad also shared a wide literary circle and were among the founders of the Iranian Writers' Association. The two had no children, but they took on parental-like roles with respect to many students and young writers. In 1981 Daneshvar wrote about her late husband in a short monograph called *Ghorub-e Jalal*, translated by Farzaneh Milani and Jo-Anne Hart as "Jalal's Sunset" (1986) and by Maryam Mafi as "The Loss of Jalal" (1989b).

Daneshvar published five volumes of short stories, many of which first graced the pages of several different literary magazines, including *Omid* and *Banu*, and the newspaper *Kayhan*. In 1961 she published her second collection, *Shahri chon behesht* (A City Like Paradise), and her third collection, *Be ki salam konam?* (To Whom Should I Say Hello?), was published in 1980. *Az parandeh-ha-ye mohajer bepors* (Ask the Migratory Birds) was published in 1997, and *Entekhab* (Choice) in 2007. Several of these short stories have been translated and published in English in two collections: *Daneshvar's Playhouse*, translated by Maryam Mafi (1989a), and *Sutra and Other Stories*, translated by Hasan Javadi and Amin Neshati (1994). A number of her short stories have also appeared in English in multiauthored anthologies, including *Modern Persian Short Stories* (Southgate 1980), *Strange Times, My Dear* (Mozaffari 2005), *Afsaneh: Short Stories by Iranian Women* (Basmenji 2005), and *Tablet and Pen: Literary Landscapes from the Modern Middle East* (Aslan 2011). (For a more complete list, see Motlagh 2022).

In addition to *Savushun* and *Jazireh-ye sargardani*, Daneshvar published a third novel, *Sarban sargardan* (Wandering Cameleer) (2001), and wrote a fourth, *Kuh-e sargardan* (Wandering Mountain), which has not been published. *Jazireh-ye sargardani* and *Sarban sargardan* were intended to be part of a trilogy, of which *Kuh-e sargardan* was to be the third book. In 2004 Daneshvar announced that *Kuh-e sargardan* was about to be published, but various delays ensued. It is widely believed that the manuscript was having difficulty getting approval for publication from the Iranian government (Ahmad 2015, 153). In addition, after 2007 Daneshvar began experiencing more health problems, and her closest adviser in publishing, Alireza Haidari, died in 2008. It was later reported by *Nafeh Monthly Literary Journal* that the manuscript had been lost since 2007 (ISNA [2010]; see also *Voice of America* [2014]).

All of Daneshvar's novels are historical fiction, and all draw heavily on her own personal experiences. Each is set at a critical juncture in Iran's twentieth-century history; thus, they provide windows into the most important topics of their times, whether political, social, or intellectual. As indicated earlier, *Savushun* is set in the 1940s during the World War II occupation of much of Iran by outside political powers—the British in the south and the Russians in the north. Daneshvar was eighteen and living in Iran when World War II started, and she was twenty-four when it ended, helping her to paint a very realistic picture of the period. This era and especially 1941, the year that Reza Shah was deposed by the Allied Powers because he was believed to be supportive of Nazi Germany, is one of the most decisive periods of Iran's recent history. The Allies replaced Reza

Shah with his son and crown prince, Mohammad Reza Shah Pahlavi, then only twenty-two years old.

Daneshvar's two subsequently published novels are set at the end of the Pahlavi period and the beginning of the Islamic Republic era. *Jazireh-ye sargardani* (*Island of Bewilderment*) makes multiple references as well to political events of the 1950s and 1960s which laid the foundation for the 1977–79 revolution. In particular, the British- and US-supported ousting of democratically elected Prime Minister Mohammad Mosaddeq in 1953 and the subsequent facilitation of Mohammad Reza Shah's assumption of dictatorial powers are referenced repeatedly in *Island of Bewilderment.* The second book in the planned trilogy, *Sarban sargardan*, traces the lives of some of the same characters as they mature and as they are impacted by the growing unrest of the mid- to late 1970s. This book takes the story through the departure of the shah, Khomeini's arrival from France, the roaming of teenage armed supporters of Khomeini in search of "dissidents," and the beginning of the Iraq-Iran War in September 1980. It is presumed that *Kuh-e sargardan* was set in the 1980s as the Islamic government became more fully established, which may at least partially explain the publishing delays.

The title *Jazireh-ye sargardani* has been interpreted by some as an allusion to Iran (so famously referred to by President Jimmy Carter in 1977, on the eve of the revolution, as "an island of stability"). The title of the second book, *Sarban sargardan*, is said to refer to Ayatollah Khomeini, who was a source of inspiration for some of the revolutionary forces and whose faction prevailed in the post-revolutionary power struggle. Though the characters in *Island of Bewilderment* seem to be searching for philosophical and practical answers to the problems of their lives and their society, there is hope for a better future, similar to the feeling many Iranians had right before the revolution. In *Sarban sargardan*, however, everything happens contrary to expectations, just as happened in the early postrevolutionary period in Iran—with the suppression of opposition groups, the collapse of Iran's economy, rising inflation, and the onset of the war with Iraq.

Island of Bewilderment is autobiographical in many respects. Not only is the author present in the novel as Hasti's mentor and friend, but so are her husband, Jalal Al-e Ahmad; their friend, the political theorist Khalil

Maleki (1901–69); and such contemporary writers as Gholam-Hossein Sa'edi (1935–85). Hasti is in many ways like Simin Daneshvar—for example, in her desire to be an independent woman, in her delay of marriage, and in her reluctance to prioritize political action over art. As a mentee of Simin, the character Hasti repeats words, opinions, and sentiments she has heard expressed by Simin, and those tend to be opinions and sentiments that the author Daneshvar has expressed in other places as well, such as in her letter to the reader published in *Daneshvar's Playhouse* (Daneshvar 1989a, 155–70).

In other cases, the problems and actions of characters are quite parallel to events in Daneshvar's own life or in the lives of her friends. For example, the character Simin is confronted and questioned by a "student" she suspects to be an agent of the secret police. Whether or not exactly such an incident actually occurred in her life, we know that the writer Simin Daneshvar was shown written evidence toward the end of her teaching career that the secret police had actively blocked her promotion to a tenured position (Milani 1992, 183). As another example, when the author Simin Daneshvar describes one of the characters going to observe her son from afar in front of his school, she seems to be recalling actions of her friend, the noted modern feminist poet of Iran Forough Farrokhzad (1934–67), who was not allowed to see her son after her divorce from his father.

In addition, in the author's portrayals of the three generations of women—Hasti, Mother Eshi, and Grandmother—she seems to be reflecting, to some extent, on three periods of her own life. In her portrayal of Grandmother, in particular, Daneshvar explores issues of aging and reflects on the passage of time and the reverberation of memories. These issues are also explored through the characterization of the ailing Professor Mani and his wife and the aging British expat.

When Daneshvar first began writing fiction, her depiction of the often mundane, daily lives of ordinary people was unusual in Persian literature, as was her focus on female characters, who are almost always her main protagonists. In *Island of Bewilderment*, Hasti, Mother Eshi, and Grandmother are the best developed characters. Their thoughts, dreams, and inner lives are shared with the reader in a way that those of other characters are not. Passages that enter into Hasti's mind are found throughout the book, and most of a chapter each is devoted to the thoughts and dreams of Mother Eshi and Grandmother.

All three of these female characters are strong, independent women, each in her own style. Grandmother, though traditional in many ways, was effectively a single mother, supporting her grandchildren while furthering her own education; speaking out in class and challenging her (male) professors; "mothering" her younger college classmates; and serving as a pillar of the community in her urban neighborhood. Mother Eshi spends freely of her husband's money, goes where and when she likes without consulting a male guardian, and by the end of the story is planning to pursue high school and college degrees for herself. The only character who approaches the common, Western image of the oppressed Middle Eastern woman is Salim's mother, Mrs. Farrokhi. Though holding wealth of her own and physically comfortable, she is ignored by her husband, unhappy in her marriage, psychologically depressed, and pathologically obese. Yet, she seems to cling to the notion that a bad husband is better than no husband.

Issues of gender and women's rights and their nonobservance in much of Iranian society figure prominently in all the works of Simin Daneshvar. At times, she uses satire to bring forth these issues, strengthening their impact on the reader. At other times the narrator and/or the characters discuss and display various positions on these issues. For example, in *Island of Bewilderment*, the character Simin discusses these issues in her classes and consciously tries to set an example of female strength for her students. Elsewhere in the book, Salim and Hasti exchange opinions about the proper roles of women, especially as wives and mothers; Morad promotes the independence of the women in his life and encourages their political participation; and Mother Eshi strives for gender equality by emulating the romantic activities of men.

Many Persian proper names carry meanings, of which Persian-language readers would be aware, although those meanings would not always be at the top of their minds (just as in English the names May and Rose, Buzz and Rich, Johnson and Smith carry meanings). It does not seem to be coincidental, however, that Daneshvar chose the name Hasti, which means "existence," for her main character. When that meaning is brought to the fore by the words or thoughts of the characters, we have so indicated in the translation. Though less of a point is made of it, Salim means "flawless," Morad means "desire," and Eshrat means "pleasure." Similarly, Pakdel, Morad's family name, means "purehearted." As the reader of the novel will recognize, the qualities associated with the meanings of these names do bear some resemblance to the personalities and behavior of these characters.

The political message of *Island of Bewilderment* is somewhat mixed. Overall, the book is critical of the excesses of the Pahlavi era—the conspicuous consumption of some classes, the privileging of Western culture, and the living conditions in the slums and shantytowns of southern Tehran, for example. It is also sympathetic toward the political ideals and activism of youth. On the other hand, Hasti refuses to adopt the position of any particular political party, just as Simin Daneshvar refused to join even the party headed by her close friend Khalil Maleki (Daneshvar 1989, 165). That an entire chapter is given to the description of Nowruz, the Persian New Year, and the Zoroastrian and pre-Islamic ideology and customs associated with it; that most of the characters in the book are not particularly religious; that the only cleric in the book is not portrayed very positively—these features have been taken by some as an indication that the author was pushing back against the Islamic identity promoted for Iran by the government in 1993 when the book was published (Ahmad 2015).

Yet the situations described and the range of actions and opinions expressed by the characters seem quite realistic for the 1970s (rather than shaped by the 1990s) to the translators, particularly to Higgins, who was completing her doctoral studies in Tehran in 1969–71 and was a Fulbright Lecturer at Tehran University in 1977–78. About the same age then as Hasti, her closest friends were mostly college-educated Iranian youth, some recently returned from studies abroad, and their topics of conversation included many of the themes, events, and intellectual, philosophical, and political ideas referenced in this book. Thus, she could bring some firsthand familiarity to rendering descriptions and dialogue of the book into English prose.

To assist the reader not well acquainted with twentieth-century Iranian history and Persian literature, we have added a list of characters and persons mentioned in the novel. An asterisk indicates those who are real people. Anyone who would like more information about any of these people beyond the very brief identification we provide can find it for most with a simple internet search. For more information on Iran in the 1950s, 1960s, and 1970s, we recommend the relevant chapters from histories of modern Iran by Abrahamian (1982), Amanat (2017), Ansari (2003), and Richard (2019).

In addition to the characters and persons mentioned list, we provide a glossary defining the various titles, terms of endearment, places, special days, and culturally specific practices mentioned in the book. We have made some minimal additions to the text, such as parenthetical explanations of certain references and the indication that certain lines are well-known quotes from Persian poetry easily identified by readers of the original text.

With respect to the spelling of names of people and places, we have followed the transliteration scheme of the Association for Iranian Studies due to its simplicity, except that we have not distinguished between the long and short *a*. The Persian letter *'ayn*, which is a soft glottal stop, is omitted in the novel from the initial position when it is not pronounced, and it is marked by /'/ in the medial position. The letter *hamza* is marked by /'/. In the list of persons mentioned, the *'ayn* is shown when the full transliterated name of a historical personage is included in the identification. If the Latinized form of a proper personal or place name is commonly used, the name is not transliterated here.

We would like to thank Rachel Cohen and two anonymous reviewers for their careful reading of the manuscript and their many useful corrections and suggestions, and Leila Rahimi Bahmany for reviewing selected portions of the text. Also, Simin Shabani clarified for us many details concerning Tehran of the 1970s and selected customs and sayings based on her long residence in the city and her extensive reading. We would also like to thank the management of Kharazmi Publishers for permission to publish this translation and Hadi Hosseinzadegan of Qoqnoos Publishers for putting us in touch with them. The cover image is an untitled painting by Sohrab Sepehri (1928–80), the Iranian artist-poet mentioned in the novel. The painting is held by the Tehran Museum of Contemporary Art.

The book was originally dedicated by Simin Daneshvar to Shirin and Dr. Abdolhossein Sheikh.

Due to both its subject matter and its literary qualities, *Island of Bewilderment* is deserving of wider appreciation within the worldwide audience of English-language readers. We hope you find this novel by the experienced and highly regarded writer Simin Daneshvar interesting, entertaining, and informative.

References

Abrahamian, Ervand. 1982. *Iran between Two Revolutions.* Princeton, NJ: Princeton Univ. Press.

Ahmad, Razi. 2015. "A Postcolonial Reading of Simin Daneshvar's Novels: The Spiritual and the Material Domains in *Savushun*, *Jazira-ye Sargardani*, and *Sarban-e Sargardan*." In *Persian Language, Literature, and Culture: New Leaves, Fresh Looks*, edited by Kamran Talattof, 141–62. New York: Routledge.

Al-e Ahmad, Jalal. 1978. *Gharbzadegi* [Weststruckness]. Tehran: Ravaq Publishers.

Amanat, Abbas. 2017. *Iran: A Modern History.* New Haven, CT: Yale Univ. Press.

Ansari, Ali M. 2003. *Modern Iran since 1921: The Pahlavis and After.* London: Longman.

Aslan, Reza, ed. 2011. *Tablet and Pen: Literary Landscapes from the Modern Middle East.* New York: W. W. Norton.

Basmenji, Kaveh, ed. 2005. *Afsaneh: Short Stories by Iranian Women.* London: Saqi Books.

BBC Persian. 2013. *Simin saken-e jazire-ye sargardani* [Simin, Resident of a Wandering Island]. YouTube, March 30, 2013. https://www.youtube.com/watch?v=uPy5_O-44VQ.

Daneshvar, Simin. 1948. *Atash-e khamoush* [The Quenched Fire]. Tehran: Elmi.

———. 1961. *Shahri chon behesht* [A City Like Paradise]. Tehran: Kharazmi.

———. 1969. *Savushun.* Tehran: Kharazmi Publishing House.

———. 1980. *Be ki salam konam?* [To Whom Should I Say Hello?]. Tehran: Kharazmi Publishing House.

———. 1981. *Ghorub-e Jalal* [The Sunset of Jalal]. Tehran: Ravaq.

———. 1989. "'My Heart Aches for Your Suffering and Patience': A Letter to the Reader." In *Daneshvar's Playhouse*, translated by Maryam Mafi, 155–70. Washington, DC: Mage Publishers.

———. 1993. *Jazireh-ye sargardani* [Island of Bewilderment]. Tehran: Kharazmi Publishing House.

———. 1997 *Az parandeh-ha-ye mohajer bepors* [Ask the Migratory Birds]. Tehran: Nashr-e no.

———. 2001. *Sarban sargardan* [Wandering Cameleer]. Tehran: Kharazmi Publishing House.

———. 2007. *Entekhab* [Choice]. Tehran: Qatreh Publishers.

Ghanoonparvar, M. R., trans. 1990. *Savushun: A Novel about Modern Iran.* Washington, DC: Mage.

Green, John. 1982. "Translators' Introduction." In *Garbzadegi [Weststruckness].* Translated by John Green and Ahmad Alizadeh, vii–xviii. Lexington, KY: Mazda.

Green, John, and Ahmad Alizadeh, trans. 1982. *Garbzadegi [Weststruckness].* Lexington, KY: Mazda.

ISNA. 2010. "Majera-ye gomshodan-e akharin roman-e Simin-e Daneshvar" [Story of the Loss of Simin Daneshvar's Last Novel]. Khabar Online, https://www.khabaronline.ir/news/100924/%D9%85%D8%A7%D8%AC%D8%B1%D8%A7%DB%8C-%DA%AF%D9%85%D8%B4%D8%AF%D9%86-%D8%A2%D8%AE%D8%B1%DB%8C%D9%86-%D8%B1%D9%85%D8%A7%D9%86-%D8%B3%DB%8C%D9%85%DB%8C%D9%86-%D8%AF%D8%A7%D9%86%D8%B4%D9%88%D8%B1.

Javadi, Hasan, and Amin Neshati, trans. 1994. *Sutra and Other Stories.* Washington, DC: Mage.

Khalifi, Azadeh, and Jalil Moshayedi. 2019. "The Study of Modernism in Simin Daneshvar's Novel *Wondering Island.*" *International Journal of English Language & Translation Studies* 7, no. 1 (2019): 25–34.

Mafi, Maryam, trans. 1989a. *Daneshvar's Playhouse.* Washington, DC: Mage.

———. 1989b. "The Loss of Jalal." In *Daneshvar's Playhouse*, 131–53. Washington, DC: Mage.

———. 1989c. "Translator's Afterword." In *Daneshvar's Playhouse*, 173–83. Washington, DC: Mage.

Milani, Farzaneh. 1992. *Veils and Words: The Emerging Voices of Iranian Women Writers.* Syracuse, NY: Syracuse Univ. Press.

Milani, Farzaneh, and Jo-Ann Hart, trans. 1986. "Jalal's Sunset." *Iranian Studies* 19, no. 1 (1986): 47–63.

Motlagh, Amy. 2022. "The Persian Short Story and Its Histories of Translation." In *The Routledge Handbook of Persian Literary Translation*, edited by

Pouneh Shabani-Jadidi, Patricia J. Higgins, and Michelle Quay, 145–59. New York: Routledge.

Mozaffari, Nahid, ed. 2005. *Strange Times, My Dear.* New York: Arcade Publishing.

Richard, Yann. 2019. *Iran: A Social and Political History since the Qajars.* Cambridge: Cambridge Univ. Press.

Rooney, Terrie. 2003. "Daneshvar, Simin 1921–." In *Contemporary Authors*, vol. 206, 93–96.

Southgate, Minoo, trans. 1980. *Modern Persian Short Stories.* Washington, DC: Three Continents Press.

Sprachman, Paul, trans. 1982. *Plagued by the West.* Delmar, NY: Caravan Books.

Voice of America Farsi. 2014. "Sarnevesht-e raz-alud-e akharin ketab-e Simin-e Daneshvar" [The Mysterious Biography of Simin Daneshvar's Last Book]. VOA News Online, https://ir.voanews.com/persiannewsiran/simin-daneshvar-writer-iran-book-lost.

Zand, Roxane, trans. 1991. *A Persian Requiem.* New York: George Braziller.

Island of Bewilderment

1

It was not yet dawn. Light from the window fell on Hasti's eyelids and found its way into her heart. A star in her heart winked back. She rose and sat on her bed. Everything was fine. For a moment, like all trusting optimists, she believed that day had been born from the heart of night like the water of life from within the primordial darkness, but the light only lasted a moment: morning had been tarnished at the very beginning by its own lie.

Hasti removed the wax-soaked cotton wads from her ears, and the snoring of her grandmother, who was sleeping in the bed opposite hers, merged with the darkness. Darkness and sound. Hasti lay down and closed her eyes.

She was dreaming. She is in unknown territory. She's sweating from excessive heat; her dress is stuck to her body; she's panting from thirst. She sees trees she doesn't recognize with burnt leaves and broken limbs. They throw no shadow. Several women with black, head-to-toe, Arab-style chadors are coming forward, their hands holding the pots that are on their heads. The chins and necks of the women have tattooed images of scorpions, snakes; no, this one is an image of a star, and that woman has an image of the crescent moon on her chin. Hasti's eyes do not see clearly enough to recognize all the images. She asks a woman with an image of a scorpion under her throat, the tail of the scorpion reaching to her chin, "These trees . . . ?" The woman answers offhandedly, "Cedar trees." Hasti thinks that she is referring to the two trees in paradise . . . of which the poet Hafez says one should not expect kindness.

Yet Hasti looks for kindness from one burnt tree and sits under it. There is no shade but one can lean against it. The ground beneath the tree is covered with dead sparrows, their wings broken . . . It seems that blood has also been spilled. Cartridge shells are everywhere. Several cats and dogs are coming, paying no attention to one another. Each is missing either a forepaw or a hind paw. All of them are blind. It is as though a mortar shell has fallen and wounded them. The cats are meowing. The dogs are howling. Perhaps they are hungry. Don't they see all those dead sparrows under the trees? The odor of carcasses . . . Perhaps they are saying silently, "Is there no one to respond to our cries?"

Hasti passes a ruined wall, goes over bricks and cartridge shells, and arrives at a burnt lawn. She knows it's a lawn because of the sign beside it: PLEASE DO NOT WALK ON THE LAWN. So much dirt is spread over the lawn—it has so many pits—and there's a metal cylinder the size of the hot water heater in their house. A collapsed building can be seen in the distance. Several closed doors are visible. Hasti sees herself groping the ground, but she can't find a key.

Hasti sees two skeletons coming forward in long, jerky strides. They stand in front of her. They hug each other and kiss.

And now Hasti is standing next to a water well. There is neither pulley nor rope.

A voice says, "Those who had the rope and those who had the key, they have all vanished."

Grandmother was saying, "I have been standing in the waiting room, eyes on the route of the train of death." And now each breath, which splits and scratches her chest, sounds like a train that has barely arrived before it starts off again.

Hasti awoke. The vanguard of true dawn had yet to appear.

As quietly as a cat, Grandmother got up from bed. She took the kettle of water from beside the charcoal heater at the end of the room and went outside to relieve herself and cleanse herself for prayer. She returned in the same quiet manner, taking her prayer bundle out of the wardrobe. It was a full and precious bundle that held Grandmother's dearest possessions. A little prayer rug with a drawing of an altar; within the arch of the two-columned altar was the spot for spreading the prayer cloth. Grandmother's mother and others before her had probably spread their prayer rugs at the same place, in the same house, and positioned their foreheads in prostration on the same spot. The Quran was also the same Quran from which all of Grandmother's now-buried ancestors had heard or read and felt in their souls the word of God. It was a handwritten Quran that had been illuminated. In the margin at the beginning of each sura a picture of a cypress tree gave one peace and the good tidings that God is kind and forgiving.

Once, Grandmother knew the word of God completely by heart. But now, where has that memory gone? Hasti had bought a magnifying glass for her. Grandmother kissed the Quran and placed it on top of the prayer rug.

The album of photos of her son and his faded letters were also in the prayer bundle. There, too, was her son's agate ring, which Grandmother herself had removed from his blood-splattered finger.

Grandmother stood to pray. Depending on the degree of her strength or her agitation about the day ahead, she contented herself with only one morning prayer, or she added more. Many times, Hasti had counted four or five, even up to ten times that Grandmother had stood in prayer and finished over and over again, until the sun shone on her face where time had left its mark, with lines and spots and wrinkles and bags and hollows.

That day, Grandmother said only one morning prayer. When she had finished, she asked, "Hasti dear, are you awake?" She repeated her usual mantra: "Be more powerful than the sun and rise sooner than it does." But today she also said something new: "There's plenty of time for sleeping to boot. We are all going to sleep hundreds of thousands of years in the earth . . ."

Hasti ignored the remainder of Grandmother's words, which were about the Resurrection and the trumpet of the angel Israfil. She thought, alluding to Khayyam's poem, *If luck is with us, we will grow like blades of grass by the side of a stream; but as for me, I would be happy being no more than the potters' clay, O Khayyam.*

She wished she could sleep until noon. She wished she could just stretch out and read Truman Capote's *In Cold Blood.*

That Friday Grandmother was expecting a visitor. Akhtar Iran was coming, and together they would remove the charcoal heater. Although it was early in the season, Hasti had bought an Aladdin portable kerosene heater from the first paycheck that she had received. A magic lamp.

Hasti yawned, stood up, and opened the window. The weather was mild. The sun was shining and dancing on the dry branches of the trees in the courtyard. The sun kissed the branches and gave the welcome news that spring was on its way. But one could not trust even the sun's good tidings. Spring weather sometimes gets delayed. Hasti remembered that once it had snowed in Tehran on the third day of spring. *Was it the third or the fourth*?

When the doorbell rang Hasti was ready, except for carrying out her mother's instructions. Her mother had said to wear her New Year's clothes. Yesterday evening Hasti had stopped by Marusa's, her mother's Russian seamstress, but her dark red suit was not ready. Her mother had said to go to the hairdresser and to sleep in a way that her hairdo would not be spoiled. She had advised that she stick her forehead to the pillow. Hasti had gone to the hairdresser, but she had slept like a normal person, and the curls and ringlets of her hair had been disturbed. Her mother had said to paint her nails dark red, put on dark red lipstick, and take off the grease of the lipstick with a facial tissue. She should do this two or three times—the tried-and-true secret of invisible makeup. Hasti had not done any of this.

Hasti opened the door. Her mother's husband's driver was standing next to the back door of the car. He said hello and closed the button of his coat with much difficulty. His stomach pressed on the button, which was about to pop off.

"Just a minute," Hasti said, and she went back into the house.

Grandmother was sitting by the charcoal heater looking at the courtyard through the open window. Hasti hugged her from behind and kissed her white hair.

When they arrived at Pahlavi Avenue, the gate of the Marble Palace was open. Here and there gardeners were trimming the trees, sifting dirt, and planting seedlings in the edges of the little garden plots. They were arranging, clipping, and grooming it all. Whenever Mr. Ganjur, her mother's husband, wanted to get rid of bothersome people, he would give his address by saying, "Pahlavi Avenue, next to the shah's house." But the Marble Palace wasn't the shah's house, nor was Mr. Ganjur's house next to it.

The gate to Mother Eshi's garden was open. Workers were painting the pool blue. The car stopped by the veranda off the family room. As

Hasti had foreseen, the button on the driver's coat could not withstand the pressure of his stomach. He jumped out of the driver's seat with his coat unbuttoned.

The family room was warm and clean. Hasti saw her mother in her deep blue, woolen dressing gown standing next to the closed door of the sitting room, her ear glued to the door . . . When she saw Hasti, she left her post and came to her side. She kissed her, scrutinized her head to toe, and said, "Oh, my God! Didn't I say to wear your New Year's outfit?"

When Hasti explained that it wasn't ready, her mother said angrily, "How dare this Russian bear, Marusa, not finish my child's clothes on time!" She pulled aside the edge of Hasti's coat. "Thank God you've worn a black skirt. Take off your coat and skirt so that I can give them to Pasita to iron."

Hasti opened the button of her coat. "You're not showing me off for marriage, are you?" As she took off her coat she added, "You know that I hate showing myself off."

Hasti, wearing her mother's peach-colored dressing gown, was sitting on the sofa in the family room, her coat and skirt beside her. She stirred her tea and drew in the scent of Darjeeling as though it were caressing her soul. Her mother was sitting in the armchair across from her, thinking.

"Well?" Hasti said.

"Keshvar, the dealer," her mother replied, "has been here since early morning to see Ahmad. You know that Ahmad borrows and lends money and takes interest. He takes 3 percent interest. And Keshvar deposits jewelry with him."

Mother Eshi rose, returned to her post, and put her ear to the closed door. "I hope God will put it in Ahmad's heart to take a piece of jewelry for me as his profit," she said softly. "I would even be happy with emerald."

When she sat, she laughed and said, "You won't believe what a blaze I set aflame last night. I danced the Baba Karam at Dr. Bahari's party, and I out-flirted all the American women. Dr. Bahari said, 'Well done!'"

Hasti laughed. "Now you want a reward?"

"Well, of course!"

"Couldn't you lower your expectation a bit," Hasti said, "and be happy, for example, with turquoise?"

"No. Emerald." Mother Eshi thought for a moment and added, "Hasti, do you remember that deaf and dumb Seyyed who came here a couple months ago and stayed for two weeks? He told the fortunes of our American friends by using sign language, and Ahmad interpreted for them. For me he signed that I would soon come into possession of a jewel or something, but Ahmad denied it. He said that he didn't give any such sign . . ."

"That deaf and dumb Seyyed is a charlatan," Hasti said. "He is neither deaf nor dumb . . ."

The door of the sitting room opened, and Keshvar and Mr. Ganjur came out. Hasti rose and greeted them. Mr. Ganjur ran his hand through his salt-and-pepper hair and pulled up his pajama bottoms. He sat next to Mother Eshi, lit a cigarette, and yelled, "Naneh Agha, bring tea! Make sure it's freshly brewed."

A bell for summoning the household help was on the table. Mother Eshi pressed her finger on its button.

Hasti stood in front of Parviz's aquarium, which was installed on the wall of the room. She turned on its electric light and entertained herself watching the exotic fish that glided and wriggled among the rocks, moss, and miniature plants and the bubbles that rose from the aerator. No, it wasn't a scene worth painting. It was a superficially joyful object for the spoiled sons of those who charge interest, though it's religiously forbidden, and serve as fixers for Americans, however much they themselves say they are educational experts. They also have misleadingly good-looking bodies and a style that causes American women around them to say, "Oh, how handsome!"

Hasti heard Mr. Ganjur saying to Mother Eshi, "Pretty woman, don't forget when you are returning from Bowling Center to give Parviz and Taqi Khan a ride home from the zoo," and Mother Eshi saying, "What do you mean? How could I forget?"

Keshvar was sitting on the sofa. Plump with a peaches-and-cream complexion, she was wearing a chador and made a show of veiling her face in front of Mr. Ganjur. Hasti sat next to her.

Pasita entered carrying Parviz's cat.

"Well, where's the tea?" Mr. Ganjur asked.

Pasita answered in English. "Naneh Agha is bringing it." She gave the cat to Mother Eshi and said in English, "I don't know what has become of Lady. I gave her meat; she didn't eat it. I gave her milk; she didn't touch it. I think the animal is sad. Parviz should have taken her with him to the zoo, so she could visit her relatives."

Mr. Ganjur bit on the corner of his salt-and-pepper mustache and laughed.

Lady sat on Mother Eshi's lap as Mother Eshi petted her long white fur. The cat yawned and then closed her rose-colored mouth and shut her big blue eyes. The interior of her ears was pinkish, and her nose was the same color. Mother Eshi pressed her cheek on the cat's head. Then she put the cat on the floor. She rose, took a ball of wool from her knitting bag that was under the sofa, and tossed it in front of the cat. At first the cat crouched defensively; then she attacked the meadow-green ball, bit it, and began to play with it . . .

In her broken English, Mother Eshi explained to Pasita that she should not be afraid, that there was nothing wrong with the cat.

When Mr. Ganjur had finished his tea, he rose, pulled his pajama bottoms up, and went to the sitting room.

"Mother Eshi," Keshvar asked, "don't you want to remove the hair from your legs?"

It was strange that everyone, not just Parviz and Hasti and Shahin, but even the Filipina maid, the Afghan cook, Taqi Khan, the driver, Naneh Agha, Keshvar, and friends and acquaintances all called the lady of the house "Mother Eshi." Mother Eshi didn't mind, either. Mr. Ganjur sometimes called her "pretty woman," sometimes "Mother Eshi," and when he was angry with her, he would yell, "Hey, you!" Since Mother Eshi would not respond, he would yell, "Hey, I'm talking to you, Eshrat," and Hasti would be offended.

Mother Eshi gave Hasti's coat and skirt to Pasita and said in her own special English, "You take; you good brush, iron, and bring soon. Understand?" Pasita understood.

Mother Eshi remembered Keshvar's question and explained that the hair on her legs had not grown out yet. "I'm postponing hair removal," she said, “until a few days before New Year’s.” Then she put her head to Keshvar’s ear and whispered.

Keshvar said loudly, “I told him, by God. He said, ‘Leave it for her New Year’s gift.’”

Several strands of yarn had gotten loose from the ball of green wool that had been on the carpet. Hasti was rolling the strands around the ball and thinking. *From the time Pasita brought Lady to the family room to the time that she lovingly took her away was a short scene worthy of filming. It would be good for people whose hearts were happy. Perhaps people whose hearts were sad would also be happy for a few moments. At least to the extent that they would be from an antianxiety pill . . . People don’t realize it, but colors, scenes, touches, scents, and tastes, if they caress the senses, drive away anxiety. On the other hand, darkness, clamor, ugliness, harshness, putrid smells, and dirty colors disturb the senses, and after a while, they shatter the nerves.*

With her tiny green eyes, Keshvar cast an admiring look at Hasti and asked Mother Eshi, “Are you ready to marry off your daughter?”

“It depends!” Mother Eshi said. “Who will be the groom?”

“The groom works at Omran Bank,” Keshvar said. “And he produced the play *Khaleh Suskeh* (Auntie Cockroach) that’s on television and in theaters. Have you seen it?”

“No.”

Keshvar turned to Hasti. “You haven’t seen it either?” Hasti answered that they didn’t have a television.

Keshvar chanted from *Khaleh Suskeh,* “I’m going to find a hubby . . . a hubby and a half . . .”

“Mother Eshi,” Mr. Ganjur yelled from the sitting room, “tell Navidi to take Keshvar Khanom home while you’re getting ready!”

Hasti accompanied her mother to the bedroom and sat on the double bed with its blue suede bedspread. The sheer curtains on the glass paneled interior doors were light blue, and the window curtains dark blue. Navy blue silk tassels were hanging from the ends of the curtains like earrings. Lately, whenever Hasti had come into her mother’s bedroom, she had thought that if it were done in green, it would be more calming. But Mr. Ganjur had bought all the furnishings for the bedroom by the lot at an inexpensive price from an American family whose mission in Iran had come to an end, and so it cannot be made green.

Hasti turned on the switch and light spread poetically from the canopy above the bed. She also turned on the tape player and . . . disco . . . rock and roll, and then probably the twist . . . She turned off the tape player. There were several pieces of gum without their blue covers on the table next to the bed. She put a piece in her mouth and chewed. The scent of mint cooled her mouth. *Maybe Mr. Ganjur has bad breath*, she thought.

Mother Eshi placed a box in Hasti's hand and said, "I must give you your New Year's gift now. This Russian bear, Marusa . . ."

Hasti pulled the violet ribbon that was arranged like a flower on the violet, flowered wrapping paper and opened the box. A violet sweater, of violet wool and violet silk. At the corner on the left side of the sweater, there was a little square of silk. The wide ribbon of a larger invisible square of wool surrounded the small square, and, in the same way, invisible ribbons of silk and wool were repeated and spread over the sweater. One ribbon, two inches wide, of dark color surrounded the wrists. The garment looked unreal. She kissed her mother and asked, "Shall I wear it today?"

"Of course!"

Mother Eshi's hand touched the bell on the bedside table. "This Pasita," she said, "her head's in the clouds . . ." She searched for violet nail polish and violet lipstick in the drawer of her dressing table.

Mother Eshi put on black slacks. She fastened her bra and put a flowered, beige silk blouse over her bare body. At the bottom of the blouse there were two ribbons that served as a belt. Mother Eshi brought the two ends of the ribbons forward and knotted them. A section of her midriff was visible. The blackness of the slacks made the whiteness of her midriff look like ivory, but the weather was still too cold for a person to show off an ivory-like strip of her stomach. She threw a beige mink jacket over her shoulders.

As they were leaving, Mother Eshi shouted, "Bye-bye, Ahmad!" and said to Hasti, "What a miser! Now he's placing the jewelry in a steel box, and only he knows the secret of its lock."

On their way to Bowling Center, Mother Eshi spoke a little English. Ostensibly, this was so that the driver wouldn't learn the family secrets, but in reality, she was practicing her English. She had been studying English for several years at the Iran–America Society so that she would not be speechless in front of American friends. They, especially the women among them, did not bother to learn Persian. A few of the men knew Persian, but neither did the flirting of Mother Eshi nor the flattery of Mr. Ganjur attract the attention of that limited number. But the stilted accents of the couple when they spoke English did attract attention, and sometimes it caused boisterous laughter.

Hasti, too, had studied English at that society in hopes of becoming an English teacher in the high schools of the capital, but it didn't happen. Touran Jan used to say that, for women, teaching is more sensible than any other work. In front of the class, you are your own boss. You have to work only with a number of innocent children. If you are a sympathetic, knowledgeable, and kind teacher, you can, according to the poet Sa'di, draw them to school even on weekends. And Simin used to say, "The attractiveness of teaching is that half of it is knowledge and the other half is acting. The acting entertains people."

Hasti could have asked Mr. Ganjur for a favor, and in the wink of an eye he could have made it happen. Mr. Ganjur used to say, "The Ministry of Education is desperately searching for English teachers. All the students have turned to the study of English." But Hasti didn't say a word. She didn't even divulge to Mother Eshi her motive for studying English.

When they turned onto Old Shemiran Road, Mother Eshi revealed her reason for arranging this date with her daughter, for beseeching her to agree, and for making sure she would definitely come. She stressed that in the sauna Hasti should be friendly to Mrs. Farrokhi. Why? Because she has a son who is a gentleman in every sense of the word and who comes on Fridays to pick up his mother.

"How many times do I need to repeat that I'm disgusted by traditional marriage?" Hasti said angrily. She turned to the driver and said in Persian, "Mr. Navidi, drop me off right here." It wasn't far from there to her house on Valiabad Street.

Her mother told the driver, "Never mind what she says; just drive on." She hugged Hasti. "For my sake, just this one time." And in Persian she said, "For God's sake . . ." She continued in broken English, "Let Morad go.

He thin and weak. He always restless. Besides, he hasn't come to ask for you. And he not like me."

"He will come to ask for my hand," Hasti said. "If he doesn't, I will take steps myself."

"You like him that much?"

"He's the only man I know who will not exploit me," Hasti said. "He makes it possible for me to be the new woman that I want to be."

Mother Eshi said in Persian, "There are new and old among women?"

One day Simin had spoken in class so much about what a woman should and shouldn't be. She had said that because of the special situation of being a woman, the wife always stays in place in the husband's home, while the man, in contrast, advances day by day, and the gap between them continually grows. Eventually, a deep abyss divides them and makes their marriage stale and meaningless.

They undressed in a room adjoining the sauna. Although Mother Eshi was plump, she had a well-proportioned figure. That's because she attended to her body so much. Her breasts had nursed three children, but they were still firm and upright. Hasti had seen her nurse Parviz. She didn't bend down. Rather, she would hold the baby's head up and put her nipple in his mouth. Mother Eshi's eyes were black, just like Hasti's, and when she gazed seductively from under those bowed eyebrows, those slightly puffy eyelids, and those long eyelashes, it made even Hasti's heart flutter. Hasti couldn't remember the original shape of her mother's nose. This nose had been operated on three times until it came out looking just like Elizabeth Taylor's.

Mother Eshi gathered her blonde hair to the top of her head and clipped it. Hasti knew that she colored her hair and sometimes rinsed it with boiled chamomile and sometimes with crushed nigella seeds to give it a shine. The waves and curls of that golden hair that came to the top of her shoulders were produced by the experienced hands of the well-known beautician Farhad. All the chic women of Tehran would give an arm and a leg to get an appointment with him.

Very fat and totally naked women were sitting on the steps of the sauna. A slender woman was stretched out on the floor. When she saw Mother Eshi, she stood, and they kissed one another. You could see that the woman had been swimming in a bikini during the summer. Mother Eshi asked how her back was, and she said it was better. She complained that she had lain in the sun by the sea so much that summer, making her sweat, and now, too, the sauna was making her sweat. This woman could not be Mrs. Farrokhi, however much Mother Eshi kissed her. She was too young to have a grown son, especially "a gentleman in every sense of the word."

Mother Eshi sat on the third step next to the fat women. They were all sweating. Perspiration sat on Mother Eshi's nose, and Hasti also felt herself becoming damp from sweat. She looked at all the women and compared her mother to the others. *Of all of them*, she thought, *she is the most beautiful, but she won't sit as a model for me.* Hasti decided to keep all these naked bodies in her memory, so that when she arrived home, she could draw them and compare the results with her BA project, for which she had won first *mention*. (In the Faculty of Fine Arts, expressions like this, in languages other than Persian, were often used.) Her BA project was the naked bodies of women who had sought relief for incurable pains in the hot baths of Sare'in. When Professor Mani had seen her painting he had said, "It's Dante's inferno!"

Raya entered and slammed the door of the sauna. Hasti suddenly feared that the door wouldn't open again and that she would be burnt to a crisp in that hell that was not Dante's. It was a pointless destiny—a person on her way to be shown off to Mrs. Farrokhi burnt to a crisp.

Raya was thin, and her skin was the color of a yellow carrot. She was wearing only shorts, and her breasts would fit in Hasti's palms. She had a pitcher in her hand. Many stones, some smooth, some rough, had been scattered on and around the heater. An electric light peeked out from time to time from among them, and from time to time it glared. Raya filled her fist with liquid from the pitcher and tossed it on the stones. The stones sizzled and emitted steam and a pleasant scent. Mother Eshi explained that the pitcher contained a few drops of eucalyptus extract in water.

A woman with frizzy black hair crouched next to Hasti on the floor of the sauna and told Raya, "Sprinkle again." Then she complained, "They didn't tell us as kids that women are supposed to be thin. So we ate on and on, and so we grew fat. Rice, rich soups, fried potatoes, animal fat. Now how much trouble we must go through to lose one pound. Look at me. I get fat just from drinking water. I weighed myself; I was 175 pounds. After swimming, sauna, massage, and exercise, I'm two pounds lighter. But when I drink one glass of water, my weight returns to what it was before."

The slender woman, who was once again resting on her back on the floor of the sauna, said, "Then don't drink water, my dear."

The 175-pound, frizzy-haired woman answered, "I can't. My heart calls out for water." Facing Hasti, she asked, "Why have you come to the sauna? Your figure is perfect."

Hasti didn't know why she submitted to her mother's wishes and her plans. She didn't know why her attachment and that of her brother Shahin to Mother Eshi had no bounds. Was it her attractiveness that seduced them? Did Hasti, deep in her heart, prefer the world in which her mother lived? Did her mother's world open doors to her that she couldn't even approach in her life with Grandmother? But Hasti considered those doors of opportunity pointless and the people behind them a group of hollow bourgeois consumers, as did Morad, who attributed numerous other characteristics to them as well. Morad had told her many times, "If you want to be authentic, you'll turn your back on your mother and leave that foolish class." Morad himself intended to leave his paternal home.

Hasti turned to the 175-pound, frizzy-haired woman, but the woman was making an appointment with Raya and bargaining to move forward her turn at massage. Hasti now became determined to do a painting of the sauna and title it *Carefree, Fat Nudes*. She didn't know why she suddenly thought of Biafra, people thin as a spindle and straw-like children whose ribs could be counted but whose stomachs bulged out. Their stomachs were empty, so why did they bulge? She had asked Morad when he had shown her photos of those people. Morad had talked on and on, concluding, "Swimming with the current is easy, but against the current it's hard . . . Yet . . . Although it takes more effort, it gives value to life."

Hasti felt that one of her legs was being pulled by her mother and the other by Morad, just like the two legs of a puppet. And then there were Touran Jan and Simin.

A woman with a mountain of flesh entered and slammed the door. Again, Hasti feared that the door wouldn't open and that she would be melted in that furnace. Enormous breasts fell on the woman's stomach, and her thighs were so thick that nothing could be seen. She was a multilayered woman, completely naked, yet all that flesh wasn't firm. When she stretched out her arms to give her hands to Mother Eshi, the flesh of her arms hung loose and limp. At a sign from her mother, Hasti rose and was introduced to Mrs. Farrokhi.

Mrs. Farrokhi narrowed her eyes and looked Hasti over, although there was no need for her to squint. Two small pillows of flesh in place of eyelids had naturally narrowed her eyes. Mrs. Farrokhi could not seem to get enough of looking Hasti up and down and surveying her face. Her narrowed gaze traversed back and forth, embracing her. Hasti got goose bumps from that all-encompassing look.

"Eshrat," Mrs. Farrokhi said, "burn incense when you get home, though I don't have an evil eye." So, that look was a look of admiration.

Hasti moved away from her mother and Mrs. Farrokhi, who sat side by side on the first step. A jack would have been necessary to raise that enormous body up to the third step. Hasti sat on the floor of the sauna next to the frizzy-haired woman and hugged her knees. The frizzy-haired woman said, "Now I see why you came to the sauna." And she laughed.

Hasti was drowsy. She closed her eyes and put her head on her knees. She heard her mother's voice: "She's twenty-two." And she counted the first lie. She had taken four years off her life.

Again, her mother's voice: "I was fifteen years old when Hasti was born. Shahin is three years younger."

If only Hasti could go to sleep completely, but Mrs. Farrokhi and curiosity did not allow that. This transient, fleeting voice reached her ears: "I didn't want to phone her; if I had known I wouldn't have gone. This woman showed me so much arrogance. How can I explain that gesture? She stood and put her hands on her hips . . . 'I don't poke into the business of others.' I understood well. I'm not stupid . . . She didn't say anything . . . No, she wouldn't go anywhere. She wouldn't come anywhere. What happened that they became so busy? Did her husband become the minister of war? Did he become prime minister? It's as though I've killed someone in their family. As if it were *my* fault that Mina Khanom became our daughter-in-law. Anyone would say the same. Really . . . I told Farrokh A'zam, 'She prays, then she sings. After prayer she dances. She doesn't even pick up the prayer rug.' I don't want a sloppy bride like this. They found each other themselves . . . They danced around jerkily with one another at a gathering . . . They call it a *party.* That damned Morad had given the party."

Hasti suddenly woke up. Was she talking about her Morad? No! Her Morad wasn't damned, and he wasn't into parties and dancing around jerkily. Hasti closed her eyes again and heard Mrs. Farrokhi's voice. "This time I'm going to find the bride myself. She has nothing? Even better! Thankfully, God has given everything to me. I'm not looking for the wealth of others."

"All the same," Mother Eshi said, "my daughter is not without resources. Ahmad is very rich. He would give his life for Hasti. I'm sure a good dowry . . ." Hasti thought that if she counted her mother's lies, she would soon lose track.

No, they were actually closing the deal. They were making plans, and they were carrying them out . . . Until the hundred thousandth lie . . . What remained was meeting in person the "gentleman in every sense of the word." If Mother Eshi liked him, it would be all done.

Hasti stood up. Her head was spinning. She waited until the vertigo had passed. "Mother Eshi," she said, "I'm going to the indoor pool to swim."

"You don't have a swimsuit . . . ," Mother Eshi said.

"My dear," Mrs. Farrokhi added, "don't rent a swimsuit from Raya . . . You can catch a thousand diseases." Without a response from Hasti, she continued, "Anyway, my dear, you should have swum first and then come to the sauna. That's the *right* way."

"I brought a swimsuit," Hasti said. She went toward the door, and again fear that the door wouldn't open haunted her. The door was airtight. Hasti turned the round handle to the left and then to the right.

"Dear," Mrs. Farrokhi yelled, "don't fiddle with the door handle; it'll break!"

Her mother rose.

The frizzy-haired woman also rose and said, "If the door doesn't open, all of us will soon be grilled meat."

Her mother came to the door. She pushed in the button at the center of the handle and turned the handle. Opening the door, she laughed and said, "After you swim, come to the exercise room."

"Sorry," Hasti said as she left, "for frightening all of you. I'm so clumsy."

"It happens," Mrs. Farrokhi said. Hasti was glad that she hadn't said "dear."

Hasti entrusted her body to the tepid water of the swimming pool and welcomed the kisses of the water on her skin. She no longer feared any closed door. There was good reason that she couldn't tear her heart from Mother Eshi. She was indebted to her for this happiness and calmness, and for many other joys as well. The caress of the water was like the blessings of her mother. It was like good tidings and good wishes: Morad will come to give New Year's greetings the fourth day of the new year—your birthday—and you'll wear your violet wool and silk sweater. You'll show Mrs. Farrokhi several more examples of your clumsiness. Morad will bring you a bouquet of flowers. But as soon as his eyes fall upon your sweater, he'll say, "Hasti dearest, take off this fancy sweater. My dear, right now millions of people in India are hungry . . ."

Hasti had met the wife of the Indian ambassador at Mr. Ganjur's house. The ambassador's mission in Iran had come to an end, and the ambassador's wife was worried about her dog. She was worried that her beloved dog would become sick on the plane. She spoke of a shot that the Pasteur Institute was supposed to give dogs, and she asked Mr. Ganjur if he could convince the Pasteur Institute to provide a certificate saying that they had given the shot even though they had not. Although the English of the ambassador's wife was unfamiliar to Hasti's ear and she didn't understand most of what she said, she understood the ambassador's wife to say, "These kinds of formalities are obligatory, whether you are an ambassador or not."

Mr. Ganjur scratched his head and said, "Let me see what I can do. I can prepare an inoculation booklet and place an affirmative sign next to 'inoculation done,' but it will need a stamp. The stamp of the doctor . . ."

Hasti became so angry that she interrupted her mother's husband. "Ma'am," she said, "millions of people are dying of hunger in India and you are thinking of your pet dog that . . ."

The ambassador's wife pulled the corner of her silk sari over her head and took a cigarette from the inlaid box on the table. Mr. Ganjur gave Hasti an angry look.

Hasti found her mother stretched out on a table in the exercise room. Raya switched on the electricity, and Mother Eshi and the table both began to shake . . . Then she took a round disc that seemed to be made in imitation of a flying saucer and connected it to a metal cylinder with a base shaped like a spaceship. With this she set upon Mother Eshi's ivory-like stomach. She drew the flying saucer back, she pushed it forward, and she turned it around, and then it was the turn of the thighs and the flank . . . Other women were lying on other tables in the exercise room, and other Rayas, fatter and taller or shorter, but none thinner, had set upon them. It was like surgical operations on hospital beds. But Mrs. Farrokhi was sitting up on a table and watching Hasti, who was still wearing her swimsuit. No ship had been launched into space, but Raya poured oil from a bottle into the palm of her hand and greased every part of Mother Eshi's body that she planned to rub and pound and slap and turn.

In another room they had mummified the frizzy-haired woman—not her whole body, only her face, neck, shoulders, and hands. With care and some splitting and cracking, she stood and walked. Her ankles had also been mummified. Names and images competed with one another in Hasti's mind . . . Queen Nefertiti . . . Frankenstein's bride . . . But Hasti remembered that she had never seen an image of a mummified, 175-pound Queen Nefertiti. Queen Nefertiti, what a swan-like, beautiful neck she had.

Mother Eshi lay down on the table in place of the frizzy-haired woman, and Raya mummified her. Royal Petroleum Jelly, hormone lotion, atomic water spray—all these words that were rightly appropriate for the space age. Morad said that Sartre had said, "Two-thirds of people these days live in poverty and need, so that the other third . . ." Among them, women who took turns to become mummified, without any awareness of the situation.

Mrs. Farrokhi in her Karakul lambskin coat and Mother Eshi in her mink jacket ahead, and Hasti after them, all came out the door of Bowling Center. They found Salim, Mrs. Farrokhi's son, sitting behind the wheel of a black BMW. Mrs. Farrokhi said, "Thank you, dear."

Salim Farrokhi got out of the car, came forward, and said hello. Mother Eshi did not shake hands with him, but Hasti extended her hand when she was introduced. Salim did not take her hand, and Mrs. Farrokhi explained. "Dear, he doesn't shake hands with unrelated women."

Hasti had only cast him half a glance and had seen his reddish-brown beard. She decided to try a different approach and not look at him again, but she couldn't.

Salim took his mother's hand to help her across the culvert. This task was more appropriate for a crane than for Salim, who was shorter than Morad but just as thin.

Mother Eshi looked at her watch and said, "I have a suggestion. I'll send Navidi after Parviz at the zoo, and Mr. Farrokhi can take us all home."

"I'd be pleased to," Mr. Farrokhi responded. He had a deep, protective voice.

"Now that they have the opportunity," Mother Eshi said, "let them go to Bowling Center restaurant and have coffee." Then she added, "If they have Turkish coffee, I can even read their fortunes."

In the restaurant, they sat at a table next to a window overlooking Old Shemiran Road. Jazz music did not allow them to hear one another. Salim stood and went to the information desk. When he returned, the clamor of the jazz subsided.

Hasti heard Salim ask, "Mother, may I help you take off your coat?" His mother made an excuse, saying that she was afraid she would catch cold and that was why she had worn a fur coat.

"Hasti Jan," Mother Eshi said, "take off your coat. Show Mrs. Farrokhi the sweater that you knit yourself." Hasti stubbornly refused.

Her mother was reading Salim's fortune, her intent transparent. *Way too transparent*! Hasti thought. She said that a dark-eyed girl with turned-up eyelashes; a clear, high forehead; and full lips, round chin, and dimples in both cheeks when she smiles . . . will appear on his path . . . It was so blatant that Mrs. Farrokhi also understood. She snorted and said, "For heaven's sake, Eshrat."

"Hasti," Mother Eshi said, "turn your cup upside down so I can read your fortune."

"I read my own fortune."

"Okay, do so. Let me see."

"I mean," Hasti said, "that beyond the essence of my spirit, I don't believe in any fortune."

And she didn't know how it happened, but her eyes met those of Salim. His eyes sparkled. *This guy has strangely feverish eyes, large and oval.* The color of his eyes was between blue and gray, and it looked as though they had eyeliner drawn around them. The pupils of his eyes caught the light, and the light moved around in them. The eyes changed color with changes in the amount of light. Even the shape of the eyes changed with movement of the head, and the oval shape became elongated. Fear gripped Hasti as her heart dropped.

2

Those two sentences had ensnared Salim, not Hasti's high forehead, nor the dimples on her cheeks when she smiled.

When Hasti returned home from the office, Grandmother said, "Salim called and asked permission to take you out for coffee, and . . . I didn't let him finish. I said, 'We have coffee; come have coffee here. Then I can meet you, too.' I hope that wasn't the wrong thing to do."

Hasti took a shower. All these years she had been enamored of Morad, and Morad hadn't said anything, and now the persons closest to her were driving her toward marriage with someone else. Grandmother favored an ordinary life devoid of excitement. Her mother's reasoning was this: the number of suitors will become fewer day by day, and in the end, you will become a stale, old maid. If she became Salim's wife, she could, with the windfall of the Farrokhi family money, at least fulfill her brother Shahin's lifelong wish and send him to America.

But Morad's voice was in her ear, and Morad's close-set eyes remained etched in her mind. In real life, Morad's eyes were never focused on one point. They were always darting about in search of something unseen. But his voice always circulated around a single subject. Morad would say, "Consumption patterns must be changed," and Hasti would tease him and say, "Yes, and we should all have bedsheets full of holes, like a sieve."

Hasti knew why, of all things, bedsheets had come to mind: just recently Mother Eshi had bought Russian sheets from a shop at the end of Lalezar Street. "However much you wash and iron them," she had said, "they won't wear out. Even American women buy Russian bedsheets." And Hasti had said, "And Russian people eat American wheat."

Hasti was debating whether to wear her New Year's outfit or her mother's gift of the alternating matte and glossy violet sweater. Salim had not seen either one. She put on the dark red jacket and skirt and reserved the sweater for the day Morad would visit. She fixed her hair and makeup. Now that everyone wanted to sell her, let the price be high.

Salim arrived. He had a bouquet of Persian violets in his hand. He gave the flowers to Hasti and said, "Prelude to New Year's." He did not say where he had picked or bought them. And he did not listen to Hasti's insistence that it was not necessary to remove his shoes. Hasti knew that she should put a pair of slippers in front of her guest's feet, but the only men's slippers in the house were Shahin's plastic ones that, aside from being too big for Salim's feet, were badly worn.

Hasti put a side table in front of the armchair in which Salim had sat, and she put a tray with coffee-making supplies on the table. Salim asked, "Shall I make some for you, too?"

"Yes, please."

Salim didn't look at Hasti. He had given her the one modest glance allowed by his religion that day at the Bowling Center restaurant. But Hasti searched for the magnetism of his gaze and thought, *The eyes of this guy cannot be forgotten. They contain a supernatural secret. If, as Grandmother says, "God is manifest in humans, His glow reflected especially in the eyes and the gaze, more than in other senses," Salim's eyes are proof of this.*

Salim poured a teaspoon of Nescafé from the container into a cup, added a spoonful of sugar, poured in a little boiling water, and mixed it well until it foamed. Then he poured boiling water and stirred again. He stood and gave the cup of coffee to Hasti. Grandmother had put the bouquet of Persian violets in a small crystal vase on the tray. "What refinement you've shown," Salim said, "to have put my gift flowers on the tray."

"The refinement is not mine," Hasti replied. "It is Grandmother's."

Grandmother entered. She had changed her clothes and wore her New Year's prayer chador. Her face had been freshly washed, and her appearance, with that white hair, was spiritual, like one who has just finished praying.

Hasti sighed in relief and left the stage and the conversation to Grandmother and Salim. Sometimes she heard what they were saying; sometimes she didn't. She didn't hear them when her mind was caught up in thoughts of Morad.

Grandmother was clearly pleased with Salim. She asked what he had studied and what his father's work was. Salim said that in England he had studied the history of religions and that he had written his master's thesis on comparative mysticism. He said that his father was a button merchant in the grand bazaar (his friends called him "button man") and that he himself was obliged to work in his father's business. Since he had joined, the business had expanded, and now they also import braid, edgings, lace, and women's decorative items. Touran Jan asked, "Why 'obliged'?"

"I wanted to become a university professor," Salim said, "but they didn't accept me. I don't have a doctorate." And Hasti had no idea that worthless buttons could get a person's wife into an elite sauna and a person's son to England.

Then Salim talked about his father's activism during the Mosaddeq era. Another reason they had not employed him at Tehran University, he said, is that his father was a supporter of Mosaddeq and that he and Shamshiri had attracted a large number of bazaar merchants to the cause.

Now it was Touran Khanom's turn to say that her son was martyred as a follower of the old man, Mosaddeq—that he was shot near the Parliament building—and to show Salim the photo of Hasti's father that hung on the living room wall.

Salim rose and stood in front of the photo. Father's photo looked out at Hasti every day from its black frame. A young man with a thin, curled mustache. His face seemed freshly shaved and his hair just out from the barber's shop, neat and brilliantined. New jacket and slacks on his body, a bow tie at his neck. Grandmother would say to Hasti, "Your eyes are just like his." Mother Eshi would say, "The old woman is talking nonsense. Your eyes are just like mine."

Salim didn't move from in front of the photo. It was as though he were asking Hasti's hand from her father's image. Then Salim's attention was drawn to the photo of Mosaddeq to the right of Hasti's father's image. Mosaddeq, in a black cloak, squatting in the corner next to a wall in his place of banishment, Ahmadabad. A cane was positioned diagonally between his legs. He had signed the photo years ago and had sent it to Touran Khanom, the mother of a martyr . . . Touran Khanom had always told Hasti, "Name your son Mosaddeq."

Touran Khanom recited:

O heart, did you see that the beloved did not come?
The dust came, yet the rider did not.

She added, "This is the saddest poem that Omid composed for the old man, Mohammad of Ahmadabad."

Salim looked at the picture of Khalil Maleki, whose jacket had been thrown over his shoulder and whose shining eyes were fixed on the camera. Even in the photo his large bald head shone from cleanliness. This picture was inscribed "Dedicated to the light of my eyes, Hasti Nourian."

Salim turned to Hasti and said, "So you knew Khalil Maleki well?"

"I knew Mr. Maleki during the last two years of his life," Hasti responded. "He used to say to me, 'Hasti, you be my eyes, and I'll be your knowledge.' He would speak about Marxism in simple words, and I would write them down. But every day that I went there, he would say, 'First, go say hello to Sabiheh.'"

"Was he afraid of his wife?" Salim asked.

"Not at all! He respected her."

"Maleki was a great man," Salim said. "He was the first person to propose communism without Moscow—before Tito, even before Nehru. He shook the foundation of that ideology on this side of the world. But few people heard his voice. Perhaps he had spoken in an arid desert or into a well. He had come too early . . ."

Hasti remembered the last night when she, along with Jalal and Simin, had accompanied Maleki home. Sabiheh Khanom was crying, and Jalal suggested that if in the house . . . Hasti prepared coffee in the kitchen. Simin asked Maleki, "Why? Why?" And Maleki said, "Simin Khanom, your heroes will not always remain heroes. We turned to Tito, who had no faith in freedom. We gave our hearts to Nehru, and we were disappointed." And Simin said, "Trust only in yourself." And Maleki had cried. In July of that year Maleki died, and in September, Jalal.

An image of Jalal Al-e Ahmad was on the adjacent wall. Salim gave it a perfunctory look and said, "I have seen this photo of Jalal."

"It's the last photo of Jalal," Hasti said. "Monajjemi, the engineer, took it at Jalal's cottage in Asalem."

Salim sat, and Hasti welcomed his look into her eyes. What secrets did those eyes hold? What to call them? What best described them? Magnetism? Attraction? A door to the unknown heart? Those eyes pulled Hasti into a sea—no, a calm ocean—and then carried her to a secure shore and protected her. And those know-it-all eyebrows? Why know-it-all? Those eyebrows held a thousand questions in reserve.

"More than anything," Salim continued, "Maleki's strong antenna detected weakness in the whole Soviet system and the dictatorship of the proletariat." He swallowed and added, "A system that had the name of socialism but whose customs were a type of state socialism, or, in Maleki's words, state capitalism."

"But Maleki himself was a socialist," Hasti responded, "a freedom-seeking, Iranian socialist, stressing the rights and interests of the small and unfortunate nation of Iran . . ."

Salim finished Hasti's sentence: "While the Stalin regime established the Tudeh Party to sacrifice Iran's interests to the immediate interests of the Soviets—in the case of the northern oil, in the disturbances in Azerbaijan, in opposition to the National Movement and other Iranian anti-despotic movements . . ."

All three were silent. Grandmother left and returned with her son's photo album. She faced Salim and said, "Mr. Farrokhi, come here and sit on the sofa so I can show you photos of my son and of Hasti as a child." She sighed and added, "Those were the days."

"What happened that your son was martyred?" Salim asked.

Grandmother breathed heavily. "Mosaddeq was coming out of the Parliament building. He said, 'Right here, where the people are, is the Parliament, not in there . . . ' There was no stool. My son bent down and Mosaddeq stood on his back and gave a speech, and my child was shot."

Salim combed his beard with his fingers and was deep in thought. Hasti searched for the gaze of his eyes, but Salim's eyes were traveling far away. That night they appeared more gray than blue. Perhaps his gray jacket and trousers had spread their color to his eyes. *Why had he not worn a tie? He had taken the first step of a marriage proposal, hadn't he?*

"Your son's name wasn't Reza, was it?" Salim asked.

"No."

Hasti knew the photos of the album by heart. Grandmother was turning pages and explaining on and on. The first photo was an image of a chubby child, dressed from head to toe, as though he was packaged, like a baby bear that does not control his hands and feet. They had placed him on a table, and in front of him was his birthday cake that had only one lit candle. And then other photos: the same child lying naked on his stomach, his head raised, and like a lizard, his tongue sticking out. How hard they must have worked to get the child to raise his head and look at the camera. Of course, the photographer must have said, "Look at the birdie," but sticking out the little tongue was no doubt the initiative of the child himself.

Then the same child on Touran Jan's lap. The same child in the arms of his father. The same child standing under a tree with Mehrmah Khanom holding his hand—Mehrmah Khanom who was not much more than a child herself. The same child sitting on a chair wearing short trousers and a jacket—he even has a bow tie. And other birthday photos with lit candles to which the passage of time had added one for each year, until it had reached eighteen lit candles. And now the child, through the blessing of time, has also grown a mustache.

They arrived at the wedding photos. Salim's attention was captured. "Why has the bride's photo been cut out?" he asked.

Touran Khanom answered, "I cut it out myself. That slut—that woman no longer had a place in my life. Not even one year had passed since my young son had departed when she left and married her first suitor. Shahin had not even turned one."

So much the better, Hasti thought. If not, Mother Eshi would have nagged her and Shahin their whole lives, saying that she had wasted away her youth for them.

Photos of Mother Eshi had sometimes been completely cut out, sometimes partially. One place the upper part of her body was gone, but her hand and lower body cradled Shahin who was sleeping in her lap in swaddling clothes. In that photo Hasti sat in the arms of her father. She had tilted her head and was looking at him. "She was a clever girl," Grandmother said. "She would do anything for her father. Every day, when it was time for him to come home, she would sit by the door, and when her father arrived, she would clutch his legs so tightly."

Hasti remembered being motherless as more difficult than being fatherless. Even at five years of age she had wanted to take her mother's breast in her hand and, not suckling, put her head over her mother's heart and go to sleep to the tune of its beat. One time she climbed onto Grandmother's lap and took her breast in her hand and called her "Mother Tutu." Grandmother had become silent and had frowned. Hasti had called Touran Jan "Mother" or "Mother Tutu" several more times, and again Grandmother had frowned, until finally she lost her temper. She placed her course pack on the kitchen table and yelled at her grandchild, "Your mother is that slut, not me. Don't call me 'Mother' any longer or I'll smack you!"

"Can I call Mehrmah Khanom 'Mother?'" Hasti had asked.

"No."

"Akhtar Iran?"

"No."

Nevertheless, we should be fair. Although Grandmother didn't have time to caress or fondle them, she took good care of her grandchildren. In her senior years, she returned to her studies so that she could be relieved from the constant thoughts of her son, and also so that she could get a degree and advance from elementary school teacher to secondary school teacher.

Grandmother and Salim had become deeply engrossed in conversation. They weren't talking about trivial things. They spoke seriously of history, God, and mysticism.

Salim was saying, "We must come to know God a new way. We must build a new history. With the transformation of the *Renaissance*, Satan inserted himself into history. It is our duty to drive Satan away."

Hasti listened carefully. The words of this guy were fresh and unrelated to Morad's words. She interrupted. "In my opinion, the era of rebirth or, in your words, *Renaissance*, is the greatest of human transitions. It's a turning point in human history; the *Renaissance*'s focus on humanity is the most significant development that humans have achieved."

"*Humanity*, yes," Salim said, "*humanism*, no. People, whether left, right, or moderate, must first and foremost become truly human and humanitarian. But the seed of colonialism and exploitation of the rest of the world was planted by the *humanism* of the West. Even now, colonized countries imitate the West. These countries want the Western world to remain just as it is. Taqizadeh said, 'Iran should become Westernized.' But in my opinion, our era is the final stage of the transformation of the *Renaissance*. At the very least, countries like ours should not whole-heartedly grasp the colonialism born of the *Renaissance*. Countries of the Third World must look to the future."

"One cannot wholly negate everything Western," Hasti replied. "Western science, *technology*, art, philosophy, and ideas like *socialism* . . . We can at least gain inspiration from them."

"We have had and do have sources of inspiration of our own," Salim said.

"He means the Quran, Islam, and mysticism," Grandmother said.

"Revolutionary Islam," Salim added. "Revolutionary messianism. This type of religiousness is a departure from the advocacy of a Western system and from immoral *modernism*."

Grandmother put her hand on her chest and said, "It's as though you are speaking from my heart."

"The Irish turned blindly to a Marxist revolution," Salim continued. "Some countries have fixed their eyes on the Middle Ages. We should find refuge in Islam, and the totality of our own Islam."

Just like Morad, Hasti thought, *this guy lectures people, but the subject of the lectures is different. And he uses so many foreign words. This is such a charming habit. Why doesn't Grandmother leave the two of us alone*?

Hasti responded to Salim. "You mean return to ancient times? You mean despite being historic and having a long history behind us, acting exactly against history?"

Salim criticized her. "With such a mentality, how is it that you have hung Jalal Al-e Ahmad's photo on the wall of your room?"

Hasti cocked her head. "I was and am very attached to Jalal Al-e Ahmad. He was a man who had—how shall I say it?—a halo . . ."

"*Charisma*," Salim said.

"But a person," Hasti continued, "doesn't necessarily agree completely with all the opinions even of one's beloved. His wife, Simin, speaks about *ideology*-strickenness. She says that all Third World countries, and even Western countries, are *ideology*-stricken. 'Have correct political understanding, yes,' she says, 'but not *ideology*-strickenness of any kind.' Excuse me for stealing some of your catch words and style of speaking."

Salim laughed. "I should meet this Simin Daneshvar and . . . ," he said.

Hasti finished Salim's sentence: "And finish her off for training such impudent students."

Salim became serious. "Having a correct political *conception*, yes, but denying religious *ideology*, no. Most people worldwide are religious. Humans need *metaphysics*, a refuge, a divine supporter beyond the powers of this world. In my opinion, appealing to religion and to mysticism in an autonomous way is a natural act."

"Contemporary humanity," Hasti said, "is becoming empty and hollow. It's traversing the last stages of the industrial age. It's tasting the *information* age. Contemporary humanity is in a state of eruption—an eruption the consequences of which are worse than those of the Mongol invasion. In my view, the end of human civilization has arrived." She hesitated and added, "Our era is a Kafkaesque era. It's a reflection of Kafka's depressed subconscious and restless character."

Salim looked at her with astonishment and said, "If you turn to God and put your trust completely in God, you won't be so despairing."

"My mother and my grandmother say that when I began to speak, the first word that I said was *ouch*. The first word is important."

"It was just a word," Salim said. "The idea that the first word a child utters shapes his destiny is a superstition."

Hasti had to laugh. That was so similar to what Morad had told her: "Girl, banish these superstitions from your mind."

Salim began to comb his beard with his fingers again. And then he combed his hair with all ten fingers. Hasti thought for a moment of going to get a comb and putting it in Salim's hands. It was laughable, it seemed so inappropriate; beard and hair did not require this much combing. And in her heart, she said, *Man, my laughter was from happiness. I was happy that you, despite your religiousness, are not superstitious and that you and Morad have suggested to me one concept through two different expressions.*

"Mr. Farrokhi," Grandmother said, "you were saying . . . ?"

Salim bit his lip and said, "The problem of humanity is not the arrival of the information age; the problem of humanity is Satan-strickenness, Miss Hasti Nourian."

Hasti wanted to say, "You mean my inappropriate laugh," but she didn't.

"Satan is the carnal self," Touran Khanom said.

"We have individual Satans and a group Satan," Salim said. "In our era it is the group Satan. He has filled the entire earth. Humanity today considers itself God. This itself is a type of Satan-strickenness. The path of salvation is revolutionary messianism." The annoyance had gone from his voice.

Hasti recited:

Past the course of the moon,
Yet, too far out of the sun's reach.

"Who composed that poem?" Salim asked.

"Mehdi Akhavan-Sales."

Salim took a notebook and pencil from the pocket of his jacket and asked Hasti to recite the poem again so that he could write it down. He put the notebook on the arm of the chair and said, "Perhaps you are right, and humanity will destroy itself with space research and nuclear weapons. But I'm hopeful that there will be a change in human life . . . a new way of safeguarding everyone's security. We must struggle and fight to reach that goal, however. Individual prosperity is not enough."

Again, Hasti disagreed. "If you want my opinion, Nietzsche's prediction is correct that the distressed world will become full of clamor and commotion (just like the coppersmiths' bazaar), full of narcotics, full of promiscuity. Our days are dark days."

"These dark days," Salim responded, "will come to an end, and humanity will come out victorious. The visible and invisible worlds, it is also in the Quran . . . ," but he didn't continue his sentence.

And again, the silence of three people.

It was Salim who resumed speaking. "I wasn't aware that Iranian women have become informed and knowledgeable to this extent. My mother says that you are a painter and no more than twenty-two years old."

"I'm twenty-six years old."

"And this talk . . . ?"

"I have taken several classes with professors I admire. It's possible that I have inadvertently stolen their words."

Again silence.

Salim seemed to be thinking, and Hasti imagined that he was weighing whether he should take such a pretentious wife or whether he should leave by the same route he had come. She stood, put the vase of violets on the table in the middle of the room, and took the coffee-making supplies to the kitchen. She opened the refrigerator to bring out a bowl of fruit and saw that meat had been prepared for cutlets. Mint and tarragon had been put in a basket. Red radishes had taken the shape of roses. She took out the bowl of fruit. Washed lettuce was in the strainer on the table in the kitchen.

Hasti realized that Grandmother planned to keep Salim for dinner. With all that leg pain of hers, she had gone to Darvazeh Dowlat and bought fresh herbs, symbol of New Year's, from Mohammad Aqa, along with expensive fruit, ground meat, and lettuce. She planned to tie the marital knot firmly that very night between Hasti and Salim, with his rust-brown beard. A youth whom she had never seen . . . whom she didn't know . . . She had only heard of his qualities from Hasti. Grandmother had never made such provisions for Morad.

Hasti put the bowl of fruit on the table and heard Grandmother saying, "But what I want is for people to make peace with one another on earth. Now, if the path to this is, as one of Hasti's friends says, Marxism, so be it, as long as it doesn't bring God down from heaven to earth."

Hasti filled a plate with an apple and a large orange and went looking for a fruit knife and fork. She heard Salim's voice saying, "I believe in the last words of Dr. Shariati, who said, 'Freedom, equality, mysticism.' But I know that Marxism is also a type of West-strickenness—the same West-strickenness that has been going on, in my opinion, since the *Renaissance*."

Salim took the orange and attacked it with the knife. The knife was old and blunt. "Marxism accepts modernity," he said. "Therefore, religion becomes the opiate of the people. I don't agree that God should be disregarded or that the proletariat should consider the world their property. In the meantime, I'm sure the continuation of Western imperialism is not the remedy, whether Marxism or black reaction, whether alcoholism or emphasis on sexuality."

Salim gave up on peeling the orange and took the apple. Hasti knew that a knife that wouldn't cut an orange wouldn't cut the skin of an apple, either. She left and brought a kitchen knife that had a serrated blade and put it in front of Salim, but Salim had eaten the apple unpeeled. Hasti used the kitchen knife to peel for him the largest orange there was in the bowl; she separated the sections and put them on a clean plate.

A smile appeared on Salim's closed lips. "Hasti Khanom, don't be so despondent."

"What should one hope for?" Hasti asked.

"Hope for a God who is all-embracing."

Hasti responded: "Simin says that ancient Indians predicted that our era would be an apocalyptic one in which the earth would be annihilated, and that this apocalypse had already begun 2,500 ago. But she herself is an optimistic person. She believes that humanity will finally arrive at a rational solution and get life in order."

Touran Khanom became angry. "All these nonsensical words that this wicked witch has put in your head; I'm fed up with this witch."

Hasti pounded on the arms of the chair with both fists and said, "Don't call Simin a witch!"

Salim was calmly eating the orange; he didn't even raise his head. Hasti's contrariness, her doubts, even her anger—none of these had yet driven him away. He took his notebook from the arm of the chair, opened it, and said, "What I have thought about from time to time, or have heard from someone, or have read somewhere and have liked, I jot down. This is the eighteenth notebook. I want to read several pieces of it so that you will know me better." He paused and added, "In my opinion, your problem is bewilderment, a mystical bewilderment."

It was the first time that Hasti had heard such a phrase. It was the first time that someone had examined her emotional state and had given a name to that state. *Naming is important*, she thought. *When you give a name to something or some state, part of the issue has been resolved.* "What is mystical bewilderment?" she asked. "It's not the case, is it, that, because you have researched mysticism, you connect every ailment to mysticism?"

Salim read: "O Infinity, who are You? Are You the core of an atom around which electrons rotate? Is it because of the explosion of one mother atom, which was You, that life has begun? That existence originated? From You we have separated and to You we shall return?"

Hasti was tempted to say, "It's like the literary sections of the magazines, *Today's Woman* and *Women's Ettelaat*, except at a higher level." But she didn't. She contented herself with saying only, "Then God is a woman?"

Salim became indignant. "God is beyond gender, Miss Nourian."

Hasti made amends. She felt she was playing cat and mouse, pushing away with one hand, and drawing in with the other. "I long for a God," she said, "that is love and hope and whose manifestations are conditions that attract me in humans and in the world." And the words slipped out: "And a look that is also in your eyes and a smile that with those closed lips . . ."

Salim sat up straight and fixed his eyes on her. It was as though concern for religious modesty had left him. That look seemed so deep and so warm . . . His voice had the same warmth. "God is both love and hope," he said. "Just as Sa'di said, 'It is closer to us than the veins of our neck. It pulls us, and from Its pull, the longing for union rises in us . . . ' The jugular vein."

For the first time Hasti welcomed her entrance into another world, a world beyond the one she had experienced until then. Magical eyes and a deep voice, as if from an exalted world, had tamed and calmed her. Did it mean that if she became Salim's wife, that condition would continue?

Salim stood and said, "Well, I should go," and he turned toward Grandmother. "May Hasti Khanom and I have permission to . . ."

Grandmother interrupted him and said, "Please stay for supper and dine with us paupers."

Salim happily accepted and wanted to phone his mother. Hasti went to the bedroom, brought the phone, and connected it. Salim dialed standing right there and listened for a while. He hung up and dialed the number again, and then again.

Grandmother returned to the room and worriedly whispered in Hasti's ear, "The cutlet mixture has become runny. I wish I had not grated the onions."

Hasti laughed and said, "My dear, add a little chickpea flour."

"We don't have any."

Salim dialed the number again, and apparently no one answered, since he said, "I will take my leave. My mother is expecting me for dinner."

"It's clear that our food is not worthy of you," Hasti said, "especially since the cutlet mixture has become runny."

"I'll go home," Salim said, "and let them know and then return for supper. And I'm perfectly happy with crumbly cutlet." He put his hand to his beard and said, "Hasti Khanom, will you come with me?"

Hasti blurted out, "Why not?"

She went to the bedroom to get her purse. Grandmother followed her. "Cover your head with a scarf, dear. Please."

Hasti stubbornly refused. "He must accept me as I am. If he doesn't want to, all the better."

When Hasti returned to the living room, Salim said, "If I make a request of you, will you agree?"

Automatically, Hasti said, "Of course."

"I ask you to put on a scarf."

The scarf was in Grandmother's hand.

Salim started the car. "As the proverb goes," he said, "'The night is long and the dervish awake.'" The two did not speak until they were near Mokhber al-Dowleh Square. The streetlights were on.

"Do you see that statue?" Hasti asked. "A worker is slapping the head of a villager." Since Salim didn't express an opinion, she continued, "This intersection is waffling between being a square and being an intersection. It's neither this nor that."

The knot of the scarf was pressing on Hasti's Adam's apple, and she thought she would suffocate. She loosened the knot.

They stopped behind a red light. "Now let's proceed to the main issues," Salim said. "I was too shy to discuss them in front of your grandmother. I talked so much. I must have bored you."

"On the contrary, your talk was refreshing, and I also expressed my opinions freely."

"Despite your expression of opinions different from mine, you're exactly what I've been looking for. My mother has introduced ten girls to me up to now . . ."

"And she'd probably seen most of them in the sauna!"

"It's a good tradition, after all. In the old days they selected girls in the public bath; now it's in the sauna."

There was a large crowd in Sepah Square. This one was a real square. The swarm of men, women, and children was such that people had poured off the sidewalks into the street. Taxis, vans, buses, passenger cars, motorcycles, bicycles, and handcarts, full or empty, all searched for a way through the crowd. They went forward a foot and stopped. Swear words were on everyone's lips. There were many helpless policemen, and the few police officers were even more helpless. Salim stopped so that a man holding the hands of two small boys, one in each of his hands, could pass. A woman with a child in her arms followed them.

There was no opportunity for conversation until they reached Sepah Avenue. Salim began. "We can spend some more time together and perhaps both of us, or maybe only me, will end up in love."

Hasti grinned and said, "And me probably in a headscarf!"

"This is not a difficult obligation . . ." Salim said, "since my intention is pure and in accordance with religion." He laughed and added, "With a scarf, our socializing is not against Sharia law, provided the two parties agree. But I must tell you that I have some commitments with respect to my mother."

"But your father's alive."

"My father is always either taking a temporary wife or getting rid of one."

"Well, he's a Muslim man, after all."

She shouldn't have said that, and now that she had, she should make amends. *Why*, she asked herself, *do I cause him pain? He who has told us about his beliefs. From the very beginning, I should have said "no" and spared him, as well as myself and Grandmother, with her runny cutlet mixture.* When they reached Hasanabad intersection, she offered her opinion: "This one, too, is waffling between being a square and being an intersection."

The light was red, and Salim put on the brakes. The congestion in the Hasanabad intersection was no less than that in Sepah Square. The line of men and women at the Mihan Cinema box office was disorderly. *The people of Iran*, Hasti thought, *will never become accustomed to lines, not until eternity.* There was a fight, too, and they even exchanged blows. The light turned green and turned red again, and there was no way forward. Some people selling black market tickets were wandering about up to three hundred feet from the theater. They would whisper into their customers' ears, and, with a glance to the left and the right, they would sell tickets and search their pockets for change. Or they wouldn't finish their transactions and would turn their backs on their customers. Hasti wondered what film they were showing.

Salim put the car in gear, and it moved forward. "Do you know what film they are showing?" Hasti asked.

"*Vaxi, Taxi*, something like that . . . with Raj Kapoor."

"Mr. Farrokhi," Hasti said, "it's natural that you should protect your mother."

"I'm my mother's only joy," Salim replied. "My sisters have married and left home. My older brother shows up once a year. My mother takes refuge from anger by eating and sleeping. I've convinced her to go on a diet and to go to the sauna, to exercise and get massages. Excessive weight is dangerous for her."

"I know a good doctor," Hasti said. "Dr. Bahari. Perhaps with diet pills . . ."

"She made a date with your mother to go see Dr. Bahari, but I'm worried that those pills will be harmful to her."

Salim turned into a street to the right and stopped beside a large gate. The light above the gate was on, but Salim didn't get out of the car.

"So you live in the same neighborhood as Professor Mani," Hasti said.

"You know Professor Mani?"

"He was my professor."

"I'm a stranger in this town, it seems. Your mother said that you have finished your studies at the Faculty of Fine Arts. But I didn't know that Professor Mani was your professor."

"He's retired now, but I still have the honor of working with him at the Ministry of Art and Culture."

"That reminds me of another issue I want to discuss," Salim said. "Do you want to continue working after marriage?"

"Of course."

"Why?"

"For financial independence. You well know that the result of men's economic dominance is the greater exploitation of women."

"Most Iranian men," Salim said, "at least 70 percent of them, are not ready to tolerate the economic independence of women—that is, they don't accept the reason that women have sought financial independence. Listen to me: You think that if you have financial independence, you will be less exploited. No. If you are married to an unsuitable man, he will take your monthly salary and say, 'It's in my house that you work, and the time that you should spend in service to me, my children, my family, and my relatives, you work in an office.' Then you must again extend your hand to your husband and request your own money back from him for the expenses of toiletries, the hairdresser, clothes, etc."

"You are in no way an unsuitable man," Hasti said. "You are a refined and wise young man, and you will not exploit your wife, whether she works or not."

"I look at the matter differently," Salim said. "I don't want my wife to work, whether at home or at the office. She will be tired enough if she only takes care of the children and her husband. Think about it: waking children from sweet sleep at the crack of dawn and passing them like footballs from aunt to aunt to grandmother so that a woman can go to work—is that right?"

"Several nurseries have opened, and more . . ."

"Measles, scarlet fever, whooping cough—colds and sore throats at the very least—await children there. They get them from each other. Since mothers are going to work, they leave the children no matter what their health."

"More vaccines have been developed . . ."

Salim thought a moment and continued. "Some men become suspicious of their wives' work in offices and lose trust in their wives. Why? Because . . ." And he was silent.

Hasti finished Salim's sentence. "Because they fear that other men will cause their wives to stray. Or what's more, that their wives will give up their feminine identity."

"That is also an issue," Salim said. "But even though I have not seen you more than two times, I trust you." He paused and asked, "Now do you agree that we see one another for a while?"

"Certainly," Hasti said. "But I should tell you the truth. I'm expecting a proposal from a friend I've known for years, but he keeps evading the issue and is not ready to take a wife. I'll give him an ultimatum, and the next person to whom I will extend a hand will be you."

Salim pressed his eyes closed. He bit his lip. "Does your mother know about this?" he asked.

"My mother has never taken him seriously."

"How about your grandmother?"

"Grandmother loves him like her own child, but she doesn't think he's appropriate as a husband for me."

"Are you in love with him?" Salim asked.

"Yes."

Salim put his hand on the door handle. Hasti knew, or thought she knew, what Salim was thinking. *He's thinking how much time, energy, and hope have been uselessly spent; how much he has shown off his knowledge. He asks himself, "What monsters are these?" and "Why didn't Hasti who, at twenty-six years of age, can spout out all those mouth-filling words, say the last word first?"*

Salim opened the car door, and it occurred to Hasti that he would go and leave her there until she became tired and left. "Wait a minute," she said. Salim shut the door and turned to Hasti. "Forgetting him will not be easy," Hasti said, "but know that if I come to you, it will be with all my heart, body, and soul."

Salim put his head between his hands, and Hasti thought, *When he raises his head he'll whine, "Why do you women play with the feelings of young men? Why do you all do the same thing—deceive young men and their mothers, draw them to your home, and in the end confess that you are in love with someone else?" His tone will no longer sound enchanting, his look will no longer have that magnetism, and he will say bitterly, "Miss Nourian, even if you are able to forget, the echo of the music of first love will forever mix with the beat of your heart, and so you will not be able to come to me with all your heart, body, and soul." Yes, then he'll bring forth yet another long piece of literature, but this time, from the depths of his own mind.*

In contrast to Hasti's expectation, what Salim said was not another long piece of literature, and it did not have the meaning that Hasti had imagined. Salim said, "As Dowlatshah, the Qajar poet, says, 'And whom will the beloved choose? And whom will she desire?'" And then he displayed even greater magnanimity. "It is obvious that a girl of your perfection, truthfulness, and sensitivity cannot remain, until twenty-six years of age, a virgin emotionally. I understand that completely. So both of us will wait."

"And we will continue our relationship. I enjoy our conversation."

As Salim got out of the car, he asked, "Won't you come in and say hello to my mother?"

"No," Hasti said. "I'll wait for you right here."

The big gate was half open, and Hasti heard the sound of Salim's footsteps on the sand for a time before a light went on and a door opened and closed. And the tops of the tree branches that hung over the large gate greeted Hasti.

There was no news of Salim, and again Hasti thought that he had left her in the lurch and it would be over right then. She knew the area well. Professor Mani's house was at the end of the same street. She could go to Professor Mani's house. No, it was too late, and Professor Mani was ill. Well, she could take a bus or van or whatever other vehicle came by and return home.

When Salim returned, he handed Hasti a package as he sat behind the wheel.

Hasti first pulled from the package a small jar with a tag taped onto it. "What's this?" she asked.

"Chickpea flour."

Then she brought out a fruit. "Is this a bitter citron?" she asked.

"No. It is a bergamot orange. I picked it from the greenhouse. The potted plant is so large with all these branches and leaves, but this year it produced only this one bergamot orange."

As they set off Salim asked, "Do you know the story of the bitter orange and bergamot girl?"

"In our childhood, Mehrmah Khanom told it to us several times . . ." Hasti smelled the bergamot orange and pressed it to her cheek.

"When I was picking it," Salim said, "I heard its voice saying, 'Oh, don't pluck! Ouch, he plucked!' But would it separate from the branch?"

When they arrived at the house, Hasti went to the kitchen and gave the jar of chickpea flour to Grandmother. But the cutlet had already been fried and spread on a plate, and Grandmother had poured the thinly cut potatoes into the frying pan. They sizzled. "I went to Teimur Khan's house," she said, "and got chickpea flour from his wife."

The fresh bread and carnelian-colored quince jam, the fig jam, and the basket of herbs on the dinner table were a testament to Grandmother's effort, and Hasti knew that tonight, due to aching legs, sleep would not come to Touran Jan's eyes.

Salim asked about Hasti's brother, and Hasti explained that tonight Shahin had taken Mother Eshi and Parviz to the cinema. Afterward they would probably give Parviz hazelnut ice cream, and Mother Eshi probably wanted fried sausages and mustard, and probably they wouldn't have found a means to get home yet. Salim noted that Eshrat Khanom has a car and driver.

Grandmother, who was tossing the salad, said, "Shahin doesn't set foot in his mother's husband's car, and he doesn't go to their house either." She laughed and said, "I don't know how my former daughter-in-law could get on a bus with those high-heeled shoes, or into a van or a taxi with those . . ."

To keep Grandmother from saying anything more, Hasti explained that sometimes Shahin takes Mother Eshi to a restaurant, or he gets tokens and they have lunch together in the Faculty of Dentistry cafeteria. "The reason for tonight's outing is that Parviz really wanted to see the film *Pinocchio*."

Salim praised Grandmother's fig jam and asked, "You mean Shahin Khan is studying dentistry?"

"No," Hasti said. "It's just that the food at the Faculty of Dentistry is better." She said that Shahin is in his fourth year at the Faculty of Law, in the field of political law, and that his favorite professor is Hamid Khan who, for New Year's this year, will go on a field trip with all the fourth-year students.

When Salim had given his thanks, said good-bye, and left, Grandmother put her hand on her lower back, sat in the armchair, and rubbed her knees. "Girl," she said, "you spoke so much nonsense today. You showed yourself to be more bitter than horseradish. Why? I don't have a good opinion of your mother, but she's found a perfect suitor for you."

"All the time the offended figure of Morad was before my eyes."

Hasti tossed and turned. Sleep had left her. The thought of Salim's eyes—eyes that seemed as though their owner was not of this world, that seemed to be searching for or seeing something far, far away—and of his magnanimity did not let her rest.

Simin had taught her that whatever model she chose for her painting, she should pay attention to the eyes more than to all the other parts of the body. Simin had said, "From the gaze you will discover the secret of the model's spirit." In the words of Hegel, she had added, "'The eyes are the body, and the gaze a spirit that has appeared in them.' It's like a jewel in the heart of a stone. The jewel is the spirit of the stone, but finding it is difficult. You must get to the hidden jewel by going through the stone; that is, through the solid body." And she had said, "Sight is superior to all other senses, and the blessing of the gaze, the look, the view, the wink, the watch is superior to and more mysterious than words, smiles, touch, taste, scent. In general, to look, stare, fix your eyes, or see is better than all the other windows that link us to this world."

And Grandmother would talk about the evil eye and would always burn wild rue incense for herself and Shahin and Hasti, and she would say that the gaze has so much power that it can cause a rock to burst. How well she remembered the evil eyes that had dried out perfectly shaped trees. That . . .

Hasti remembered the bergamot orange that Salim had given her and that Grandmother had put on the heater under the photo of her son. She had said, "This is a bergamot," and Hasti had said, "No. It's a bergamot orange." Touran Jan had said, "Bergamot orange and bergamot are one and the same thing. We will make jam of it, and another night, when he comes . . ."

"No," Hasti had said. "Leave it right there under the photo of my father." Then she had kissed Touran Jan and said, "My poor dear, how hard you worked to show us in good light!"

Why had Salim given her a bergamot orange? Why had he reminded Hasti of the story of the bitter orange and bergamot girl? Had he wanted to say, "If I want to pick you, will you yell, 'Ouch, he plucked; ouch, he plucked!'? Will you want to say, 'Don't pluck; it will hurt me. After all, here is my heart, here is my mind . . . '?" The memory of Mehrmah, the memory of the story of the bitter orange and bergamot girl, the memory of Salim's eyes, the memory of Morad . . .

Hasti's eyes grew hot, and tears ran silently down her cheeks. *Does all this attention to Salim's eyes*, she thought, *and all these mental associations foretell the tearing of my heart from Morad*? Eyes have the blessing of tears. Tears of joy and happiness, tears of sorrow, and Hasti counted tears of mystical bewilderment too. *Yes, tears. They are the extract and crystallization of all bitterness, all happiness, all ambiguity in a person's spirit. But tears are bitter because people's misfortune is greater than their good fortune. Through the years, many dynasties had been overthrown, but the dynasty of tears still rules over people.*

Hasti became aware of the associations and the depictions in her mind. Did she want to enter into the realm of poetry? Poetry was also dear, like eyes, and Simin would say, "The gradual perfection of every art is when it comes close to poetry." But when she thought deeply about it, she realized that, from the time that one of the painters of the day, Sohrab Sepehri, had also become a poet, the desire of most painters was to become a poet-painter. A poet, like Sepehri, who wanted "to give a jasmine flower to the beggar" and who would say his prayers toward a red rose and whose father, when he died, saw all policemen as poets.

3

When Grandmother had come to clean up the room, she had found Salim's notebook, which had fallen beside the armchair.

"Where is it now?" Hasti asked.

"Next to the bergamot."

Hasti grabbed the notebook and started turning the pages. She skipped the sections written in Arabic and French. She didn't understand the short English expressions, even though they had been written in a good hand. Even the Persian notes were only sometimes comprehensible to her. The title of the notebook was "Letters to God," and it was divided into five sections: Mysticism, India, Islam, China, and Miscellaneous. Of the writers' names, she knew Rumi well, but she didn't know Ibn Arabi. In the section on India, she didn't know the meaning of *avatar*, but she could read the names Sathya Sai Baba and Maharishi Mahesh Yogi. Of the third name, only Bhagavan was legible. Salim's Persian and Arabic handwriting was not that good.

In the Mysticism section, several pages were written in Persian, and Hasti devoured the words and the sentences.

The Burden of Trust

I like the expression *the burden of trust*. Both Rumi and Hafez as well as others have talked about it. It is obvious that all of them have borrowed the term from the Quran. Seriously, what is the burden of trust that neither the sky, nor the earth, nor the mountains agreed to carry it, yet humans did? Did humans agree because of ignorance? And did this very ignorance cause them to attain favor and knowledge? And was this oppression that they brought upon themselves superior to all justice? Some say that the burden of trust is sorrow because God created humans out of a mud similar to potters' mud using teardrops that angels had shed for forty years. So humans are made of sadness. Rumi has interpreted the burden of trust to be human free will and freedom. The sky and the earth ran away from freedom. And of course, the mountains could not have accepted it because God had secured them in place like "a pin in the earth." I have another idea—that the burden of trust is the love that takes humans to the valley of faith. I don't know why I thought of Moses, who heard God, and Mohammad, who saw God.

But the reason I'm thinking about the burden of trust tonight is a girl I have just met. I think this girl is the burden of trust that I will carry on my shoulders and take to the valley of faith. She is well-mannered and gracious. My mother liked her, too. I have only seen her once. She said, "I read my own fortune." The only problem with this girl is her broken family. Nor does she know anything about religion.

On the next page, the passage likening God to the nucleus of an atom and the explosion of the mother atom . . . that Salim had read to Hasti and Grandmother.

In the section on India, Hasti's attention was drawn to the passage below:

We are like a balloon whose string is in the hand of God. He pulls us in whichever direction he wills. He flies us in the sky and pulls the string on earth . . . and how fragile we are. With one flick we burst and vanish.

Under that passage Salim had made a comment:

So what happens to the "will"? Didn't God give humans the will even to throw themselves into the abyss of sin? And hasn't the stain of sin made them distinct from the rest of creation?

God, You gave me the thread to weave the silk cloth of my life. May it never happen that I weave a cheap rug out of it . . .

Hasti's heart tightened. Neither was Salim's outlook like that of Morad, nor were the words that he composed or had adopted. Who was right?

As soon as she closed the door of the house, Hasti was sorry. She wanted to return, call her secretary, Fakhri, and tell her that she was not coming to the office that day. There were many excuses she could use: "I'm going to the carpet company to see the antique rugs; maybe one of the designs will be useful for us." "I'm going to the Museum of Ancient Iran's storage room to see Marlik pottery." Maybe . . .

Instead of all this, she would go to Tehran University to Simin's class. She wouldn't go to listen to her teach for two hours, but would figure out how to find her alone and what to tell her. Finding Simin alone was never easy. She had tried it many times. Usually, students, both male and female, surround her after class and pour down the wide staircase beside her and behind her. And in the corridor another crowd joins her and assails her with questions. Simin's eyes shine. *These are all my children.* Marami comes from the faculty administration office and shouts, "Ladies and gentlemen, disperse. The professor is tired."

Simin goes to the department office, and Hasti follows her. The secretary is sitting at her desk rapidly knitting something. One of her friends, a well-dressed woman, is sitting on the chair next to her and filing her nails. A large table is in the center of the room with chairs set around it. The department office is the meeting room, the office of the secretary and registrar, and the lunchroom for the secretary and her friends. It is also the professors' lounge, the place for advising, and the place for students and professors to bargain over grades. Amidst all these activities, Hasti once observed the secretary using the meeting table to take a pattern out of an issue of *Burda* magazine to make a dress for a friend. She was tracing the pattern, and her friend was sitting on a chair basting. Both students and professors testify, however, that the secretary is the best in her work and that she provides a shoulder for all of them to cry on.

Hasti had heard that the secretary's well-dressed friend was a member of university security. She knows that Simin would suggest having lunch together in a quiet corner of the faculty cafeteria. They would stand in line for a while, where one cannot express certain views or use certain words. Simin would get the food coupons and ask Hasti, "Do you want a soft drink?" Hasti would like a Pepsi, which they don't have. Okay, Coke? They don't have it. Bubble Up? Canada Dry? 7up? They have 7up. They would wait for a table to be free and then sit awaiting the food.

One of the others waiting for food would come and greet Simin Khanom and compliment her on her interview published in *Kayhan* newspaper. He would say that His Majesty, the shah, has also read it, and that they have asked the newspaper to send the second part of the interview to the royal court. Then, the second liar. The third liar. The fourth one would say that he has read her novel *Savushun* and would ask the meaning of the title. Simin would say, "It's explained in the book itself, if you've read it." The person would say, "I swear I have read it three times." Simin would say, "You will understand it if you read it the fourth time." A woman would come, a man; old and young, everyone lies. Simin would say to Hasti, "They say this to all writers, whereas they haven't read even one line of their writing. In addition, most of them have come to eye you."

This one would be the cheekiest of all. He would tighten the knot of his tie, bring a chair, put it next to Simin and Hasti's table, and sit down. Then he would ask Simin what new jokes she had heard. And he would start: "A person from Qazvin . . ." "A person from Rasht . . ." "A person from Isfahan . . ."

Panting, Hasti entered her office. Fakhri was sitting at the desk typing the annual report. Her body moved back and forth with the clicking of the keys, and her ponytail bounced up and down. But the Aleppo boil on her cheek was fixed in its place.

Hasti was overjoyed by the tidiness of her desk. She picked up a pencil and tried to draw Salim's eyes on a piece of paper. She drew several, but none of the drawings reflected the secret of Salim's eyes. The key to this secret was not even in Salim's own hands. The servant brought tea.

Simin or Professor Mani, from which one should she seek help?

Hasti remembers the day when she was supposed to meet with Professor Mani and Simin to determine her undergraduate thesis topic. She and Simin have already sat at the meeting table and have had tea, too. The department secretary is knitting. Her friend comes in with a box of pastry and offers some to the three of them. She has just been promoted. In the security office, no one's reward is overlooked. Ajami, the department servant, comes in. He has a pox scar on his face, and he is wearing a blue coverall jacket. He whispers in Simin's ear.

Simin says, "Invite him in, but when Professor Mani arrives, he must leave." A middle-aged man with a closely shaven head and a dark red shirt comes in and sits down. The department secretary and her friend leave the room with the box of pastry.

The red-shirted man says, "Professor Daneshvar, I have two questions."

"You're not a student in our department, are you?" Simin asks.

The red-shirted man says, "No."

"What do you study?"

"Political law."

"May I see your student ID card?"

"I don't have it with me."

"So how were you able to enter the university campus? No one is allowed in without a card."

"Well, now I'm here."

"You're too big to be able to enter through the fence," Simin says. "And you don't have wings that would enable you to fly over the fence."

"Meaning?"

"You know well what I mean."

The red-shirted man puts his hand on his heart and says, "I swear that I am not a SAVAK agent."

"Let's get to your questions, then."

"Why don't you continue on Jalal Al-e Ahmad's path?"

Simin smiles. "Because I'm not Jalal Al-e Ahmad. Everyone acts according to their own nature and temperament."

The red-shirted man speaks sarcastically. "Your nature requires you to give financial aid to the families of political prisoners? To use the influence of your family and try to follow the cases of political prisoners? And to protect them? To go to Evin Prison to visit them and encourage them?"

"I don't have the resources to help financially on a large scale," Simin says. "But sometimes I give a bit of financial help to friends whose husbands are political prisoners. This is not a crime, is it? Actually, none of the things that you have mentioned is a crime. Besides, what does any of this have to do with you? You said you're not a SAVAK agent, didn't you?"

The red-shirted man says, "With all due respect, both you and your deceased husband liked showing off, liked being a topic of discussion. As a matter of fact, what you do is a kind of self-promotion, yet in a feminine way, covertly, and . . ."

Simin laughs and says, "Mister, if it is self-promotion, why would it be covert?" She becomes serious and asks, "So, next question?"

The red-shirted man says, "It's rumored that SAVAK killed Jalal Al-e Ahmad. I want to hear it from you that . . ."

"Why don't you ask Chief Nassiri?" Simin says.

Professor Mani enters. Simin and Hasti stand up, and the red-shirted man stands, too. As he is leaving, he remembers to be empathetic. "Professor Daneshvar, I want only good for you. Why should your class be like a travelers' inn or a mosque, where anyone who desires can enter?"

Hasti breathes in relief that the red-shirted man has finally left, though without saying good-bye.

Professor Mani is fat. His face has turned red, and his eyes are a bit red, too. He has a small mouth.

After a lengthy discussion, Simin suggests, "Because Hasti is skillful at drawing nude bodies, and she is a woman as well, she should go to Sare'in, to the Gavmish Goli hot springs pool when it is the women's hour. She can draw at least fifty women and children in various positions and movements, naked and bare." She pauses and then continues, "Jalal and I went to Sare'in together, to the inferno. I'm prepared to give her my notes about it."

"How about Jalal's notes?" Professor Mani asks.

"No," Simin says, "not Jalal's notes, because we are talking about a feminine perspective and mentality. When it was the women's hour at the pool, Jalal was not allowed to enter."

"What a pity!"

Fakhri came in and placed the annual report that she had typed in front of Hasti. Hasti thanked her. She wasn't in the mood to read a report. She picked up the phone and called her house. She told Grandmother that she would come home late that afternoon. Grandmother had to know all the details. Where is she going? Why is she going? When is she coming home?

Hasti explained that she would go either to Simin's house in Tajrish or to Professor Mani's house. If she goes to Simin's house, which is far away, she might sleep over there. Grandmother emphasized that she should definitely call from there and inform her. *Well, she's old and lonely, and . . .* "But Shahin is with you!" Hasti said.

The annual report lay there waiting on the desk, unread, and Hasti remembered the afternoon that she had gone to visit Simin when she was sick . . .

Haji Ma'sumeh opens the door and greets her. She is heavyset and, in her own words, "leggy." She's wearing the green wool jacket and slacks that Simin had brought from England. Over that, she's wearing Simin's sheepskin vest that Roya had sent her as a gift from Mashhad.

Hasti enters. The room is hot, and there's a pan of scented water on the heater. The air smells of chamomile. Simin picks up a bottle of rubbing alcohol from the medicine tray that is on the table and says, "Rub some alcohol under your nose."

Hasti sits at the dining table. A master's thesis by one of the students is on the table, and a thick, open book is in front of Simin.

Haji Ma'sumeh brings tea and biscuits for Hasti and sweet-lemon juice for Simin. "Hasti Khanom," she says, "I implore you to stay the night. I have prepared turnip soup for the lady, and I'll run out and buy some kebab for you and me, with two bottles of Pepsi."

She shows her dentures to Hasti, and asks, "Do you like them? I just got them." As far as Hasti remembers, three of Simin's servants fancied getting dentures while they were in her house. They kept going and coming, pulled some teeth, made molds, and then put in the dentures. The dentures would hurt; again, they would go, and now it is okay . . .

Hasti knows that Haji Ma'sumeh is a hermaphrodite; she is neither a man nor a woman, but has in her some traces of both sexes. On her chin a bit of hair grows, which she removes. Her chest is flat, but she has shaped her eyebrows. She has a manly voice. She has covered her long black hair with a yellow and green headscarf.

"Haji Ma'sumeh," Hasti asks, "why are you wearing the lady's clothes?"

Simin laughs and finishes Hasti's words. "The lady is not dead yet!"

"I swear to the Mecca pilgrimage I have made," Haji Ma'sumeh says. "May the sacred black stone shame me if I lie. The lady is cool. She doesn't mind."

Hasti knows that Haji Ma'sumeh has neither gone to Mecca, nor has she seen the sacred black stone up close. Only once, as a man, she had been the servant of a haji whose job was selling cement, plaster powder, and limestone.

"Ma'am," Haji Ma'sumeh asks, "once I've finished shoveling the snow, may I go to the religious ceremony at the Arzani house?"

"Go."

"May I take some sugar and some tea, too?"

"Take some."

"Is there anything you need?"

She brings water and pours it into the pan on the heater. She takes a handful of dried chamomile flowers from the box next to the heater, adds it, and stirs with her finger. Then she brings kerosene and pours it into the heater's storage tank.

When Haji Ma'sumeh leaves, Simin says, "I must find someone else and fire her. I've heard from the neighbors that she smuggles opium. She's transformed this house into a hangout for people from Qaen . . . Her brother, Jeffrey . . ."

Hasti laughs and asks, "You've changed Ja'far's name to Jeffrey?"

"Haven't you seen his frizzy, afro hair, full of small curls . . . ?"

"The summer theft was the work of Jeffrey and his fellow townsmen," Hasti says. "But you never told me the whole story."

"Well, I was sleeping in the courtyard under the mosquito net," Simin says. "Haji Ma'sumeh came and woke me and said there was a thief. I saw she was holding a long stick with a soft brush at its end to clean spiderwebs. 'You go ahead,' I said. 'I'll follow.' I waited until the thieves had left."

Hasti laughs hard and loud.

"When I came in, I saw that the lights were on and the whole house was a mess. They had taken a few pieces of jewelry and nine thousand tomans. When the neighbors and the police came, everyone said that they suspected Haji Ma'sumeh and her fellow townsmen. But I didn't let them arrest her. Marshal Naneh said that she had heard Haji Ma'sumeh's 'Oh, thief . . . Oh, thief . . . ,' but she had not heard any footsteps. Only that amber necklace that Jalal had brought me from Russia was especially precious to me."

Someone knocks, someone rings the bell. Hasti opens the door. Someone has brought halva to commemorate a death. From Jamshid Khan's house. The woman is holding a tray on which there are four plates of halva. "Isn't Haji Ma'sumeh here?" she asks.

"No." Hasti says. "She has gone to the Arzani house for a religious ceremony."

"Well," the woman says, "it is the night of the saint's martyrdom, after all . . . Hasn't the lady gone, too?"

"The lady is ill."

"If possible," the woman says, "please put the halva on another plate. We don't have many plates."

Hasti goes to the kitchen and does as the woman has requested.

"I'll come to visit the lady as soon as I'm free," the woman says. Then she thinks and adds, "No, I won't have time tonight. I must go to the religious ceremony at the Arzani house, too. Otherwise, his wife will bombard me with a thousand sarcastic remarks tomorrow, saying that I have ignored her religious ceremony . . ."

The phone rings. The telephone is on a small table in the hallway. Hasti picks up the receiver. A young girl's voice asks, "Is this the Al-e Ahmad house?"

Hasti gives an affirmative reply.

The voice says, "I am Mrs. Arzani's granddaughter. Please go and ask my grandmother to come to the phone . . ."

"My dear," Hasti says, "Haji Ma'sumeh is not home, and the lady is ill. As for me, I don't know where your grandmother lives."

"The lady knows the address," the voice says. "You can ask her. It won't kill you, will it?"

Hasti hangs up.

Again someone knocks. Hasti opens the door to Marshal Naneh. Marshal Naneh is the servant of the Honorable Major. She comes in. Her heavy cheeks hang from beneath her eyes all the way to her double chin. She's wearing the major's trousers, which are tattered at the knees. The front of her blouse is greasy and filthy. She's also wearing the major's military jacket, which is both tight and short, its epaulettes torn. A black scarf covers her head. "Say hello to the lady," she says, "and tell her that the major's wife has asked her to give her Leila Khanom's magazines. She has said, 'I swear to God that I didn't cut out the pictures.'"

"What's the name of the magazine?"

"Its name was on the tip of my tongue, but I've forgotten it. Please call the major's wife and ask her."

"Leila Khanom is not home. Tell your lady that we don't know where she has put the magazines."

"But she will be upset," Marshal Naneh says. "You can't imagine how bitter she can be."

"Naneh Jan, go. Godspeed."

"She has the grudge of a camel," Marshal Naneh says.

Hasti goes to Simin. "Simin Khanom," she says angrily, "what kind of a life is it that you have created for yourself? The other day, that SAVAK guy said that your class is a travelers' inn. Now I see that your house is a travelers' inn, too. Sell this old place; it's become a coffeehouse! Go live in an apartment, and don't give your address or telephone number to anyone. Isn't it a shame to waste your precious time this way?"

"Why are you standing?" Simin asks maternally. "Sit down and take it easy. I admit that I don't have more than seven or eight major flaws and ten or twelve minor ones. My first flaw is that I have *naïve* written on my forehead."

Hasti sits and says, "And anyone who spends time with you immediately discovers your gullibility."

"You mean they read the *naïve* on my forehead?"

"And you let them use you."

"You mean I let them take advantage of me." Simin laughs and adds, "I created you myself, and now you are confronting me?"

Hasti has calmed down. "I have been created by a mother and a father," she says, "neither of whom has parented me."

"I meant something else completely," Simin says.

"Creating with respect to emotions and intellect," Hasti says. "But you taught me yourself that wherever I see wrong, I should say something."

"It's true, but in this corner of the world, where we live, social institutions either don't exist, or if they do exist, they don't work. Therefore, all of us will gradually become social workers. But I can't live in an apartment. In an apartment, I feel that I'm hanging between earth and sky, suspended in the air. I feel that I'm suffocating, especially at sunset. Besides, every corner of this house holds a memory for me."

Hasti respects Simin's silence.

"I need this courtyard," Simin says, "with its arches and pool, and the sitting room with its wall heater."

"And probably the grapevine trellis with its shade where you sit and write," Hasti adds.

"And the pine trees," Simin says, "and the plants and the doves and the sparrows. And the neighbor's pigeons that drink water from the pool and raise their heads and give thanks to God. When I caress the trees, their leaves tremble with joy under my hand. I know that they like me, too. I like the leaves more than the flowers. No one thinks of the leaves. How long they wait for a single flower to bloom."

"Do you also like the cockroaches, the mosquitos, the lizards, the flies, and the mice?" Hasti asks.

"They have become completely extinct in this house. There are lots of insecticides. There are traps for the mice, and nothing beats the reproduction of cats."

"Who feeds the cats?"

"The neighbor lady. She has even chosen a name for each one: George Washington, Denis Papin, Shahnaz Pahlavi, Ardeshir Zahedi."

Hasti laughs.

"The neighbor lady curls her hair just like Denis Papin. She says that she saw a picture of Denis Papin in her elementary school or junior high school textbook. She says, 'He was the inventor of the steam machine. He was an important man.'"

Simin puts the thermometer under her tongue and looks at her watch. She has a fever of only one degree. She takes an antibiotic pill. Haji

Ma'sumeh has put everything on a tray on the dining table: a bottle of water, a glass, the pills, and the bottles of syrup that she had fetched from the pharmacy. All this after she had put the neighbor's safe on her shoulder and carried it to their storeroom. Then the towel, and then the newspaper that she had run out herself to buy.

Simin puts the newspaper on the table and motions to Hasti to put the pot of hot scented water on the newspaper. Hasti burns her hand. Simin covers her head with the towel and breathes in the chamomile vapor. Then she puts nose drops in her nose.

"The potholder was next to the heater," she tells Hasti. "There's Vali ointment for your burn in the medicine cabinet. In the right-hand side."

Hasti thinks of the person who created Vali ointment. There was a rumor that its creator had held a sit-in in front of the Ministry of Health. He had wanted to set a part of his body on fire and then apply the Vali ointment to show the officials its miracle so that he could get a permit to distribute it. Hasti didn't know if the creator of Vali ointment had actually done this or not.

"I've come to visit you and see how you are," Hasti says, "but I've upset you. Maybe you are doing the right thing." She thinks for a second and asks, "Do you remember Faridi?"

"That damn Tudeh Party student?"

"Yes."

"He's in prison now."

Hasti continues. "After Maleki and Jalal died, he told me, 'I'm going to Simin's house to find out from her if Maleki's supporters are thinking of reinstating the League of Socialists and who their candidate is. This issue is important to the party.'"

"So that they could tarnish the candidate right away."

"He had come to visit you, and you had not divulged anything about this issue. But . . ."

"I know what you're going to say. But he looked poor, and it was raining that day, and I knew that he didn't have the money to pay for his return taxi."

"He always wore your purple wool sweater and tied your violet scarf over it. Most likely, he's still wearing it now, in prison."

Simin puts her hands on her temples, closes her eyes, and says, "All these lost, shepherdless lambs."

Simin opens her eyes and says, "See, when that woman brings halva, you eat the halva, but to avoid being used you do not even say 'May God bless the deceased's soul.' Marshal Naneh wanted the fashion magazine *Burda*. The magazines are in Leila's wardrobe in her room. Of course, they cut out the patterns of the dresses they like and then swear to God that it wasn't them, but it was. The Arzani house is not that far. As Haji Ma'sumeh would say, you could just run and get the grandmother. Maybe her granddaughter had important business with her."

Simin continues. "Now, we'll make plans for ourselves and raise ourselves from the triviality of life."

"So let's disconnect the phone." Hasti says.

"No," Simin says. "Maybe your own grandmother wants to reach you."

Simin picks up the thesis and says, "This is the master's thesis of a girl who has done research on the mystical and philosophical works of Sheikh al-Ishraq (Master of Illumination), Shahab al-Din Sohravardi: *Treatise of the Bird, The Red Intellect, The Chant of Gabriel's Wing, On the Reality of Love.*"

She thinks a moment and adds, "Did you know that Sohravardi was killed in his youth? Murdered Master, Martyred Master, and all like him are taken out this way in their youth. But what do we ourselves do with each other? As long as we are alive, we deny each other, and when one of us is executed, we throw flowers at his feet."

She thinks a moment again and adds, "Even worse, some of us go whichever way the wind blows and try to drive from the stage those who have remained pure, using slander, false accusation, and swear words. Whereas, if, as Akhavan-Sales puts it, 'This old uncle of ours, history, doesn't say the last word, the people will.'"

Simin picks up a tangerine, peels it, and offers it to Hasti. "Have some fruit, or halva." Hasti prefers the halva.

"Today I read this thesis," Simin says. "I used *On the Reality of Love* in my own thesis. I was reading a section of it when you arrived. I was mesmerized. Read the parts which I have underlined with a red pencil. Of course, I have interpreted it."

Hasti laughs and says, "So that I become mesmerized, too? Then, as Rumi says, 'Who shall take us home?'"

Simin pays no attention to Hasti's humor. "You might find it a little disjointed. We don't have time to read it all."

Hasti looks at Simin's thesis. Worried, she says, "Simin Khanom, the print is too small. I can't distinguish all the letters."

"Maybe you need glasses," Simin says. "You must see an eye doctor." She takes her own glasses from her housedress pocket and gives them to Hasti. "Put on my glasses, but please, when it comes to your painting, see only through your own lenses!"

So, how about what you and the likes of you have taught me? Hasti thinks. *How about what I have read and heard*?

It is as if Simin has read her mind. You could tell from her reply. "Events and past experiences, if you do not become obsessed with them; what you have learned and what you know, even if you might have forgotten them; the sum of all of these leaves knowledge in your mind so that you will be able to see the world with awareness and through your own lenses. But Hasti Jan, don't remain, until the end of your life, the mindless appendage of those who have taught you, and don't become their talking parrot, either. You must doubt what you have heard, learned, and read. Maybe I will become a fossil. The likes of me have been wrong."

Hasti is still thoughtful.

"Read, my dear," Simin says. "You'll be late. I'll close my eyes, and, with the ecstasy I have due to my fever, I'll fly the heavens. Then we will listen to music. I have two new records. One is *My Slender-Waisted Beloved*, sung by an Afghan, and the other is *You Have Two Dark Eyes*, sung and played by Bijan Mofid. He is another martyred sheikh. He is destroying himself all on his own."

Hasti puts on Simin's glasses and says, "Wow! This is much better!"

"They suit you, too," Simin says. "By the way, where do things stand with Morad?"

"Nowhere."

"As Sohravardi would say, you have left the spirit land only to arrive at nowhere land."

Hasti reads, "God created wisdom, which is the same as the enlightened or superior being. This primordial light has three characteristics or three forms: knowledge of the truth, knowledge of the self, and knowledge of that which did not exist, but then did."

Simin explains, "Meaning that it was possible that it would not come into existence."

Hasti reads, "From the first of these characteristics, that pertains only to the one God—that is, it has to do with absolute perfect knowledge—beauty came into existence. From the second of these characteristics—that is, the one that pertains to the self—came love. And from the third characteristic, sorrow emerged."

Simin sighs and says, "So it was possible that sorrow wouldn't emerge. So 'love' is the answer to problems."

Hasti reads, "These three—that is, beauty, love, and sorrow, all of which have been created from one source—are brothers. Beauty, the oldest of the brothers, looked within himself and found the finest divine blessings in himself. He smiled and one thousand angels came into existence. Love, the middle brother, who was close to Beauty, was moved by Beauty's smile. He was struck by Beauty and infatuated with his perfection. And because after any union, separation appears, the youngest brother, who was called Sorrow, joined Love. And with this mixture, the heavens and earth came into being."

"Did you understand?" Simin asks.

"No."

"In Sohravardi's opinion, the creation of the universe is indebted to beauty, love, and sorrow. These three brothers are the three allegorical forms of enlightened or superior being, which is the primordial creation, meaning wisdom."

Hasti turns the pages until she gets to the red lines. "After forty days, when humans were created, the inhabitants of the kingdom of heaven wished to meet them. Beauty said, 'I will go to meet them first.' So he mounted God's steed and came to the place where humans were. He found the place very pleasant. He settled there. Love followed him. He wanted to settle there, too. His forehead hit the wall of terror, and he fell. Sorrow took his hand. Love opened his eyes and saw the angels who had all gathered there. He looked at them. They had surrendered themselves to Beauty and bestowed their kingdom on him, and they all joined Beauty's court. When they came close, Love, who was commander, made Sorrow his deputy and commanded everyone to kiss the ground from afar because Beauty could not bear intimacy. When the angels saw Beauty, everyone knelt and kissed the ground, and humans were ornamented in the angels' robes."

Hasti turns the pages again. "Beauty was waiting in nowhere land for a long time until Joseph was created. Beauty went and hung onto Joseph such that no room remained for Love. Hopeless, Love came to the youngest brother, Sorrow, who was in the desert of bewilderment. Sorrow said, 'We were both at the service of Beauty and have our status due to him. He is our master. Now the right thing to do is that each of us go in a separate direction and follow the path of God and asceticism until one day we will have the chance to serve the master again.' So Sorrow went to Canaan to see Jacob . . .

"And Jacob gave all that he had. He even gave him the pupil of his eyes and named the monastery of his body the House of Sorrows. Love, as personified by Joseph, went to Egypt and asked for the address of the beloved and ended up in Zuleikha's chamber.

"But Love would not take everyone in and would not show himself to just anyone, and if he wanted to go somewhere, first he would send Sorrow to empty the house and give the good news that the promised one is coming. Then Love would arrive and go all around the house. He would destroy the irregularities and right the wrongs. Then he would set off for the court of Beauty. So when Love gives us the capacity for union, we must surrender to it.

"Love has been extracted from a vine, which is a plant that emerges in the garden, at the foot of the tree. First it makes its roots firm in the ground. Then it raises its head and wraps itself around the tree. It continues growing until it covers the whole tree, and it takes all the moisture and energy of the tree until the tree dries out . . .

"Love is a servant who was raised in the primordial time and place, and his duty is guarding the two worlds. Wherever he sets foot, the wild bull of self must be sacrificed, yet not everyone is worthy of this sacrifice."

The phone rings, and Hasti picks it up. It's Touran Jan.

"Why haven't you come?"

"I'll be on my way right away."

"If only this clinging witch could let you be. Is it my fault that she's barren?"

Simin laughs and says, "Your grandmother doesn't like me. Well, I steal you from her, and she's left all alone."

"Before I leave, tell me if you agree with such words and ideas."

"No. Joy and love are part of human nature. Why should love wrap itself around the human body like a vine around a tree and dry out the leaves and branches of this most precious tree in the world? But if you wish to sacrifice the bull of self for Morad, and become the Zuleikha of your time, it's up to you."

"Is he worth it?" Hasti asks.

Simin does not answer.

Much later, Hasti reads Sohravardi's book *On the Reality of Love* with Morad and asks him his opinion. "Let me read it again," Morad says, "and I'll write my opinion for you."

Morad's writing was in the desk drawer in Hasti's office. She found it and read:

> My dear Hasti,
>
> This vast and comprehensive book of sorrows that constitutes our literature, save for a few exceptions, is born from our despotic culture, and in our era, from our colonial-despotic culture. It's precisely because of this that we find in it an ambiguous reality which is at times nightmarish and, at other times, exemplary. But fortunately, Rumi and Hafez, who are at the peak of our culture, were not that fond of sorrow. Sometimes I ask myself, "Isn't it about time that the poets and writers who express the essence of our era try to surpass these two?"
>
> Your Morad

Hasti was trying to depict the secret in Salim's eyes on paper, and she was asking herself, *Is Morad what I really desire, or is neither of them*?

From beyond the centuries, Sohravardi had taken Hasti's heart in his fist to reveal the secret of love to her. A whisper from a faraway road was murmuring in her ears, "Well done, love; well done the love that we possess, O God!"

Fakhri came to Hasti's desk. The annual report had not been touched. Hasti had drawn at least ten eyes on the paper and was drawing another one but from the side. And the trash can was full of crumpled paper. She didn't even raise her head. Fakhri put her finger on one of the drawings and said, "What mysterious eyes!"

Then she said, "Miss Nourian, you haven't read the report!"

"I'll read it in the afternoon."

Hasti dialed Professor Mani's house to make an appointment. She said that, if it were no trouble, she would visit him that afternoon. The professor postponed it until later. He had discovered that A'lam al-Dowleh had a few photographs of Qajar women, and he wanted to go there that afternoon and get them from the old man for free, if he could.

4

Every afternoon, when Hasti came home, Grandmother would say, "So, tell me. What's new?" And Hasti would report . . . Well, that afternoon she would go from the office to Professor Mani's house . . . And . . .

Hasti had decided that Professor Mani, more than Simin, had seen ups and downs in life, and his wife undoubtedly knew about love, since she had come all the way from Czechoslovakia to Tehran with him and, in the professor's words, "had stuck with me for a good thirty years." He would say to his students, "Come, admire our forbearance and sympathize with us."

And another report . . . that early morning on New Year's Day, she should go to Mother Eshi's house and set up their New Year's table. Since she had a thousand other tasks for Hasti, Mother Eshi had said, "Go to bed early so that you won't be tired. Ahmad has invited a slew of foreign guests for the turning of the year, so that they can see New Year ceremonies in an Iranian family." And Grandmother had said nothing because Hasti had said, "They have invited Salim, too."

In contrast to Hasti's expectations, it wasn't long before a taxi stopped in front of her at the start of Shahabad Avenue. It had four passengers. A man sitting next to the driver got out, Hasti took the place beside the driver, and the man got in again. The driver was fat, and the man wasn't skinny, either. It was as though they had Hasti pressed in a laundry mangle. The gearshift was hitting Hasti's leg as the driver kept shifting, and she kept pulling away. It was clear that the man next to her had eaten a lot of garlic at lunch time.

Hasti told the driver to stop at the Shah Avenue intersection, and the driver stopped right there in the middle of the street. The man grumbled and got out. While waiting for change Hasti said to the man, "Well, if you are going a long way, you shouldn't have gotten out to begin with."

"I always sit next to the window, sister," the man said. As he got back into the car, he passed gas loudly. He turned to the three women in the back seat and said, "Swear to God, that was the cars lined up behind the taxi honking their horns."

Hasti arrived at the end of Pahlavi Avenue by means of another taxi. She had planned to catch a third taxi, but she changed her mind. It wasn't far to Professor Mani's house. The one time that she had to cross the wide street, finding a way among cars and people and pleading with her hands and eyes for some drivers to just tap once on the brakes and stop was, in Touran Jan's words, "more than enough for her and her ancestors."

She had been to Professor Mani's house many times to show him her drawings. She could go from the outer courtyard to the inner courtyard with her eyes shut. Both courtyards were built of brick and had decorative brick arches in the architectural style of the Qajar era, but the brick did not seem old. It seemed that someone had polished all those algebraic designs on the surface of the arches with a pumice stone—probably Gholam Reza, the gardener, cook, servant, and handyman for both courtyards. The professor had not touched the shape of the building or its decoration. He had only added to the house this century's creature comforts.

Triangular blue tiles had been placed all around the little garden plots, and the small pools had also been lined with blue tiles. Gold and red fish moved gracefully in the pools. Over the inner courtyard pool, at the top of the arch, there was a carved lion head that seemed to be yawning. Hasti knew that the professor had bequeathed all his belongings, after his death and that of his wife, to the Faculty of Fine Arts. It was going to the right owners—if only that rich museum is not looted, and if those involved in the property's transfer and delivery don't each one pocket a few pieces of its relics. The couple had no children.

The professor's wife took Hasti to the sitting room. The first time that Hasti had seen her, she was middle-aged, and her remaining good looks gave notice of the beauty of her youth. Photos of the woman that were dispersed here and there, in the niches, on the walls, and on the tables, bore witness to this fact. But now . . . It was as though time had scattered the dust of old age on her face and her limbs, as though from head to foot soft ashes had been sprinkled. Her silver hair had only a few strands of gold. Time had drawn lines around her blue eyes. Between her eyebrows two parallel lines had been placed in remembrance, nostalgia even. Her gray clothes accentuated the curvature of her back. Tired, she moved slowly. As if apologizing for her gray slippers being so big, she asked, "Is there an herbal remedy for corns?"

She told Hasti, "Go to kitchen and make tea or coffee with milk for you."

"Shall I make some for you too?" Hasti asked.

"No, thank you," the woman said in broken Persian. "If you drink coffee or tea, you not sleep until morning."

The niches of the living room were filled with antiques. In one narrow niche there was a green crystal decanter; the bouquet of various colored flowers on its body appeared to have been presented to the niche. Next to the decanter, a place on the wall had been given to a notched plate in the middle of which was a picture of the last Qajar shah, Ahmad Shah, who seemed to be sighing for the bouquet of flowers on the crystal decanter. In another niche, a water pipe, its tube curled and its silver top jewel-studded, waited to be put to work, but Hasti knew that it would just have to keep waiting. From the crystal pot on which the water pipe was fixed, a picture of Naser al-Din Shah Qajar, with his full, curved mustache, stared at Hasti. "New buy," the woman said.

Hasti's attention was drawn to a photo of a young woman that she had not seen anywhere. It was in a golden frame in a niche above the head of the sofa. The woman's dress was like sailors' clothing. Two unframed photos had been attached to the walls of the niche on the two sides of the image of the woman. Hasti couldn't see them well. She stood up to go observe the pictures more closely. The woman also stood. "Let me go see!" she said. "He gone to take a shower."

"He's shaving," Hasti said. "I hear the sound of the electric razor."

The woman's eyes rounded. "He didn't shower?"

The photo on the right was of a woman in a chador and a face veil that had been pushed back onto the top of her head. With its folds and creases, the face veil formed a half circle above the woman's head and hung beside her ears. The eyes of the woman smiled. Her connected eyebrows had clearly been widened with black dye. The photo on the left showed a woman whose narrow, clinging pants revealed the curves of her legs up to the top of her knees, and above that, a short, full skirt with a flowered edge . . . She looked like a ballet dancer.

Hasti picked up a photo of the professor's wife as a young woman. It was like a picture postcard of a Western woman, a postcard that had been tastefully retouched. The woman returned and said, "He come soon." Hasti looked at her. Now she looked like a photo that had been crumbled and then smoothed out with the hand, a photo that had not been retouched at all. *Couldn't one iron the back of the picture? No. The passage of time is not compatible with this type of ironing.*

Professor Mani entered, and, after greeting Hasti, he sat on the sofa, put his hand over his heart, and said to his wife, "My dear, this battery is not strong anymore. One day it will stop working." His wife gave him a handkerchief to clean the perspiration from his face, which had turned beet red.

A tear came to the blue eyes of the woman. "My turn first," she said. "This my second country, and I cannot go back my first country. It is under heel of Russians. If you go, I have not strength."

Professor Mani took the withered hand of his wife, sat her down beside him, and kissed her hair. "You have all these friends and acquaintances," he said. "Hasti, too. She won't let you be alone. Isn't that so, Hasti?"

Hasti chattered boldly. "Why speak of death now? Speak of life. I have come to announce that I have found another semi-suitor. If I give him a little push, he will fall into the trap. I've come to ask you, should I give him that little push, or not? Unfortunately, love for Morad has tied my hands behind my back."

The professor stretched out, and his wife pulled a blanket from beneath the sofa to spread on him. She sat by his feet and began massaging them. "Give him a shove with your shoulders," the professor said. "He has only a few faults. His bushy beard is an impediment to kissing. He also fingers prayer beads." He laughed and began coughing.

"He also fingers prayer beads?" Hasti thought for a moment and said, "Are you speaking of someone in particular?"

"Salim Farrokhi," Professor Mani said. "He was here last night. Ostensibly, he had come to inquire after my health, but he sat here until 11:00 p.m. asking about you. My wife and I yawned so much that he finally left."

"But," Hasti said, "he has shown himself to me to be well mannered."

"And so he is," the professor responded. "We've been neighbors for years, and I know him well. A better suitor won't come your way. My wife and I pushed him enough. Hold the wedding while I'm still alive."

"But Professor," Hasti said, "what shall I do about Morad?"

"What do you love about Morad?"

"First, I love his strong personality . . ."

"Morad not have strong personality," the professor's wife said. "He neurotic."

"It's become all the fashion," the professor said, "for artistic women to pick artistic men; educated, intellectual women, educated, intellectual men. Of course, this is exciting, and they have much to talk about with each other. But I doubt that in private they can also satisfy each other's needs. At least, they can't all do so."

The professor's wife said, "Hush! Stop!"

The professor stopped joking. "Look, girl, you are wasting your youth on Morad. You've been waiting years for him to propose. Your feelings for him are due to familiarity and habit, his kindness, and your own imagination." He dropped the seriousness and made a joke: "Perhaps I should add 'sexual attraction' as well. Should I?"

Hasti blushed. "Have you kissed him even once?" the professor asked.

Hasti lowered her head.

"You haven't gone beyond kissing?"

"No."

"Don't say anything to Salim, but let go of Morad. As my wife said, Morad is confused and disturbed. He's all mixed up. Both of you have been students of mine, and I love you both. But Morad would be a difficult husband."

"I saw likes of Morad in my first country," the professor's wife said. "Here, too, I saw them . . . Their heads are in air. Idealist . . . *dreamer* is the right word. In the end, they married to politics and bring family ill fortune. If you become Salim's wife, your heart gradually awaken."

"She means," the professor added, "that little by little, he will grow on you. When you have children, with his kindness and your familiarity with him, a quiet love will find a place in your heart—as long as you don't make love with him while thinking of Morad!" He laughed and began coughing.

The woman left the room and returned with a teapot and tea glasses on a tray. "Quince-seed water is warm," she said. The professor corrected, "Quince-seed brew . . . ," and he sat up. His wife brought out a backrest from under the divan, put it behind him, and arranged the blanket over his shoulders.

"Love for Morad aside," Hasti said, "I don't like Salim's opinions. I'm afraid he is hidebound and fanatical."

In French, the professor's wife asked the professor the meaning of *hidebound* and *fanatical.* When she had understood, she said, "You in the east, he in the west, you rub each other . . ."

The professor laughed. "She means, 'You'll polish each other,'" and he poured quince seed brew from the teapot into the small glass.

"You will polish each other and meet in middle of sky," the woman said.

"Perhaps," Hasti said. "Perhaps we won't polish each other, and then continued tolerance and forbearance—a lot of tolerance! In the end, it will bring a person's blood to a boil."

She hesitated and added, "I've talked a lot. I'm afraid it's getting late and I won't find a ride home. But there's another problem: Salim is against his wife working."

"He has money," the professor's wife said. "You stay home and paint."

"But if I'm not in society, if I don't associate with people and don't work, where will I find subjects for my painting?"

"A good idea," the professor's wife said. "Become a painting teacher at girl school."

Hasti remembered her efforts to become a painting teacher and then remembered her study of English. Her last hope had been Mr. Hitti, Ministry of Education teaching expert. She had written him a letter in proper English and requested a personal interview. A long time passed, and no answer came. She went by Mr. Hitti's office many times—at times that

Mr. Ganjur, her mother's husband, was not there. She made friends with Mr. Hitti's pretty secretary. She even drew a profile of her that had shown her to be even more beautiful than she was. Finally, the secretary opened up and said that they had investigated at the Faculty of Fine Arts, and Mr. Hitti had written at the bottom of the letter, "Because of her political opinions, she is not qualified to be a teacher."

Hasti had exploded. "That is what democracy means in free countries—countries other than the Soviet Union!" She regretted that she had sacrificed a drawing. For every Tom, Dick, and Harry, a drawing . . . Professor Mani had come to her rescue, and, with himself as a guarantor, he had placed her in the Ministry of Art and Culture.

And now what Professor Mani was saying made her angry again. "I would love to go to class one more time and die while lecturing. All those hands that write down whatever you say. All those eyes that are fixed on a person. All those ears. The eyes, ears, and hands of adolescents and youths. Then these eyes, ears, and hands become old, but perhaps a memory of you remains in their mind, and sometimes they may repeat the memory for their children and grandchildren. Then, even if a person no longer exists, he will continue to live in their memories and minds. Unfortunately, there are always one or two SAVAK agents among the students. What are they doing?"

"They report," Hasti said, "and because they report, they will not have this memory."

"Perhaps," the professor said, "what you teach will break and shatter something in them. Then their memories of you will be more colorful than those of the others."

Hasti had to walk to the corner of Pahlavi Avenue. Every now and then she had stopped and put her hand out for a taxi or a minivan. She even thought of buying a bus ticket, but the long line of those waiting for a bus dissuaded her. Three buses came and passed by without stopping. Those waiting moved a bit, but after the buses had passed, they were still in the same place they had been.

The streetlights came on. A car honked its horn. Hasti went to the sidewalk and took a few steps. She sensed that the car was coming along with her. Hasti sped up. She had decided to take refuge in a shop or to turn down a small side street when a man called her name. She turned around and saw Salim's black BMW and he himself in a blue wool sweater behind the wheel.

Hasti sat next to Salim and they set off. She breathed easily again. She guessed that Professor Mani had telephoned Salim so that he would come look for her, and Salim confirmed that he had. Salim spoke about the antiques, the long-lasting love of Professor Mani and his wife, and the fact that he was still working. Hasti noted that one day a week he comes to the Office of Artistic Creation to consult and that she herself had invited him.

"You mean artistic creation also has an office?" Salim asked.

"Here, everything has an office."

"Professor Mani believes he gets energy from associating with youth," Salim said. "He said that he wants to die while painting, on the condition that his wife is by his side."

Hasti laughed and said, "Simin wants to die while writing a love story full of joy and hope."

They had arrived at the midpoint of Pahlavi Avenue. "Do you have anything to do tonight?" Hasti asked.

"No."

"Then come see us."

Before they arrived at Reza Shah Avenue, Hasti made a request: "Can you stop here so I can do a little shopping?"

"What do you want to buy? I'll go myself and buy it for you."

Hasti pointed to a sandwich shop and said, "Next to that sandwich shop . . . But I want to shop myself."

Salim was shocked. "This is no place for a woman. It's full of rough, drunk men. They come in the evening to, in their own words, 'get wasted.'" But he stopped.

Hasti opened the door of the car, hurriedly entered the shop, and stood in front of the counter. In fact, there was not one other woman there. Some hands busy, others extended, smoke and moist, stale air, and voices calling out:

"A beer and a chicken sandwich."

"A Coke and hearts and liver."

"Sausage, pickles, and white bread."

"And to drink?"

"A small Qazvin vodka with ice."

"Potato salad and . . ."

A man in white coveralls was standing behind the counter. He had a pen behind each ear, and a notepad and several pieces of carbon paper were in front of him. He wrote price slips of the orders and gave them to the customers. He gave the second copy to one of several men who were moving around him. They also wore white coveralls, and they were working hard. Apparently, one of the pens was out of ink. The man with the pen behind his ear threw the nonworking pen on the table and said, "What is this?"

The bowl of potato salad was empty. One of the men pulled another bowl out of the cooler.

Hasti looked behind herself. Next to a long, dark table that was attached to the wall, the men were, as Salim had said, "getting wasted."

"To your health."

"Thanks."

"Cheers."

"Good health."

"Tops up."

"Pass that hot sauce."

"Monsieur, the ketchup is finished . . ."

"Mustard . . ."

At last, Hasti was able to give her order. "One cooked chicken, five white bread rolls, pickles, bologna . . ." A man in street clothes came up and whispered to the man with the pens behind his ear, who now had no pen behind his ear, and waited. The man wrote up Hasti's order slip, separated the first copy, and gave it to the man in street clothes. That pen was no longer working either, and monsieur threw it down, too.

Hasti's eyes followed the man carrying the order slip who sat behind the cash register, and in that fog and smoke she saw Salim standing next to the cash register. Salim came over to Hasti at the counter and said imperiously, "Go sit in the car, please. The door is unlocked."

When Salim came to the car, he put the package of purchases on the seat. Hasti was enraged. She was tempted to get out right there as Salim was starting the car. Silence, until Salim said, "Really, that was no place for you." *From now on*, Hasti thought, *forbearance* . . . "O bergamot girl, don't be offended by me."

"The three wise monkeys," Hasti said bitterly. "Be blind, be deaf, be dumb."

"How does that story go?" Salim asked.

"One day Professor Mani showed a picture of the three wise monkeys on the classroom screen. It's a well-known image in Indian art, mostly in the form of statues. One of the monkeys has his hands over his eyes, one over his ears, and the last one over his mouth. That describes the condition of women in our little world."

"In no way do I deny the efforts of women," Salim said, "or of men, but it should be in a righteous way."

When they arrived at the house, Hasti said, "Please, come in. We are *your* guests."

Shahin came to greet them, and Hasti made introductions. "This is my brother, Shahin, the long-necked, the big-nosed," she said playfully.

Salim and Shahin went into the living room. Hasti saw Grandmother engaged in the evening prayer in the bedroom. She put the package of food above her prayer rug and said softly, "Salim is here."

To confirm that she heard her, Grandmother said loudly in the middle of her prayers, "God is great!"

Hasti turned on the stove and put the kettle on the burner. She washed her hands and face and put on a touch of makeup. Other than plates of butter and cheese and a few eggs, there was nothing in the refrigerator.

When Hasti brought tea, Salim and Shahin stood up. Shahin's golden hair sparkled in the lamplight, and Hasti noticed that Shahin had also lit the Aladdin kerosene heater.

"Mr. Farrokhi," Shahin was saying, "it appears that you are a follower of Dr. Ali Shariati."

"No. I prefer Jalal Al-e Ahmad."

"A chubby professor," Shahin said, "who uses big words so that no one notices how short he is, analyzed Jalal in class one day. He said, 'In his short life, how often he changed opinions . . . ,' and he arrived at the conclusion that Jalal was not a normal person. Very angrily, he said, 'May he be damned before me.'"

"Jalal was searching . . . ," Salim said. He got up and stood next to the picture of Jalal. He shook his head and murmured, "His bandaged, broken hand on top of a cane. Jalal's hands were indeed broken and bound."

He came back, sat, and continued. "In any case, Al-e Ahmad did not fall into Buddhist mysticism. He was not under the influence of Jewish literature. In the end, he found himself on the path to salvation. He had even put his commitment to Kasravi and Khalil Maleki behind him."

"Another day," Shahin said, "the same chubby professor analyzed Maleki and said, 'Maleki was a Tudeh Party member, and he remained one until the end of his life.' He said that he had heard with his own two ears, from Maleki himself, that if, after the split, Radio Moscow had not abandoned them, the party would have completely fallen into the hands of the reformists. We booed the professor."

Hasti was relieved that Shahin, with his childish behavior, had not revealed that it was Morad who had booed the professor and the others had followed his lead.

Shahin was saying, "The chubby professor took his overcoat from the back of the chair and hurriedly left the room. Then he returned to the class victoriously with the head of the faculty. The head of the faculty went to the pulpit—that is, behind the podium, and gave a lengthy lecture that students must be like this and like that, and more of this type of nonsense."

"I'd like to know," Salim said, "what the head of the faculty said in more detail."

"He said, 'You should be lenient and tolerate the opinions of others.' One of the students . . ."

Hasti thanked God that, again, Shahin did not mention Morad's name.

". . . probed the root of the word *lenience* and proved that *lenience* means 'carelessness.' The head of the faculty said, 'No, my dear; *lenience* means 'forbearance'; that is, civility. In India, temples, mosques, and synagogues are side by side on the same street.' That student was quick with an answer. 'Religious lenience,' he said, 'is different from tolerating someone putting a brand on the forehead of great people who have had the most painful destinies, especially Maleki, who is no longer alive to defend himself. Slinging mud on Maleki doesn't make either the professor or you a great person . . . '"

"My notebook is in the pocket of my jacket . . . ," Salim said.

Hasti rose, took Salim's notebook from beside the bergamot orange, and gave it to him. Salim, whose color until then had been pale, became flushed in the cheeks. "Did you read it, Miss Nourian?" he asked.

Hasti lied.

Salim asked for a pen. After writing a few lines, he said, "You were saying, Shahin Khan?"

"The chubby professor blew up and said, 'That troublemaker of a boy and his girlfriend come to my class just to cause trouble.' He pointed toward us and said, 'These eight people are professional troublemakers, and none of them are students in my class. They are not even students of this faculty. I'm a professor who made the shah laugh. Do you remember? He had asked me, "How long was the beard of Fath Ali Shah Qajar?" "Your Excellency," I said, "one cubit." "How much is one cubit?" he asked. I raised my arm and showed him and said, "From the elbow to the middle finger."'

"The students laughed, even us professional troublemakers. The head of the faculty said, 'Those who are not members of this class, leave immediately.' We were obliged to get up, that student and his girlfriend in front, then the rest of us following them. At the door, that student said, 'Professor, you taught us lenience and civility in practice as a final lesson!' The chubby professor exploded and shouted, 'You skinny boy, you go under the trees with your girlfriend . . . '"

Hasti thought that Salim must have guessed that the girlfriend was none other than Hasti herself. All three were silent until Salim asked, "Hasti Khanom, the other night you said that Maleki spoke about Marxism in simple language and you wrote down what he said. Do you have what you wrote?"

"No," Hasti said. "When I went to prison, Grandmother burned the notes."

"Many Marxists," Salim said, "have not read Marxist literature, but you . . ." Suddenly, Hasti's words registered with him, and he asked, "Then you have also been in prison? Why did you go to prison?"

"On 16 Azar," Hasti said, "we sat in strike around the statue of the shah, used toilet paper to wrap the statue in swaddling clothes, and scattered garbage at the foot of the statue. Those on the balconies were also shouting slogans from atop the verandas."

"Those on the balconies?" Salim said.

"Those on the balconies were the girls, with heavy makeup, dressed in the latest fashion, who were shouting slogans in the strikes. As soon as they sensed danger, they would flee inside and hide."

Hasti continued. "What a welcome the women inmates of Qasr Prison gave us. They sang songs for us. They had crammed thirty or forty people into one room. At bedtime, so that a few of us could sleep, a number of inmates stood with their back to the wall, singing, 'Night of the Karun River, such a . . .'"

"How many days were you in prison?" Salim asked.

"Two months. The first day of interrogation, I was in good spirits and happy. The interrogator said, 'Are you laughing at us? Now I'll show you.' He took a police baton and hit my head. The scalp tore, and blood flowed onto the white skirt and jacket that my mother . . ."

Shahin interrupted. "Hasti was more unhappy about the white jacket and skirt than about her head . . ." And he laughed. But Salim and Hasti didn't even smile.

It was apparent that Shahin intended, by whatever means possible, to get Salim to like him. The poor kid didn't know how and with what words and language to find a way into his heart. He started off on one topic. He started another topic, until he arrived at an end that he imagined would impress Salim. "Mr. Farrokhi," he said, "I do traditional body building. Would you like to see my room?"

"First let me have a cup of tea," Salim said. He took his cup, stood up, and asked, "Where's the kitchen?"

Hasti rose from her place, took the cup from his hand, and said, "I'll bring the kettle and the teapot here."

In the kitchen, Grandmother was preparing a sauce to go over the chicken. Hasti greeted her and explained that Salim had paid for the supper.

"Hasti!" Touran Jan said. "Send Shahin to buy fruit, lettuce, and tomatoes."

Hasti turned on the stove, filled the kettle with water, and placed it on the burner. "You mean on a fool's errand?" she said, "Since he keeps boasting to Salim about Morad and his girlfriend?"

"Has he used names?"

"No, but Salim is not stupid, although he pretends that he doesn't know."

Shahin went ahead to his room to turn on the overhead light and the table lamp, and Hasti and Salim followed. Dumbbells, chains, and a push-up board were in the corner of the room. A picture of Mosaddeq on trial that Hasti had drawn years ago and had given to Shahin as a gift was pinned to the wall above Shahin's bed. The face of the old man, mouth open, one hand raised and pointing, eyes astounded, all reflected a shout of anger, incredulousness. It was a historical allusion, a legendary allusion—a memento to centuries past and current that at the same time illustrated Mosaddeq's firm will and wisdom.

Salim was staring at the picture. "Is this a charcoal drawing?" he asked, then added, "No doubt Hasti Khanom drew it." He also asked why the picture didn't have a frame and glass over it and said that it would be a shame if all that effort were wasted.

Shahin made excuses, saying that he had not had an opportunity yet to frame it. What he didn't say was that he didn't have the money and that Grandmother, although she has money in a savings account for Shahin, had postponed so often giving him the money to buy a frame for his idol, Mosaddeq, that Shahin had let it go.

Salim was not taking his attention away from the drawing. "Hasti Khanom," he said, "may your hands be steady, your eyes always sharp, and your mind always keen."

Hasti laughed and said, "May it be so!"

Salim continued. "You have summarized the whole existence of Mosaddeq in this drawing. Even more, the drawing is the essence of all the Mosaddeqs that this country has seen. Brave old man!"

"I look at the other side of the case, too," Hasti said. "Didn't the shah and his sister suffer by submitting themselves to such plots? Even for one moment? Suffer from their own plots and from going along with the plot of foreigners?"

Salim turned and looked at her. His eyes remained lost in Hasti's eyes, and thunder and lightning were reverberating in Hasti's heart. Tonight, because of his blue turtleneck sweater, his eyes appeared more blue than gray. If Hasti could get those eyes on paper, perhaps she would be freed from them. But those eyes that seemed to be on the route to the presence of God, what harm could there be in them?

"All of them wanted money and power," Salim said. "Money and power turn a person's heart to stone."

On two other walls, all sorts of pictures of the wrestler Takhti reminded the viewer of another champion: Takhti on a champions' platform. Takhti while wresting. Takhti with his new bride. Takhti in suit and tie. Even an image that had been cut out of the newspaper of Takhti's lifeless corpse. Salim went from one picture to another, and Shahin recited the slogans, "'The world champion Takhti.' 'Champion of champions.' Winner of three gold medals—with that modest appearance. Child of the poor, south side of town. Idol of young men."

Salim's attention was drawn to a photo that showed Sha'ban Ja'fari's body-building club. Sha'ban Ja'fari was in the middle, and the athletes were standing in rows next to and behind him and on the steps. Their upper bodies were bare, and from the images of those in front, it appeared that they all wore tight, traditional body-building leggings. Those situated in the front had chains in their hands. The last figure on the right was Shahin, who appeared to be younger than the others.

Salim put his hand on Shahin's shoulder, and, as though he were dealing with a young child, said, "Let's see, my dear. When you place a drawing of Mosaddeq above your head, and here and there on your walls the images of Takhti . . ."

Shahin interrupted Salim and said, "I have ten more pictures of Takhti. Do you want to see them?"

"No . . . ," Salim said. He took his hand off of Shahin's shoulder and added, "I mean a photo of brainless Sha'ban has no place in this room. Sha'ban Ja'fari's title is Crown Giver."

Shahin pouted. He took the picture from the wall and tore it to pieces. He had hung it because he wanted to have his own picture in the room too. "Besides," he said, "no one saw brainless Sha'ban in the club. One only heard the sounds of his yells and shouts that echoed under the arches. Anyway, it was the only traditional body-building club here."

At dinner, Shahin really took over center stage. First, he agreed with Salim and said, "I'm in the fourth year of political law, but I'm stupid and dull-witted." Then he reminisced that the same chubby professor, much before he talked about Jalal and Maleki, had, in his words, "analyzed" Mosaddeq's personality. "Mosaddeq," he had said, "had thrown himself into the lap of the Tudeh Party, and his being a leftist was the cause of his downfall."

Grandmother and Hasti were shocked by Shahin's next statement, because Shahin attributed to himself Morad's words in answer to the chubby professor and also his words after class. Hasti remembered that for several days after that class, Shahin was very agitated and had become ill from the fact that he had not known or said these things himself. However much Grandmother consoled him, saying, "Dear boy, you too will grow up and develop opinions," he did not believe it, not until Teimur Khan, at Grandmother's request, took him to Sha'ban Ja'fari's club.

Salim's color seemed paler than before, but he ate supper with a good appetite. Touran Jan had fixed her eyes on him, and her prayer chador had slipped off her head. *I hope,* Hasti thought, *she won't bring incense to burn for Salim, swing her fist full of incense around Salim's head, then put it on his shoulder and heart and repeat her incantation, "May the evil eyes of the jealous be destroyed, both those of the family and those of others."* She had burned incense for Morad three or four times, and Morad, with laughing eyes, was attentive to her words and gestures. She had done this hundreds of times for Hasti, Shahin, herself, Mehrmah Khanom, Teimur Khan and his wife and children, and even Akhtar Iran . . .

Shahin did not let up and again repeated Morad's words. "Mr. Farrokhi, in my opinion the British, with the rich archives of their Ministry of Foreign Affairs and their government as a whole, caused Americans to be frightened about communist influence . . . The government always makes a bugaboo out of the Tudeh Party and . . ."

"That's right," Salim said, "but the Tudeh Party will not be the agent that changes the status quo. The Tudeh Party, no; the masses of the people, yes. It will be the masses of the people with their well-rooted beliefs and in spite of their ignorance, poverty, and lack of resources."

Salim thought, scratched his beard, and continued. "You should have said to that chubby professor that Mosaddeq, even though he had royal blood and was from the aristocracy, was a nationalist, a *democrat*, a *liberal*, and a *radical*. Therefore, he couldn't proclaim the Tudeh Party illegal. Mosaddeq's associates were also not of one mind and not organized. A strong Iranian and nationalist party was not supporting him."

Hasti was close to saying "you use so many foreign words," but she didn't. She brought up Maleki and his supporters, saying that they knew what they were doing. She added, "It was for the same reason that, after the fall of Mosaddeq, they sent Maleki to Falak al-Aflak Prison and put him in the same cell as his archenemies—that is, the fanatical Tudeh Party members . . . What agony . . . One of them wanted to kill Maleki in the middle of the night. Maleki told me himself. And if he had killed him, how much agony he himself would have borne. I know him."

"Is he still a Tudeh adherent?" Salim asked.

"I don't know," Hasti said. "But I do know that the attraction of Marxism remains in a person's mind for a long time. Governorship of the proletariat . . ."

Grandmother began to speak. "God forbid." She pulled her prayer chador onto her head and said, "I never become tired of discussing Mosaddeq." She turned to Hasti. "Hasti, how many times did I go to Ahmadabad to see him? With this backache and leg pain of mine? I used to tell myself, 'If I have to go on my knees, I will still go to see him.' I also went the day of his funeral procession. I'm proud of the fact that my son was martyred for the old man."

Suddenly she cried and recited Akhavan-Sales's poem for Mosaddeq,

My heart burned for your pain and patience.
O gardener, spring did not come.

Hasti rose and drew Grandmother's head to her chest. She pulled a tissue from the box on the table and wiped away her grandmother's tears. Salim lowered his head. What secrets did those eyes now reveal? Grief, uselessness, disillusionment, perplexity, disgust for oppression? Hasti thought, *The Mosaddeq era addressed to some extent the disorientation of the Iranian people.* She said, "Too bad that Mosaddeq didn't proclaim a republic. In any case, politics dirties a person's hands. If Mosaddeq had smashed the idol of himself . . ."

"Meaning," Salim said, "that he should have abandoned his idealism and puritanism?"

Hasti surprised herself. How logical and relaxed she had become. Bitterness and hopelessness had left her at peace. Was that condition due to the blessing of those eyes that were no longer moist but had glued their lashes together?

When they got up from supper, Salim put his hand on Shahin's shoulder and said, "You are neither stupid nor dull-witted."

"Because," Shahin said happily, "my favorite professor, Hamid Enayat, taught us reflection and deliberate assessment of matters."

Salim turned to Grandmother and said, "You have raised bright and knowledgeable children. These two should fill your son's empty place. I think you have shed enough tears for that deceased . . ."

Grandmother corrected Salim. "For that martyr. But every time talk of Mosaddeq comes up, I start to cry. Yet I'm certain that Mosaddeq moved the heart strings of the Iranian people, and, in the end, they will do wonders!"

"God willing," Salim said.

Hasti believed this was a way of saying good night to two bothersome people who, until then, had not let him and Hasti be alone.

Hasti was sitting in the living room in the armchair watching Salim, who had put his hand on his back and was pacing. "The weather is unpredictable," Hasti said. "I wish you had put on your jacket."

"I was in a hurry," Salim said, "but I've had this backache for a while."

"Have you seen a doctor?" Hasti asked.

Salim answered, "Each doctor says something different. One doctor says, 'It's arthritis; exercise.' Another says, 'It's a slipped disc; don't move.' A third says, 'Back pain is a nervous affliction.'"

Hasti offered her own opinion. "You're not a nervous person. You've caught a cold. I'll go get the hot-water bottle."

Salim asked that she kindly bring a blanket, too.

When she turned on the kitchen light, Grandmother raised her head from the kitchen table and asked, "Did you get a proposal?"

Hasti searched in the kitchen cabinet for the hot-water bottle. A kettle full of boiling water was on the Aladdin heater in the living room. She heard it gurgling.

Movement appears at the bottom first. There's news. One bubble rises from the bottom to the surface and confirms the news. The second bubble joins it and pulls it to the bottom. Small bubbles at the sides and sometimes in the middle swear that the news was correct. They give way to large protruding bubbles. And they are not even jealous. No one has ever been jealous of bubbles. Large bubbles join together, separate, and join again. Like waves in the sea. It is as though the languages of heart and mind have been mixed. Bubbles sparkling at the top in happiness. The water in the kettle has come to a boil. Open the lid of the kettle. You see the steam. Steam doesn't have the shape or color of water, but its essence is water. Just like reality and art.

Hasti asked Touran Jan, "Which blanket should I take? Our blankets are all worn out. A clean, new potholder. A dishcloth . . ."

Touran Jan slapped her own face and said, "God, give me death. I put the evil eye on the poor child."

Hasti went to Shahin's room. The light was on and Shahin was sitting on his bed with his hand under his chin. When he saw Hasti he said, "Should I say 'Congratulations'?"

"Oh, Shahin," Hasti said, "you show-off. Stand up now."

She took Shahin's blanket off the bed, shook it, and began to fold it with the side that looked newer on the outside. Shahin apologized. "Sister, to make amends for our poverty, I claimed knowledge. It's true that these words were not my words. Also, Morad said most of these words later, not in class."

Hasti came to the living room with a hot-water bottle, a used dishcloth, and a blanket. She poured water from the kettle into the hot-water bottle and watched Salim, who had closed his eyes and appeared to be at peace with the world. It seemed as though his spirit had separated from his body—that he had taken refuge in the city of God. His breathing was calm and harmonious. Hasti went to pull the blanket over him. His eyes opened. He stood, put the hot-water bottle on his lower back, and wrapped the blanket around himself. Hasti went toward the wall heater to turn it on, too, but the heater was out of kerosene. She didn't know whether they had kerosene in the house.

"Had you fallen asleep?" she asked Salim.

"No. I was concentrating my thoughts to chase away the pain. You call this kind of state 'spaced out.'"

Hasti sat in an armchair and was silent. *What kind of people are these men*? she thought. *Just when they see the girl becoming a little gentle, they become agitated. Man, I was waiting for you to say, "I was deep into spiritual contemplation." But when you came out of that state, you brought me a bouquet of thorns.*

Grandmother entered with a full fist and the wire mesh on which she steamed rice. She put the wire mesh on the Aladdin heater, which no longer held the kettle. She circulated her full fist around Salim's head and recited her incantation. When the incense smoke had filled the room, Hasti asked Grandmother, "Do we have any kerosene?" Grandmother motioned with her head that they did and kept moving her lips.

Hasti returned with the kerosene container. She was lighting the heater when she thought of chamomile incense. She knew that whatever they might not have at home, they had chamomile flowers. They also had a clean, glazed bowl. She carried the kettle and the space heater out of the room. The scent of chamomile filled the room.

"If you could please bring a cup," Salim said, "I'll drink some chamomile tea . . ."

Hasti brought a ladle, a tea strainer, and a cup on a tray to the living room. Luckily, Salim's eyes were closed this time.

Hasti's eyes were fixed on Salim's gift, the bergamot orange, not yet shriveled, under her father's photo. Salim had followed her gaze. "The bergamot girl," he said, "is looking at her twin sister."

Hasti smiled and said, "Grandmother wanted to make jam from its rind, but I didn't let her."

How quickly she had forgotten Salim's spaced-out state! How quickly she had come out of this thought that people are like trees, each one alone in the desert.

"Are you feeling better?" she asked.

"A little."

"Salim Khan, what do you think?"

"About what?"

"About political struggle."

"For the moment, *j'étudie*."

"Studying," Hasti said. "When you speak, it is as though you are reciting poetry, even when you use old Persian. But you spoil your poetry with foreign words."

Salim fell deep into thought. It was a while before he asked, "What's your political opinion?"

"I'm neither here nor there. Sometimes I think I'm a leftist humanist and a follower of Khalil Maleki, and sometimes I think I believe in the power of religious momentum, or, as you might say, religious *dynamism*, and am a follower of Jalal Al-e Ahmad. Sometimes I think I will resort solely to art, art with a correct political and social take, but which take is correct? I don't know."

"For the moment, I recommend the latter."

"Is political struggle exclusive to men?"

"No, but you don't have the *potentiel* and *capacité* for political struggle. Resort to art, provided that, from the metaphysical world of balance, equilibrium, and refinement, you make way for reality, you inject reality."

"I believe in my own personal God," Hasti said.

Salim leaned his head on the arm of the chair and said, "Tell me about your personal God."

"My personal God is the first letter of the alphabet—that is, the source of human knowledge and art, the great player of creation, and we in this world are no more than puppets . . . It's possible that what I've said is not my own, that I have read or heard it somewhere. But I believe in these words."

Salim lifted his head and said, "And the giver of moral courage, the breath of eternal happiness, the first energy, the deliverer of wanderers, most of it by Sathya Sai Baba—so you *have* read my eighteenth notebook."

Caught in the lie, all of Hasti's body started to burn. She was close to tears. She remembered the phrase *half-slaughtered chicken* as if it were she herself. The intelligence and memory of Salim came out in a frightening form for her, and she was helpless. She sighed. She could only say, "Shame is the worst condition afflicting humans. If we don't move heaven and earth to make amends, we will burst."

"Shame?"

Salim consoled Hasti this way: "I intentionally left my notebook so that you would read it. You said you didn't read it . . ."

"Don't be magnanimous; that makes it worse."

"And don't *idolize* me."

Salim continued warmly, "Dear Hasti Khanom, we are all a mixture of strengths and weaknesses. No one is absolutely bad or good."

Hasti held her tears and said, "There are scoundrels and rogues who are absolutely evil."

"That's true, but only God is innocent of all sins. God is absolute goodness. Now tell me, did you give your friend an ultimatum?"

"No. He's gone to Mashhad."

Salim sat up straight and said, "Mashhad?" He asked why Hasti's friend had gone to Mashhad this time of year. Hasti was surprised at Salim's curiosity. She thought that she only needed to give Morad an ultimatum. She thought that Morad's answer would be negative—that he would not take up the ball and chain of marriage to Hasti. Then it would be only Hasti and Salim. Salim, with his meticulousness, moral support, and helpfulness in addition to his magnanimity, helped her to clear thoughts of Morad from her mind. Now, what did it matter that he had said, "In your view, I was spaced out," that he had mentioned to her face her lie that she hadn't read the eighteenth notebook, though she had read it? *One cannot always be courteous, especially when one also has a backache. Hadn't he said himself, "No one is absolutely bad or good?" I also think that if I were absolutely good, I would be boring, and I would no longer be lively and cheerful.*

"I know what you were thinking," Salim said.

"What was I thinking?"

"You were thinking of answering me this way: 'My friend has gone to Mashhad on pilgrimage, and he will bring me gifts of a camel load of love, prayer beads, and veils.'"

Hasti froze, smiled bitterly, and said, "And a kilo of camel milk and one top-quality lizard."

Salim laughed and closed his eyes. "Excuse me. When this back pain begins, I become agitated. But bergamot girl, they bring camel milk and lizards from Arabia, not Mashhad. Your friend will bring from Mashhad saffron and rock candy for Grandmother."

"Do you want an aspirin?" Hasti asked.

"Yes, please; two." Salim took the aspirin. He closed his eyes and said, "Tearing myself away and leaving this house are difficult for me. Meanwhile, I'm very curious to know what you *were* thinking about."

"It wasn't a thought, really. It was just a notion that passed because there is no possibility of putting it into action."

Salim insisted, and from Hasti's mouth emerged, "For a moment I had the notion to come sit next to you, put my head on your shoulder, cry, and say, 'Salim, help me,' and then kiss your eyes."

Salim stood up abruptly and let go of both the blanket and the hot-water bottle. He went to the heater, sat on the floor, and glued his back to the warm side of the heater. He put his hand on his beard, combed his hair with his fingers, and said nothing.

Hasti respected his silence at first. Finally, she couldn't wait longer, and she asked, "Then, what would you have done?"

"I don't know. I would have been torn. My heart would have said, 'Dry her tears and embrace her,' but my mind would have said, 'Softly take her head off your shoulder and sit to one side. If this is the first act of her giving her heart to you, there will be enough time for embracing when she becomes your wife.'"

"Will your heart," Hasti said, "or, in Grandmother's words, your lust, win or your mind?"

"I don't know." He thought and said, "Hasti, come, right now, let's get married. While my rival hasn't come back and taken you from my grasp . . ."

"How?" Hasti asked. "This time of night, notary offices are closed."

"We ourselves can execute a temporary marriage," Salim said. "You say, 'I give myself,' and I say, 'I accept.' Then we write our holy union on paper and we both sign it."

"It's that simple?"

"It's that simple. The union of husband and wife in Islam is the most progressive of unions. The agreement of the parties alone is sufficient."

"The rival," Hasti said, "will not take me from your grasp. It is several years that he has been leaving me waiting. But in any case, I owe him the opportunity of an ultimatum. He will show up on the fourth day of the New Year. I didn't tell you that the fourth is my birthday."

Salim asked forgiveness in advance for his impudence and then asked, "Have you ever fallen into such a temptation with that friend of yours?"

Hasti remembered Professor Mani's warning. "Absolutely not! In all these years we have not even touched each other."

"I guessed as much."

Hasti laughed in her heart. Was she laughing at Salim or at the thought of how easily men believe certain lies—lies that show their superiority and satisfy their pride?

When saying good-bye, Salim did not extend his hand to Hasti. Hasti didn't have such an expectation, either. "Hasti Khanom," he said, "we can have a happy life together." He paused and added, "Really, why did your friend go to Mashhad? I was set to go as well, but I stayed to see where our relationship would lead." Then he asked, "Your friend's name is not Hadi, is it?"

"No."

"It's not Farhad Dorafshan?"

"No."

"Firuz Dorafshan?"

"No. Only I did have one classmate by the name of Farkhondeh Dorafshan. The kids gave her the nickname 'Wishing Tree.'"

"Why 'Wishing Tree'?"

"She was always saying, 'I wish I knew what I should do.' 'I wish I knew what should be done.' 'I wish I knew what can be done.'"

"I'll wait for your phone call," Salim said.

Suddenly, he remembered the chamomile water. "The chamomile water has boiled away, and your glazed bowl has been scorched."

5

Hasti rose. She had counted. Grandmother had finished her fifth round of prayers and was standing for the sixth when the pale sun of the last day of winter peeked through the window. Grandmother went to get the photo album of her son, his worn and yellowed letters, and the three poems that he had composed during his lifetime—one, advice for teachers like himself; one, counsel for parents; one, guidance for students. All three poems had been published in the Ministry of Education's journal, *Education and Socialization*. Grandmother looked for her glasses and found them.

Hasti opened the window and looked out into the courtyard. At the front, the sun said hello to the top branches of the weeping willow—a tree that had its head down, not out of shame but as its usual habit. It seemed as though the sun also kissed it. Then the sun rested on the pine trees, and, as a good deed, it went to visit the naked trees too. "Good morning," it said and gave them the good news that they would soon bring out their green New Year's clothes and, if they were patient, their buds and flowers would form colorful patterns on their clothing. The trees shook their heads as though they were complaining, "But we haven't bathed." The sun shone with a smile and said, "May your sorrow be short. The sky has a lump in its throat and when it bursts into tears, it will wash you from head to foot." The trees did not believe the sun. They didn't have much of a memory. Again, they shook their heads, and the sun said, "Each day I will be warmer and shine on you more than the day before. Don't you remember?" The trees were coy and said, "But when it hails it will rip and wreck our clothes." The sun laughed boisterously and said, "Then you *do* remember."

A morning songbird called, and the sparrows answered happily from among the needles of the pine trees. They were deliberating about spring. The sun was teasing the violet jasmine bush that was under the window, quoting the poet and satirist, Obeyd Zakani, "'You have made merry without me.' You have even started budding." *It happens suddenly,* Hasti thought, *like a miracle.* The naked trees that survived the winter find new life by sucking in the essence of the earth and the spirit of the sun and the moon, and by becoming moist from the sky's tears of enthusiasm. In the morning one day, you see that a powdery green substance has been scattered all over them. A little later, their clothes are completely and perfectly ready with those bright colors—green, yellow, blue, red, violet, purple, white, orange, pink, and maroon. You say to yourself, "What beautiful makeup they're wearing. And with what mastery the dressmaker of creation has decorated them." No, my dear, this dressmaker rarely uses black, gray, navy blue, and brown. Look at the rainbow. It's imitating their makeup, and because it's imitating, it's short-lived . . . Oh, the sweat of the sun is golden, the light of the moon is silver, the raindrops are pearls, and the trees are ornamented by all these divine jewels.

Grandmother said, "God is great!" in the middle of her prayers to get Hasti's attention. Her voice was rough and commanding, and Hasti knew that she should close the window. If she had softly asked Hasti to swear by the sun and its light, the poetry of Hasti's mind would not have inclined toward such bitterness that she would say to herself, *The sky is a lie. It's no more than accumulated air. The moon is a cold, dark, stony place, and the sun is just a mass of fused matter.*

Hasti put on her dark red skirt and jacket and touched up her face. She looked at herself in the mirror. Soon those large black eyes will seem even larger behind glasses.

As a gift for Grandmother, she had bought a navy blue wool cardigan that had been wrapped in blue flowered paper. She put the package on Grandmother's bed. For Shahin she had bought a bottle of Sauvage cologne, which she put on his bed. Shahin's room seemed neat and empty without him. Dust had settled on the dumbbells, chains, and push-up board in the corner of the room, and the air of the room was heavy and stuffy.

Last night she had packed in her bag a wool sweater, a pair of jeans, a pair of slippers for herself, and her gifts for Parviz and Mr. Ganjur. Her gift for Mr. Ganjur was the same as her gift for Shahin and had been wrapped in the same paper. Her gift for Parviz was a child's drawing notebook and a cardboard box of variously colored pencils. And for her mother she will buy some tulips on the way. She knew that when she gives Parviz his gift, he will curl his lip and complain, "I told you to buy a lovebird for my gift," and her mother will say, "And I told you several times, lovebirds are not good omens."

Hasti went to the kitchen, where Grandmother was setting out breakfast. "Touran Jan, shall I set up your New Year's table?" she asked.

"Don't bother," Grandmother said. "I'll do it myself."

Touran Khanom put the dishes of butter and jam on the kitchen table and said irritably, "You go, Miss Artist, and set the splendid table of that slut. You know well how to set up lifeless nature, though the fish for the table are alive."

Anger was in the air. She had awakened on the wrong side of the bed. And that on a morning that held good tidings.

Courtesy until when? She poured tea for Grandmother and asked, "My dear, when will you forget your grudge against my mother? At least, she gave you two grandchildren from her womb."

"Forget my grudge? The first anniversary of your father's martyrdom had not even passed when that slut went and married that garage owner, Grease Monkey. She never acknowledged that they had martyred your father. She always said, 'He was shot accidentally.' That hussy was still living in this house when she went to the Valiabad bathhouse attendant and gave me away, saying, 'So and so has passed menopause.'"

"My dear," Hasti said, "today is the celebration of New Year's; don't spoil it for me."

Touran Khanom stood, put her hand on her hip, and said, "It's a New Year's celebration for you, but not for me, a stay-at-home old woman. I suffered all this torment until you grew up, but your heart is not with me."

Out of breath, Grandmother sat on a chair. She took a fresh breath and said, "Your eyes are on the colorful table of that slut . . . God forgive me."

She calmed down a bit and said, "For God's sake, confess that both of you are so close to her. Do you know why Morad is leaving you waiting? Because you are like your mother. A learned, intellectual person like Morad is weary of that type of woman. Women who are controlled by their sexual desires. Lewd and lusty women. You, with your wisdom, grace, and art . . ."

But when Hasti kissed her good-bye, she had become calm. Grandmother embraced her and opened her closed fist in the palm of Hasti's hand. It was an antique gold coin. "Come home early tonight, won't you?" she said.

"Okay."

"If Salim is also there, he'll probably bring you home; bring him in."

"Sure."

After Hasti left, Grandmother said to herself, *Well, old woman, now you're left alone with your foolishness. I've heard many times that solitude is a quality of God. Good! This quality befits only God. I'm among His servants, and I will endure. Didn't God create me in His own image? Didn't He put His light in my heart? Is this kind of talk only good for the classroom? Didn't Morad say, quoting Sartre, "I struggle; therefore, I am?" Well, I also struggle. With everything—with old age, with backache, with leg pain. What do I fear? That I won't be able to breathe, and that I will die alone in this house?*

I'll sit on the veranda, on the padded wooden chair, under the sun. The light of the sun will warm my hollow bones. The essence of life no longer circulates freely in my veins and in my nerves and bones. It has been sucked out. First, I'll loosen the muscles of my eyes. No. First I'll moisten my hand towel with cold water. I'll squeeze it and put it on my eyes. Ten times. I'll loosen my jaw. My tongue, my dentures, my skull. From the top of the head to the tip of the toes, I'll relax my whole body and dream. And when the entire body is relaxed, the brain wouldn't dare become stressed. My heart wouldn't dare become agitated.

I needlessly picked on my little child, Hasti. But what can I do? I can't help it. A human being has a thousand kinds of moods. I didn't want to spend my New Year's Day in solitude and quiet. How often Hasti has quoted from Goethe that "solitude is the secret of knowledge." One day I said to Hasti and Morad, "It's all someone else's words. What do you say yourselves? What are your words?"

God help me, I'm feeling agitated again. It's fine. I'll swear at bitchy Eshrat and arrogant Simin as much as I want.

A voice in her head was speaking loudly, as though it were just last night: "We travel uphill by ourselves. Or, with a slap on the back and a kick on the bottom, they make us travel up. Or we fall down not having reached the summit. But when we have arrived at the summit, we put the gears in neutral, and, without braking, we go downhill speedily."

And a man's voice: "My wife loves a bit of danger and driving. All she is thinking is brake, gear, bearing, distributor wire, and clutch . . ."

And a woman's voice, laughing: "As a child, I loved horses."

A man's voice: "And in the end you married an ass."

A woman's voice: "No. In the end I found my own horse."

With pride and haughtiness, she came and sat up straight in the armchair and crossed her legs. It was as though the queen were sitting there, smoking a cigarette and speaking philosophically. *When she was talking about going downhill, she was referring to me. However much Hasti swore, "My dear, she doesn't taunt. She speaks frankly and directly. You were busy entertaining. Didn't you notice the subject of the conversation? Morad had asked, 'Simin Khanom, what is life?' You only heard the last words, and those words she quoted from another writer." I yelled at my little child, "Don't defend that woman so much."*

She had worked so hard entertaining. She had put on her glasses and cleaned the red currants three times. Cumin, chicken, sautéed onions, what a waste!

"I have colitis," the husband said, and he ate bread, cheese, and walnuts. He didn't even see the herbs that were arranged like a painting. "Wife," he said, "why don't you take my share?" The woman poured a serving spoonful of red currant rice on her plate, and Touran Khanom cut up the chicken fillet and put it on her plate. She ate it reluctantly, with only a fork, as though she were eating ashes. Of course, she praised Madam's cooking, and then she ate salad and said that she didn't want to become fat.

Again, Hasti was defensive. "Touran Jan," she said, "I had not invited them for dinner. You urged them to stay." And Touran Jan said, "How can one be too full to eat two bites?" But when they went for a return visit, how many tiny sweets she offered Touran Jan. "You must have some," she said, "They're Shirazi sweets." It was as though Touran Khanom had come through a famine. Touran Jan had asked, "Did you make them yourself?" "No," she said. "I know nothing about cooking." *Grown woman, why shouldn't you have learned to cook?*

Touran Khanom went to the dining room. On a side table in front of a mirror on the wall, she spread a white tablecloth and a rectangular piece of cardboard that she had bought the day before from Mohammad Aqa. On the cardboard six items symbolic of New Year's had been pasted within clear plastic pockets: half an apple in the middle, garlic, vinegar, lotus fruit, ground sumac, and coins. At the top of the cardboard "O cupbearer! Congratulations on the coming of the New Year," from a poem by Hafez, was written. She took the Quran out of the small rug in her prayer bundle, kissed it, and put it at the top of the cardboard. From in front of the kitchen window she took the wheat that she had sprouted herself and sprinkled it with a little water. For prosperity, she also placed a saucer of rice at the corner of the tablecloth.

If Hasti becomes Salim's wife, she thought, *Salim has a car, and next year, before or after the turning of the year, he'll take everyone to Shah Abdol Azim Shrine, to the resting place of his father-in-law. He'll bring his mother also. This won't be a problem for Salim. Touran Jan goes with Hasti! He'll take Touran Jan along with Hasti to their house. She's a good companion for Salim's mother. Touran Jan will rent her house, sell her belongings, and send Shahin to America without worry. She won't be stressed any more over every penny that's spent.* With this hope, she was rid of her heart palpitation.

In the old days, before she had leg pains, she went every year to her son's grave. She took rose water and halva. She gave money to the cemetery custodian. She washed the gravestone of her poor son with rose water. HOSSEIN NOURIAN had been written on the stone, and the year of his birth and death had been etched in smaller print below his name. "Cousin," Mehrmah had said, "hire Mr. Shoghal to compose a poem about the incident and have them carve it on his gravestone."

She would reserve a little rose water and pour a few drops on each of the graves of her husband, her mother, and her father. They were all together. They were only missing Touran. Her grave had been prepared next to the grave of her son. She had lain in her own grave and "tried it on," so to speak. It was tight. She gave instructions to have it widened. Her gravestone was also prepared, except that it didn't have the date of death. Well, if she were to die, Salim or Morad or Hasti or Shahin would have them carve the date of death on the gravestone. For the expenses of her wrapping and burial, she had placed five thousand tomans in the fold of the winding sheet that she had purchased from Karbala. She had also written her will and put it on top of her winding sheet.

Again agitation. It felt as if someone was squeezing her heart in their fist. She couldn't breathe. Her mouth was sour and dry. Her ears made a scratching sound, as though someone was pulling their fingernails down a blackboard. Her knees hurt so much that she couldn't think of anything else. She wished she could die right then. Everything was ready.

At nightfall, or in the middle of the night, Salim and Hasti would come, and they would find her body. Salim would bring a Quran reciter, and he would put a lit candle at her head. She thought she should tie a kerchief under her chin right now so that her mouth wouldn't be hanging crooked. When her eyes fell upon the Angel of Death, she would remember to close them firmly. If not, her protruding eyes would jump out and whoever unveiled her face in the grave would think that she still had her eyes on the material world. When they put the tombstone at Mehrmah's head, her left eye was open. It was as though she were asking, "Why me?"

She could no longer stay in the padded wooden chair on the veranda in the sun. Her legs took her to the door of the building, and she opened it. No, the roll-up steel door of Teimur Khan's motorcycle repair shop was down. A large lock fastened at the bottom showed that this door would not be opened anytime soon.

The shop was the garage of Touran Jan's house, and Teimur Khan was her tenant. She had not taken key money, nor had she, like other property owners, raised the rent as much as a cent all these years. She had even chosen and gotten a wife for Teimur Khan—the most modest of her students, Maryam. She had gone herself to propose to the family and had held the engagement party. She had run Akhtar Iran and Mehrmah around in circles. She had held the wedding feast, too, in her own house. She had paved the way to bring the bride to the groom's house. Mohammad Aqa had put the mirror in front of the bride. She had taken the bride and groom to

Teimur Khan's house, which was only a few steps away from the courtyard door of her own house. She herself had put their hands together and had placed a large antique gold coin in the palm of the bride, as a present on her unveiling. She had raised the lace veil. Of course, Teimur Khan had also given the bride a present on her unveiling. She had recited all the prayers for good fortune and, of course, burned incense of wild rue seed and circulated it over their heads.

She herself had named their first son Mohsen, but however much she worked with the child, he didn't make much progress. He had learned the alphabet, but he wrote the lines of his assignments vertically, not horizontally. With all her efforts, he didn't learn the multiplication tables beyond five times five is twenty-five, and besides that, instead of "times tables," he said "fines tables." As soon as he began to grow a mustache, he rode a bicycle. Sometimes he stood straight up on the bike and rode. Later he became bolder and rode a motorcycle. He motioned to his neighbor's daughter, Farideh, who was usually hanging around on the veranda opposite the shop. He sat Farideh on the back of the motorcycle. He did minor adjustments to the exhaust pipe of the motorcycle until the putt-putt motor, as he called it, finally made so much noise and drove the neighbors crazy.

No, Mohsen could not be put on the right path until, on the advice of Touran Khanom, he joined the army. Touran Khanom persuaded him to sign up for the motor corps, learn to drive, and, while in the army, get a driver's license; he didn't get it then, but he did later. Touran Khanom didn't forgive any rent for the shop, but she did distribute three months of rent over later months and persuaded Teimur Khan to buy a minivan for Mohsen on installments. Now Mohsen had gotten on the right path. Whether it was the blessing of the minivan or the army, neither Teimur Khan nor Touran Khanom knew.

Mohsen would get up at four in the morning, go to Amin al-Sultan Square with the minivan, and buy fresh fruits and vegetables. Mohammad Aqa's shop was his first stop. Then Mohsen would set off, and he would drive and sell his produce in the alleys and byways from Darvazeh Dowlat to the area close to his father's shop. He would stop next to Touran Khanom's house and shout, "Herbs for rice, herbs for stew, herbs for salad," and, depending on the season, "cucumbers, tomatoes, squash, eggplant, watermelon, cantaloupe, tangerines, sweet lemons, oranges. Housewives, run. Housewives, come and get it. Run, run." Women with their baskets would gather around the minivan of "Mohsen Run," or just "Run." One would say, "Run, don't forget fava beans." Another would say, "Peas, fingerling potatoes, and green beans." And a third would want herbs from Varamin for salad. Mohsen Run would sweat and make promises. When it came to large potatoes and onions, Mohsen would sweat more.

Touran Khanom would also buy from Run, or she would stand watching. She had taught him to be cheerful. Now if he sweats, so be it. Also, not to overcharge. She lined up the women so that Mohsen would not be distracted. She knew most of the women and asked about the health of their children one by one. She recommended brewed Shirazi oregano tea or diluted mint extract for diarrhea, and for constipation, plum juice, sap of the manna ash tree, or soaked figs. The women stood on one foot and then the other, but Touran Khanom asked after the health of all their relatives. When Run pulled currency from the back pocket of his trousers to add more to it, Touran would say, "Dear child, God bless your money." Mohsen would say, "Madam, it's a long time before the installments are finished." Touran Khanom would go home and get a fist full of wild rue to circle around Mohsen's head, and she would recite the incantation.

When Touran Khanom had given the house a cleaning, she would wash her hands and face and put her prayer chador on her head. She would put a pot of tea, a sugar bowl, and two glasses on a tray and go to see Teimur Khan in his shop, where she would sit on a stool. Teimur Khan's shop was full of children's tricycles, bicycles, and motorcycles, broken and new. On the opposite side of the shop, a picture of a girl motorcycle rider spanned the entire wall. The girl's eyes were slanted, and her hair was windblown. She seemed so cheerful, as though she were driving on the royal road to good fortune.

Teimur Khan would oil or fasten a chain. He would change a horn and test it out. He would change the light bulbs or disassemble a motorcycle while listening to Madam. His hands were greasy and black, and he had a thick mustache that he called a mustachio. He never shaved his mustachio. At first his mustache was bristly until Madam had taught Maryam to pound a bit of the fat tail from a sheep, spread it on a gauze cloth, and bind it to her husband's mustachio. The mustachio became very smooth, but Maryam couldn't stand the smell of the tail fat. She told Madam so, but she didn't complain. Finding a husband is not an easy task at any time.

When a motorcycle was fixed, it would be placed in a corner of the shop. Teimur Khan would wash his hands, drink a glass of tea, and feel refreshed. He would murmur, "O lovers, O lovers, Master Rumi has arrived," or, "During the day, all I am thinking, and during the night all I am saying, is 'Why am I neglectful of my own heart?'"

When he stood up to go get a bicycle or tricycle, he would put his hand on his back and say cheerfully, "Ya Ali, you are the problem solver." When he finished work, he would take the kettle of boiling water off the kerosene burner, brew fresh tea with Touran Khanom's teapot, and recite poetry that he knew Madam would like.

Well, the old woman, who didn't go to the theater, the cinema, or concerts, wanted very much to see Amir Arsalan's show at Sangalaj Theater. Morad had bought tickets for her, too, but it was a long way, especially with such leg pain and backache! Shahin had said, "When Entezami came from the center of the hall onto the stage holding Shams Vazir, who had turned into a dog, and said, 'This poor animal . . . ,' the hall began to shake from the roar of the audience's laughter." *By the way, was it Shams Vazir or Qamar Vazir*? It had been several years that Touran Khanom had feared enclosed halls. She couldn't breathe, and her heart would beat rapidly. Her concert, cinema, and theater were the songs of Teimur Khan, and Teimur Khan sang just for her, and only for her, these verses based on Rumi's poetry:

That person who came to know you, O Master Ali,
    What should he do with his life? Ali, Ali
What should he do with his wife and children?
    Ali, Ali, Ali
The one who is mad about you, what should he do with the two worlds?
    O Master Ali.

And Madam would also murmur under her breath.

One day, the poem of Shahriar:

Go, O pauper, knock on the door of Imam Ali's house,
By God, through Ali, I came to know God.

She wrote in good handwriting and took for Teimur Khan,

The Truth is Ali, Ali, Ali.
Say, "Ali, Ali, Ali."

No, it was clear that today the concert hall of Teimur Khan was closed. Mohsen's minivan wasn't there, so he wasn't there, either. She had bought a handheld loudspeaker for Mohsen as a New Year's gift. If her legs weren't hurting, she would have gone to see Mohammad Aqa's New Year's display again. His wife would be standing behind the till. Multicolored fish would be tossing and turning in large, red and blue plastic basins full of water. Several wide-mouth bowls full of water would be hosting two or three fish each. Mint, small radishes, and scallions would be spread on top of each other. There would be newly arrived New Year's herbs that Run had brought for Mohammad Aqa just yesterday. Mohammad Aqa would sprinkle the herbs with water. On a large stool in the corner of the shop, there would be sprouted wheat and lentils in melamine plates, bunches of candles, cups of sprouted wheat porridge, and green and red candlesticks that looked like eight-petal lotus flowers.

She closed the door of the building, came in, and sat on the veranda in the padded wooden chair again. With a concave mirror in one hand, tweezers in the other, and glasses on her eyes, she tried to pull out the hairs from among the wrinkles under her eyebrows. She felt the kiss of the sun on her white hair. Too bad that no poet had compared old age to spring, since old age, if not accompanied by illness, is pleasant. She tried to make herself happy with this idea that in old age one has a lot of time to think, has intelligence and patience, and can transfer one's experience to others. Furthermore, a brain like hers, that has been active all life long, does not grow old with the aging of the body. *A human body is brittle and has not evolved much, but the brain (of course, not everyone's brain) has the potential for much more growth than the body has. Didn't Sakkaki learn syntax at seventy? And wasn't he the greatest grammarian of his time?*

She decided to free her mind so that she could defeat time with mental associations and imagery. She decided to revive herself with the trees, to travel with the clouds, if they came, and to fly with the birds. *O human being, trees grow old later than you. All winter they sleep until they are rejuvenated in the spring. If only you too had this cycle and succession.*

The sky frowned for no reason and dragged the sun behind a few pieces of cloud so that the clouds would gather together and pour tears. Their tears are in anticipation of the joy of spring, a gift to the celebration of earth and time. This morning one of them had envied Hasti. Hasti was at the peak of youth, but she didn't know the value of love, spring, and youth. When Touran herself was young, she had a heart that beat with hope and desire. There was always joy in her heart. She always imagined that a happy occurrence was awaiting her. She always thought that the whole world had extended her a hand, saying, "Come. It all belongs to you." *But God save us from the young people of this era who waste their youth. They're sloppy. They become full of themselves. Some of them are in a hurry to receive their share from life—as large a share as possible and as soon as possible. Some of them are wounded and even perish.*

The clouds came in search of their friends, stuck to them, and pulled the sun into their own insecure hiding place. Touran's heart beat and suddenly, like a wall clock, gave a single, loud chime. *Clang.* And for a moment, it stopped. Under her breath she said, "Fly with the birds. No, migrate." She closed her eyes tightly and put her hands over her eyes. In the grave, when she uncovered Mehrmah's face, her left eye had come out of the socket. Touran Jan had been shocked. She had closed Mehrmah's eye.

Her heart had deceived her. It was tick ticking again. She had told Dr. Ovanesian, "Sometimes my heart stops." The doctor had said in his Armenian accent, "It's old age." Touran Jan had said, "Then fear seizes me, and my heart beats fast." The doctor said again, "It's old age." Touran Jan heard, "Aspirin." She had asked, "Doctor, how much aspirin should I take?"

She gazed into the courtyard, and her eyes traveled from tree to tree. She had planted the cypresses and pines that remain green in winter so that her heart would be warmed by their greenness. When it snowed, they became bent and crooked. When she was middle-aged, she knocked the snow from them with a shovel, straightened them, and tied strings around them. Later on, that had become the task of the prince—that is, Shahin. Now they had bent down due to separation from the sun; their greenness had become dark brown. The sun had rescued itself from the claws of a piece of persistent cloud. Her heartbeat had become even. She sensed a murmur amid the light of the sun and among the trees. She listened. The murmur had a message: don't cover your body against the spring breeze.

The clouds had become malicious; they covered the face of the sun and it rained. God save us! Too bad Mehrmah was not alive. She would persuade her to phone Simin and Eshrat and insult them as much as she could. Mehrmah would put a tissue in front of her mouth, and Touran would glue her ear to the telephone receiver. Her lips would move, but they would make no sound.

If Mehrmah were alive, she would bring her to live with her. Mehrmah would, of course, agree. She didn't get along with her daughter-in-law. When her daughter-in-law had become settled in her husband's parental home, they had turned Mehrmah's room into the children's room and had moved Mehrmah to a damp room close to the entrance. Old age is that same damp room close to the entrance, with its musty odor . . . Her daughter-in-law didn't allow her to embrace her grandchildren. "You're a transmitter of disease," she said. "Microbes, viruses." And Touran Jan thought that the virus of old age had afflicted her soul. Her cousin, Mehrmah, was five years younger than she was.

The telephone rang. "Whoever you are," Touran Jan said, "for God's sake, don't hang up." Standing up was not easy. Her right leg had gone to sleep. She put her hands on the arms of the chair, said, "Ya Ali," and crawled on all fours from the veranda to the bedroom. When she picked up the receiver, she was panting.

A man's voice asked, "Is this the Nourian house?"

"Yes, yes. Who's calling?"

"Hello, Touran Jan. This is Morad."

"Hello! God bless you, Morad Jan. Where are you?"

"I'm calling from Mashhad. Touran Jan, get a ticket and come with Hasti to Mashhad. Remember what a good time we had when we went together to Sare'in and Tabriz? In my hotel . . ."

"Morad Jan, dear, who will take care of the house?"

"Lock the doors."

"Morad Jan, Hasti has only five days off."

"May I speak to Hasti? I miss her so much! Her existence is my all. You know that yourself."

"Morad, my love. Hasti has gone to her ungrateful mother's house for drudgework, and I'm all alone."

Suddenly the line went dead. Touran Jan sat down right there on Hasti's bed. Why had she said, "My love?" Because she was all alone?

She couldn't get off the bed. The muscles of her legs had cramped. The telephone rang again, and Morad asked why the call had been cut off. He urged them to come to Mashhad by plane and reminded Touran Jan that she herself had said, "Money is for spending." He added that not seeing Hasti until the eleventh of the month was more than he could bear. Suddenly, Touran had a brief, passing impulse to say, "Why don't you marry Hasti so that always . . . ," but she didn't. If she had stirred up the conversation, she thought, the telephone call would last much longer.

Morad tempted Touran Jan by suggesting that she could make a pilgrimage and he and Hasti could see new people, hear new talk, and learn a world of new things. Touran Jan listed so many reasons that they couldn't come, trying to convince Morad not to expect them. She decided to tell Hasti no more than that Morad would not be coming until the eleventh of the month, but she couldn't.

Someone pounded on the courtyard door with the knocker, and Touran Jan shouted, "Whoever you are, for God's sake, don't leave." She put her hands on her knees, stood up, came tottering to the veranda, and yelled, "I'm coming, I'm coming." She sat on a step and stood on the next one, sat and stood, sat and stood again, until her feet reached the courtyard pavement. She held on to the trees with her hands and arrived at the courtyard door. She couldn't open the door's wooden bolt. She took a stone from the ground and hit the end of the bolt. When the bolt was open, she couldn't open the door. "Whoever you are," she yelled, "are you still there?" She recognized the voice of Mohsen Run, who said, "Madam, it's me."

"My dear, push on the door so that it will open."

Mohsen gave Madam a cut-glass bowl full of sprouted wheat porridge. Touran Jan asked him to hold her hand and take her to the veranda. "Let me go lock the door of my minivan," Mohsen said. "I'll be right back."

Touran Jan went out the courtyard door, and her gaze traveled from Mohsen's minivan to the street. She squinted to watch the coming and going on Sepahsalar Garden Street, but her eyes weren't strong enough.

When Mohsen had bolted the door, he said, "Madam, the wooden bolt and the door itself have both swollen. One day soon I'll bring a saw and a plane and fix them."

"What time is it, dear?" Madam asked.

"It's 9:30."

"It's only 9:30? You're not mistaken?" And she thought, *Until Doomsday—that is, at least until eight at night—I must endure.* Out loud she said, "There was a clock as big as this house. I hanged myself on its large hand and stopped the movement of time."

Alarmed, Mohsen asked, "You hanged yourself? Who rescued you?"

"No," Touran said. "I was reading a book that had this sentence."

Mohsen put Touran Jan on his back, took her into the building, and sat her down on Shahin's bed. Then he left and returned, bringing the bowl of porridge. "My dear," Touran said, "put the porridge on the New Year's table, in the dining room. And come back after the turning of the year to get your gift. My gifts bring good luck."

"Can't I get my gift right now?"

"My dear, you're no longer a child who wants lollipops. Come in the evening. Now leave through the side door. Remember to close the door firmly."

She was in good spirits. Her legs were also better. Yes, a young man had carried her, had taken her through the courtyard and up the steps of the veranda, and had lain her down on Shahin's bed. That young man gave off the scent of youth. The scent of a human being. That young man will come after the turning of the year and will be all smiles at the sight of the handheld loudspeaker. From now on, he will be able to announce his fresh produce with the loudspeaker and not strain his throat. Perhaps Teimur Khan and his wife will also come and afterward go to the home of

Mohsen's maternal grandparents. She had given Teimur Khan as a present her late husband's watch on a silver chain. Teimur Khan had oiled the watch and fixed it himself. "What a good watch!" he had said. She had set aside for Maryam a thin, silk, prayer chador that she had bought in Baghdad from a specialty shop. That fellow's shop had so many steps! She had not worn that prayer chador more than once.

She stood and, with the corner of her prayer chador, cleaned off the dust that had settled on the drawing of Mosaddeq. *Truly, money is for spending!* She decided that while Shahin was away she would persuade Hasti to take the picture to be framed. Hasti had quoted someone who had seen the picture and had said, "This drawing is the essence of all the Mosaddeqs that this country has seen during its long history." Who was she quoting? She couldn't remember. *If you ask me what I ate yesterday, I won't remember. But how many memories and poems have fixed themselves in my mind over the long run. I remember them all.*

It's afternoon. Touran persuades Mehrmah to phone Simin and swear at her. "Well, shall I teach her a good lesson?" Mehrmah asks.

"Say what I have taught you." And she glues her own ear to the telephone receiver. The aggressive voice of a young man answers the phone. After an exchange, it becomes clear that it's Haji Ma'sumeh's brother.

Then Haji Ma'sumeh comes to the phone. "The lady is not in."

"The lady has gone to . . . screw herself?" Mehrmah asks.

"If I could lay my hands on you," Ma'sumeh says, "I'd tear you apart. You jerk."

Another time, and this time Simin herself answers the phone. "You shrew of a witch," Mehrmah says, "why don't you keep your hands off other people's children?"

"Who are you?"

"I'm the mother of a boy that you have led astray, you demon."

"He's my student? Where is he now?"

"He's become a guerrilla fighter, and it's all your fault, you devious bastard."

"Leave my mother out of it," Simin says.

"You're the source of all evil," Mehrmah says. "Why don't you just die and leave us alone?"

"Look, dear woman, all I do is teach. Of course, my teaching is related to politics and society."

"And you divert the children."

"No. I never impose any opinions on students, neither my opinions nor those of others. These lost souls . . ."

Mehrmah starts crying. Touran Jan hits Mehrmah's head with her hand.

"Are you crying?" Simin asks. "For a moment, I thought that you phoned me just to harass me. Has your son been arrested?"

"Not yet," Mehrmah says, and her crying becomes stronger. With no preamble, she asks, "Are you putting a curse on me?"

"Why should I curse you?" Simin says. "I don't believe in curses and the evil eye and such superstitions, anyway."

Silence. Mehrmah sighs.

"If your son is really in danger," Simin says, "you can bring him to my house tonight at 11:00 p.m. I'll hide him. Don't ring the doorbell. Just flick twice on the windowpane. Okay?"

Mehrmah's tears have stopped. Touran Jan hit her on the head as a sign to continue. Touran Jan's lips silently curse. "So that Haji Ma'sumeh and her brother can report him and collect the reward?" Mehrmah says.

"I have prohibited Haji Ma'sumeh's brother from setting foot here."

"Your prohibition is like your teaching. When I called an hour ago, Haji Ma'sumeh's brother answered the phone."

"I'll hide him," Simin says, "in a place that, if Haji Ma'sumeh's brother does come, he won't notice, and for this, I trust Haji Ma'sumeh. Whatever tricks she plays, she doesn't report anyone. Will you bring your son tonight?"

Touran puts her hand on Mehrmah's shoulder and motions with her head to say yes. Mehrmah bites her lip. "Okay."

Mehrmah hangs up and says, crying, "Cousin, I don't like what you just did. Why? Why did you make me harass an old, lonely widow this way? Poor woman, she's barren. She has enough trouble of her own. Now she will also be waiting."

Hasti comes home from the college. She puts her hand around Mehrmah's neck and kisses her. She shows Touran Jan and her cousin the drawing of a nude body that she has made that day. "Why are his eyes closed?" Mehrmah asks.

"However much I told him," Hasti says, "'Raise you head, man, so that I can see your eyes,' he didn't. I had no choice but to draw his eyes this way."

"Drawing portraits is forbidden," Touran says. "Drawing the naked body of an unrelated man is doubly forbidden. God will ask you on Judgment Day to make this portrait come alive, and since you cannot . . ."

Hasti laughs and says, "Then He will send me directly to hell."

Mehrmah and Touran Jan go to the kitchen to cook a potato omelet. Akhtar Iran married and left Touran Jan's house some time ago. Touran had cared for her since she was a little child, taught her to work. And she, in turn, had taken care of the children and Madam . . . until Teimur Khan cajoled Karim Aqa in the traditional body-building club and brought him to ask for the hand of Akhtar Iran . . . At that same first glance, Karim Aqa had made Akhtar Iran lose the little mind that she had. Akhtar Iran fell head over heels in love with Karim Aqa. Touran Jan put together a trousseau for her. She sent Akhtar Iran, with her flat nose and puffy face—just like a potato omelet—and her tiny eyes to her marital home. "But she's cute and lovely," Karim Aqa said. With Madam's permission, Akhtar Iran named her son Amir Shahin. Now Karim Aqa calls the child Amir in memory of the first imam, whose title was Amir; Akhtar Iran calls him Shahin; and the child has become completely confused.

Mehrmah and Touran Jan agree to make the next day's phone call. An upsetting call to Eshrat. Of course, when Hasti and Shahin are out. The cousins are one soul in two bodies. They are very dear to one another and quick to forgive each other.

Eshrat herself answers the phone. "Slutty bitch of a witch," Mehrmah says, "listen. Hear what I have to say."

"If you have nothing to do and are in the mood to swear," Eshrat says, "go ahead, and I will surely follow suit."

"You who left your children motherless," Mehrmah says, "and went to marry that garage owner Grease Monkey less than a year after the death of your young, heroic husband. Now, why don't you leave the children alone? You have made them pigeons with two homes."

"Why are you huffing and puffing?" Eshrat says. "They have recorded my rights on paper and given you a copy. Now listen carefully. I didn't have children to not see them."

"But who raised your children?"

"I know it's you or Mehrmah or Akhtar Iran. You have put a tissue over the mouthpiece of the phone and changed your voice so that I won't recognize you. I know who encouraged you. That decrepit old crone. Grease Monkey is a name that old crone calls my husband. Tell her, 'I did well to free myself from that dilapidated house and from you, old woman, who smell like a corpse.'"

"Wrong, you jerk!" Mehrmah says. "I am none of the people you mentioned. But if by 'old crone' you mean Touran Khanom Nourian, I swear on the spirit of my father who was a descendant of the Prophet . . ."

"May a descendant of the Prophet strike you down! Well, you were saying? I'm entertained by your words."

"I swear by the spirit of my ancestors, Mrs. Nourian is not aware of my phone call. Mrs. Nourian is a literature teacher in high schools of the capital, and she doesn't consider you important enough to even respond to your hello."

"Don't joke," Eshrat says. "I know what she's burned up about. Her son was neither a hero nor a martyr for Mosaddeq. Ask this literature teacher which imam it was who was eaten by a bear in Baghdad. It wasn't an imam; it was the Prophet. It wasn't Baghdad; it was Canaan. It wasn't a bear; it was a wolf. And the wolf didn't eat him, either. His brothers spread the word around that . . ."

"You shameless witch of a shrew!" Mehrmah says. "You're even denying the martyrdom of your first husband?"

"What martyrdom? First of all, 'witch of a shrew' is you and seven generations of your ungodly ancestors. Second, Hossein and I were going to Lalezar to shop. After such a long time, he wanted to buy a summer dress for me and a prayer chador for his goddamned mother."

"Why goddamned?" Mehrmah asks. "Touran Khanom hasn't died yet, despite what you hope. She'll live to be a hundred. Goddamn yourself, you whore."

Eshrat laughs and says, "Whore suits me. What was I saying, Mehrmah Khanom, my dear?"

"You were saying you had gone to buy clothes."

"Yes, I remember it well. We were crossing Ekbatan Street. We saw that a big crowd had formed. There were several soldiers with rifles too. A young man had fallen on the ground. Blood was flowing from him."

"The same young man who had written on the wall with his own blood EITHER MOSADDEQ OR DEATH."

Eshrat continues. "More soldiers with rifles were arriving. Several shots were fired. Hossein and I and two other people took cover and sat on the ground behind a car that was parked near the wall, beside that same poor young man. There was a lot of commotion, but there was no more gunfire. Hossein took a little peek from behind the car. He was shot right in the middle of the forehead. I tore my hair. He had died instantly . . ." Now Eshrat's voice breaks. She hangs up.

Mehrmah no longer sees her cousin next to her. Touran sits on Hasti's bed. She pounds her hands on her knees and cries.

Touran Jan wiped her eyes. She hit her head with her fist and yelled, "Leave me alone. Child-snatcher Simin. Bitch Eshrat. Godforsaken Mehrmah. Short-lived Hossein."

When she had calmed down, she said to herself, *Get up, old woman. Didn't you say, "I struggle; therefore, I am?" Stand up and think about lunch for yourself. Get up and soak the rice for supper. If you continue chewing on your memories this way, you'll be crazy by nightfall. Hasti and Salim will come, and you will prepare a nice supper for them. But what will you eat for lunch? Not lentil rice left over from last night.*

She went to the bathroom and washed her face. She moistened her facecloth, wrung it out, and put it on her eyes. She brought a spoon. She sat at the New Year's table and ate the sprouted wheat porridge to the bottom of the bowl.

6

It wasn't easy for Hasti to get to work right away. When she got out of the taxi, she saw a truck blocking her path. The cab of the truck had gone through the gateway of the large garden, but the body could not. There wasn't even a narrow space on either side of the truck that Hasti could use to get to the building. Hasti wasn't a large cushion with a crimson, carpeted, design-laden cover that one of the workers could pick up and toss from atop the truck to a worker standing below in the garden. Three workers were in the garden catching the cushions, putting them on their heads, and carrying them to the building. Two others stood on cushions to pass them along.

Hasti placed the flowerpot of tulips, her purse, and her bag by the wall. At first, she stood watching the movements, and sometimes the pauses, of the workers. Then she crouched down with her back to the wall. A white Peugeot stopped a bit beyond the truck. A man jumped out of the car, and a woman who was sitting next to him called, "Hasti Khanom, come help." Hasti stood. The woman was Keshvar, the dealer, and she had a large bundle on her lap.

The man suddenly ran, embraced Hasti, and twirled her around in the air. Hasti struggled to escape. The man put her down and said, "My, how you've grown! You've become a real woman!"

"Bijan? Is it you?" Hasti asked.

"Johnny Dollar, your private eye!" Bijan replied.

"But you look like Anthony Perkins."

"The image of my father as a youth."

Bijan said that he had entered the country five days ago. He had wanted to tour Europe for two or three months, but Papa Ganjur had telephoned and said that he needed him. So he came.

Bijan and Hasti took the bundle from Keshvar's lap. Keshvar got out of the car and sat on the edge of the channel of clear water that was flowing between the street and the garden wall—flowing quickly enough to disturb her reflected image.

Bijan and Hasti were chatting. Bijan was saying that when he went to America, Hasti was a little girl of ten or eleven. He said that he had earned two master's degrees, one in journalism and one in industrial administration. Hasti asked what connection these two fields could possibly have with one another, and Bijan said, "That's me! I wanted to stretch it out. Fourteen years."

Then Bijan asked about Hasti's life, and then they started to talk about memories they had of each other.

"Do you remember the year that my father bought me a bicycle as a New Year's gift?" Bijan said, "And I rode it around the pool? I fell in the pool, and the bicycle fell on top of me. My father jumped in the pool with his clothes on and rescued me. Blood came out of my nose. My head had hit the spout of the pool. You still had a pacifier in your mouth. For a long time, you couldn't stand being without a pacifier. You came and put your pacifier in my mouth."

Hasti did not remember.

Bijan asked whether she remembered their house in the Monirieh district of Tehran. Hasti answered that she had vague memories of that house. "I had failed my sixth-grade elementary school exam," Bijan said, "and out of embarrassment, I had lain down in the closet with my father's cloak over me. You came and brought me two little muffins. Then you left and returned with your doll, gave it to me, and told me the story of the bitter orange and bergamot girl. At noon my father came home. He had bought me a wristwatch. He called out, 'Bijan, apple of my eye, where are you? What grade did you get, son?' You came out of the closet and said, 'Shush. Bijan got an ouchy. He's sleeping.' My father didn't scold me. He fastened the watch on my wrist. Your mother came, too. She kissed me and said, 'One year in the seventy or eighty years of a person's lifespan is nothing.' And she took me to the basement sink and made me wash my face."

The truck backed up as far as the metal grate over the channel. Two workers came, grasped two sides of a carton, and brought it out from the seat next to the driver. Two more came and did the same with the second, third, and fourth cartons. Paper and pen in hand, the driver came to Bijan and said, "Sign for this."

Bijan read aloud, "Kashan-woven crimson cushions, sixty. Cartons containing Japanese flower-bird china table settings and sundries, four. Altogether, 274 pieces. Wages of cleaning workers . . . Wages of delivery . . ."

Bijan placed the paper on the hood of the truck and was about to sign it when Hasti said in English, "You're signing without receiving the delivery?"

Bijan said in English, "Since the day I arrived, I have taken on the nonindustrial administration of this strange party. Don't worry." Hasti thought, *He has barely arrived, and they have assigned him this drudgery.*

Bijan selected two workers and told them to stay. One of them asked, "Until when?"

"Until whenever your work is done," Bijan said. "Your wages are hourly . . ."

The group set off with the bundle on the head of one of the workers, a canvas bag in the hand of the other worker, the flowerpot of tulips in Bijan's hands, and Hasti with her bag and purse. As for Keshvar, her own weight was enough. "Bijan, lock the car," Hasti said. "In fact, why don't you bring the car in?"

"I may have a need for it later."

But still, he gave the flowerpot to Keshvar and returned.

Diamond-clear water was pouring into the pool, and it was moving quickly. In fact, the pool was about to overflow. Along the edges of the little garden plots, the violets had set their eyes on the clear, blue, pool water and requested with their gaze that it reach them, too. The water said that their gaiety was flawless. All of the greenhouse's ornamental flowers had been put out to watch. *Freedom,* Hasti thought, *for even one moment is a windfall. Tomorrow they will be imprisoned in their glass house again.*

Hasti entered the family room wearing jeans, a wool sweater, and slippers. The chores had been assigned. The director was obviously Bijan. Hasti's position: artistic advisor. Pasita, Naneh Agha, and Taghi Khan had also joined the group. Lady had mixed herself in as well and was rubbing herself on Pasita's legs. Pasita was scratching the cat under her chin, and Lady's eyes were closed. One of the workers wanted to hold the cat. Lady scratched him. As for Keshvar, she had gone to the sitting room to put the contents of the bundle in their proper places.

The main living room had been completely emptied of chairs, tables, and decorations. Only the carpet and the television grimaced at one another. The ceiling chandeliers shone, even though the lights were not on. In the next room, which was the dining room, everything was yawning in its own place. In the room on the other side, a platform had been set up in the center and a rug thrown over it. These two side rooms were separated from the main living room by two arches facing each other.

Bijan put his hand on Pasita's back and told her in English to go get the picture from Keshvar. When Pasita brought the picture, Hasti said, "Bijan, the television doesn't belong here with the New Year's tablecloth spread on the floor and the cushions along the walls. Let's move the television to the dining room and in its place put a picture of Zoroaster."

Bijan scratched his chin and said, "But the turning of the year will be announced on television."

"Yes," Hasti said, "but the announcement can be heard from the dining room. Besides, no one wants to listen to the speeches of the shah, the queen, the crown prince, and the prime minister."

It was not an impossible task. Two workers were nearby, and they had a bag full of tools.

Under Bijan's direction, the workers spread the cushions around the living room; only the space under the arches was exempt. Thirty pairs exactly—cushions for sitting and cushions for leaning against. Bijan and Hasti sat comfortably cross-legged next to one another on one cushion. "But," Bijan said, "these Americans are not able to sit cross-legged, unless they do yoga."

Bijan took Hasti to his bedroom. Pasita was taking the Japanese flower-bird dishes out of a carton, Taghi Khan was dusting them, and Naneh Agha was filling the flower-bird bowls with sprouted wheat porridge. Then the wooden spoons with embossed handles. Then the rose water sprinklers. Hasti took one of the small, flower-bird bowls and examined it inside and out. "It's an imitation of Chinese flower-bird dishes," she said, "but it's machine-made." No one's ear was tuned into an art history lesson, not even Bijan's.

"Everything's ready," Bijan said. "You tell me, which ones shall we send out first?"

Hasti spoke and Bijan wrote. "First, the printed tablecloth. Then the side plates, knives, and forks. Then the sprouted lentils and wheat. Then the potted hyacinths. Then the crystal bowls containing fish. Then the bowls of sprouted wheat porridge with small bowls . . ."

Hasti taught Pasita to cut the fresh garlic with a knife into the shape of tuberose flowers and to split the pomegranates and place them on the fruit bowl ready to eat. She told Naneh Agha to pour rose water into the sprinklers and asked where the red ribbon and candles were.

"How many candles shall I buy?" Bijan asked.

"Seven."

Bijan took the workers in his car, and when he returned with the red ribbon and candles, the large, symmetrically printed tablecloth had each of the symbols of spring and New Year's in its proper spot. Hasti put the candles in the middle of each plate of sprouted lentils and wheat and tied a ribbon around each one. It was as though, at the sight of the red ribbon, the pieces of split pomegranate on top of the baskets of fruit recognized their own kind and boasted to them.

"Wow!" Bijan said. "All these colors and such abundance! How good it is for the eyes, the nerves, and the taste buds."

"If the eyes see only dark and neutral colors," Hasti said, "their owner becomes emotionally depressed. When the senses confront ugliness and harshness, it makes a person crazy."

"Girl," Bijan said, "you know a lot."

"What you two said?" Pasita asked.

Bijan explained to her in English, and Pasita nodded her head. Her slanted eyes shone, and she said in her broken Persian, "My eyes so happy."

Pasita went to get the place cards. "Did you know that Pasita means 'morsel'?" Bijan asked. Hasti didn't know.

"This unfortunate morsel," Bijan said, "has a BA in midwifery, and all the males of this household, thinking she is a luscious morsel, want to taste her. The male guests, too. My father pinches her cheek. I even saw the Afghan cook touch her breasts. But Pasita spends Sundays with her boyfriend from her own country. Through my father, she changes her salary into dollars and sends it to her family in the Philippines."

"Most foreign families," Hasti said, "and some well-to-do Iranian families have one of these 'Pasitas.'" She wanted to add, "And you touch her back." But she didn't.

Pasita brought the cards. "Read them," Bijan said, "and I'll tell you where to put them."

"Mr. and Mrs. Ganjur."

"Put it on the center cushion."

"Mr. and Mrs. Hitti."

"Put it on the cushion to the right of my father."

"La'l Beigom and Sir Edward."

"To the left."

Pasita read and read until she arrived at Hasti Khanom and Salim Farrokhi.

"No, no," Hasti said in Persian. "Don't seat me next to Salim Farrokhi. He won't sit next to an unrelated woman."

Bijan laughed. "Then he is a sheikh, and you have placed the Quran and a picture of Imam Ali at the head of the tablecloth for his sake. From now on I'm going to call him Sheikh."

Hasti frowned. "You'll do no such thing!"

"Then it's a serious matter. I apologize."

"Look," Hasti said, "Islam accepts both our New Year's and the Zoroastrian religion. I have placed the Quran and the portrait of Imam Ali next to the image of the Prophet Zoroaster."

They also put together a small New Year's display table in the dining room for the children. They completed the display with sweets, fruit, nuts, and sprouted wheat porridge. In the end, the pot of tulips Hasti had brought was of use. It took its place in the middle of the dining room table, even though one of its flowers had broken off. Hasti put the flower in a clay pot on the outer surface of which, with so much skill and patience, wheat had been grown. Hasti asked Naneh Agha how she had done it, and Naneh Agha explained that first she had covered the body of the pot with one of the lady's nylon stockings. Then she had planted all the young sprouts, one by one, on the stocking and had filled the pot with water. Every other day she had changed the water in the pot and sprinkled the sprouts with a splash of water.

Hasti sat on the family room sofa and started to paint three white eggs to put on top of a dish full of colored eggs. Bijan helped, acting as a "gofer," and he watched as Hasti drew a miniature, coquettish lady on the first egg. "That looks like Mother Eshi," Bijan said, "but thinner."

"Mother Eshi requested it herself," Hasti said. "It's for Peggy . . ."

"No, my dear sister. It's for Murray, Peggy's husband."

Hasti laughed and said, "His name is Mardan Khan. Peggy and all his other friends call him Murray. I'm the only one who says Mr. Tavassoli."

Bijan recited a well-known verse by Iraj Mirza: "His name was Ali Mardan Khan. The lady of the house had no peace from him." "And neither did the Pasita of the house," he added.

"Have you met him?" Hasti asked.

"No, but I've heard about him. My father says that since he returned from America, he has hit like a wolf upon the flock of women, whether married or unmarried. A harem . . ."

Changing the subject, he said, "I didn't know that you did miniature drawings, too. I was told that the method of teaching here is just like that in America, with the unit system, and that the schools of art that are taught are Western ones."

"That's correct," Hasti said. "Mr. Hitti is an educational expert, and your father . . ."

She wanted to say, "is everyone's fixer." But she didn't. Instead, she said, "And your father works under the supervision of Tavassoli, who is Hitti's assistant."

She thought and added, "An easy means of neocolonialism."

"I've heard," Bijan said, "that most of the college professors have been educated in foreign countries."

Hasti smiled bitterly and said, "Another easy means of cutting people off from their national identity and character."

"You're repeating Jalal Al-e Ahmad's words," Bijan said.

"You mean you've read Al-e Ahmad's books?" Hasti asked.

"My father sent me all kinds of books," Bijan said, "and Mother Eshi, all kinds of dried herbs, ground saffron, cumin seeds, red currants . . ."

And he left the family room.

Hasti remained, debating what to draw on the egg dedicated to Mrs. Hitti that would reflect her hate and grudge and that, at the same time, the most important guest at the New Year's ceremony, Mr. Ganjur's boss, would not recognize it. *Grudge and hatred for whom*? she thought. *More than anything, for Mr. Hitti and then for, in Grandmother's terms, the garage owner Grease Monkey*. Ahmad Ganjur was indeed a garage owner originally. Now he had expanded the garage and entrusted it to Ja'far Aqa. Ja'far Aqa discovers with one look the secret of any problem in large trucks, and with a few commands the problem is fixed. And if not, he takes off his coat and lies under the truck himself. It's a done deal.

Most of what Hasti knew about Ahmad Ganjur was what Mother Eshi had said or was from the taunts that Grandmother had leveled at her son's replacement. Mother Eshi would say, "He joined the Iran-America Society and studied English, and he became close to Americans. He even went to New York for two or three months and spent several months in London on his way home. He also went to California one time with Bijan to find a place and furnishings for him and to set up a savings account so that Bijan could live from the bank interest. I don't know how many hundreds of thousands of dollars he took; he wouldn't say."

Grandmother would smile bitterly and say, "I know what he's up to. He fooled the Americans and went to Khorramshahr and Bushehr and learned English from the porters in those two cities. And when he returned, he lied, saying that he had been to America and that he had been to England."

Mother Eshi would say, "He became a manager in the Point Four Program."

Grandmother would say, "He became a dealer for the Point Four Program."

Mother Eshi would say, "He was a translator in the Advising Office of the Royal Armed Forces."

Grandmother would say, "He waxed the boots of the American sergeants."

Mother Eshi would say, "He went to the Franklin Publishing Organization and translated American literature. Or he edited the manuscripts of other translators."

Grandmother would say, "He picked up the scent of dollars there and went into the paper business. Then he sponged off them in the transport and delivery of paper for the printing presses."

Hasti herself was a witness to this type of parasitism. Ahmad Ganjur would say, "The establishment of the middle school cycle in Iran was among my initiatives." He would say, "The least benefit of the American system in place of the French system, which I have set in motion, is the changing of our students' grades to the equivalent grades in American colleges." But Hasti, who had stuck her head into every nook and cranny of the Ministry of Education in her efforts to become a teacher and had finally written a letter to Mr. Hitti, understood that the work of her mother's husband was as a dealer and errand boy, but of a very remunerative type. She knew that Ahmad Ganjur rents houses for Americans who come to Iran. He gets them maids. He goes to the airport. He takes a sign on which the name of the American traveler has been written. He waits in the airport lounge and circulates with the sign until he finds the American traveler, with or without a family, and takes them to their prearranged and all-prepared home and life.

Hasti suddenly noticed that the Atlantic Ocean was depicted on the egg that was to be Mrs. Hitti's gift, along with the Statue of Liberty, with her back toward the sea and her torch out. The scene was illuminated by light from the lamps along the ocean and beside the Statue of Liberty, her back turned to the rest of the world. When Bijan saw the drawing, he said, "I know why you did this, but for my sake, not for the sake of my father, turn the statue toward the ocean and light her torch."

Hasti put the egg aside to give as a gift to Morad. She had also knit him a blue-green sweater. She was sure that Morad would put on the sweater in front of Hasti and Grandmother and that he would kiss both of Hasti's hands.

Hasti chose an egg that had been dyed blue and drew a skyscraper on it with the lights of most of its windows lit. On the blue background, a boat was loose without a rudder and without passengers. For La'l Beigom she drew a Qajar woman who seemed to be dancing. She had seen the picture in Professor Mani's house, and, with her mediation, Sir Edward had bought it for his wife, who was from Karachi. Finding a similar one would not be difficult for Professor Mani, and with money from the sale of this picture he could change the worn-out pipes of his building.

Sir Edward had served long enough in the colonies, the semicolonies, and the regions under the influence of the British government that it was hard to tell that one day, long ago, he had been English. His wife and two sons were still living in London, but the only communication that he had with his wife was a check that he sent every month. Every place that Sir Edward had served he had taken a local wife. Most recently, during the time of Ayub Khan, when he was the governor of Karachi, he took La'l Beigom. La'l Beigom had told Hasti all of this, and she had added that now, here, he is an expert in the Government Employees Office. Hasti knew that his present occupation was no less important than being the governor of Karachi.

At two in the afternoon, according Bijan's schedule, the residents were to take their places on the veranda in front of the family room. Hasti, in her dark red jacket and skirt, came to the veranda before everyone else. She gazed at the ornamental flowers, trees, and plants and the pool filled to the brim with water. The sun after the rain had animated them such that they suggested to Hasti, come, make all this permanent, but not on eggs. No one wants to look at a drawing with a microscope.

Mother Eshi came to the veranda next, and Hasti was surprised. Her mother was usually the last person to join a group. Of course, it takes time to do her makeup. Mother Eshi wore a long white dress with silver and gold threads embedded in the fabric. The two sides of the skirt were slit to the knees. If not, walking and sitting in such a tight skirt would have been impossible. The green of her emerald necklace winked at the greenness of all the green there was in this world. Farhad, the matchless beautician, had given her long blonde hair as many curls and ringlets as he could.

The sun was shining generously on that golden hair and dress when Mr. Ganjur also arrived. He wore white trousers and a wide white tunic that extended to his ankles, and he had wound a cord three times around his waist. On his head he had a white skullcap with decorated edges, and on his feet, cotton peasant shoes that were even whiter. When Mother Eshi saw him, she said, "Oh, Ahmad Jan, what kind of a getup is this?"

"Pretty woman," Ahmad Ganjur said, "don't you get it? This is the dress of a Zoroastrian priest." He put his hand on his belt and said, "The name of this three-tasseled cord is *kosti*." He kissed his wife's hair and said, "My beautiful peach!" He coughed and added, "Now, come on, tell me. How much of a tip did you give to Farhad?"

Mother Eshi pouted. "Only a thousand tomans."

"And that's little?" Ahmad Ganjur said.

"Are you serious?" Mother Eshi said. "Firuzeh bought him a Porsche sports car for New Year's and parked it in front of his beauty shop. She put its key on its gold chain in his hand. Farhad kissed her hand. He kissed her face as well."

Next Bijan and Parviz arrived. Parviz's dress was an exact copy of his father's, but brand new. Before Mother Eshi could open her mouth, Ganjur said, "This is the priest's child." Hasti pressed her eyes together and bit her lip.

Parviz had taken Mother Eshi's hand, but he was fixated on what he was wearing. His golden hair stuck out from under his skullcap. Hasti's eyes turned to Bijan. A red carnation in the buttonhole of his gray jacket collar was a miniature of spring. In answer to Hasti's look, Bijan shrugged his shoulders.

And now Pasita arrived at the veranda—with rouge, eye shadow, and lipstick. Ganjur smiled when he saw her. Pasita was wearing a loose dress trimmed with silver and gold braid. The red, green, and yellow hues on the body of the dress and on the sleeves admired each other's colorful beauty. She wore a triangular gold shawl on her head. On top of the shawl, a long, wide scarf was arranged in such a way that the front had folds and pleats, and one of its corners fell down her back to the shin.

"Bijan Jan, have you started a costume ball?" Mother Eshi asked.

Bijan answered, "This is the dress of an aristocratic Zoroastrian woman." But his eyes fled Hasti's look.

"Then shouldn't you have prepared one for me?" Mother Eshi scolded. "I'm the wife of the priest, after all."

Bijan changed the subject. For the *n*th time he reminded them that the language of the party would be English. "Except among ourselves and in exceptional circumstances."

First, a Hillman car entered through the garden gate and stopped in front of the veranda. La'l Beigom and Sir Edward came to the veranda. The driver came after them with a gift box in his hand and then set off after Parviz. La'l Beigom was wearing white satin slacks and a purple shirt that fell to her knees. She had on her head a violet brocade scarf that had been tied around her neck and hung from the left shoulder. Ahmad Ganjur introduced only Bijan, saying, "A youth freshly arrived from America." This phrase left a good taste in his mouth. He said the same thing to Peggy and Murray, who had come next.

Peggy's son and daughter went looking for Parviz and asked in English, "Where do we put the gifts?"

"Have you put your name on them?" Parviz asked. They had. Parviz told them: "On the hall table."

Parviz was in the same class as Murray's son. Mr. Ganjur was so well-connected that, along with the grandson of the private doctor to one of the princes, Parviz had been accepted into Tehran American School—a school for American children only, with 100 percent American teachers.

Murray put his hand on Bijan's back and said in Persian, "So, you have just come back from America? Have you lost your mind that you have returned to this godforsaken place? But on the other hand, here money grows on trees. You just need to reach up and collect it." Then he went looking for Mother Eshi, rubbed his hand on his narrow mustache, and said, "May I die for you. You have become like a tree in full bloom."

Moher Eshi replied, "It *is* spring, honey!"

When Mr. Hitti's Cadillac stopped in front of the veranda, Ahmad Ganjur, in his Zoroastrian priest's dress, jumped down from the steps of the veranda and opened the car door. Helen, Mr. Hitti's daughter, got out first. She was wearing a long dress of Isfahani block-print cotton, and two camel bells were hanging from her belt—one small bell and the other larger. She had fastened anklets with charms on her ankles. When she came up the stairs the bells and charms jingled. The fringe of her long shawl seemed to be real gold braid.

Mother Eshi embraced Mrs. Hitti, and they exchanged kisses—first the left cheek and then the right like Americans do. Mr. Hitti was shorter than Mother Eshi, so Mother Eshi could plant her lips on the bald spot in the middle of Mr. Hitti's head. Hasti could see the place that her mother's lipstick had left its mark on that head.

Now Mr. Hitti introduced to Ganjur a tall man whose back was a little stooped and whose blond hair was a little receding. "The archaeologist Mr. Crossley." Mr. Crossley asked forgiveness for coming without an invitation. Mr. Hitti interrupted saying it would be a shame if he were not to see Iranians' New Year's celebration. Ganjur used the same phrase to introduce Bijan that he had already repeated many times—a youth fresh from America—and called Hasti his daughter. Mr. Hitti wanted to kiss Hasti, but Hasti excused herself, saying she was Muslim. And after that more guests arrived, none of whom Hasti had seen or recognized, except for Dr. Bahari and his wife.

When the guests saw the New Year's display, the adjective *marvelous* broke the record in their descriptions of it, and then other exclamations followed: Oh, my God! Extraordinary! How colorful! Every color under the sun! Unbelievable! It's a fairytale! It's dreamlike! I must be dreaming! Beyond beautiful!

Only the Italian wife of Dr. Bahari said, "A work of art completely Eastern." She said that in Italian, and Dr. Bahari translated it. Murray said in Persian, "Well done, Mother Eshi. Bravo!" Mother Eshi moved her head, and a section of her hair flowed onto her right shoulder like a golden waterfall.

Murray sat cross-legged on the cushion comfortably, and, facing the guests, he challenged them, "Can anyone sit like me?" Peggy stretched out next to him and said, "Murray, sit like us." Mr. Crossley sat next to Hasti.

Naneh Agha brought the shiny, golden, boiling samovar and placed it on a corner of the tablecloth, and Pasita sat next to the samovar. Naneh Agha left and returned bringing a flaming brazier. She took a handful of wild rue from a crystal bowl, circled her full fist around the tablecloth, made some motions in the air, and poured the rue on the brazier.

Ahmad Ganjur, standing behind Pasita, began to explain the benefits of wild rue incense and the meaning of Naneh Agha's movements. Then he took three pomegranate boughs that were at the corner of the tablecloth and said, "Well done." He asked all the guests to join him in saying, "Well done," which they did. He had started to speak about the holy branch when the telephone that was in the family room rang. Ganjur interrupted himself to say, "Hasti, my daughter, get up and answer the phone."

Hasti recognized Mrs. Farrokhi's voice, and Mrs. Farrokhi recognized hers. Mrs. Farrokhi explained that in the morning Salim was well. He took a shower. He intended to come, but he caught a cold, and now his back hurts so much that he can barely move. "Don't be waiting for him, dear," she said. Hasti breathed a sigh of relief, though she expressed sorrow, and she wished Mrs. Farrokhi a Happy New Year in advance.

"Dr. Bahari is here," she added. "Would you like him to come to the phone?"

"The doctor came, dear," Mrs. Farrokhi said. "He examined him and gave him an injection."

When Hasti returned to the living room, Ganjur was talking about the holy fire, and there was the scent of myrrh and frankincense in the air. Ganjur said that the scent is a reminder that we are expecting the arrival of the spirits.

With the holy branch in his hand and the ritual cord at his waist, Ahmad Ganjur took a few steps and began his main speech. "At New Year's, the universe is renewed. The celebration of New Year's is the celebration of the birth of the earth and the sky. The spirits, or *farvahar*, from which the month of Farvardin got its name, come to the earth and become guests of the living. These spirits are humans' guardian angels in the sky. They are also spirits of the departed. Now we are awaiting the spirits of our departed."

La'l Beigom clasped her hands together and said, "My God! Then the sky of Iran is full of angels."

Ahmad Ganjur continued. "The spirits are forces that come from Ahura, and after a person's death they return to Ahura. These spirits are parts of our God or Ahura. They mix with our soul and guide our soul. These spirits are our spiritual twins. Before us they were in the sky, and with us they came to earth."

"That's very interesting," Mr. Crossley said. "It's similar to Plato's ideas."

Ahmad Ganjur chewed on the corner of his salt-and-pepper mustache and said, "Plato got it from us." He glanced at his watch and said, "Hasti, my daughter, light the candles." Hasti did so. Ganjur took a few more steps and said, "The world of light is the realm of Ahura Mazda. At the moment of the turning of the year, the spirits of the departed come to earth, become guests of the living, and participate in the joy of the family. So the house must be clean, the clothes new, the tablecloth fully laden and well arranged, and the family's oven lit. The spirits become happy with greenness and freshness, and they give their blessing. But if they see the living wretched and on bad terms with one another, they become offended by the disaffection of the family. They curse and they leave."

He raised the pomegranate boughs in his hand above his head, fixed his eyes on the ceiling, and said, "O spirits of our departed, come, come. We are ready. You are most welcome!" Murray put his hand over his mouth and laughed. Ganjur gave him a beseeching look and continued. "The pomegranate is a symbol of the breasts of women when they give birth, so it is an indication of fertility."

Murray roared with laughter and said in Persian, "May I die for the pomegranate, this sexy tree."

Ganjur said with a serious voice, "Meanwhile, the pomegranate tree is holy because its blossoms resemble flames. The display that you see on the tablecloth is a sign of joy and abundance of riches and a symbol of Ahura Mazda, who presides over the six Amesha Spenta."

This time Murray counted on his fingers and said, "With Ahura Mazda, it's seven."

"That's right," Ganjur said. "Seven items whose names begin with the letter *S*."

He was silent for a moment. It was as though he had forgotten the rest of his speech. Bijan helped him out. "Papa, what are the Amesha Spenta?"

Ganjur smiled. "Amesha Spenta are attributes of Ahura or manifestations of him. Ahura Mazda directs the world with their help, and the number seven is holy."

"You all know," La'l Beigom said, "that I am a Muslim. I want to say that in Islam too we have seven favored angels: Gabriel, Michael . . ."

Ganjur did not allow La'l Beigom to finish her words. "Zoroastrians," he said, "put the Avesta at the head of the New Year's tablecloth, and we Muslims put the Quran there." With the branches, he pointed to the holy Quran.

"Now what if an Iranian were a Jew?" Mr. Hitti asked.

Bijan interrupted. "Well, in that case, he would place the Torah there."

Ahmad Ganjur, with the branches pointed toward the sprouted wheat and lentils, continued. "Greens are a symbol of abundance of riches and fertility. This porridge is made of germinated wheat, and you know that wheat is the holiest of plants. It's the first meal that Adam ate."

Murray laughed and said, "Eve tricked Adam, and Satan had tricked Eve. And God kicked all three out of heaven."

Peggy hit Murray's shoulder and said, "Don't joke around so much. Let him finish his talk. I didn't know Ahmad was so knowledgeable."

And Ahmad presented his knowledge with even more self-confidence. "Eating porridge brings fertility."

Murray exploded into laughter and said, "We will all test it tonight."

"Murray," Peggy said, "won't you just shut up?"

Ganjur shook the holy branches in the air and warned, "Tsk, tsk! I said at the moment of the turning of the year you must be happy. If not . . ."

Murray did not let up. He finished Ganjur's sentence: "And if not, the spirits will be upset and leave us."

Ahmad Ganjur said to Murray in Persian, "Mardan, for your children's sake, just this one night, don't be a spoilsport."

He pointed at the service-berry and continued. "The service-berry blossom is the love potion that leads to fertility. It's a symbol of cosmological fertility. If you stand under the service tree in spring, you will smell semen."

Murray put his hand over his mouth. Nevertheless, he could not restrain himself. "And you will become horny," he said.

Ganjur pointed at the garlic and said, "Garlic is a medicinal plant. However devilish its smell, because of its medical benefits, it's exceptional." And facing Hasti he said, "My daughter, get up and remove the green cloth from the nougats."

Hasti removed the cloth and was surprised that so many gold one-Pahlavi coins had been poured over the nougats. Who had poured the coins on the nougats? And when? And why had they not trusted her?

"My daughter," Ganjur said, "turn on the television, but mute the sound." She went to the dining room and saw Parviz seated at the table in his child priest's clothes. He and the children of the guests had eaten up all the food. Hasti didn't know which button to push. She tried several until finally the first button from the top turned the television on, and the voice of a man who was praising New Year's filled the room. "Hasti Jan," Mother Eshi said, "turn the fifth button to the left." But Hasti didn't know if that was the fifth button from the top or from the bottom. Finally, Parviz came to her aid.

When she returned to the living room, Ganjur was saying, "The coin is a sign of good luck, and sumac . . ."

"And sumac," Murray said, "makes a person's mouth water." He added in Persian, "May I die for . . ."

Then Ahmad Ganjur talked about the hyacinth—that it was a rare flower, and he said the apple is a symbol of fertility and birth. And he told the story of the dervish who had given the barren king and queen a magic apple and explained that before having sex, the king should eat one half of the apple and the queen the other, and their barrenness was cured.

Murray pointed at the apples in the fruit basket and asked, "Ahmad, are these apples also magical?" And everyone laughed.

Bijan looked at his watch, went to the television, and turned up the sound. "May God change our lives for the best!" Hasti thought, *Just change our lives.* And *clang* . . . New Year's had officially come to the feast of the earth.

All of the guests except Mrs. Hitti stood up—some with difficulty and La'l Beigom easily. Mrs. Hitti said that her leg had gone to sleep. They all clapped and showered each other with kisses. Hasti got goose bumps from Mr. Crossley's kisses. Then Ganjur put his hand in the pocket of his tunic and took out a box with a white velvet cover. Three golden bangles that were connected with each other at one spot and three golden chains that continued this connection. At the end of each chain, there was a bunch of emeralds, diamonds, and rubies, in order. He put the bangles on Mother Eshi's wrist and showered her hand, neck, and lips with kisses. Mother Eshi showed the bangles to everyone, and Ganjur said that green, white, and red are the colors of the Iranian flag . . . "I love my country. Every bit of my existence is bound to this land of Ahura."

"Pretty woman," he said to Mother Eshi, "pass around the nougats and gold coins," and he warned that the gift for each one is a single gold coin. "It's a good omen. Until the end of the year your pocket will be full and you will be successful in your work. But the number one is a sign that God is one and has no equal."

Dr. Bahari exploded in laughter and said, "Ahmad is cheating here. His Excellency Zoroaster did not write any such thing."

Mother Eshi passed around the nougats and coins, and everyone, even the children and even Hasti, Pasita, Bijan, and Parviz, took one coin and a handful of nougats. Hasti had put paper tissues here and there on the tablecloth.

Keshvar the dealer, Navidi the driver, Taghi Khan, the Afghan cook, Naneh Agha, and Lady all came into the adjacent hall. Lady went toward Parviz and placed herself in his arms. The master of the house took the bowl of nougats and coins from his wife. As he gave each one of them a coin and a handful of nougats with his own hand, everyone kissed it. Hasti delivered the paper tissues on time.

Hasti took the empty Japanese flower-bird bowl to Bijan's room, put it on his bed, and closed the door. When she returned, everyone was sitting in his or her place, and Keshvar and the servants were sitting on the platform in the side room—Keshvar and Naneh Agha cross-legged and the men on two knees. Ahmad Ganjur had eaten the first egg that had been put on the mirror. Facing Hasti, he said, "My daughter, the saltshaker."

Hasti went to the dining table and brought the saltshaker. Ganjur said to Hasti, "I ate the first egg for the health of my eldest child, and I am eating the second one for your health, my dear, and the third for the health of Parviz."

Dr. Bahari tittered and said, "It's good that you don't have eight children. If you ate eight eggs, you'd have a stomachache!"

"Then you would treat me!" Ganjur said.

Mother Eshi gave the gift eggs to Mrs. Hitti, La'l Banu, and Peggy and said, "They're real paintings. Hasti drew them." Then Pasita passed around the bowl containing the colored eggs.

Ahmad Ganjur's speech would not end. Without anyone asking, he went toward the egg, the simplest sign of fertility and birth, and he asked himself, "Now, why is it placed on a mirror . . . ? When the cosmological bull tosses the earth from one horn to the other at the moment of the turning of the year, the egg on the mirror will shake. But the mirror is also sacred. You see life in the mirror."

"What is the meaning of the fish in the water?" Mr. Crossley asked.

"Water is the sign of Anahita, the angel of water . . . but fish? I don't know about that. Perhaps Bijan knows."

"Fish are also a symbol of Anahita," Bijan said, "because without water, they can't live."

"And now," Mother Eshi said, "the spirits are present at the New Year's tablecloth, tasting from among the seven *S* items."

The eating then began, and Hasti was among the main people serving. She felt she was playing a part in a silent film run at a fast speed. All the servants were acting with her in this fast-forwarded film. Naneh Agha poured tea, and Pasita passed it around. Hasti, in her stocking feet, was in the middle of the tablecloth pouring porridge into the small flower-bird bowls, and Bijan was placing them in front of the guests. He too had removed his shoes.

Parviz had released Lady, and the children were giving him their empty plates. He was striding down the middle of the tablecloth in his new peasant shoes, filling the plates with food. Lady also came to the tablecloth and sniffed at the fresh chicken and fish on the flower-bird platter. Bijan picked her up and put her in Naneh Agha's lap. Naneh Agha put a piece of cheese in the cat's mouth. At the suggestion of Mother Eshi, they went to get Mrs. Hakimi's homemade sweets. Baklava, coconut Turkish delight, almond Turkish delight, mulberry-shaped marzipan, honey candies, crispy treats, rosettes, and . . . La'l Beigom said the sweets were peerless and asked where she could get them. Mother Eshi gave her the address of Par Confectionary. Then fruit and nuts. They ate little fruit, but lots of pistachios.

Guided by Taghi Khan, Haji Firuz came into the side room, with his tambourine, red clothes, and trumpet hat, singing, "I say hello to my master, my master, the dear one." Hasti didn't know why, but he mistook Mr. Crossley for Ahmad Ganjur. Perhaps because he was closer at hand. Haji Firuz approached him from the side room, hit his tambourine, then put his hand under Mr. Crossley's chin, and sang, "My master, raise your head . . . My master, why don't you smile?" Mr. Crossley gave Haji Firuz a shove. He fell into Hasti's lap and let go of his tambourine, which Hasti snatched from the air. The tambourine gave an alarming, loud sound.

"Go to hell," Mr. Crossley yelled, "you n****r! Get away from me. You stink!"

Bijan took Haji Firuz's arm and helped him up, and Hasti put the tambourine in his hand. Bijan led Haji Firuz to the side room next to the platform and whispered something in his ear. But Haji Firuz was silent. He struggled to free himself. Meanwhile, Hasti told Mr. Crossley that Haji Firuz was not Black, that he had blackened his face with soot. "And even if he were . . ." Hasti felt her voice shaking.

Bijan had calmed down Haji Firuz, and he resumed playing and singing, though devoid of gaiety and full of offense. When he sang, "Snap, snap the fingers, snap," and, at the direction of Ganjur, they all tried to snap their fingers, it was as though Haji Firuz were singing a funeral dirge. Hasti turned and looked at him. Two white furrows of tears were running down his black face. Hasti got up and seated Haji Firuz on the platform. She returned to the living room where she emptied a silver tray of dirty glasses and put nuts, fruit, and sweets in flower-bird bowls. Nothing remained of the porridge. She took the tray to the side hall and placed it on the platform in front of Haji Firuz. "It's New Year's, after all," she said. "Please eat something. That guy was way out of line."

Taghi Khan brought several crystal carafes on a silver tray and placed it next to Pasita. Each carafe was filled to the brim with red wine. Then he collected glasses and looked for the tray that they had been on, but couldn't find it. Navidi brought the crystal cups that had also been spread on a silver tray. The Afghan cook brought plates containing caviar sandwiches. Taghi Khan had left and returned with the largest steel tray in the house. With Pasita's help, he collected the empty or half-finished dishes and cleared half of the tablecloth. Now there was space for the chicken and pickle sandwiches. Those containing the "pearl of the Caspian Sea," in Ahmad Ganjur's terms, had been gobbled up as soon as they had been served. "I kiss the tiniest bits of this land of Ahura, especially its caviar."

Hasti went to the family room and saw that the table in the center of the room was full of balls, tanks, airplanes, ships, astronauts, and crumpled gift wrap. She knew that Ganjur had told the guests to bring gifts only for Parviz, so as not to burden them with expense. But when had Parviz gone after the toys? Probably when he had become bored with his father's speech.

Hasti decided to leave quietly. She went to the bedroom to get her purse from her mother's dressing table, and her eyes fell upon a color photo of Salim. Why was Salim's photo there? Well, probably Mrs. Farrokhi had given the photo to Mother Eshi so that she would show it to Hasti. If she liked the picture, they would set a date for a meeting. But why was the photo of Salim on the table now? She picked up the photo. It had been taken in London. Those same eyes, that same gaze. The same looks except for the mustache and beard. In the corner of the photo, "To my dear mother" and "February." What year? It was not legible, or Hasti's eyes were not seeing well enough to read it. Salim was wearing a dark blue suit with shiny gold buttons, and he also wore a tie. He was sitting on a chair with a blue velvet cover. The arms and back of the chair had been engraved, and they looked golden. Salim had leaned so calmly that it was as though he were a statue of Buddha in a state of meditation. But with his eyes open. That night in Grandmother's house his eyes had been closed. He had said to Hasti, "In your view, I was spacing out." She put the photo in her purse.

She took Parviz's gift out of her bag. She also took out the box of Sauvage cologne. She wanted to write on the box, *Mr. Ganjur, I have not been, am not, and will not be your daughter. As long as I remember, Mother Eshi even begged that Shahin and I call you "Papa Ahmad." Never*! But the gift wrap completely covered the box of cologne and was full of flowers, drawings, and pictures. She signed the corner of the box, returned to the family room, and put the gifts for father and son on top of one another on the table. She heard the sound of cheers and of Bijan's voice saying in Persian, "Father, I'll take Haji Firuz and pick up the performing minstrels." When he came to the family room, Hasti said, "Bijan Jan, take me home, too, on your way."

"I understand," Bijan said.

They went together to the veranda. Cars had filled every empty spot in the garden, and several drivers were sitting on a rug on the veranda around a tablecloth that had been spread before them. Navidi was in charge of the group. They were all eating and drinking. When they saw Bijan and Hasti, several rose. Bijan put his hand on the shoulder of one and said, "Relax." Navidi wanted to get up, but he couldn't. Once again, his stomach had caused the button of his new jacket to pop off.

Haji Firuz came to the veranda too. He had a closed handkerchief in his hand. *Whose handkerchief was it? And who had given it to him*? Bijan took his wallet from the back pocket of his trousers and crammed several bills, without counting them, into Haji Firuz's closed handkerchief.

A minivan honked and stuck its nose into the garden. The driver realized that no more cars could come in. Five men got out of the car, and Bijan said, "Hasti, wait a moment until I pass them on to Qoli, the Afghan, and return."

Hasti told Haji Firuz, "That American man didn't even have an invitation. He thought that you were a Black man. Most Americans don't like Blacks."

"I know," Haji Firuz said. "That young man told me."

"Where are you going next?"

"College intersection. There's a party with foreigners there, too."

"There are two white grooves on your cheeks."

"That young man gave me some black shoe polish."

A man with a large pot on his head was coming forward. Another man had a smaller pot on his head. A third had put on his head a tray on which there were several large and small pots. A fourth had on his head a tray on which a white cloth had been spread, and the tray on the head of the fifth man was just the same as that on the head of the fourth man, but the fifth man had a bunch of skewers in his hand as well. Hasti laughed so hard she couldn't breathe. Several of the drivers looked at her. Were they among the gluttons? She was reminded of Obeyd Zakani's tale *Mouse and Cat*. The mice, who had heard of the repentance of the cat and his asceticism and piety, put on large trays whatever food they had in their nests and made it a gift. They were also five and came one after another, and in the end, the cat got the five chosen mice . . . Then Hasti remembered that Vali, in directing Sa'edi's play, *Stick-wielding People of Varzil*, had used this very scene, and how appropriate.

Bijan had been gone a long time. The five chosen mice had put their loads on the ground next to the veranda, and Navidi had given each one of them a bottle of Pepsi. Hasti had thought that her mother had been talking about a costume ball. Hasti herself thought of puppet shows and bald heroes, but Ganjur had luxuriant salt-and-pepper hair. If Salim had been there—which, thank God, he wasn't—he would have said, "Inferiority complex and Weststruckness and satisfying them by means of Eaststruckness." He would have said, "It's showing off history and tradition to a people enamored with history but with only a short history of their own."

If it were Morad, he would have made a big fuss. He would have yelled, "Consumption, consumption! Weapons, weapons! Oil, copper, uranium, the Middle East, the Third World, the Gulf!" He would have looked at Parviz's toys and would have said, "The real ones, except for the astronauts, are all stored in His Majesty's arsenal." Maybe he would also have talked about the hungry people of India and Biafra.

Haji Firuz sat next to Bijan in the white Peugeot. Bijan showed him where the mirror was, and he polished his face with the black shoe polish. Hasti sat in the back. Silence. When Haji Firuz got out, Hasti sat in his place next to Bijan and said, "You wrote your father's speech about New Year's and the seven display items very well."

Bijan added, "Especially considering the audience members who are mad about sex."

"Where did you get all this material in the space of just five days?" Hasti asked.

"In fact," Bijan said, "I'm an absolute expert on the New Year's ceremony. Every year at USC we put on a New Year's festival. My father would send me sprouted wheat, service-berries, wild rue, and whatever books of Pourdavoud, articles of Dr. Farahvashi, and whatever else had been written about New Year's. A speech about New Year's was always my responsibility."

Hasti was too tired to ask, where or what is USC?

Bijan pushed in the car's lighter. He lit a cigarette and said, "Three whole nights this old man paced the floor, memorizing my writing. He repeated it back to me, and I corrected his pronunciation. And, indeed, he did a fine job."

He stopped at a red light at the Darvazeh Dowlat intersection. The street was empty. Most of the shops were closed. There wasn't even a policeman at the intersection. The light was still red when Bijan moved the car forward. He put out the cigarette in the car's ashtray, which was full of half-smoked or not even half-smoked cigarettes, and said, "This man has done so much for me."

Hasti didn't say anything.

"Are you disappointed?" Bijan asked.

"Bijan," Hasti said, "you are like my brother. When they cut your umbilical cord from your mother, you were still emotionally attached, but little by little you became free. Listen to me: Also cut your emotional cord with your father. Let go of this strong attachment. If not, he will pull you along with himself to the bottom of the pit."

"And you," Bijan said, "should do the same with Mother Eshi, however much I love her like my own mother. This woman has never spoken to me disrespectfully." He thought for a moment and continued. "But I can't do this, and neither can you. Me, because I am indebted to my father and I don't want to be ungrateful and break his heart. You, because with the help of your mother, you find access to a world that prepares you for reality. Your mother is looking for suitors for you . . ."

Hasti smiled bitterly and finished Bijan's words: "And she is finding rich, sheikhly suitors."

"I never said such a thing," Bijan said, "and I never will."

When they arrived at Valiabad Street, Hasti saw Grandmother sitting on a stool in front of the house door with the door lamp lit. She told Bijan, "Let me out right here."

7

Was it right for Hasti to make a drawing for Salim on the fiberboard that Morad had given her for New Year's last year? Morad had polished that fiberboard so much that it looked like ivory. In cutting it, he had observed the golden ratio. He had told Hasti, "One cannot disassociate oneself from the past. Review the manuscript illustrations in the college library. Start with the medieval manuscripts, like *Khavas al-Advieh* (Properties of Spices) and *Manafe' al-Hayawan* (Benefits of Animals), and finish with contemporary miniatures, even the ones for sale. There are some skilled miniaturists who work on fiberboard or ivory on Manuchehri Street. I didn't have the money to buy ivory for you. We'll go together."

And they had gone together.

When Grandmother had said that Morad wasn't coming for her birthday, Hasti was secretly happy. That day was the day of Mrs. Farrokhi's gathering.

The day after the New Year's party, Mother Eshi had phoned Hasti looking for the book *Ajayeb al-Makhluqat va Gharayeb al-Mowjoudat* (The Wonders of Creation and the Oddities of What Exists). Complaint after complaint. "I never expected you to leave without saying good-bye! Many of the guests were asking Ahmad, 'Where's your beautiful daughter?' Especially Mr. Crossley, who was quite taken with you. Murray came to our rescue. 'She went to see her fiancé . . . ,' he said, 'and anything for my dear girl.' But it's a shame that you didn't see the play by the performing minstrels. You won't believe what they did on the platform. They played and sang and shook their hips and grimaced and did somersaults and turns . . . Of course, in the end the platform broke and they all fell. The guests thought that this was part of the performance."

"So they didn't put on a play?" Hasti had asked.

"They did. After dinner they put on the Uncle New Year play. A thin-bearded man got on top of two others who had arranged themselves like a donkey. The thin-bearded man held a fan, and he fanned himself as he ascended the throne in place of a king. The vizier and ministers and several women surrounded him. Pasita had mixed herself in. That little devil became the thin-bearded man's favorite wife, and the man flirted with her as much as he could."

"Was it the drama *Mir-e Nowruzi* (New Year's King)?" Hasti had asked. "Or the comedy *Kuse bar neshin* (The Thin-Bearded Man Sitting on Top)?"

"Bijan, who was translating, said 'Uncle New Year,' and he said, 'He's similar to Santa Claus of the Christians, except that he has left behind his pack of gifts.'"

"Really," Mother Eshi had asked, "why didn't you stay? Don't spend so much time with that old hyena . . ." Then she had sincerely apologized and had said, "Don't spend so much time with Grandmother, or you'll waste away."

Hasti had spoken of fatigue and Mother Eshi of sympathizing. When Hasti had asked her to say more about the play, Mother Eshi had said, "Even the children were saying that they'd never had so much fun in their lives. That thin-bearded man who had sat in the place of the king was supposed to have two Black servants who would make funny gestures. Ahmad didn't allow them to blacken their faces."

"For Mr. Crossley's sake," Hasti had said.

"Yes, and Bijan was in a foul mood. Indeed, from the time that he returned, he was in a bad mood. Mr. Crossley called him 'Bij.' He looked him in the eye and said, 'My name is Bijan, sir.'"

Hasti had said good-bye.

"Wait," Mother Eshi had said. "I have something more to say to you. Why are you angry with me? And was it you who took Salim's photo from the dressing table?"

Hasti had answered the second question affirmatively, and Mother Eshi had said that she had wanted to show her guests her future son-in-law—that when Hasti had said Salim was not coming, she understood that Grandmother had cast an evil eye on the poor child.

Mother Eshi had asked Hasti to swear that she would come the day of Mrs. Farrokhi's gathering, and Hasti had said that she would. Mother Eshi's boisterous laugh seemed to Hasti the sign of a marriage marketplace. She thought her mother had also snapped her fingers in joy. Mother Eshi had thanked God that Hasti had broken up with that half-witted boy, and Hasti had said, "It's not broken off yet."

Hasti sat at the dining table. She put Salim's gift bergamot orange and his photo on the table and arranged the painting tools on a plastic sheet next to her. Grandmother had put on Hasti's gift cardigan and was sitting with her back to the wall of the dining room, awaiting guests and reading *Zad al-Ma'ad* (Provisions for the Hereafter) with a magnifying glass that was also a gift from Hasti.

Hasti had had the basic drawing in mind since last night when she knew that Morad was not coming. A large circle, a fresh bergamot orange with its branch and leaves in the middle of the circle, a circle within another circle. Light from above. Light of the surroundings and light from the interior. All over in the drawing, Salim's eyes: in profile, straight on, three-quarters forward, even his closed eyes.

Hasti's hand started working. Her mind suggested various pictures.

You can draw one luminous, protective, half-opened hand above the larger circle.

Is love that clear?

Well, you can draw a bird in flight facing the open eyes and full face of Salim that is above the bergamot orange.

Would that be seen as a "yes" to Salim's request for my hand?

You can draw a vague sketch of your own naked body inside the bergamot orange.

Would that be seen as my request for Salim's hand? Besides, the bergamot orange itself is said to have concealed within it the bitter orange and bergamot girl.

Decorate around the bergamot orange with miniature-like drawings?

No, I'll draw a branch and leaves on the bergamot orange.

If it were not fiberboard, but rather a large canvas, all of this could be drawn.

Grandmother's voice broke the train of her thoughts. "Why does no one ring the doorbell of this house?"

"Teimur Khan and Akhtar Iran each came last night with their families."

Why doesn't Grandmother understand that she cannot have many guests? Before her leg pain took from her the ability to walk long distances, most mornings Grandmother went to this or that hospital to visit one of her age mates, and most afternoons she went to the funeral service of one of them. She used to say herself, "If only I had the joy of attending at least a circumcision party."

As for Hasti, she had set a date with her friends for the first Friday of each new year, to go to a restaurant for lunch, each person at their own expense, to exchange New Year's greetings.

She remembered Brigadier General and his orderly. A brigadier general who was retired but had an orderly, thanks to the good offices of his nephew, Lieutenant General Tondar. A brigadier general whose house was a few houses above and across from the shop of Teimur Khan. A brigadier general who would sit, New Year's or not, in the frontage of his house, which was a fairly wide space, put his swollen feet on a footstool, and place the canes that the German doctors had sent home with him at his two sides. There he would seat his visitors, whether the visits they were making were socially obligatory or not, on the steps that ended at the porch of the house, or they would seat themselves. The gathering of the neighbors and passersby around Brigadier General resulted in the formation of, in Teimur Khan's terms, a kind of neighborhood or quarter council.

Hasti looked at Grandmother. The book *Zad al-Ma'ad* was closed, the magnifying glass was on top of it, and both were on Grandmother's lap. She seemed to be dozing off. "Touran Jan," Hasti said, "recite a poem. Please recite Attar's *The Conference of the Birds* so that my hand, eyes, and mind work more sharply and with more strength."

Grandmother didn't do it. Hasti wanted to raise her spirits. "I don't think there is any woman your age who knows so much poetry."

"What do you mean? Your Simin Khanom surely does!"

"Simin Khanom has gone to Shiraz."

"To hell with her."

Hasti didn't want to get mad and say, "What wrong has Simin done to you?" So she said, "I wish that Mehrmah Khanom were alive and would tell me the story of the bitter orange and bergamot girl."

Grandmother opened her eyes. "Where are you, Mehrmah? If you were alive, you would certainly have stayed with your cousin. Whatever poetry I have memorized was done during the time that I had given you shelter."

The doorbell rang. Hasti, with the help of Brigadier General's orderly, opened each of the two sides of the door to give passage to Brigadier General and his canes. The ends of the canes rested on four bent prongs, to the bottom of which thick rubber had been pounded. With the help of his orderly, Brigadier General sat in the armchair in the living room, and Hasti assigned the orderly to one of the dining room chairs. Their New Year sweets were Grandmother's favorites: Turkish delight, *masghati*, rice cookies, and of fruit, long-lasting ones: apples and oranges.

After she had served tea and offered sweets and fruit, Hasti sat across from Brigadier General and asked, "Did you have a good time in Germany?"

"I was in the hospital the whole time."

"Which city was it?"

"It was Germany. I don't know which city. My son Emad knows. They took us straight from the airport to the hospital. The lieutenant general had made the arrangements."

"You had surgery?"

"No. They said at my age it was impossible."

"Did they say what your ailment is?"

"Emad knows. It's long and complicated. Emad said, 'It's erosion of the bones of the pelvis . . . ' They should, with plastic or, I don't know, with nylon, or I don't know with what . . . In any case, they should take out the bones and replace them with artificial bones. They told us to buy these two canes." And he put his hands on both of his claw-footed canes, which had been placed at the two sides of the chair. It was as though he were caressing them.

Hasti left the conversation to Grandmother and Brigadier General and returned to her drawing in the dining room. Brigadier General's orderly had eaten everything Hasti had put in front of him. He took his plates, knife, and tea glass to the kitchen, washed them, dried them, and put them away, and now he was absorbed in Hasti's drawing.

"Do you like it, Asadollah Khan?" Hasti asked.

"Draw one of these and give it to me as a New Year's gift. I'll hang it in my room. Being far from home is a bad thing."

"You mean you are uncomfortable here?" Hasti asked softly.

"Brigadier General," Asadollah Khan whispered, "is like my father, but when Aqa Emad comes once a week, he slaps my face."

"But why?"

"I don't know. It's just like that. One time he hit me with a water hose. My back turned black and blue. The attendant at the Valiabad bathhouse told me so."

"Well, tell Brigadier General."

Asadollah Khan murmured more softly. "Brigadier General is like a timid mouse. He fears Aqa Emad. Every time Aqa Emad comes, he asks his father, 'Are you still alive?' Whatever provisions there are in the house, he gathers them up, puts them in his car, and leaves right away."

"Then conceal the provisions."

"What should I do?"

"Hide them."

"I had hidden them the time he hit me with the hose."

"Do you want me to tell Brigadier General?"

"No, no. He'll kill me."

Hasti couldn't think of anything else to do. "How many months are left in your term of service?" she asked.

"One year, one month, and seven days. If they allow me to leave . . ."

"Why wouldn't they allow it?"

"Well, maybe they won't allow it."

"What town do you come from?"

"It's not a town. Our village is near Saveh."

Hasti changed the subject and asked in a louder voice, "Do you like my drawing?"

"Very much."

"What have I drawn?"

"You've drawn two suns, one inside the other. Also, you've drawn seven or eight stars like eyes. But stars don't come out in the daytime. Draw one sun. There aren't two suns . . ."

When a car horn blared, Asadollah jumped up. "Aqa Emad. They have come to give New Year's greetings. When the lieutenant general has returned from greeting the shah . . ."

This lieutenant general, Hasti had heard from Brigadier General, gets a New Year's gift of one gold Pahlavi coin from the shah . . . from the majestic hand of His Highness . . . But his wife would put a bunch of new ten toman notes within the pages of a Quran and would give them herself as gifts to women, children, and men, old and young, and to orderlies, from whatever part of Tehran they were, and they would rush to get it. Brigadier General is of the opinion that the dresses of the lieutenant general's wife are splendid. Brigadier General likes the word *splendid*.

Grandmother's eyes were closed, but, contrary to what Hasti imagined, she was not napping. She had let her mind wander.

Mehrmah, who had broken off relations with her son and his family and had found refuge in her cousin's house, says, "Cousin, you sit and study. Rewrite your notes neatly. I'll keep the children busy, and Akhtar Iran will do the housework."

Hasti jumps into the arms of Mehrmah and says, "The story of the bitter orange and bergamot . . ."

"Once upon a time, a devil was lying down under a tree. He asked, 'With what did he pluck?' Someone said, 'With tongs.' He said, 'It can't be done with tongs . . . '"

"All of my classmates are young," Touran Jan complains. "They call me 'the old one.'"

"Cousin," Mehrmah says, "you are more knowledgeable than all of them put together. You outdo the professors, too. You've said that yourself."

Touran Jan walks around the courtyard memorizing Attar's *The Conference of the Birds*. She recites it for Mehrmah. She has forgotten only two couplets.

How full were the wells of their minds! What strong ropes they were holding that they could pull so much eloquent literature from their minds.

"If we leave Hafez aside," Foruzanfar said, "then Persian poetry worthy of scrutiny . . ."

"Professor, classical Persian poetry should have ended with Hafez, and Nima . . ."

"Venerable lady, don't spin such nonsense."

Several professors and several final year students, among them an old lady, have been standing in the cloakroom entrance to the Faculty of Literature meeting hall. They are awaiting a former minister. The former minister's speech is about the tribes of Iran. He's late. A professor who has recently become a senator shifts from one foot to the other. He cracks his knuckles. Since he has become a senator, he has grown a goatee. Last year he had a messy gray beard.

As though it were yesterday. Memories from a long time ago nail themselves firmly into the brain. But ask me, "What did you eat yesterday?" I won't remember. But no, wait. I do remember. I ate the sprouted wheat porridge that Mohsen Run had brought. Nevertheless, old age means living in the past . . .

The professor's patience is wearing thin. He turns to a professor who Touran doesn't recognize and complains, "Why doesn't this fellow come? Does he think he's still a minister? I must appear in the royal court and have dinner with His Highness."

Touran Jan had heard that the professor had become a senator from his wife. They saw each other in the Valiabad bathhouse. They had even washed each other's back when the bath attendant wasn't there. They had poured warm water on each other's head. The professor's wife had said, "My husband has become a senator." She had advised Touran Khanom to do her thesis with another professor. "My husband doesn't have time anymore."

Touran Khanom had grumbled and said that it was no longer possible. "Why did the professor need to become a senator?" she had asked. "Isn't his merit and accomplishment already acknowledged by all?"

"Well," the professor's wife had said, "he was going to lose this piece of property that we have. Two of the children want to study medicine."

In time, Touran Jan had thought, *everyone shows their true colors. I don't know what charm the people of Iran have, what tool they possess that they can separate the pure from the impure.*

The former minister still has not come. The senator professor turns to the other professor, strokes his goatee, and says, "Let's forget about listening to this fellow's nonsense. Whenever I see him, I feel as if I'm being knifed."

The unrecognized professor says, "Maybe one day he will be useful. You made one blunder. That's enough."

"What did I do?" the senator professor asks.

"You acted like an amateur. You wrote a poem for Mosaddeq, and like a *true friend,* he ordered that they broadcast your poem three times on the radio. It was an original poem."

The senator professor discreetly signals to the other with his eyes and eyebrows that he should drop the subject. But the other professor still recites the poem:

O Mosaddeq, you are a man, a true man.
    You are in battle with the devil and with evil.
O Mosaddeq, we say your praise.
    . . .

"Sir," the senator professor says, "I adore heroes."

Laughing loudly, the unrecognized professor says, "One hero is Mosaddeq. One hero is the shah."

"Careful. I'll set fire to your mustache to get even with you."

"You see that I don't have a mustache." The unrecognized professor continues, "Why did you let him get his hands on your poem? You could have recited it for him and left."

"He was slick. He took it from me, hid it under his pillow, and played sick." No, another person had said *played sick* another time, on another occasion. That other person had said, "Putting his head under a blanket and crying were among Mosaddeq's weapons. And always at the perfect time." Touran Jan remembered. Khalil Maleki had said it. He had said it to Hasti . . .

The speaker enters. He's thinly built, and he's wet from head to toe. So, it's raining and they haven't realized it. He couldn't get a taxi. The senator professor goes forward, says hello, bows, and helps the former minister and main speaker take off his wet overcoat. He hangs the speaker's overcoat on the coatrack. He also hangs his wet hat. "We were just talking about you," he says.

Touran Khanom knew that the "talking about you" professor would assign her thesis to another professor, and he did. Touran Khanom was disappointed because the senator professor was more enthusiastic, and, as he himself had said many times, in Persian literature up to Hafez, there was nothing that he did not know.

Most of the students had accepted Mrs. Nourian. Only a few students still called her "the old one." She had lent her neat notes in her good handwriting to most of them, on the condition that they keep them only one night. Boys and girls would go to her and pour out their hearts. The girls' concerns were related to either love or political confusion. The boys were more distressed about politics, and as soon as their political faction matured, they began thinking about establishing a new faction. She would mediate, and she often helped lovers unite. Arranging two abortions. Arranging the marriage of a girl three months pregnant. Convincing the notary public to predate the marriage by three months. Of course, the notary public was a longtime acquaintance, but in this kind of matter some "convincing" was still necessary.

She gathered those caught up in politics, boys and girls, around herself and gave them motherly advice to stick to their studies—that politics can't be trusted, that politics is passing, that politics is for gaining power, and that they well knew what power and money do to a person. Some said that there was something in the air that drew them to politics, and one of them asked, "But wasn't your own son martyred in support of Mosaddeq?"

The deniers would say "no." But most of those who accepted Mrs. Nourian gathered either around the heater or around the warmth of her soul, and she described what had happened. And each time it brought forgotten details to mind.

Mosaddeq had broken off with Parliament, and Hossein Nourian had arranged with his friends to accompany Mosaddeq from his house to the

Parliament building and carry him above their heads into the building. The friends don't come. Hossein goes and makes himself a protective shield for Mosaddeq.

It's February 28, 1953. The shah has left. Ruffians have set off from the palace to the door of Mosaddeq's house. Hossein goes and speaks from atop a stool. "Long live the national leader of Iran," he shouts, "Dr. Mohammad Mosaddeq!" The thugs assault him. A certain lady comes to his rescue and pulls him off the stool. If not, he would have been martyred right then . . .

Mosaddeq comes out of the Parliament building. He says loudly, "It's a den of thieves in there. The nation is here." Hossein Nourian bends over . . . Mosaddeq stands on his back to speak until they can bring a stool. Hossein realizes that a soldier has pointed his rifle at Mosaddeq. Hossein shouts to Mosaddeq, "Sir, get down!" Baring his own chest, he says, "Shoot here, you scoundrel," and the scoundrel shoots . . . Most of the girls and some of the boys shed tears. Crying, Touran Khanom wipes their tears.

Touran Khanom brings to the college the signed photo of Mosaddeq that he has dedicated "To the mother of the martyr Hossein Nourian." She shows it to her classmates. She has attached this photo to the wall above the head of her bed. She greets the photo every morning. Mosaddeq has addressed Mrs. Nourian as "Dear Sister."

Hossein Nourian is the hero of heroes, and the mother of this legendary hero gains more respect day by day. Her classmates have accepted Mrs. Nourian's belief that the only path is the path of Mosaddeq.

The "talking about you" professor had recited a poem for Mosaddeq. Hossein Nourian gets the poem from Mosaddeq and takes it to Radio Tehran. He asks one of his closest friends to read the poem every morning, noon, and night . . . five or six times . . .

Touran Khanom emboldens one of the students whom she has united with his beloved to mention the subject of modern poetry, if the senator professor comes, in order to provoke the professor. Since he has become a senator, the professor comes to class late and brushes off students seeking guidance from him.

The professor comes and sits at his desk. He points to his head and says, "Half of my head is aching."

The emboldened student says, “Professor, today tell us your views on modern poetry. Your headache will get better.”

The professor smiles bitterly and scratches his goatee. He softens his voice and says, “It’s nonsense, sir. It’s absurd.” He takes a piece of paper from the pocket of his jacket and reads, “‘The dark blue cave runs, it screams loudly.’ Right from the belly of the poet! The meter is not right, nor is the rhyme. One long hemistich, one short . . .”

Touran Khanom raises her hand, and the professor’s voice becomes softer than before. “Venerable lady, you who wept for the beginning of the decline of Persian literature in the sixteenth century will now weep blood for the decline of modern Persian literature. Americans are fanning the flames of these absurdities.”

“So there’s a fire, Professor?” Touran Khanom asks. “In my opinion, new poetry is the blood of our poets that has fallen drop by drop onto paper in the form of words. In the very lack of equality of hemistiches, a kind of meter and order can be observed, and there’s a kind of harmony and cohesion in the complete work. But reading it takes patience. One should get used to it.” Without waiting for the professor’s permission, she recites, “My farm remained dry, and so did all thoughts.” She adds, “No one knows better than Nima the fear and repression of his era . . .”

“Enough, old woman!” the professor shouts. “You have added to my headache. I can’t gather my thoughts now.”

When the professor had not yet become a senator, he would take his hat by its brim and cram it onto his head. Once he became a senator, he would take his hat off the table, level the two sides with his hands, push the center of his hat in, and straighten the brim . . . It seems he has returned to his old habits. He grabs the brim of his hat and crams it onto his head. He picks up his silver-headed cane and says, “Now my whole head hurts.” Then, in a deep voice, he says to Mrs. Nourian, “Tell this lowly poet with his absurd poems, ‘The Pahlavis have served this country very well.’ And they have served you, old woman, more than all the others, enabling you to take center stage in your old age!”

But at the elementary school where Mrs. Nourian was working, no one cared about the martyrdom of her young son, nor about the path of Mosaddeq. Touran Khanom was a sixth-grade elementary school teacher.

One day that she was missing her son and spoke about his martyrdom, she saw the girls' eyes staring at her in horror. When she talked about Mosaddeq, the girls chattered. The principal of the school was formerly a member of the Women's Center. Mrs. Sediqeh Dowlatabadi, head of the center, looked dignified in the long white dress she was wearing. One night she had introduced the principal to Her Highness Shams, and Her Highness had shaken her hand. Everyone became aware of this "hand-shaking." Mrs. Dowlatabadi gave a fantastic speech . . .

The head of the Parent Teacher Association is a retired director general of the Ministry of Foreign Affairs. Under the direction of Mrs. Nourian, the sixth-grade girls are preparing a performance for the end-of-the-year celebration. The first play is *Khayyam Night.* The invitation cards also include the title *Khayyam Night.* The math teacher, who is of the first sex—that is, male—has agreed to play the role of Khayyam. And in the second play, he has agreed to play the role of Bozorgmehr in Anushirvan's court.

Touran Khanom pulled out whatever she thought she had in her closet. The girls also brought from their houses, either by their father's car or by taxi, other things needed. They cut and sewed for many days. With Mehrmah's help, Touran Khanom spent three nights making a beard from cotton and wool and a crown of cardboard for Anushirvan, and she drew pictures of jewels on the cardboard crown. The head of the Parent Teacher Association sent by minivan two cushions with golden pillowcases and a platform. They painted the platform as a throne, and put jewels on it in harmony with those on the cardboard crown.

Touran Khanom is sitting next to the head of the Parent Teacher Association. The hall is full of students' parents and family members and of relatives of the teachers and the principal. Touran Khanom has brought Mehrmah and Hasti with her.

Akhtar Iran remained home to watch Shahin. She tied the child's leg with a long rope to a large stone that is in the corner of the courtyard so that he couldn't stray from her sight. With that rope on his leg, Shahin could go one paving stone's distance from the pool and return. Akhtar Iran sat to clean herbs.

The performance has begun. The girls have sung the national anthem while everyone stood and then sat. Khayyam, with his white beard, has leaned on two cushions. His beard has been attached a little crookedly. It will probably fall off. A young, angelic girl in a silk dress comes onstage. A decanter and a goblet are in her hands. She pours wine from the decanter into the goblet. With smooth movements, she walks and strolls gracefully. Khayyam removes his hand from his beard and takes the goblet from the girl. But now the beard has separated from his chin. With his left hand, Khayyam puts the beard in its place, and oddly, the beard is now level. The decanter in hand and with shining hair, the girl stretches her free hand toward Khayyam and sings, "O Khayyam, if you are drunk with wine, be merry. If you sit with a rosy-faced beloved, be merry."

The math teacher—Khayyam—drains the goblet, which contains Pepsi. But he fears extending his goblet toward the girl. Perhaps the beard will decide to fall again. The girl bends and pours Pepsi from the decanter into Khayyam's goblet. She twirls, a few more graceful steps, and she sings!

> O Khayyam, who said there will be a hell?
> Who went to hell and who returned from heaven?

The head of the Parent Teacher Association shakes his head and says, "Bless you, Firdowsi." He whispers in Mrs. Nourian's ear, "'This tomb is my resting place.' From Rostam Farrokhzad's letter to his brother."

Mrs. Nourian understands the retired director general saying *Firdowsi* instead of *Ferdowsi* and is of the opinion that Persian-speaking Turks like him are full of life. But she doesn't understand the relationship between the phrase *From Rostam Farrokhzad's letter to his brother* and this night of Khayyam.

The second play, that of Bozorgmehr and Anushirvan, with the same beard of Khayyam and with the same actor. This time the beard falls off several times. The math teacher bends and picks up the beard from the floor, and finally he dispenses with the beard altogether.

When the performance is finished and the lights come on, everyone applauds. The beardless Khayyam-Bozorgmehr and all the actors come onstage and take bows.

A woman comes toward Touran Jan, along with the angelic girl who had played the part of Khayyam's beloved. The woman has a dark complexion. She says, "Mrs. Nourian, my name is Simin . . . , and this niece of mine, Leila, is a student and admirer of yours."

Touran Jan shakes her hand and asks, "How were the plays?"

Simin laughs and says, "I laughed a lot. I enjoyed their simplicity and their innocence. But I think a mistake was made in the play of Anushirvan and Bozorgmehr."

"What mistake?"

"When Bozorgmehr discovered the secret of chess, he was not yet in prison and had not been blinded. In the performance, they brought Bozorgmehr in prison clothes and in a neck iron and chains to Anushirvan. A blind Bozorgmehr would not have been able to discover the secret of chess and then invent backgammon in response to the gift of the Indians. But it's not important. It's not important at all."

"No, it is important. What else?"

"The words that Bozorgmehr used about fate are true in India also. Our countries, both countries, were, and are, fated." Simin sighs and adds, "Our countries are the crossroads of history and the crossroads of events."

Simin extends her hand to take her leave, but Mrs. Nourian asks about other mistakes in the play. Simin smiles and says, "You know, Mrs. Nourian, Leila said to me, 'Auntie, tonight wear your wedding dress. I want my favorite teacher to like you.'"

"Still, please go on."

"Well," Simin says, "if the gift-bearing Indians spoke in pretend Hindi, that is, in a made-up language, it would be more comical . . . If Anushirvan's cardboard crown that had been hanging from the ceiling was balanced and Anushirvan was not obliged to raise himself in order to put his head in the crown, it would be better. But this itself made me laugh a lot. And when the precisely aimed crown fell from the ceiling onto Anushirvan's head and went down to his shoulders, I nearly died of laughter. The scuffle of the actors and Indian messengers to take the crown from Anushirvan's head, and that finally they brought scissors . . . My God, I was bent with laughter."

Touran Jan doesn't even smile. "What else?" she asks.

"Well, from a historical perspective, when the Roman messengers came, Bozorgmehr *was* in prison and *had been* blinded. They brought him out of prison, and when he answered the Romans' questions, Anushirvan again gave instructions to take him back to the dungeon. But in this play, Bozorgmehr seemed comfortable and sat down with his neck iron and chains and white robe, this time completely beardless. And when the shah ordered the singers to sing, minstrels to play, and dancers to dance, Bozorgmehr really enjoyed it. With eyes completely sighted—and, excuse my language—with ogling eyes, he looked all of them up and down."

"If the Romans also spoke with an invented language," Touran Jan says, "it would be better."

After Simin leaves, Touran Jan says to Mehrmah, "That shameless, pompous witch. She shook my self-confidence. To hell with her. I will continue my studies . . ."

"Cousin," Mehrmah says, "she didn't know that you are the one who staged these plays. Besides, you yourself asked."

"Shut up!" Touran Jan says, "Shut up! Shut your trap!"

Oh, that she hadn't said that. Oh, that her hand had been broken and she hadn't hit Mehrmah on her head so often . . . Oh that . . .

Touran has just come home from high school . . . The test questions had been difficult. Two or three of the students had turned in blank papers. Touran Jan is thinking.

The telephone rings. A male voice asks, "Are you Mrs. Touran Nourian?"

"Yes."

"A woman has been in an accident. We found your phone number in her calendar."

Touran Jan's teeth are chattering uncontrollably. "What does she look like?" she asks.

"She's short with a rather dark complexion, and she's wearing a wig."

Touran hits her head and says, "God, have mercy. My dear cousin. My sweet Mehrmah."

At Amir Alam Hospital, she's directed to her cousin's room. Blood has fallen on the floor from the hallway into the room. The mattress is bloody. The sheet that has been pulled over Mehrmah is bloody. A man and woman are standing next to the bed. "A jeep hit her on Takht-e Jamshid

Street," the woman says, "just above the embassy, and it left. It left in such a hurry that no one could get its plate number. A crowd gathered. One of the shopkeepers said, 'I saw that jeep come out of the embassy.'"

"A taxi driver stopped," the man says. "God bless him. I picked her up and laid her down on the back seat. She was alive. I asked her, 'Sister, whom shall I notify?' She pointed to her purse that was in this woman's hand. This woman and I got in the front seat. The taxi had an accident at the Dowlat intersection. She fell from the back seat to the floor of the car. She was no longer alive."

Touran Khanom looks at the man and the woman. The clothes of both are bloody. "Truly," she says, "you two are both Good Samaritans."

Hasti heard Grandmother's voice clearly this time. "*Horrible Tehran*! Day by day you become more horrible. Oh, Moshfeq Kazemi, where are you? My dear Mehrmah, where are you?"

Again, her voice became a murmur and was mixed with snoring. Hasti made the last leaf on the bergamot orange greener. Done. She gathered up her supplies.

She looked at Grandmother. Her eyes were shut. The buttons of her cardigan were open. The buttons of the blouse under her cardigan were also open. Her left breast had been taken out. She had put her hand under the head of an imaginary child, and she said loudly, "Suckle, my dear one. Suckle, light of my life."

Hasti was frightened. What if Touran Jan has lost her mind? But she remembered that Grandmother often talked loudly in her sleep, or she snored.

Mehrmah Khanom had measured the size of Hasti's ear with cotton. She had melted the wax and poured it in the hollow of the cotton. When the wax became hardened, she had made the cotton into a ball and said, "At bedtime, put this in your ears, and you won't hear a thing, even if a bomb goes off . . ."

"Hossein Jan," Grandmother said, "don't sit on the downspout. You'll fall. Hey, what are you doing on the rooftop? Why have you all gathered on the rooftop? Father, Cousin, Mehrmah, Hossein?

"I'm not coming. My prayer chador is lost. My black chador is torn. It wouldn't be right for me to come to the world of the dead in a torn chador.

"Mehrmah, let go of Eshrat's hand. It wasn't right for a twenty-year-old woman to rot in the home of her first husband until the end of her life.

"Eh, now you have taken Simin's hand. Where are you taking her? What wrong has she done?

"Me? I have erred.

"Well, on whom should I pour out my anger? On whomever is handy.

"Whether innocent or guilty.

"Hossein, my dear. See, didn't I say Hossein will fall? Catch him, catch him."

A firecracker exploded in the alley. Hasti asked herself, "Do the kids want to set off firecrackers from New Year's until Doomsday? Roman rockets? Make noise and bang on house doors for candy?"

She looked at Grandmother. Tears were falling from her cheeks to her lap, and her left breast was still in her hand. She sat next to her and wiped away her tears with her finger.

Grandmother opened her eyes. "Were you dreaming?" Hasti asked.

"All the dead had come to the rooftop. The dead numbered more than the living. They wanted to take me."

8

Bijan was driving, and Mother Eshi was saying that she had sent Mrs. Hakimi's Shirazi cookies to Mrs. Farrokhi this morning . . . a lot of them. She had told Navidi to entrust the cookies to Nanny and to say that Mrs. Ganjur has sent them. "Then press your foot on the gas and leave quickly. Otherwise, she'll tip you the money for the cookies as a New Year's gift."

The garden door was open, and Bijan drove up to the building. As they climbed the stairs, Mother Eshi said, "When you congratulate Mrs. Farrokhi on the New Year, kiss her hand." Hasti didn't say anything. She had wrapped Salim's gift in white paper and had put it in her purse.

Mrs. Farrokhi, a silk prayer chador on her head, sat in the living room on a sofa with threadbare brown velvet upholstery, beside her a younger, slightly thinner woman. There was no room for any other being. But in front of Mother Eshi both beings rose, without jack and crane. Then smacks and kisses. "Many happy returns. May God give you a long life, Eshrat. What wonderful cookies! Qodsi and I have picked at them."

"A bit more than picking, Mother!" Qodsi said.

Mrs. Farrokhi kissed Hasti's cheek, and Hasti kissed hers. "Nanny," Mrs. Farrokhi shouted, "come see your bride." Nanny came from behind a table on which there were two open bundles—in one bundle, a row of folded black chadors, and in the other, a row of prayer chadors. Nanny covered Hasti's face from forehead to chin with kisses.

Hasti surveyed the side tables full of plates of fruit, bowls of cookies, dishes of nuts, and even bowls of sugar, but she didn't see a single box of tissues. There was no other door anywhere around the room, and Polish chairs had been placed on four platforms. Mother Eshi sat next to Qodsi while Hasti traversed the length of the room and sat at the other end. She could hear her mother laughing and chatting with Qodsi, and she heard her mother ask, "Why haven't you come to the sauna?" Qodsi said she had gone to Isfahan to bring Niku, her husband's niece. Hasti saw her mother pout.

Nanny was not fat, but the woman who, like Hasti, had a scarf on her head and served tea, was fat. "Ladies," Qodsi said loudly, "please have some cookies. Help yourselves."

To flee from Qodsi's eyes, which were looking her up and down, Hasti gazed at the ceiling. A chandelier hung there, but the light was gloomy, reflecting the wornness of the house. The mosaic of tiny mirrors that covered the ceiling was coated in soot, pieces of the mirrors had fallen, and the flowers and bushes of the plaster molding had broken. All was the fault of the passage of time, but even more so the fault of the large iron heater that was burning in the corner of the room. The heater pipe passed through a hole in a window of the French doors and was emitting smoke into the garden. The moldings had rotted around the fanlight windows above the doors, windows that once had had their own special color. The living room was the twin of Professor Mani's living room, and the two houses had probably been built at the same time.

Women were arriving. Those who were wearing a black chador were taking their chadors off and handing them to Nanny. Nanny was putting a prayer chador on each head and then folding the black chadors and putting them in the black chador bundle.

When the fat woman offered Hasti another glass of tea, Hasti asked softly, "Where's the restroom?"

"Do you want the Western style or the regular one? The regular one is at the end of the garden."

Hasti wanted the Western style, and, leaving her tea untouched, she followed the fat woman. They passed the serving pantry next to the living room, where a samovar was boiling; they passed a hallway in which the side carpet had lost color years ago, not from shyness in front of Hasti's beauty.

The fat woman opened a door and switched on the light. The bathtub and the sink sparkled in whiteness, white tiles all over, everywhere. Light seeped from the cracks around a closed door to the room adjacent to the bathroom. A voice said, "Who's there?"

"Aqa Salim," the fat woman said, "it's me, Taji. I've brought one of the guests."

Salim's voice: "Is the garden door open?"

"Yes."

Hasti washed her face. She took the gift from her purse and shut off the bathroom light. She closed the bathroom door and knocked on the closed door next to the bathroom. Salim's voice: "Farhad, come in."

Salim was lying on the floor. Seeing Hasti, he quickly sat up. He put his hand on his back and said, "Ow!" Hasti left her purse and gift on a wooden bench next to Salim's bed. There was only one pillow on the bed.

"Hello," Hasti said. "Happy New Year. Let me help you lie down."

"Impossible. You're an unrelated woman."

"If a temporary marriage can happen, we can become brother and sister temporarily, too."

"Put that pillow behind me," Salim said, "and give me a hand." Hasti did exactly what Salim had requested.

"Look in the medicine cabinet," Salim said. "There's a bottle labeled IBUPROFEN . . ." Hasti found the medicine.

"It can't be taken on an empty stomach," Salim said. "Can you go get me an apple or a cookie?" As Hasti started out, Salim added, "Happy New Year. So, you have kept your promise. The first person to whom you have extended your hand is me."

"My friend is not coming so soon after all."

The living room was full, and the cashmere box had been closed over the black chadors. The box of prayer chadors was empty. Hasti took a plate full of the remaining fruit and also a knife and fork from the side tables. Mrs. Farrokhi should tell Nanny or Taji to clear the plates covered in fruit peelings and the shells of seeds, pistachios, and hazelnuts, but Mrs. Farrokhi was busy smoking a water pipe. Hasti asked Taji for a small tray and two glasses of tea from the serving pantry.

In Salim's room she put the tray on the wooden bench. She peeled an apple and, using a fork, put a piece in Salim's mouth. Salim's eyes had become sunken and his color pale. *Was this backache business going to continue for life?*

There were two taps on the door, and Salim said, "Hadi, come in."

A tall man entered wearing a new, dark gray winter jacket. It was Farhad Dorafshan, the brother of Farkhondeh Dorafshan, but while Farkhondeh was tall and thin, her brother was broad shouldered. Farkhondeh's eyes were not red. Her brother's eyes were. Farkhondeh did not have a week's growth of beard. Her brother did.

Hadi—that is, Farhad—put Hasti's purse to one side and then sat on Hasti's gift, which was smashed to pieces. Hasti began to cry. In her heart she said, *The big oaf*!

"Sister," Salim asked, "why are you crying?"

"This guy has destroyed my fiberboard."

"I'll buy you as much fiberboard as you want."

"I had drawn a picture on it for you."

"Well," the big oaf said, "you can draw another one."

Crying, Hasti said good-bye and asked, "Where's the restroom?"

The big oaf got up. He opened the door at the head of Salim's bed and turned on the bathroom light.

Hasti washed her face and hands. She waited. Sneakily, she flushed the toilet unnecessarily. She turned off the bathroom light. She opened and closed the door between the bathroom and the hallway. She felt her way back and sat on the toilet lid.

Farhad's voice: "She's from which of your father's wives? The one in Monirieh Square? The one in Jaleh Square? The one at Absardar Crossroads? Are you sleepy?"

Salim's voice: "I took a pill. I'm dizzy."

Farhad's voice: "This sis of yours, why does she cry at the drop of a hat?"

Salim's voice: "She's sensitive. I wish I could see what she drew for me."

Farhad's voice: "Is this fruit for eating?"

Salim's voice: "Of course."

Silence.

Farhad's voice: "How's the business of finding a wife going?"

Salim's voice: "It's going nowhere. From the time it was rumored that a man was in search of a wife, the mothers of spinsters and marriageable girls have come swarming, bearing photos and elaborate descriptions. My sister went to Isfahan and brought Niku, the niece of her husband. For years she never set foot here, but now they have settled in."

Farhad's voice: "Is the girl pretty?"

Salim's voice: "Which girl?"

Farhad's voice: "Niku."

Salim's voice: "She's very beautiful. She'll finish high school this year. She wears a prayer chador, and she comes and sits next to my mattress. She peels tangerines for me, and she secretly looks at me."

The sound of laughter. Farhad's voice: "So you have gone beyond the one glance permitted by religious law?"

Salim's voice: "But unfortunately, I have fallen in love."

"Why 'unfortunately'?"

"The girl I have fallen in love with has a thousand and one flaws, both religiously and socially. With respect to opinions also, she is the exact opposite of me. She isn't pretty, either. And she's old. Meanwhile, she is also in love with another man."

"And she's probably both pregnant and a virgin, too. What a mess! You and I have been classmates and friends for twelve years. You were always known for your intellect and wisdom. Do you really want to involve yourself in such a mess?"

Salim's voice: "It's out of my control."

"You are not a person to allow things to be out of your control. Stamp out such an inappropriate love."

"And we shall see what Fortunata has in store for me . . ."

"Who on earth is Fortunata?"

"The god of destiny."

Hasti had become tired. She scolded herself. Why had she asked Salim where the restroom was when she had been there half an hour before? Grandmother eavesdropped. Mother Eshi eavesdropped. And now Hasti . . . Why, in the big oaf's terms, didn't she stamp out such an ugly habit? She had been sitting on the toilet lid for a while. *Since the beginning of patriarchy*, she thought, *most women have eavesdropped, lied, endured, and compromised because they have not had a way into the serious world of men. Why had their blood never come to a boil*? And why doesn't she stand up, open the bathroom door, and spit in the big oaf's face? Is this the modern woman that she wants to be? Has she rushed things too much? Has the temptation of Salim's wealth pushed her to this? If there were a Gillette razor, she could commit hari-kari. But she could only see an electric razor on a shelf above the sink. Salim had a beard, after all, a reddish-brown beard.

Don't men tell lies? she thought. *Hadn't Salim presented me as his religious and nominal "sis?" Women have lied and do lie from fear of men. Men lie from fear of whom? Oh, my God, the world, especially this part of the world, has been rotten. A healthy, normal person has been one who has a strong mask . . . In any case, men have been the first sex, and they have had the right to come to a boil, and when someone comes to a boil, they boil over. And women have been the second sex. They should only be stressed.*

She should go and forget the cunning Salim. *A man who is in love doesn't see so many faults in his beloved . . .* She had crossed half the length of the bathroom . . . but the name "Hitti" from the mouth of the big oaf stopped her in her tracks.

"Firuz and I set a time bomb in Hitti's car. His daughter came and sat in the back seat. She was wearing a dress of Isfahani block-print cotton. She had hung camel bells from her belt . . . Her hair was just like a golden braid . . . So delicate. I felt pity. I opened the door of the car. 'Run,' I yelled. 'Run!' And since the girl didn't move, I grabbed her hand and pulled her out of the car. The driver closed the hood of the car. I said to the driver, 'Get away. There's a bomb in the car.' Hitti came. The driver warned him . . . I ran away . . . What an explosion!"

Salim's voice: "Is this Hitti a military advisor?"

"No. He's an educational advisor." Pause.

Farhad's voice: "May I stay here several nights?"

"Of course."

Farhad's voice: "We have been exposed. We had left Farkhondeh in Mashhad, and Firuz and I came back. I phoned you . . ."

Groping, Hasti took herself back to the covered toilet seat and sat down. Hearing that Farkhondeh, her classmate, "the wishing tree girl," had ended up in politics, Hasti could no longer move from there.

Farhad's voice: "One day I had gone to Mount Sangi with the guys from the center. Dr. Shariati kept falling behind. I turned and said, 'Doctor, why aren't you coming?' A stranger came to my side. 'Aren't you Farhad Dorafshan?' he asked. I said, 'No.' 'Have you heard of Mr. Hitti?' he asked. I said, 'No. Why?' Dr. Shariati had reached us. 'Hadi,' he asked, 'what is the matter?' I said, 'Nothing.'

"Another time we saw that stranger in the courtyard of Imam Reza Shrine. We were praying behind the prayer leader, Sheikh Sa'id. Baktash was very drunk. He didn't have a prayer stone. He took the prayer stone from in front of me, broke it in half, and put half in front of himself and half in front of me. Dr. Shariati came toward Baktash and said, 'Leave the line of men praying before the crowd attacks you.'

"Again I saw the same stranger. I believe he also knows about the Bagheshah incident. Do you remember? Behind Bagheshah Park, Firuz and I half strangled a secret policeman who had followed us. The fellow died in the military hospital."

Silence.

Farhad's voice: "I'm very tired, Salim. Come, let's do something. Give your sis to me, and get off your high horse and take Farkhondeh. Both of us will take wives. We'll have children . . . We'll plant flowers . . . We'll read books. We'll go work on a farm in the Afjeh suburbs."

Salim's voice: "What do you like about my sister?"

"The way her eyes look . . . When she cried, I wanted to get up and kiss her tears, lick them away."

Salim's voice: "My sister needs glasses. She concentrates all her power in her eyes in order to see well. Then her eyes become like those of someone who has received a vision."

Hasti's inner voice: *O wicked Salim. Even I myself didn't know that my eyes always looked like that.*

Farhad's voice: "Ring the bell so that your sister will come. I'll speak with her a bit, and I'll be cheered up."

"My sister has left home already. She has a husband and two children."

Farhad's voice: "At least you take Farkhondeh."

"Do you remember that the first girl I met was Farkhondeh?"

Farhad's voice: "Who didn't please you. I wish someone would be found to take Farkhondeh."

Salim's voice: "And free the family of her."

Farhad's voice: "No. She has done that on her own."

Pause.

"You have a picture of Che Guevara, don't you? A large picture in which he has a cigar between his lips?"

Salim's voice: "A Havana cigar. What do you want it for?"

"I want to look at it."

Hasti didn't know what they were doing that they didn't speak. She could hear them walking and picking things up and putting them down. Were they searching for the picture of Che Guevara? She heard the ruffling of papers. What if the big oaf comes to the restroom? What would he do if he came face-to-face with Hasti? He would strangle her, wouldn't he? As Grandmother would say, it was as though a kitten were clawing at Hasti's heart. It was as though they had put a broom in ice water and were drawing it down her spine.

Farhad's voice: "For now, ten pictures. Aqa Sheikh Sa'id said, 'First let's begin with the slums.' You know, Salim, armed struggle must be learned. It doesn't just happen by itself. In time, I will join the Palestinians."

Salim's voice: "Take a Palestinian wife, too."

Farhad related everything . . . They have never gotten together all in the same place . . . That in hiding and in their Mashhadi friends' houses, they would gather in tens or twenties . . . That one night in Cheragh Maznian's house, forty or fifty people had come.

Yes, they had also talked about an alliance. Aqa Sheikh Sa'id had said, "Anger is human nature. It exists in animals, too. Just as roses have thorns." Baktash had said, "Humans get angry quickly, and they don't always act wisely. When an animal is full, it doesn't hunt any more. But humans do . . ."

Hasti wanted to get out of the trap that she had built for herself. She had become tired and was no longer listening well. She was worried that Bijan might have come after them and now her mother and Mrs. Farrokhi and Nanny and Taji were calling her. She guessed that Baktash was none other than Morad. But wasn't Marzieh the alias of Farkhondeh? No, Farkhondeh didn't have that much sense to have formed an opinion about a front's struggle against colonialism. But perhaps she had recently found such sense. It had been some time since Hasti had seen Farkhondeh.

Farhad's voice: "Ring the bell. Ask them to bring a glass of tea for me."

There was the sound of the bell. *If the big oaf drinks tea, then he'll certainly come to the restroom.* Hasti touched the wall and took herself to the main door of the restroom that opened into the hallway. She took the door handle in her hand and waited for Taji.

Salim's voice: "So, you were saying?"

"What was I saying?"

"You were speaking about the group."

Farhad said that Baktash didn't yield to anyone easily. He had said to Aqa Sheikh Sa'id that we will help you until you come to power, and then you will put us aside . . . He was of the opinion that Baktash gave priority to political action over armed action, but his friend, Morteza, had said that guerrilla forces are the seed of the party . . . "Guerrilla forces," he had said, "can bring into motion the revolutionary force of the masses . . ." He had also said, "The nation should be delivered from putrid intellectualism . . . The myth of stability and the island of stability should be broken." Aqa Sheikh Sa'id had said, "Oh, bless the one who says that."

Hasti decided to open the bathroom door and turn on the bathroom light and the faucet . . . to pretend that another guest has come to the restroom . . . But Salim would surely ask, "Who is it?" Didn't he ask that the first time she had thrown herself into this dungeon?

There was a knock on the door. Taji's voice: "Aqa Salim, what would you like?"

Farhad ordered tea, bread, and cheese. It would be good if Salim asked Taji to come in and take away the plate of fruit peelings and the tea glasses. But Salim didn't request it, and Hasti cursed to herself.

Salim's voice: "I don't believe in armed struggle, either. Armed struggle destroys the possibility of democracy, as long as it is secret . . . And armed struggle is necessarily secret."

Farhad's voice: "Look, Salim Jan. Party politics is no longer of any use. How long should we preach that the workers and the peasants are downtrodden? Don't they know that themselves? How long should we say, 'We will improve your situation'? They don't trust us. They only trust preachers. Once Aqa Sheikh Sa'id went to the pulpit. You don't know what tears he wrung from the people. He even made Baktash and me cry."

"What did he say?"

"He talked of war on the path of God—that is, jihad and martyrdom. And he finished in this way—that we are heirs of the doctrine of blood and martyrdom, and the martyr is someone who is killed in jihad . . . who has been witness to the right, who has been killed on the righteous path . . . *Martyr* means 'the ruler of the world' . . . At the end he strayed from the topic and talked about Jabir ibn Abdullah Ansari, who put on pilgrims' clothes and went to Karbala. Addressing the martyr of the martyrs, Imam Hossein, he yelled, 'You are the heir of humanity! You are the heir of the prophets! You were not an atheist and nonbeliever!'"

Salim's voice: "He didn't say anything about revolutionary messianism?"

"No."

"I had told him to rely on revolutionary messianism."

"He didn't. But Dr. Shariati talked about revolutionary messianism one night in Ne'mat's house. He also spoke about major and minor religious jurisprudence. He said major religious jurisprudence is the basis of Islamic philosophy that begins with Abu Hanifa, and minor religious jurisprudence is the code of religious laws . . .

"Does this tea of your household come all the way from China?"

Salim's voice: "Probably there was no bread, or there was no cheese. There's always something missing in this house. If the girl that I told you I love marries me, she will make this a proper home."

The big oaf's voice: "A girl who is in love with another man is of no value. Dig into your pocket and hire a worthy servant or steward."

Salim's voice: "I can shape her, like wax . . ."

Farhad's voice: "And what if she shapes you?"

Salim's voice: "If she's right, let her shape me."

Farhad's voice: "Look, Salim. Since you returned from England, you've been constantly delivering religious principles to us. Can you put that aside now?"

Salim's voice: "No. I'll convince her that there is no path but the path of religion, because revolutionary intellectuals who are the sources of political information and the nerves of society do not have a direct relationship with the masses."

Hasti's inner voice: *What revolutionary intellectuals? What masses? You are a handful of quasi-intellectuals who are at each other's throats . . . And then there are the masses who don't know A from Z. And you, Salim, whom I thought would take me to a faraway land, to a safe shore, are no more than a paper tiger, a Don Quixote. You've lain back while you're stirring up most of the troubles. You're using the excuse of finding a wife, but you don't follow through. You talk about love and you want to make me soft in your hand like wax. You're dreaming. Then again there's Morad, half-witted and foolish, as my mother says—Morad without fraud and deceit—the Morad who is honest. Thank God the big oaf smashed the fiberboard on which I had drawn your eyes.*

But Salim's continuing talk did not allow her to do something she would later regret. "If the motive is the toppling of a puppet government whose backbone is American military and educational advisors, it should be carried out on the basis of firm and strong theories. A sound intellectual system should be established through a comprehensive analysis of society, economics, religion, and politics."

The instant Taji opened the door of Salim's bedroom, Hasti opened the bathroom door and fled. She went to her mother and crouched beside her. "You're so pale," her mother said. "Are you upset?"

"No."

"He didn't welcome you nicely?"

"He had a guest."

After they dropped off Mother Eshi, Hasti asked Bijan if he was free. When she heard a "yes," she asked if they could go together to Sa'i Park to take a walk or to Darband to have tea. The white Peugeot took off like a greyhound. Just before they reached Pahlavi Crossroads, Bijan asked, "Which way shall I go?"

"Straight ahead."

The gate to Sa'i Park was locked. Pahlavi Avenue was empty, and Bijan sped up. The next park was just as quiet. They passed Kourosh Department Store, and Bijan asked its name. Hasti answered, "It's the 'Whoever Knows English Can Enter' store." Bijan laughed.

"Is it always so empty?"

"No. Tehran and Shemiran traffic has no match. With respect to air pollution, Tehran is among the top cities of the world, but nearly a million people have gone on vacation, either to the north or the south."

"No one goes to the east or the west?'

"Of course. Mashhad is the number one tourist city of Iran, and Isfahan is the next."

"Miss Teacher, may I?" Bijan said.

"You asked, and I answered. Now I'll ask. Tell me more about America."

"As I told you, at first I felt rootless and deprived of identity. Later I busied myself so much with Persian books and Persian customs in order to escape exile."

"Escape exile. What an interesting phrase."

"Of course! I'm good with words!"

"What books did you read?"

"All kinds of books. Either books my father sent me or ones I got from a book exchange."

"A book exchange?"

"An Iranian professor who had built the high-voltage electricity system for Chicago had started an exchange of Persian books among students."

"We are an unfortunate, yet intelligent people," Hasti said. "We are strangers in our own land, but we go to America and build high-voltage electricity systems."

Silence. Whether the traffic light was green or not, Bijan went through, since they had not seen any police.

Bijan resumed speaking. "Hasti, I'm disappointed by the kind of literature that has recently become the fashion in Iran. The poetry is so vague that one must get assistance from astrology, and prose . . . it's all pus, blood, and slime. How well they write about the poor and the destitute."

"First," Hasti said, "the reason literature is allegorical and metaphorical is the censor, and the reason that they write about the destitute is that no one is thinking about them. Unfortunately, they lack literacy, money, and sociopolitical information."

A dog appeared in front of the car, it was not clear from where, and Bijan stomped on the brake and honked. But the dog looked at Bijan and didn't budge. Bijan was forced to pass to the left of the dog, swerving from his lane.

Bijan put a cigarette between his lips, pushed in the car's cigarette lighter, and said, "It's strange."

"What's strange?"

"You, like everyone else I have seen up to now, have become political. Everything that I have heard in these ten days is a mockery of something real. My father is saying that as soon as possible I should go and register in the shah's political party. I say, 'Father, it's a fake party. The Parliament is a sham . . . '"

"Your father has golden dreams for you. When you've stayed here for a little while, those dreams will come true."

Bijan said that his father is nostalgic for the days of the nobility. Each morning he comes to Bijan's bedroom; Bijan sees him from the corner of his eye. For a while he looks at his son, his eldest heir, the apple of his eye. He puts five hundred tomans on the table beside the bed. He wants to get Hayedeh, the daughter of the aristocrat Mo'adel al-Saltaneh, for him. When he evokes the wedding for listeners, they become enchanted by his imagination and desires.

"The bride and groom arrive by carriage at the Hilton Hotel, four lantern-holding attendants with red tulips on the two sides of the carriage . . . , wearing red clothes, the edges of their sleeves embroidered in gold . . . All the bigwigs of Tehran are present and watching, awed. They have set up a tent in the hotel ballroom . . . The bride and the groom go into the tent. The groom acts like a king. He also recites the proverb, 'The night of marriage consummation is no less than the morning of kingship.' But for the moment, the consummation is left for an appropriate time. Several cages with white doves here and there around the tent . . . One of the former tulip-holding attendants—who no longer holds tulips in his hand—opens the window. Now it's the bride's turn to come out of the tent and to free the doves one by one . . ."

Bijan laughed and said, "And probably the doves, in their fear, cover the bride's dress with their droppings." He asked, "Is everyone going crazy?"

"If *nobility*," Hasti said, "comes from the root *noble*, it is a good thing. But here nobility also means something else. Nobility in Tehran means squandering resources and showing off through excessive consumption."

Laughing, Bijan said, "Miss Teacher, what's wrong with a person having a soft, silk, dressing gown on his body, slippers on his feet? Let him sit next to a wall heater, a fine goblet in his hand. Let him listen to soft music, too, and think, *What is to be done*?"

"You see, the virus of politics has spread to you, too!"

"I said all this for your sake, to make you laugh, but you haven't. Believe me, I have heard so much talk about puppet regime, dependent government, and comprador bourgeoisie that I'm about to throw up. Everyone is political, with the minimum amount of political knowledge and the maximum amount of political pronouncement."

Bijan stopped the car at Darband Square. They got out. He locked the car doors. He tested them. Then he took Hasti's arm, and they set off.

They climbed the stairs and sat down at a table at New Park Café. Hasti asked for a cup of tea. Bijan lit a cigarette and ordered hot chocolate. He smoked the cigarette halfway down and put it out.

In spite of the cleanliness and warmth of the café, no one was there except for a few policemen sitting at the tables.

"You don't smoke cigarettes," Hasti said. "You waste them."

Bijan extended his hand palm up in front of Hasti, closed his eyes, and said, "Hasti, I'm a beggar asking for your love. Give me a kiss, for God's sake."

Hasti was startled. She sat up straight and said, "Enough of this joking!"

"Believe me, I want to take you out of this sorrowful state that you've brought upon yourself. Tell me. Maybe I can help. Did your suitor displease you?"

"I don't know. I didn't see much of him. He had a guest."

"Did his guest offend you?"

"I don't want to talk about it."

A bunch of young boys and girls swarmed into the café. The sound of their laughter filled the room. Their rosy cheeks, their shining eyes.

Hasti looked at them with regret. In her heart she recited, *"O youth, I have memories of childhood." And what kind of childhood? We always lived with the killing of our father, and our grandmother pulled us in one direction while our mother pulled us in the other.*

"I like the Pishdadian dynasty," Bijan said. But Hasti didn't laugh. She was destined to like the Ashkanian dynasty, whose name can literally mean "the tearful ones." After all, when Hasti had learned to speak, the first word that had come out of her mouth was *ouch*.

Bijan tried harder. "Let me tell you about one of my experiences in America. I was arriving at class two minutes late in the mornings. Alice, my English teacher, said, 'Bijan, it would be good if you moved from laziness and disorganization to vitality and discipline.' I said, 'Sure.' The next day I arrived one minute late. She asked, 'Didn't you move?' I said, 'Ma'am, some of my belongings were left behind. This morning I went and got them.'"

And since Hasti didn't even smile, Bijan said, "All the students laughed." And he added, "Hasti, I want to know why God has given you these shoulders."

"So that I can put the weight of my life on my back."

"No, girl. So that you can shrug them. Don't take it so seriously. Can I tell you something to do?"

"Go ahead."

"When you're all alone, laugh loudly. Little by little you will learn to laugh."

"Then they will say I've gone crazy."

"Who will say that? You're laughing in solitude."

"It's not possible to laugh in solitude."

"Something else . . . When, like today, you are sad, hum a happy tune in your heart."

Hasti recalled that when she had received her first paycheck, she had wanted to buy a radio, but instead she had bought an Aladdin heater. She remembered that one time she had felt indulgent and had wanted to buy a pot of flowers. Upside-down tulips had caught her attention—two upside-down tulips, on a long stem—as if two drops of blood had poured from the leaves.

They took Parkway Highway on their way back. Green pines, about-to-blossom crape myrtle, a smooth road, the scent of spring. "Tehran has become so large," Bijan observed. "Beautiful buildings have been constructed everywhere, but the city has become an exhibition of European and American architecture."

"I have a classmate," Hasti said, "who is an architectural engineer."

"What has he built?"

"He, too, has ended up in politics."

"What a tragedy."

"The description that he gives of Tehran is interesting, though. Shall I tell you what he says?" Hasti asked.

"Certainly."

"He says that Tehran is a dusty, brown city. It's similar to a library full of scattered books, unorganized. It has neither a title catalogue nor a subject catalogue. In this vast library, there are lots of books with pornographic pictures like *Alfieh and Shalfieh*, books on the subject of parents cursing their children, and folk stories, like *Amir Arsalan*. But there are also books on philosophy and mysticism, collections of poetry by Hafez and Rumi, and the Holy Quran. He says the city has no centrality. Nothing is in its place. Houses and cisterns have been destroyed, and shopping centers and warehouses have replaced them . . . City of high walls . . . In all, Tehran is just like the people who live there."

"Behind the high walls there is beauty," Bijan said. "But the façade of the city . . . If they decorated the domes and minarets of the mosques with bright and colorful tile work or the transoms on the houses . . ."

Hasti interrupted. "Tehran is an old, ugly, pockmarked woman, and no amount of rouge and powder can make her pits and bumps pretty."

"She's not very old. Besides, the city has become greener."

They passed a tanker truck that had released a water hose at the foot of pines and crape myrtles. The lights on the two sides of the highway had generously lit even the hills on their left. The pine saplings on the hill gave the glad tidings of a green future. The glad tidings of the small forest of spruce. *Wasn't Tehran the city of pines and spruce? Wasn't Tehran a dignified, middle-aged woman?*

"I think," Bijan said, "that this is Erect Hill. Isn't that right?"

"This is the first time I've heard that name."

Following Hasti's directions, Bijan turned into a secondary street parallel to the hill. He went up, he went down. He went back and forth. To the right, to the left. Straight road, curved road. Curve after curve. Sloping down, sloping up. At last he stopped, put his hand on the steering wheel, and said, "Now we're completely lost."

A passerby guided them to a back road. After taking it, they came out in front of the youth center on Old Shemiran Road.

They were next to the Hosseinieh Ershad Building. Bijan lit a cigarette and asked about the domed structure, its architecture and its mission. Hasti spoke about the speeches of Dr. Shariati and the large crowds that gathered round as he discussed faith, martyrdom, and revolutionary messianism.

Bijan said that he had recently read a book titled *Revolutionary Messianism*, the author of which was a resident of Kenya . . . He couldn't remember the author's name. And he smoked his cigarette to the end.

9

When Morad came, he brought Grandmother a prayer rug, a prayer stone, prayer beads, saffron, and rock candy. He hugged Grandmother and kissed her white hair. Then he hung a large turquoise pendant with a gilded chain on Hasti's neck and spun her in the air. In front of Touran Khanom, he took off his wool shirt and put on the blue-green sweater knitted for him by Hasti. He kissed Hasti's hands, too.

Hasti noticed that Morad's eyes were no longer wandering. His eyes were sometimes fixed upon a distant point, but he wasn't saying even one word about the hungry in Biafra and India, nor about excessive consumption, guns, Phantom jets, oil, the Gulf, suffocation, or torture.

Then Morad took Hasti out by bus. They got off at Pahlavi Crossroads and stood in front of the cloth an Indian peddler had spread on the sidewalk. The old woman was wearing a sari and bracelets. She was yelling, "Snake oil, coconut oil, pills for secret sicknesses, weight loss pills."

"'Secret sicknesses' means love sickness?" Hasti asked.

"No, venereal diseases," Morad said.

Slowly they made their way to Sa'i Park. It was still closed. They returned to the crossroads. They ate barbecued liver at a small store. They sat in a café, and Morad didn't even smoke.

Next Morad took Hasti to the movies. He bought the tickets from hawkers outside the cinema. It was a Jerry Lewis film. Jerry Lewis spoke Persian as though he were from the heart of lower-class Tehran. Then they went to a John Wayne film at a theater more or less opposite the first one. John Wayne's Persian outdid that of all the toughs and louts of Tehran . . . And when John Wayne sang from a Persian pop song, "Tonight is a moonlit night, and I long for my sweetheart . . ." Hasti and Morad couldn't stop laughing. And Hasti didn't think of Salim or Bijan for even one moment.

On the way back to Hasti's house, they found neither a bus nor a taxi, so they walked. Hasti was able to bring up the subject of marriage. "What were you doing in Mashhad?" she asked.

"Pondering the meaning of the universe and existence during the day," Morad said, "and mulling over the memories I have of you during the night."

"What memories?" Hasti asked.

"Memories of the first day we met, memories of our trip to Sare'in, memories of those infamous meetings of the art and culture something or other."

"Let's get married," Hasti said, "so that we have all of each other."

Morad became pensive. Near the house, he said, "Are you crazy? Imagine that we have married. We are already closer to one another than any married couple, aren't we?"

Hasti didn't urge anymore. She just said, "Come to the office one day so that we can have lunch together." She was about to say, "Give me an answer that day," but she didn't. Instead, she couldn't fall asleep that night until dawn. *Why,* she thought, *had Morad changed? Had he been disappointed by politics in Mashhad? Had he gotten married to politics, as Professor Mani's wife said, and didn't need any other marriage*?

Hasti's mind was not an organized bookcase such that she could extend her arm and take out from its shelves any memory she wanted. Maybe her mind was like a computer, although she didn't belong to the computer age herself. Only the lessons of Professor Mani and Simin had organized files in her mind because she took notes. She also took exams in their classes, and she always wanted to get an A from them. Actually, her acquaintance with Simin started this way, when, in the second semester, Simin had asked, "Who is Hasti Nourian?" With a racing heart, she had stood up. Simin had said, "You have written very well, young lady. You will become someone in this world." Simin was and is talkative. "As long as I am alive," she had added, "I will follow up on you to see how far you will go. But don't exhaust and waste yourself."

Am I exhausting and wasting myself? Hasti asked herself. *Is the path I am traveling now going nowhere? Are the tunes that Salim and Morad are playing distorted? Are they twisted? What if I leave them both and learn from Bijan how to shrug my shoulders and practice laughing at loneliness in my solitude?* But no, Morad was closer to her than all the Salims and the Bijans of this world. She took Morad's cold hands in hers and rubbed them so much that they became warm.

That day it was snowing. The male students of the Faculty of Law attacked the female students of the Faculty of Fine Arts with snowballs. One of them hugged Hasti, put a snowball down the front of her shirt, and wanted to kiss her. Hasti struggled, slipped, and fell. Snowballs were raining down from every direction. A boy took her hand and helped her up. The boy wiped the snow from Hasti's winter coat. Hasti's leg hurt. "I hope my leg's not broken," she said.

"Don't be so delicate," the boy said. Hasti leaned on him, and he took her to the Department of Architecture studio. He seated her on a stool and made coffee for her. He played Chopin's *Nocturne* on the phonograph. He said himself that it was Chopin's *Nocturne*. The boy sat on the floor, took off Hasti's shoe, and rubbed her ankle. "Don't be afraid," he said. "Your leg's not broken."

"Are you a bonesetter?" Hasti asked.

The boy laughed and said, "No, I'm Morad Pakdel."

"And I'm Hasti Nourian."

"We'll take vengeance," the boy said. "We'll gather the male students of the faculty and attack the female students of the Faculty of Law."

Maybe it was that very day that they fell in love. Or maybe it wasn't. Whenever it was, now this love couldn't be erased from their hearts. It couldn't. It couldn't.

What had Sohravardi said? He had said, "The commander of love sets up a tent in the heart." Hasti had read Sohravardi's *On the Reality of Love* several times, thanks to her secretary, Fakhri, who had photocopied it for her. Maybe Sohravardi didn't intend his text to say what Hasti had understood it to say. Hasti's interpretation was that love is the greatest mystery of creation—for love is liberating—for love gives one focus. It is not accompanied by sorrow, although attachment might have its own risks.

That day Morad had not shown up for the meeting of the Council on Artistic Creation. Hasti and Professor Mani had teamed up and convinced the council to approve Morad's membership. Professor Isa and Dr. Zandi were against it. Professor Mani described the former as someone without character, and he thought the latter was probably a member of SAVAK. And Hasti was certain about it. Always and everywhere, a Dr. Zandi, either with glasses or without, was present. The Dr. Zandi of the Council on Artistic Creation had glasses. Hasti had even seen his ID card. One day, when he was taking his handkerchief out of his pocket, the card came out too and fell on the floor. Hasti bent down and picked up the card from under the table. OFFICE OF THE PRIME MINISTER. And she saw Zandi's alias, NEJABAT. She put the card in front of Nejabat. Nejabat stared at Hasti from above his glasses. "Look, if you say anything to anyone, you're done for."

Hasti was worried about Morad. *Stupid Morad, why don't you come? What if they have arrested Morad?* Hasti thought. Because on a previous day, when they were discussing choosing the best carpet design, gilding, engraving . . . for the competition, Morad had said so many things that he shouldn't have. "Which one of them," he had said, "is about to marry now and is thinking about her trousseau?" And, "Has Ardeshir Khan once again come to take the best ones to America and present them as gifts to American senators and to Elizabeth Taylor? Perhaps caviar is not enough, since they eat it and forget about it."

Professor Isa had said, "No sir, we will display them in Kamal al-Molk Museum," and Dr. Zandi had taken notes.

Professor Mani had said, "O young man, you are naïve."

A thousand thoughts rushed into Hasti's mind. Finally, she calmed herself down, thinking, *Well, perhaps he's in his father's rooftop room drawing a front-view picture of me. He had drawn a side-view picture of me that I lost. Well, maybe he's drawing a picture of the homeless people that he so loves.* Destitute people never set foot in a painting exhibition, and the nouveau riche who do set foot there have no place in their homes to hang such paintings. They don't match their furniture and curtains.

Hasti and La'l Banu were close. One day Hasti had taken La'l Banu and Sir Edward to see the second exhibition of Morad's paintings. Sir Edward and La'l Banu stood looking at a painting that depicted a ragged old man. The old man was sitting before a fire on the sidewalk in front of a multistory building. The lights of the building were on. Chandeliers and tall standing lamps with china shades, some flowered, some not, were shining through several windows in the painting.

"La'l Banu," Hasti asked, "would you like to buy it?" La'l Banu looked at her husband.

"Absolutely not!" Sir Edward said. "Flaubert depicts an aristocratic ball and the frozen children of the poor who have stuck their noses on the window of the palace ballroom. Since time immemorial, this subject of poverty and affluence has been put forth."

"And it still is," Hasti said. In her heart, she was pleading, *Come on, stingy people, buy a painting. If you don't want it, throw it in the garbage bin. Hang it in the bathroom.* But Sir Edward had already bought from Professor Mani the painting of a Qajar woman for his wife.

Hasti couldn't take it any longer. After the Morad-less council meeting, she had asked Fakhri, her secretary, to call the carpet company and ask for Mr. Pakdel. Fakhri called many times, until finally she was able to ask Morad's father whether his son, Mr. Morad Pakdel, had been ill that he hadn't come to the council meeting. Morad's father had said, "Other than his brain that's defective, he has not been ill."

Morad came to the next meeting earlier than the others, and he was in a good mood. "My dear lady," he said to Hasti, "now you are spying on me and calling my father?" But in the council meeting, he exploded. They were choosing the best carpet design. Morad said, "For the price of one of these carpets, one can demolish a slum and build in its place inexpensive housing."

"All cities have squatters," Professor Isa said. "These are people who have invaded the cities from the villages."

Morad pounded on the table and said, "They have invaded the cities because there is no work for them in villages. Dear America delivers us wheat." He swallowed and added, "And what do they do in cities? They sell lottery tickets. They clean pools. They run errands. They guard parked cars. They carry loads."

Professor Isa turned to Morad and said, "The purpose of this council meeting is to choose the best carpet design, not to talk nonsense, nor to spout political slogans."

"Why are you so afraid of politics?" Morad asked.

"I'm not afraid of politics, but your political talk is insipid. The brains of people like you are feeble."

What if Professor Isa is right? Hasti thought. *And Morad's father is also right*? She looked at Professor Mani, who had put his hand on his heart. Hasti rang the bell and ordered the servant to bring herbal tea . . . She corrected herself, "Herbal tea for Professor Mani, and regular tea for everyone else." She noticed that the servant looked into Morad's eyes and gestured with his eyebrows.

Professor Mani put on his glasses and picked up the designs from the table one by one. He held them far away, brought them up close, and gave them to the person next to him. And with what respect and reverence he held them, as if each design were a page of the Holy Book.

Bahadori's design came in first. A bird with colorful feathers had nested in the bitter orange tree in the center of the carpet. The bird was neither a hoopoe, nor a peacock, nor a phoenix, nor a griffin, nor a bird of faith. For sure, it was not a heron. It was a bird from the heavens that had descended upon the mind of the artist like a revelation, and it had said, "Record me." The bird was ready to fly, but Hasti well knew that the warp and weft of the carpet will trap it, and the arabesques, the lotuses, the flowers, and the leaves of the design will not allow it to escape. Its wings were repeated in the triangles of the four corners of the carpet, its beak and feet lost amidst the flowers and leaves of the margins. You had to search in order to find them.

Morad made them hesitate in choosing the second-place design. He put his finger on Sadeq's jeweled lotus design. Rather thick lines surrounded geometric shapes, such as triangles, diamonds, and trapezoids, and the colorfulness of the shapes reminded one of the windows of Chehel Sotoun Palace in Isfahan, which were inlaid with small pieces of colorful glass.

"The brown color of the lotuses has overshadowed the color of the geometric shapes," Professor Mani said.

"We can tell the artist to make the lines of the lotus narrower." Morad said, and he bought Sadeq's design for the carpet company.

The design that Morad had drawn himself was ranked second. Morad didn't vote on his own design. Many large and small stars had been scattered on a dark blue background. Stars with tails, stars with halos. Moons of various shapes were key to the unity of the design. All phases of the moon had been included, from the crescent moon, as narrow as the eyebrow of the beloved, to the half-moon, to the full moon. There was no new moon. Morad's design was a deep night full of stars and moons, in which the stars and the moons had chosen their own spots. It was a night of another planet within another galaxy.

Professor Mani turned to Morad and said, "From such a harsh man as you, such a poetic work is very unexpected."

"Mr. Pakdel," Sohrab said, "hides his idealism under a veil of harshness."

Professor Mani instructed Hasti to write a note to the building engineer and ask him to come to see Morad's design and to decorate the ceiling of the dining room according to that design, such that the floor and the sky of the room are coordinated and they both reflect this unearthly night. The sky with lights and the floor with warp and weft.

Morad stood, grabbed his design, and shouted, "Didn't I say that it would be the trousseau of one of the favorite children . . ." His lips were trembling. "I don't want my design to be under the feet of those who cannot understand . . . They don't understand what eyes, hands, and minds they are setting their feet on. Didn't I say that?"

"Calm down, dear boy," Professor Mani said.

Morad turned to Hasti and asked, "Did you know, Miss Nourian?'

"Yes."

"And you too?"

And Professor Mani corrected him. "And you too, Brutus?"

Morad wrote his resignation letter while standing there, took his design, and left.

"Thank God," Professor Isa said, "that we are rid of this devious boy."

"This boy is not devious," Professor Mani said. "Whatever he says, he does."

The inlay motif design that had been sent from Tabriz was selected for the office. Professor Mani told Hasti to give the order for the desk and its accessories to the inlay workshop, to show them the design, and to emphasize that the decoration of the desk and its accessories must be made with wires of ivory and gold.

Professor Mani had another sip of herbal tea and said, "The owners of these works are not eternal. In the end, all these will be placed in museums. Young people are impatient. When you get old, you yearn to stay on the scene so that you will forget old age. You want to set forth ideas in the same way. That's when you mess things up."

Professor Isa's voice was ringing in Hasti's ears. He always arrived before the council meeting and made phone calls from Hasti's office. He even called long distance. "I have retired, but I have not cut my ties with Persian art."

"Isa Khan and I were both members of the Committee to Celebrate 2,500 Years of Monarchy," Professor Mani said. "For the march of Persian soldiers from the time of Cyrus—who Mohammad Reza Shah bid to rest in peace, because he is awake—to the present day, we ordered a ton of curly and straight beards and hair from France, and we spent so much money on the chainmail, arrows, bows, shields, spears, and clothes of the Persian army commanders and soldiers. I was present for the march. It lasted maybe an hour and a half or two hours in all, and the sun was hot. All the heads of foreign countries were sweating, and I, who am from Iran, was sweating, too. The crown prince was too hot, and a Chinese officer who was sitting next to him was fanning him with his hat. Finally, they brought fans and umbrellas, but the march was over."

Whatever he says, he does. Was this interpretation of Professor Mani the key to setting Morad on the right path and an ordinary life of going out, going to the cinema, eating barbecued liver, laughing at Jerry Lewis and John Wayne? Or had Morad entered the pit of politics and didn't talk anymore and that is why he wouldn't agree to marriage?

When they had gone to Sare'in, nothing particularly significant had happened. Nor did Morad and Jalal's discussions have anything to do with this change in the nature of Morad's behavior. But why not? Perhaps they did. Hasti didn't want to seek freedom in a love of which she was not certain.

Morad had said to Jalal, "Mr. Al-e Ahmad, why don't you enter the political ring so that we can fall in behind you?"

"I'm already involved in politics," Jalal had answered, "but my realm is the pen. If I get involved in the way you want, then you will stand aside and say, 'Go for it.'"

"Don't underestimate us," Morad had said.

They went to Sare'in by bus. Hasti and Morad were sitting in front, and Grandmother and Shahin behind them. Grandmother was going there for her leg pain, and Hasti was going to prepare drawings for her BA project. The bus was struggling to get up Heyran Mountain Pass. One mountain pass after another. The Soviet border was on their right. From Astara onward, the elevated guard posts overlooking both sides of the border were rushing past before Hasti's eyes. Each guard in one stand, with binoculars in his hand or at his eyes. But the words *patience*, *discipline*, *tolerance*, and *ability to control one's temper* did not leave Hasti's mind.

Hasti felt sick, and at the next mountain pass, she threw up. Morad rubbed the back of her neck and her shoulders. He took his own towel from his bag and asked the driver to stop the bus. The driver replied, "Right here on this slope? Do you want to kill us all?"

The voice of one of the passengers was music to Hasti's ears. "There are only three more mountain passes to go. Then we will arrive in Ardabil. My wife always feels sick, too."

If the uncertainties of reality last only three mountain passes, and then one reaches the destination, this is tolerable. But the realities of the world around Hasti are so complex that words cannot disentangle them. They cannot be explained, nor can one defend them. Rue the day we cannot tolerate them!

The next morning, Grandmother and Hasti went to Gavmish Goli—an irregular pool containing boiling hot water from the heart of the earth—giant bubbles, steam, fog, and the smell of phosphorous. Women and children resembling ghosts. Women, some in lungi, a few in underwear, most looking like Eve minus the leaf. Women at the side of the pool were either washing their own hair or their children's, rubbing their feet with pumice stone, or scrubbing their bodies. Touran Khanom, in underwear, pushed aside the shampoo and soap foam and set her foot in the hot water. She took her foot out, put it back in, and took a few steps forward until the water reached her shoulders. Then she suddenly plunged her head underwater.

Grandmother's skin was red, as was the skin of other women, and the sun was shamelessly watching the scene. A child was crying and saying, "I have an ouchy." Another child was not crying, but had an ouchy. Hasti was drawing sketch after sketch. At noon, she told Morad, "It was like Judgement Day." When Simin saw her painting, she said, "The Apocalypse." When Professor Mani saw it, he said, "Dante's inferno." Later, many years later, when Hasti had no money, he bought this "Dante's inferno." What use did he have for all those naked children and naked and half-naked women in different positions? Women sitting, standing, bending . . . All that shampoo and soap foam by the side of the pool and on the surface of the water. All those copper and plastic pitchers. Morad had said, "The red plastic pitchers that you have drawn in several places herald the betterment of this ghostly world where movements resemble the dance of the dead."

10

They needed to go visit the Foreign Artists' House and take note of any inadequacies. This house had been renovated and decorated under the supervision of Hasti and Morad. Hasti knew that the house was being prepared as a residence for foreign artists who travel to Iran, but she had not told Morad. Now it didn't matter anymore, since Morad had resigned from membership in the council some time ago. He had also set off on the right path, so he wouldn't stir up a storm like he did the day they were choosing carpet designs. He wouldn't cut off ties with Hasti, either, like he did that same day. A few days after that, he had been the first to make up, saying, "I can't stand being away from you."

When they arrived at the Foreign Artists' House, they sat in the living room on two kilim-covered sofas placed opposite one another so that Professor Mani could catch his breath. The cushions on the sofas were the true children of the kilims. They had inherited the same colors and the same geometric shapes, their colors as red as that of their mother. Professor Mani took a handkerchief from his pocket and dried the sweat from his forehead. Hasti reproached herself for not bringing the professor by taxi. Turning to Hasti, Professor Mani said, "It looks like you and Pakdel were on the same page from the outset. The design on the embroidered curtains looks great, and Pakdel has renovated the mirrorwork and the ceiling plaster quite well."

"In this house," Professor Isa said, "the foreign artists will live in the context of Persian artworks."

"So what?" Sohrab asked.

Zandi cleaned his glasses and said, "Sohrab, could you please stop acting like Pakdel . . . So that they will know Persian art and introduce it to the world."

"Well," Sohrab said, "these international freeloaders, with beard or without, male or female, but surely beautiful, could stay at hotels and visit museums."

"This place will one day be a museum, too," Professor Mani said, "and one of its virtues is that it displays some recent innovations in Iran's handicrafts. Look at the terra cotta designs. Kufi calligraphy in yellow on a blue background, free from miniatures needlessly filling the background. Of course, we didn't touch the marble bath attached to the house, nor the traditional gym, nor the fountain room. It's probably Pakdel who has fixed the fountain and turned it on. We have also added several bathrooms, Western toilets, two modern kitchens, and a central heating system."

"Why two kitchens?" Sohrab asked.

"You weren't there when we were getting approval for the Foreign Artists' House," Zandi replied. "This house has twenty-two rooms."

Some sounds came from the kitchen next to the living room. Someone opened the refrigerator and closed it. Some other sounds, and then the sizzling of something frying. Hasti was surprised. After all, *she* was holding the house key. There must be other keys, too.

A chubby woman in a red silk bathrobe came into the living room carrying a tray. When she saw all those people, she was startled. She didn't say hello. She put the tray on the engraved table in the center of the room and sat down. She wasn't short on appetite, either.

"Dr. Isa," Sohrab said, "it's a good thing that we understand the meaning of *Foreign Artists'* House. If only Pakdel were here."

Zandi took off his glasses and started to clean them. The woman swallowed her bite and took a big gulp of liquid from the ceramic cup to help the bite go down. "First of all," she said, "I'm an artist, too. You'll see my show on TV in a couple nights. Second, the boss told me to come here and rest for a few days."

"Domestic artists also have the right to stay," Professor Isa said.

Hasti heard Professor Mani asking for water, and she ran to the kitchen. The sink was full of dark blue ceramic plates and cups of the same kind. She knew that each plate and each cup had been decorated with blue twin paisleys. They had ordered them from Hamedan. She washed one of the cups, filled it with water, and returned to the living room. There was a dark blue pill in Professor Mani's hand.

When her eyes fell on Morad at her office, she cheered up. They went together to the Plan Organization cafeteria. It wasn't busy. They sat at a table. A woman with long, straight black hair was sitting opposite Hasti. Hasti had seen the woman several times in the corridors of the ministry, behind the door of this or that room, walking or standing or sitting on the staff chair. But she didn't recognize the man across from the woman. When the man turned and, with his right hand, wrote something on the palm of his left hand, she recognized him. He was the chief of staff of the ministry. And when the waiter came toward him, she knew that he had asked for the bill.

After they had ordered, Hasti said, "So?"

"So what, my dear lady?"

"Did you think about it? The answer to my question? I proposed to you."

"Look, Hasti, I don't want to bring you misfortune."

"Look, Morad," Hasti said, "the only good fortune is love. Why are you withholding it?"

"My heart is brimming with love for you . . . ," Morad replied, "but alas . . . Let's not ruin it with marriage."

"Don't give me such nonsense," Hasti said. "I've turned twenty-seven years old. Like all women, I too need a warm home with a few children whose father ought to be you!"

"I'm sorry," Morad said, "but I don't have the means."

Hasti was angry. "If you don't want to be the father of my children, then I must give in to marrying a suitor who . . ."

Morad interrupted her. "Then you will have broken my heart." He sighed and continued, "And no craftsman can be found in this world who can mend a broken heart."

Hasti raised her head and saw Mardan Khan standing at their table. After greetings, she asked, "Do you eat lunch here, too?"

"Almost every day, except Wednesdays."

Without anyone inviting him, he sat beside them. "What would you like to eat?" Morad asked.

"I've had my lunch, thank you."

"How about coffee?"

"I'll smoke a cigarette and take my leave."

Then he turned to Hasti. "Why didn't you come to our garden on Sizdah Bedar? If you had come and had tied blades of grass, as the Persian custom goes, you would have found yourself a husband." He winked at Morad, who was eyeing him.

Hasti was laughing in her heart. She saw that Morad's eyes were filled with surprise. She thought, *He must be thinking that my suitor is this very guy who just winked at him.* Of course, Mardan dyed his hair and mustache. Because of his mustache, everyone who knew him called him "Douglas Mustache," but Hasti didn't know to which Douglas this nickname referred. The woman with the long, straight hair and behind her, the chief of staff of the ministry, passed by their table. Mardan Khan looked the woman up and down and said softly, "She's not a bad piece."

"We played twenty-one with Mother Eshi," he continued. "She lost four hundred tomans. Her soft white hands with the diamond ring and red nail polish are perfect for holding cards, and for shuffling and dealing cards. May I die for . . ."

The waiter put their food in front of Hasti and Morad.

Murray motioned to Morad and asked, "Is this young man your colleague?"

"No."

"Don't be fooled by him. If he wants to marry you, I must first examine every part of him." He laughed loudly.

Hasti moaned in her heart, *Morad, why don't you slap him*? Apparently Morad had preferred eating to listening.

Murray extinguished his cigarette in the ashtray and said, "I was about to call you and invite you for next Saturday night. It's a farewell party for Hitti."

"Mr. Hitti is leaving?"

"Of course."

"So Mr. Ganjur will lose his job . . ."

"You underestimate me. I will take on Hitti's position, and Ahmad will work with me." He stood up, looked at his watch, and said, "You will come for sure, won't you? It's a pajama party."

"You mean I should come in my nightgown?" Hasti asked. "Never . . ."

"I'm not sure, you pretty girl, when you will get free from the evil of medieval ideas! Girl, how many times will you live?"

"I'm not pretty, and I'm not coming in my nightgown, either!"

"Wear whatever you want. Bijan will pick you up."

He thought for a second and said, "And now Bijan is your colleague, deputy director of the Office of Book Evaluation."

Then he left.

Morad had shaken Mardan Khan's hand firmly, and he had also eaten half of his food. But Hasti's food had become cold, and she was thinking. *I knew it. I knew it. Bijan, deputy director of the censorship office . . . Most likely Sir Edward made it happen for him. But then, I work in the same ministry. My hands are dirty, too. Professor Mani says, "Persian artwork, which I am in charge of collecting, will end up in museums one day." Perhaps Bijan can also help good books survive. But Jalal always said, "In any organization, if you don't turn with the wheels of that organization, you will be crushed."*

Grandmother said that Salim Farrokhi had called several times. Once he had spoken to Grandmother, and twice he had talked to Shahin. He had asked Touran Khanom where he could buy fiberboard and ivory, which she didn't know. But he hadn't asked that Hasti call him. His back didn't hurt anymore. One reason was that the weather was getting warmer, and another was that he had gotten a cortisone shot. He had chatted with Shahin a lot, asking about his trip, but he hadn't even sent his regards to Hasti. He hadn't even asked if she were home.

In their last encounter, Hasti had become disgusted with Salim. She knew the reason well, and she was running away from this knowledge. Salim hadn't said a word that Hasti could disagree with when she was eavesdropping in the bathroom. And if he had given shelter to Farhad Dorafshan, whose hands were tainted with blood and who had planted a bomb in Hitti's car, he had no choice, because that big oaf had been his friend for many years.

Hasti asked Grandmother and Shahin not to answer the phone anymore so that she could pick it up herself. She decided to tell Salim, *What do you want from me? I who have a thousand and one religious and social flaws, I who am not pretty, I who am old. If you think you can shape me like wax in your hand, you are mistaken. My Morad has come. I proposed to him myself. He has not agreed, but seeing him is the biggest gift that "Fortunato" has bestowed on me . . . You keep using foreign words, Aqa Salim*!

But Salim's voice on the phone was the best news, and it made Hasti forget all her hard feelings. She apologized that she had neither really wished him the best for the New Year, nor had she bid him a decent good-bye. And for taking leave from him in tears, and for not having accepted the gold coin Mrs. Farrokhi had offered her as a gift. Salim told her that he had, in fact, been offended by the latter. Hasti promised to explain the next time they met. Salim told her that with every passing day, he had missed Hasti Khanom more than before. How badly Adam and Eve needed each other!

They talked for a long time. Salim said that he had bought her a piece of ivory and several pieces of fiberboard. He had gotten the address from Professor Mani. And that Hasti must paint for her "brother" the same painting on ivory. He urged her to tell him what she had drawn. He made Hasti promise that she was going to give him his present. But for now, he was inviting her to go see an illustrated, religious narration. At any rate, making the tableaus for religious narrations was a sort of painting.

Hasti gladly accepted the invitation and asked if she could bring La'l Banu and Grandmother, which of course she could. But who is La'l Banu? La'l Banu is a Shi'a Muslim Pakistani woman who loves this sort of thing, and yes, she knows Persian, too. She attends Shi'a recitation rituals without her husband's knowledge.

Before hanging up, Hasti asked, "After the religious narration, would you like a guest?"

Salim replied, "A dear guest like you is always welcome!"

"Okay. I'll come to your place and tell you why I didn't accept the New Year's gift from your mother. If you think I'm wrong, I'll go to Mrs. Farrokhi and receive my gift."

"I'm afraid we can't meet in my house," Salim said. "We have some guests that I prefer would not meet you."

Hasti almost slammed down the receiver. *Yes, of course*, she thought. *Niku Khanom who secretly stares at you and peels tangerines for you is there. There is also Mr. Farhad Dorafshan, who has a crush on me. What kind of a disorderly household is this that you can't find a single quiet place?*

"Hello, hello? Hasti Khanom?"

"I was thinking," Hasti said, "that you could come to our humble abode . . ."

"No. With your grandmother's permission, we'll go to a restaurant and have dinner together."

Salim had brought two black chadors and a reed mat. La'l Banu and Hasti put on the chadors and followed Salim along with Touran Jan. A tableau depicting the martyrdom of Imam Hossein, the third Shi'a imam, had been hung on the wall in front of a large empty lot, and they had covered it with a curtain. A man in cleric's clothing was arranging the children, seating the taller ones behind the shorter ones. The men sat themselves behind the children, and the women, in prayer chadors, sat behind the men.

Some of the women had wrapped the chador over their chests and tied it behind their necks. Most of them had babies—sleeping, awake, or crying—in their laps. Salim spread the reed mat on the ground beside the women. The women became upset. One of them said, "The upper crust!"

The cleric came to Salim's aid, and they shook hands. Then he recited to the women a phrase from the Quran, "Whoever comes to you, welcome them." The women heard it, but they still turned their backs on the reed mat and the upper crust sitting on it.

The narrator was a dark-skinned man who had a turban-like head covering with one end of the turban hanging down from his shoulder. He was wearing a robe but not an overcloak. He asked the crowd to say "Peace be upon the Prophet" loudly, and they did so three times. He drew the corner of the curtain aside and pointed with a long stick to the image on the right side of the tableau. "Look closely. See this young man from whose grave fire is soaring? His mother has cursed him. She has raised her breast to the sky and has cursed the milk that she gave him. May you never be cursed by your parents. Say, 'Amen.'

"Look at the young butcher, who had cheated on his sale . . ."

The cleric standing beside the crowd said in Arabic, "*Wayl un-lil mutaffifin* (woe to the stingy) . . . Woe to those who cheat in sales!"

Hasti looked at the young butcher's severed hand, which had fallen in a corner like a bird. The butcher's wrist was bleeding.

The narrator pointed to a black square building on top of which was a black flag and beside it, the outline of two bare feet, and he said those were the imam's footprints. He hit his forehead and said, "Whatever wish you have, ask it from Our Holy Master, Abolfazl." Then he started reciting, "O Abbas, Ali Abbas, we have turned to you. For God's sake, O Abbas, lift this sorrow from our hearts."

The men pounded on their chests and the women wept.

The narrator drew the curtain aside again. "Look at the bridge in the other world—thinner than a hair and sharper than a sword. You will be given your record of deeds, and your sins will be weighed on a scale."

Hasti raised her head, but she didn't see Salim, and again dislike for Salim returned. "*I will soften her like wax in my hand.*" Again she remembered, "*She has a thousand and one religious and social flaws.*" *Being an orphan and poor,* she thought, *haven't been my fault, after all . . . The fact that an old woman, who is now pounding on her knees and moaning in sorrow, has raised me is not my fault. The fact that Grandmother has poured her venom into my soul drop by drop hasn't been my fault, either.*

Hasti didn't consider herself a sinner. She had done her best. She had tried to get rid of her complexes. Like a creeping vine, she had clung to Khalil Maleki, Jalal, Simin, and Professor Mani, without, in Sohravardi's words, drying them out. If she had flaws, it was not their fault. She thought how strange she seemed to the people who were sitting beside her and had turned their backs on her. Was Hasti a misfit? Was she not from this world? Was she mixed among these people by accident?

A woman without a prayer chador arrived, her head wrapped in a black scarf. Hasti recognized the woman from Simin's amber necklace, which was hanging from her neck. The necklace that Jalal had brought for Simin from Russia. So, it was not an outside thief. Impulsively, Hasti shouted, "Haji Ma'sumeh, come sit here next to me."

"Why should I sit next to you?" Haji Ma'sumeh asked. But when she recognized Hasti, she said, "Oh, my darling Hasti Khanom! What are *you* doing here?"

The cleric said in a commanding tone, "Ladies, be quiet." Haji Ma'sumeh put her hand on her necklace and sat down on the reed mat. Hasti thought, *What a small world*!

The narrator was talking about hell. The fires of hell . . . The eyes, the heads, and . . . The day of fifty thousand years, the angels of torture, the boiling cauldron, the snakes of hell . . . Then he talked about heaven. Virgin male and female angels, the fountain of heaven . . .

Haji Ma'sumeh whispered in Hasti's ear, "You're not going to tell the lady, are you?"

"No."

The narrator shouted, "Silence, sister! Woman, quiet that child."

The narrator referred to Imam Ali distributing water from the fountain of heaven among the faithful . . . Imam Reza sitting on the step, giving refuge to the deer. The hunter, with his bow and arrow, standing in front of the imam, as if aiming at Imam Reza. Both men and women shouted, "O protector of the deer!" Touran Jan also asked for help from the protector of the deer. La'l Banu's shoulders were trembling under her chador, tears had made their way down into Hasti's throat, and Haji Ma'sumeh was crying, "Accept your sinful servant so that I can come to kiss your feet in respect."

The narrator drew the curtain aside more than before, and the crowd released a huge sigh. Hasti thought that it might be the center of the scene. Imam Ali on his horse, the largest figure in the image . . . and the voice of the narrator: "My Master, Imam Ali, killing the pagan Marrat Qeis. Marrat Qeis and his horse have been split in two by Imam Ali's two-edged sword. Blood has spurted out. A halo of light around Imam Ali's head . . ."

The narrator had reached the desert of Karbala. The curtain on the image had been completely pulled aside. Several tents . . . His Holiness Zayn al-Abedin had put his head on a pillow, sleeping under the tent. His Holiness Ali Akbar had lain his head on His Holiness Imam Hossein's knee. Around this imam's head, there is a halo brighter than any other halo in the image. Her Holiness Zeinab with a white face veil. Other women in the image also all wearing face veils, with a similar cloth extending down over their chests. A woman is holding a baby, and from the description by the narrator, Hasti learns that the baby is His Holiness Ali Asghar.

And now the actual Karbala scene, as described by the cleric: "It is the night of Ashura. Our Master, Imam Hossein, is standing on top of the hill. Addressing his followers, he declares, 'You leave. My family and I will stay. I will turn out the lanterns so that you won't be embarrassed to leave.'"

The cleric hits his forehead and says, "But you were right, O Imam."

Hasti thought of Sa'edi's play *Place of Murder.* The day he was reading it to Simin, Hasti was there, too. There was also a film script that started with this very scene. Imam Hossein turned out the lanterns. Many ran away, and they set out running in history. "Gholam," Simin had said, "you have borrowed from *The Time Tunnel* television series."

The runaways were still running in history until they reached the era of Azod al-Dowleh Daylami in the tenth century. It was the day of Ashura, and the people were all in black. On the wall, above the votive water stand, was written "O Aba Abdollah al-Hossein, help us." People drank water from the stand and said, "To the memory of your thirsty lips, O Hossein." Men were pounding their chests, hitting their backs with chains, and reciting "O Hossein," and women were weeping. Hasti did not remember it all, but she did remember that the runners in history reached the Safavid era in the sixteenth century. And the poet Mohtasham Kashani was reciting an elegy for Imam Hossein in court and then . . .

Then they reached the present era. They were performing a religious street play for the night of Ashura. When they reached this very scene and Imam Hossein was about to turn out the lanterns, the runners in history did not let him. The lanterns remained on. "But you have wives and children," Imam Hossein said. One of the runners turned to the crowd and said, "Don't go. Don't go. He's right. But we will all die sometime. Why not on the path of truth?" And he turned to Imam Hossein and said, "O Imam, but you knew, didn't you? Why didn't you tell us? Why?"

"Anyone who stands by his true words," Simin said, "will win out in history."

Now Hasti was thinking of asking Simin to get Sa'edi's play *Place of Murder* from him, and Hasti would have it published by talking to Bijan, who was the deputy director at the Office of Book Evaluation. And if Bijan doesn't do it, she will know that he is turning with the wheels of that organization.

The last scene: bodiless heads, headless bodies, split horses, split camels, Imam Hossein's head on a spear.

Wailing has filled the air. Even the children are crying. Hasti cries, too. The narrator and Aqa Sheikh Sa'id cry, too. *This wailing*, Hasti thinks, *is for the thousands of years of our history. And has any runner reached the destination*?

Aqa Sheikh Sa'id sat in front, and La'l Banu, Hasti, and Touran Jan sat in back. Salim started the car. Touran Jan was still crying. In response to La'l Banu, Hasti explained that it must belong to the Qajar era. "I counted. He had drawn a hundred faces. Well, of course, they are two dimensional and very basic, but with respect to colorfulness and power of influence, it is unique."

In English, La'l Banu expressed her interest in buying such a religious tableau, and Hasti said that she would take her to Professor Mani. "He has three excellent religious tableaus—two by Qollar Aqasi and one by Modabber."

"You are not only a good artist," La'l Banu said, "you will also be a good poet. I edited, the best I could, the poem that you composed in English, and I read it to Helen Hitti. She started crying. She asked permission to add a bit to it, too, to use American folklore so that Americans will like it, and to have it published under the names of all three of us."

Hasti wanted to say, "What a concoction it will be if three people cook the soup." But she said nothing. She was staring at Salim's ear that was obviously listening. *Very few people*, she thought, *have considered the beauty of the ear. One can see pictures of ears only in biology textbooks. The ear with all those lines, angles, turns and folds, with ups and downs. In fact, having angles and protrusions is one of the mysteries of beauty . . . A cheek under which a bone protrudes . . .*

I will compose a poem for the ear, but not for Salim's ear.

At the door of the house, when Touran Jan was getting out, Hasti wanted to get out, too. "But Hasti Khanom," Salim said, "didn't we agree to have dinner together at a restaurant?"

"Yes, you invited me, but to be honest, now I have neither an appetite nor a good mood. I would like to go home and cry and think."

"But I have made a reservation."

"You can take Niku Khanom."

"Come sit in the front," Salim said. "I must talk to you."

Hasti sat next to Salim, and Salim turned off the car. "Are you jealous of Niku?" he asked.

"I was looking at your ear. I wanted to kiss your ear."

"So you *are* jealous of Niku."

"Absolutely not!"

"Why are you acting like this?"

"Like what?"

"My dear," Salim said, "you are too old to act like the fabled Christian girl—in Attar's *The Conference of the Birds*—who convinced her Muslim suitor to carry out many demeaning tasks. Nor am I Sheikh Sanan, whom you can make become a swineherd."

"You're ruining it. You started it well, but you're ruining it."

Mohsen Run came out of Teimur Khan's shop carrying his loudspeaker, Grandmother's New Year's gift. He held the loudspeaker in front of his mouth and said, "Hasti Khanom, Farideh ate cheese today and said that she wasn't afraid of cheese anymore."

Hasti rolled down the car window and said, "Tell her, 'Good going, girl.'" She explained to Salim that Farideh had been afraid of cheese since she was little.

"Sometimes," Salim said, "I think you're psychologically imbalanced. Sometimes I think you're a merciless woman."

"How come? You have only seen me a few times!"

"Because you are toying with me," Salim said. "You are pulling me this way and that. I invite you. You don't come. Just say 'no' so that I know where I stand."

"Women are not allowed to be sad?" Hasti asked. "Women are not allowed to have doubts? Women are not allowed to think?"

She told herself, *He wants to break up, and he's looking for an excuse. I could set him free by giving him a last chance.* "My friend came back," she said. "He won't get married."

Salim honked the horn several times, as if he were taking a bride.

Teimur Khan came out of his shop. When he saw those two, he was surprised, and he frowned.

"Why didn't you say this earlier? Let's go to the notary and get married right now. Then I'll take you home to introduce you. 'Father, Mother, Sister, Niku, Nanny, Taji, Hadi, Abd al-Reza, I introduce Mrs. Hasti Farrokhi, my wife.' Then you will share your sorrows with me."

"I wish I could," Hasti said. "I wish sorrows could be shared."

"What shall I do? Shall we go to the notary?"

"No."

"Shall we go to the restaurant?"

"No."

"Shall we go to my house?"

"No."

"Shall I come to your house?"

"No."

Salim opened the glove compartment and gave Hasti a package that Hasti knew contained fiberboard and ivory. "So allow me to leave," he said. "You may get out."

"I am neither mentally ill nor merciless," Hasti said. "I just don't know what I want and what I don't want."

And she got out.

Hasti drew the first sketch on the fiberboard without any previous thought. She set her subconscious, her instinct, and her soul free, and the three of them collaborated and guided her hand such that when the work was finished, Hasti was surprised. No, *surprised* was not the right word. She was shocked!

In the center, a tree that had lowered its head due to its load of bitter oranges. Bare trees or trees with few leaves surrounded the bitter orange tree. On top of each tree, a baby monster sitting and staring at the bitter orange tree. A monster sleeping under the bitter orange tree, another monster sitting above his head. A younger monster holding onto the leg of the sleeping monster.

This was not a gift that she could give to anyone. Nor was it appropriate for New Year's!

11

Bijan was wearing a black velvet suit and a black-and-white dotted necktie. It seemed as though he had also put on powder. Hasti was wearing the violet, open-necked, alternating matte and glossy sweater, her mother's gift. And she hadn't put on powder.

Murray's house had been built by an Iranian engineer in the style of Le Corbusier. The living room was hazy with cigarette smoke. Everywhere the scent of perfume, the scent of opium, and scents that Hasti didn't recognize mixed together. Hasti saw her mother dancing with Murray. Mother Eshi was wearing a white satin nightgown, and Hasti recognized her white velvet dressing gown thrown on an armchair. Ahmad Ganjur was wearing black satin pajamas. He was facing away from Hasti, and a picture of a dragon filled his entire back. On his head was a black silk cap from the top of which hung a red tassel. Peggy, who was dancing with him, wore a black nylon nightgown with no bra. A servant stood before Hasti holding a tray full of all kinds of alcoholic drinks; Hasti asked for fruit juice.

After the tango, when jazz music started to play, the young people poured onto the dance floor. Most of them were American. The girls, perhaps in imitation of Helen Hitti, were wearing dresses of Isfahani block-print cotton, with or without bells, with or without anklets. Spinning, bending and straightening, turning and twisting—the sound of the bells and anklets mixed with the rhythm of the jazz. Helen herself was wearing jeans. A young man with frizzy hair, an open collar, a woolly chest, and tight trousers, loudspeaker in hand, was singing at the top of his voice, arousing frenzy.

Hitti joined Mother Eshi, Murray, Peggy, Ganjur, and Hasti. "Americans are happy people," Ahmad Ganjur said.

"But," Hitti said, "since the time that we have devoured half the world, we feel guilty."

"And not all of them are happy, either," Hasti said. "Blacks, the remaining Indians, and soldiers from Vietnam . . ."

Peggy interrupted Hasti. "Don't mention Vietnam. I don't want to hear about it."

A woodstove that had a crescent arch on each of its four sides occupied the center of the room. The fire gave warmth from all sides, and the crackling of the firewood was the only innocent sound amid all the hullaballoo. Hasti found refuge in the quiet of one of the curves of the stove. She saw Dr. Bahari and Sir Edward at the charcoal brazier. Sir Edward took so many puffs that it seemed he had been smoking opium since he was in swaddling clothes and that his favorite toy had been the opium pipe. A hand took Hasti's and sat her down on the floor next to him. It was Mr. Crossley with his hump. La'l Banu, Ahmad Ganjur, Hitti, and Bijan also came and completed the group seated on the floor.

"Would you like some LSD or some grass?" Crossley asked Hasti.

"Don't listen to him," Bijan said. "Both are dangerous."

"Don't be afraid," Hitti said. "No one here has LSD."

"What is LSD?" Hasti asked.

"I tried it once," Bijan said. "It takes a person's spirit on an otherworldly trip, and he fears that he might not return with a sound mind."

"LSD," Hitti explained, "is a drug that was designed for the mentally ill. This drug drives the active and functional mind in a symbolic direction, and people feel reborn. The essence of existence. Existence and being are a person's feminine agents. The actions and activities of the mind are one's masculine agents."

"Long live the feminine agents!" Crossley said. He wanted to plant a kiss on Hasti's cheek, but Hasti drew herself back.

"Crossley, behave yourself," Hitti said.

Hasti turned toward Hitti and said, "Tell me more about LSD."

"Anyone who uses LSD connects directly with his subconscious mind. With his inner self." Hitti thought and added, "I have a book about hippies and a pamphlet about LSD. I'll give them to your father to give to you. Keepsakes."

Why would they place a bomb in the car of such a man? Hasti thought. Even though the same man had written that she wasn't qualified to be a teacher.

"Long live love and flowers," a voice said. "Hurrah!"

Hasti turned toward the sound of the voice. Several long-haired, bearded boys and several girls . . . Each of them with a garland of flowers around the neck. Several movie-star kisses.

Crossley asked Hasti to dance with him, but Hasti declined. She didn't know how to dance spinning and turning, and she wanted to hear what Mr. Hitti had to say.

"We've clung to Freud," Hitti continued, "while psychology since him has gained so much breadth."

"It's not all Freud's fault," Hasti said. "Encouraging drug and alcohol abuse in the West is to keep the young generation out of politics."

"So, you're a communist," Crossley said. "Totalitarian regimes are not compatible with human nature."

Hitti sighed and said, "These are bitter and depraved times. Alcohol and fear ruin the old; drugs and overindulgence, the young; and in totalitarian regimes, the deprivation of individual freedom."

Again, a voice rose from the corner in which the flower-draped boys and girls were sitting. "Long live spiritual nectar."

"What is spiritual nectar?" Hasti asked.

"Marijuana," Hitti replied, "hashish. It brings nightmares."

"Are those young people with flowers around their necks hippies?" Hasti asked.

"No. For the moment, they are just acting like hippies. If they were real hippies, they wouldn't come to a gathering of us old people. Hippies are against the older generation, society, police, law, and politics. Hippiness is the rebellion of the new generation."

Sir Edward put the opium pipe next to the brazier and said to his wife, "La'l, get up and bring me a cup of tea." Ahmad Ganjur put his hand on the floor to get up, but La'l Banu had already set off. La'l Banu was wearing a purple nightgown. The color of the gown started with light purple and played with different shades of purple until it reached the skirt and decided to be dark purple.

Sir Edward asked Hasti about the status of purchasing a religious tableau—an idea that she had put in his wife's head. He asked whether, if he were to buy the tableau, it would later become an antique. Hasti said that, in her opinion, it would.

Edward turned toward Crossley. "Was your excavation in the desert successful?" he asked.

"Yes, it was. I also took a trip to the Island of Bewilderment."

"By jeep?"

"No. By helicopter. I had requested a helicopter from you for that. I went by helicopter, and I returned by camel."

Sir Edward said that Ahmad had arranged the helicopter. Ahmad added that he had arranged the camel, too.

Hasti's attention had been so drawn to the name Island of Bewilderment that if Crossley again invited her to dance, she would agree. Crossley and Sir Edward were speaking in difficult English, and she didn't understand it all. They discussed sampling and burial of refuse for some time, and then, Crossley's long-winded speech: Getting up at 4:00 a.m., tiptoeing out of the tent, sneaking away from the wandering cameleer, making the camels wander, abandoning the excavation students and professors under the tents, being present, fresh and beard-trimmed, for breakfast at 8:00 a.m. He talked and laughed.

Hasti waited until they played a tango. It took a long time, but finally they played one. She put her hand on Crossley's shoulder and said she was ready to dance with him.

"My pleasure."

First, they traversed the dance floor diagonally in harmony with the music. Then Crossley bent Hasti and asked, "Would you like to go to America?" Hasti said nothing. He took Hasti's hand and held it up. He turned her around and said, "It can be arranged, if you are nicer to me. If you stop being a stick in the mud. How can such a mother have such a daughter?"

Just to say something, Hasti asked, "Mr. Crossley, do they throw pajama parties in America, too?"

"Some movie actors do."

Finally, Hasti was able to steer the conversation toward the subject of the Island of Bewilderment.

"It's an island surrounded by a lake of salt. On the island you are totally entrapped. Pieces of salt twenty inches long and fifteen inches wide, even larger, and in some places much smaller, surround you. During the day, when it's hot, it's not possible to put your foot on them. You go down into slime and salt, but overnight the pieces of salt freeze. I left the island by camel. It's strange that the name of the cameleer was Wandering Cameleer. The name of the opposite mountain was also Wandering Mountain."

Hasti's lips trembled. "When the pieces of salt freeze, people cannot leave the island?" she asked.

"No. It's a long way to the narrow desert road."

He spun Hasti around himself and said, "I want to suggest to the FBI—excuse me, SAVAK—that they bring political prisoners who do not confess and release them there."

The trembling spread from Hasti's lips to her whole body. With what kind of a person was she dancing? She couldn't take another step. She felt dizzy. If only that day with Salim she had not acted badly. If only when he said, "Let's go get married," she had gone. But one can't get married after wailing over history. Why didn't Salim get it? Why doesn't this tango end? In her heart she said, *You are certainly a member of the CIA. You're among the veterans of the Vietnam War who have been sent overseas as a reward. You're all in love with being overseas.*

"Are you tired?" Crossley asked.

"No, but this room is stuffy. I've become dizzy."

"Me too. I'm drunk and I've smoked grass. But I could dance with you till dawn."

Crossley guided Hasti to the veranda and seated her on a chair. He sat next to her and said, "You're delicate. You're fragile. Go mountain climbing. Practice yoga."

Since Hasti said nothing, he added, "Mrs. Hitti has shown me the painting you drew on the egg. Helen said that you are also a good poet."

"Why hasn't Mrs. Hitti come tonight?" Hasti asked.

"It's been a while since she's set foot out of the house, for some reason. She thinks the people of Iran are savages." He took Hasti's hand. "If you practice yoga, you will survive, and if not, you'll have to take refuge in drugs. But then, you will be destroyed."

Hasti withdrew her hand from Crossley's and said, "You leave. When I feel better, I'll come, too."

Hasti fixed her eyes on the pool of limpid water. *The same savage people of Iran*, she thought, *who put bombs in cars, at the last minute take mercy. But you, you all who are civilized, consign political prisoners to an island of bewilderment.* She was certain that the Island of Bewilderment was connected to her own destiny. But right now, tonight, every night, wasn't she living in the midst of the Island of Bewilderment? Hadn't Hitti said that existence and being are a person's feminine agents? Didn't her name also mean "existence"? Wasn't the nearest kin of the earth existence?

Afterward, when they had taken her and Morad to the Island of Bewilderment by helicopter, their eyes covered, and then uncovered their eyes, she would recognize the island. It was a sandy place, in the shape of a pear, skulls of the dead close to one another and far from one another. A few skulls floating on pieces of salt in the lake. Snakes, lizards, large spiders, cockroaches, and cockroaches, and cockroaches . . . Hasti closed her eyes. It seemed to her that a woman dressed in black was coming toward her with a sack in her hand. When she pulled the sack over Hasti's head, the cockroaches engulfed her head and neck.

A hand touched her shoulder. It was Crossley. He gave Hasti a filled glass. "Drink up," he said. "It's pineapple juice." He sat again and said, "Go to America. You will be wasted here."

"Mr. Crossley," Hasti asked, "do you practice yoga?"

"Definitely. Twice a day. After all, I'm an archaeologist."

Hasti's heart called out, *You are a hunter of humans. To have the strength to hunt humans, you practice yoga. To have the strength to hunt ancient civilizations . . .*

The colorful table overwhelmed Hasti with the choices of food. Mushroom sauce over steak, slivered pistachios and almonds over curry stew, chicken and pomegranate stew, Chinese food. Which of them should she choose? She looked at her mother, who filled a plate and went toward Murray. When she returned to the table without the plate, she paraded as though she were a model displaying nightclothes. She took salad for herself.

"Mother, since when are you on a diet?" Hasti asked.

"It's been a few days now. Dr. Bahari advised it. Murray also said I should lose weight."

"Keep your diet," Hasti said, "but don't hang around Mardan Khan so much."

Hasti followed Mother Eshi's look and realized that Mardan had winked and kissed the palm of his hand, held his palm toward Mother Eshi, and blew the kiss toward her. Mother Eshi left. Hasti abandoned her plate full of all kinds of food she had never tasted before and went after her mother. Halfway there, Bijan caught her arm. "Where are you going?" he asked.

"Don't you see that my mother's gone crazy?"

"Well, she's drunk."

Ahmad Ganjur also joined the group. In her heart, Hasti said, *Too bad I didn't get the sack full of cockroaches from the woman in black. I could have emptied it over the heads of all three of them.*

"Mardan Jan, you've given a good party," Ahmad Ganjur said.

Mother Eshi commented, "Murray's parties are always fabulous."

Murray responded, "I love grateful people."

Hasti saw Sir Edward and La'l Banu seated at the dining table. Using her hands, La'l was separating the bones from a piece of fish that was on a plate in front of her. She took half a sour lemon, squeezed it over the boneless fish, and put the fish in front of Sir Edward. Her long, graceful hands were the same color as the browned fish skin.

Hasti heard the voice of Ahmad Ganjur, who asked, "Hasti Jan, Sir Edward wants to buy an antique with your help?"

Murray laughed and said, "Sir Edward is an antique himself. He can't function well, either. When he comes home in the afternoon, he goes to sleep. The house must be dark and there must be no sound."

"What does La'l do?" Mother Eshi asked.

"She goes to the mosque."

After dinner Peggy seated the guests around the living room and dining room and explained that first the Iranians would put on a play and then the Americans. The Iranians' play would be in Persian. They would choose a compound word. In the first act, they would act out the first part of the word; in the second act, the second part; and in the third act, all the word. Murray gave an example. "Say they choose *New Year's*. In the first part, they act out *new*; in the second part, *year*; and in the third part, *New Year's*."

A musician with frizzy hair played on a small drum. Dr. Bahari came to the center of the living room wearing a long cloth around his waist and another long cloth over his shoulders. With bundles under their arms, Murray and Ahmad came into the imaginary bathhouse and took off their clothes except for their underwear. Dr. Bahari collected the clothes as if he were the cloak checker, and he also played the parts of the bathhouse owner and the masseur. He folded Ahmad Ganjur's Chinese pajamas and Murray's suit and put them in the bundles. Murray put his hands over his ears and pretended to go underwater in the pool. He feigned putting water in his mouth and spitting into the pool. Ahmad Ganjur closed his eyes. "By the will of God," he said, and he did what Murray had done.

Dr. Bahari, the masseur, sat in front of Mardan Khan and pretended to wash him. He put Murray's bare foot on his knee and rubbed it with a stone. Suddenly he yelled, "A genie's hoof!" Then he washed Ahmad Ganjur, and he also put shoes on his hoofs. After they left, he touched his own imaginary hoofs, said several Arabic phrases, and yelled, "Zaʿfar!"

The king of the genies, Zaʿfar, appeared with dishevelled hair, one eye on his forehead drawn with charcoal, and his upper body tattooed. He was jumping up and down with the beat of the drum. Dr. Bahari as the masseur said, "Zaʿfar, tell all the genies to come to the bath. Those two stranger genies have left. They came just for purification."

In the second act, Dr. Bahari and Ahmad Ganjur, in peasant clothes, pretended to be shoveling, weeding, and sowing. Mardan Khan, in the role of the landlord, coughed and pretended to come to his farm. The two peasants greeted him and bowed. "Where is the son of a bitch Zebarjad?" Mardan Khan asked.

"Sir, his child has diarrhea," Dr. Bahari said. "He hasn't come."

"Go bring him," the landlord said.

"Sir," Dr. Bahari said, "hasn't land reform happened? Hasn't the era of landlords and peasants come to an end?"

Ahmad Ganjur dragged Zebarjad in. Hasti had not seen him before, nor the man who played the role of the genie Za'far in the first act.

The landlord ordered that Zebarjad be beaten on the soles of the feet. Zebarjad put the soles of his bare feet up, and the first and second peasants got imaginary wooden sticks. The landlord hit the bottom of Zebarjad's feet with a stick and said, "Such boldness in my village!"

The musician beat on the drum with each stroke of the stick, and Zebarjad said, "Bastard, hit softly."

"He's right," Ahmad Ganjur said.

Hasti asked herself, "Is *bastard* the word they are portraying?"

In the third act, Mother Eshi, with gaudy rouge and lipstick, dark glasses, and her white satin nightgown, came onto the stage. She tried to dance the Baba Karam to the tune of the drumbeat, which was impossible, so she swayed lasciviously. Ahmad and Murray followed her. "Oh, lady, where are you going?" Mardan Khan asked. "Will you take me with you?" Then he invited her for dinner and ice cream, and Mother Eshi agreed to smoke a cigarette with him. Murray and Eshrat embraced and kissed each other just like American movie stars. Mother Eshi had not yet put a cigarette to her lips when Ahmad Ganjur grabbed Murray's collar. One slap, two kicks. Murray yelled, "Over a harlot?!"

Ahmad sat on the ground and cried and cried. He took his Chinese nightcap off his head, threw it onstage, and yelled, "I, the cuckold! I, the bastard! I won't follow the rules of the game! I won't say the last word, however much you deserve it! Oh, woman . . ."

La'l Banu said, "It's very clear what word you are thinking of, but I'm embarrassed to say it."

From the end of the hall Bijan said, "Whore." (In Persian, *jen* "genie" + *deh* "village" = *jendeh* "whore.")

Hasti and apparently others thought that Ahmad's tears and insults were part of the play, but the play had finished and they had clapped for Bijan. Mother Eshi and Mardan Khan had left the stage. But Ahmad Ganjur was still sitting there crying. *Even though his father has become drunk again, why doesn't Bijan come to comfort him*? For the first time, Hasti felt sorry for her mother's husband. She took his hand and pulled him up off the floor. Like an obedient lamb, Ganjur went with Hasti to the veranda. Hasti seated him on a chair and waited while the grown man cried.

"Mr. Ganjur," Hasti said, "splash some water on your face." She took Ganjur, like a child, and watched the grown man wash his face. She sat on a matted chair beside the pool with the grown man. Ahmad Ganjur sang, "I blamed crying on drunkenness . . ." He added that in the evening, his father would pour arak into the cup from under the samovar, drink it, and sing this song. He asked who wrote this song.

"Aref."

Ahmad Ganjur hit his head and asked, "What do you think I should do? Shall I admit to being a cuckold?"

"Don't allow my mother to drink. And drink less yourself."

Bijan came to the side of the pool with a cup of Turkish coffee and a glass of water. He gave the coffee to his father to drink and asked, "Father, why did you do this?"

"But, their kiss . . . It was too much."

"You kiss Pasita the same way," Bijan said. "You're even." And he left.

"I wish I could have a daughter like you," Ganjur said. "Scold your mother. Stop speaking to her and make peace on condition that she doesn't hurt me so much."

"Okay."

"Only you understand. Bijan understands, too, but I'm sending Bijan to a place where he will become the genie Za'far or the peasant Zebarjad, ill-fated like me. Like everyone around me. What do you think I should do?"

"Resign."

"With all these burdensome expenses? What work am I able to do? Shall I work as a porter or as a construction laborer?"

"The garage. With Bijan, expand the garage."

She remembered the words of Touran Jan and said in her heart, *Then you will really become the garage owner Grease Monkey.*

A voice from the living room called for Hasti. A non-native Persian-speaking voice shouted, "Hasti Nourian!" and La'l Banu came to the veranda.

In the living room, Helen Hitti, just like the referee of a wrestling match, held Hasti's hand up and said, "The original author of two poems that I will sing." Then she held up La'l Banu's hand and said, "The editor." She said that she had used the melodies of Native Americans and Blacks, had added some pieces to each of the two poems, and had given a happy ending to each. Hasti had been pleased that two people had considered her work poetry. She thought that perhaps she had also migrated to the land of poetry.

Helen sat on the floor and caressed the guitar in her lap. She played and sang:

The Cloaked Sage of Time

How much time must pass until a girl becomes a woman and a boy a man?
And how much worry should a woman endure before she's called a woman?
And how many ups and downs must a man put behind him before he's called a man?
And how long and far a flight over the ocean must a bird endure until it rests on the shore's sand?
And how many days and nights must an oceanside mountain rinse its body in the sea until it fully erodes?
And how much patience must that mountain, eroded by water, maintain until hills, cliffs, and peaks are once again formed?
My dear, the secret of all this is hidden in the heart of the cloaked sage of time.
Cling to life.

Everyone applauded. They clapped and whistled, and Hasti thought, *It's like love. The passion in her singing—the satisfaction of hearing it from someone else's mouth. It must be like union with a beloved, having the same allure and perfection. Hadn't Sohravardi said, "So when Love gives us the capacity for union, we must surrender to it"?* She wanted to put up both hands and say, "I will succumb to you, O love." Had Crossley poured vodka into her glass of pineapple juice? No. Hasti didn't put up her hands.

Next Helen played and sang:

Fear, Fear, Fear

Fear is a product they sell; if you don't buy it, it decays.
So buy it not.
I didn't buy it. "It's your turn after Malcom X and King," she said.
I looked right into the eyes of my executioner.
"Such a death gives meaning to life," I said.
"To which summits will your spirit flee?" she asked.
"Where does the scent of flowers go?" I answered.
"My spirit is that same scent of flowers."
"I have seen the abode of the Lord of this house," she said.
"A house for your sake and that of your spirit will no longer be built.
"They have broken all the beams;
"The foundation is ruined."
"With hands," I said, "with determination, and with fervor,
"One can build the house of the spirit again."

The three of them sat together. "La'l," Helen said, "what a coincidence."

"What do you mean?" Hasti asked.

"Something had happened to Helen that frightened her," La'l Banu said. "I brought your poem, *Fear*, for her that night." And Hasti thought, *What a coincidence that I should also have eavesdropped and have come to know how much you ought to be frightened.*

The musician beat the drum and announced, "It's the play Cinderella, Iranian style."

Helen stood up from beside La'l and Hasti and left.

Helen, in the role of Cinderella, sits in the imaginary kitchen. She pretends to cook. Her clothes tattered, her face soot-covered, her hair disheveled. The matchmakers sent by His Honor, the prince, knock on the door and come in. Stepmother calls her two strange daughters and they behave coquettishly. One of the matchmakers asks, "Is there no other girl in this house?"

"Well, we have a kitchen maid," Stepmother says. The matchmakers stop by the kitchen and see Cinderella. The matchmakers leave. Stepmother and daughters pretend to cut, stitch, sew, and sweep.

The musician beats on the drum: act 2. Cinderella standing behind an imaginary stove. With a wooden spoon, she pretends to stir a soup that doesn't exist. The pot also is nonexistent. Her deceased mother with two wings enters, hand in hand with a four-winged angel. The angel has a large bundle in her right hand. Cinderella flings herself into the arms of her mother. Mother and angel work hard on Cinderella, pretending to wash her, brush her hair, put makeup on her, dress her . . . and jewels, jewels, and jewels. (While they dress her, the lights go out.)

Cinderella, like the luminous sun. Mother and angel, dying from fatigue. While taking leave, the angel turns to Cinderella and says, "Remember, the moment the clock strikes twelve, flee the party and leave one of your shoes behind."

"Don't forget, dear," Mother stresses, "at the stroke of twelve, flee."

Act 3: the royal palace. Girls stand in line with mothers behind them, except for Cinderella's stepmother, who is busy putting rouge on the cheeks of her older daughter. The drum plays and the prince enters. A servant's chador has been thrown like a cloak over the shoulders of Mardan Khan. He surveys the girls. None please him. He surveys them once more. He lifts the chin of one. He opens the lips of Cinderella's younger stepsister and counts her teeth. The older stepsister bites her lip.

The musician beats the drum three times. Helen, as Cinderella, enters. "Oohs" and "aahs" from the actors and the audience. The astonished prince goes to greet Cinderella and embraces her. He caresses her, he kisses her. The girls either bite their lips or lower their heads. A musician comes on stage with Helen's guitar and plays a waltz. The prince and Cinderella dance. The drummer beats the drum twelve times, but Cinderella doesn't leave. The drummer shouts, "It's twelve o'clock!" Cinderella doesn't leave and doesn't leave.

The lights go out for a moment, and when they come back on, Cinderella is the same kitchen maid that she was before. The prince swoons and falls down. His teeth become clenched. He shakes from head to foot. His eyes seem to bulge out of their sockets. Girls, mothers, audience, drummer, and guitar player laugh boisterously. Cinderella, the kitchen maid, bends over the prince and says, "It's me. Tell them to bring water so that I can wash my face."

The prince sits up. He claps his hands and says, "Ewer and basin, brush, clothes, right away!"

Cinderella washes her face. She brushes her hair. The lights are turned off for a moment . . . And it appears the real Cinderella, not the kitchen maid and not with the clothes, jewels, and makeup of the four-winged angel and the two-winged mother, but with her own jeans, is in the arms of the prince. Girls, mothers, and audience clap to the beat of the drum and sing, "Congratulations, congratulations, congratulations on your wedding!"

12

Touran Jan was right when she said, "Why doesn't anyone knock on the door of this house? Not even a single ring of the telephone!" She would ask Hasti, "What did you do with Salim . . . ? There's no hope for Morad . . . To boot . . ."

Until finally someone did knock on the door of the house. Someone was pounding on the door with his fist, scratching on the door with his nails. It sounded as if he even kicked the door.

Hasti opened the door to a teenage boy who was wearing big sandals, without socks. On top of his tattered trousers, she recognized the blue-green sweater that she had given Morad as a gift, even though it now had many holes. All over the sweater, stains, mud, and clotted blood. Nevertheless, she recognized it. It was her own knitting.

The teenager gave Hasti a crumbled piece of paper and said, "This paper, it's from Aqa Bak."

Hasti took the letter. She recognized Morad's handwriting, but still she looked at the signature on the letter. "Baktash. M."

> Help us. Bring whatever money you have in the house. If you come with the boy, he knows the address. Otherwise, tell the taxi driver, "The shantytown, Mansour Street, Shahbaz South." Ask for Fatemeh Sabzevari's house. Tell the driver that you are a social worker.

"Wait," Hasti told the teenager. "I'll come with you." She went to the kitchen and showed the letter to Touran Jan. Touran Jan didn't have her glasses handy, so Hasti read the letter to her.

"I wish Shahin hadn't presented himself for his military duty . . . ," Grandmother said. "We have cans of pear compote; take some for him."

"If need be," Hasti asked, "may I bring him here?"

"Of course! But he's written, 'Help *us*!' Don't bring them all here!"

Hasti set off with the boy. She held out her hand in front of several taxis, but they all passed by. Just before Khaneqah Street, she got a taxi. Hasti sat in the back and told the boy to sit next to the driver. The boy searched for the door handle and clawed on the car window. The driver opened the car door, and the teenager entered, but he didn't know how to close the door. The driver closed the door and said, "What a wild creature we have here, first thing in the morning."

Hasti gave the address, and the driver grumbled, "It'll cost you a lot."

Hasti put her hand on the boy's shoulder and asked, "What is your name, sir?"

"I'm not a sir. I'm your servant, Fazlollah."

"How did you find my house?" Hasti asked.

"Aqa Morteza came with me. But I would have found it even if he hadn't come."

"What do you do?" Hasti asked. "Do you go to school?"

"We went to school once. Queen Fanar had said to. The school said, 'You slum children are wild.' We didn't have birth certificates, either."

"Why didn't you have birth certificates?"

"Well, we just didn't have them."

By then Hasti had realized where she was going. The squatter settlement—neighborhood of the undocumented. Now, why had Morad ended up there? And who are the "us" that he had written in the letter?

"What do you do now?" she asked Fazlollah.

"We pick through trash."

"Why do you pick through trash?"

"We find stuff. There are lots of things in the trash: food, toys, many, many things."

The driver looked at Hasti in the mirror and said, "I've taken many riders to the shacks of these unfortunate people. He's right. Even Queen Farah has gone there. You're probably a social worker. You do good deeds, but it's no use."

"You are doing a good deed, too," Hasti said.

"Oh, lady, whenever I go there, I feel all the world's sadness in my heart. The poor fellow is right. The end of the shantytown is Tehran's sewer. On its other side, there's the trash heap where garbage is dumped every day."

They passed by a water pump and a crowd of women with basins, plastic buckets, plastic pitchers, and pots in their hands. The taxi stopped at a muddy area beside a gutter full of sludge. It seemed as if they had gathered all the garbage in the world and thrown it into that gutter, so that the gutter would bring it to the sewer of Tehran as a souvenir. The sun was the same Tehran sun, but wasn't its heart filled with all the world's sadness from what it was seeing? Like the taxi driver's was?

They walked through passageways that you couldn't even call alleys. Empty tins from vegetable oil and kerosene containers full of construction and demolition waste, stones, and mud had been piled on top of each other to make what were perhaps called walls. The cracks between the tin containers were filled with mud and straw. Some of them had been covered with plaster, but the plaster was chipped everywhere. Thin wooden roofs or three layers of tin or torn canvas sheltered the residents of the shantytown. If Hasti were to paint their image, even the paintbrush would weep blood in sadness.

"What do you do in the winter?" she asked Fazlollah.

"We sneeze and shiver."

"How old are you?"

"How would I know?"

It seemed the path had no end. In the passageways of this matchbox city, city of the forgotten, city by the gate of a great civilization, children, roosters and chickens, cats and dogs were all wriggling together.

Hasti and Fazlollah reached a big canal over which several flimsy bridges made of wooden sticks and planks had been placed. These bridges would take the people of the shantytown to their beloved trash heap.

Beside the canal, Fazlollah pulled aside a gunnysack curtain, and they went inside a shack. The floor of the room was damp. A bearded Morad was lying on a mattress in a corner of the room. His eyes were closed, and a worn-out blanket covered him. In another corner of the room a two-burner kerosene stove was lit. On top of the stove was a pot in which something was boiling. The room was full of junk—old shoes, a radio, broken dolls, and shattered toys.

A woman entered—dark-skinned, middle-aged, with a black scarf on her head, a kerchief tied as a headband on her forehead, and a dress that came down to her ankles. Once long ago, it was a velvet dress. The woman had a withered bunch of herbs in her hand.

Hasti wanted to pound on the shack wall with both her fists, but she was scared that the roof would collapse on their heads or that the picture would fall—the picture hanging on the wall of a clergyman whose black turban meant that he was a descendent of the Prophet. The woman didn't say hello. She sat to clean the herbs. Hasti gave the woman three cans of compote. Then the woman said hello.

Hasti sat beside Morad's mattress and held his hand. It was very hot. She put her hand on his forehead, and it was even hotter. Morad opened his eyes.

"I must take you out of here as soon as possible," Hasti said.

"First," Morad replied, "you must take a man with a broken leg to the hospital . . ."

Fazlollah came in with a bag in his hand and shouted, "Onions!"

"Pour them in the *tiki*."

Morad smiled and said, "*Tiki* means 'soup.'"

Garbage soup, Hasti thought.

The middle-aged woman gave Fazlollah one of the cans of compote. "Son," she said, "take this to the welding workshop to open it. His lips have grown *tanas*."

"*Tanas*," Morad translated, "means 'swollen and cracked.'"

So, he wasn't feeling too bad, since he was able to translate.

Fatemeh Sabzevari said, "Your fiancée should buy opium from Haji." Addressing Hasti, she said, "He's hallucinating. He's become mad with fever."

Fatemeh led the way, and Hasti followed her. They passed the welding workshop. Hooked nails had fallen in a corner. Fatemeh had raised her skirt, and she was wearing men's shoes. They arrived at a shack that had a door. They knocked. Haji Ma'sumeh dressed in men's clothing opened the door to them. She still had Simin's amber necklace around her neck.

There was a rug on the floor of the room. Haji Ma'sumeh even had a television. At first, she didn't recognize Hasti, but when she did, she said, "My darling! Hasti Khanom, what brought you here? Please come in, and I'll make you some tea."

"Sell me some opium," Hasti said.

"Of course!"

"Ja'far, get up!" she shouted. Hasti just then recognized Ja'far, Haji Ma'sumeh's brother. Ja'far—Jeffrey—with his usual fuzzy hair, was lying on the rug with a stuffed bag under his head. Jeffrey got up and said hello. At Haji Ma'sumeh's indication, he took a long roll of opium from the bag. Hasti put her hand in her purse.

"I swear to the Kaaba's black stone, that I have kissed," Haji Ma'sumeh said. "I will not accept even a penny from you." Then she whispered, "Here, I'm *Mr.* Haji *Ma'sum*."

"This is too much," Hasti said.

"Keep it. It will come in handy."

Nevertheless, he, Haji Ma'sum, split the opium roll in three parts and gave one part to Hasti. From Hasti's part, he made a small ball in his hand.

Fazlollah's mother spoke with the current Haji Ma'sum in a language that Hasti couldn't understand, except for "anxious" and "Aqa Bak." She realized that Fatemeh Sabzevari was worried about Morad. Haji Ma'sum, from the city of Qaen, said, "Go! You can leave!"

Finding Haji Ma'sum in that wasteland of the homeless, where Hasti didn't know the language, was a blessing. They set out together. On the way to the house where the man with a broken leg was, Haji Ma'sum revealed to Hasti all the secrets of the shantytown . . .

"One day," he told her, "three men came. One was Morteza, who is robust and husky and has blue eyes. One was Aqa Baktash, who smuggled electricity for them and made a welding workshop, where they are now making nails for sale. He sent men to work as laborers and women to work as maids. He forbad the renting of children to beggars. He tried to teach the women to stand in line by the water pump, but the women didn't learn that. Now he has become ill . . . He has always been frail . . . All three of them have denied themselves of so much. They would cook lentils and eat them for three or four days. Cigarettes and tea, never. They would sleep on the bare floor. The man with the broken leg had gone to fix a bridge over the sewer—they themselves call it a canal—because children were falling into the water all the time and drowning. He himself fell from the bridge, and his thigh bone was shattered."

They arrived at the room of the man with the shattered thigh. His beard was fuller than Morad's beard, and Hasti thought she had seen him somewhere. When she put the opium ball in his mouth, she recognized him. It was none other than Hadi—Farhad Dorafshan. What were these three people doing in the slum of rental children?

"Where's the nearest telephone?"

"Mashhadi Baqer's shop on Shahbaz Street. What do you need it for?"

"I want to call an ambulance and get him to the hospital."

"Ambulances don't come here. State hospitals won't admit him, either. And he wouldn't go there himself. Get a taxi and take him to a private hospital."

Hasti and Haji Ma'sum stood on Shahbaz Street South and held out their hands for taxis. Some of the taxi drivers slowed down and motioned that they were going straight ahead. An empty taxi came by, and Haji Ma'sum stood in the street in front of it. The driver slammed on the brakes and stopped within an inch of him. The driver jumped out of the car, but when he saw Haji Ma'sum's stature, he changed his mind about fighting. Instead, he said, "My good man, if I had run you over, you would have ruined my life."

"Bastard," Haji Ma'sum said, "a man has broken his leg. You must take him to the hospital. If not, I'll ruin both you and your taxi." The driver seemingly succumbed to the plea of Hasti, who spoke of doing a good deed. They both got in, and the taxi stopped at the barren land in front of the shacks.

"Darling, Hasti Khanom, don't get out of the taxi," Haji Ma'sum said. "Hossein Ali will carry the man with the broken leg on his back and bring him here. I'll run and send them. You know that I have things to do."

He was right. It was not good to leave a bag full of Afghan opium alone in a shack with fuzzy-haired Jeffrey.

Hossein Ali and the driver helped put Farhad Dorafshan on the back seat. Hossein Ali shouted, "Brother, lie straight, flat on your back!" Farhad lay on his back.

By then Hasti had a plan. She would take him to the National Iranian Oil Company Hospital. She would tell the hospital guard that he was a close friend of Dr. Bahari's and that she was a social worker. Hossein Ali and Hasti sat in front.

"You make hooked nails, don't you?" Hasti asked Hossein Ali.

"Yes, sister. We sell them in the bazaar for three tomans a kilo. We make thirty to forty tomans a day." Then he added, "Aqa Baktash built the forge. God bless him."

Hasti explained to the driver that once they had taken the man with the broken leg to the hospital, they would return and take another sick man to Valiabad Street.

"I suppose you take quite a few sick people to their homes or the hospital . . . ," the driver said. Then he asked Hossein Ali, "Mister, how many sick people are there in the shantytown?"

"There have to be forty or fifty."

"What is the population of these slums?" Hasti asked.

Mister Hossein Ali said, "Aqa Morteza is counting people. Mostly, they are kids. There are so many mosquitos that the legs of young and old alike become pitted. Aqa Morteza says that it's from lack of food."

The hospital gate was open, but the gatekeeper would not let the taxi drive in. Dr. Bahari's name and the social worker position were the charm, however, and the gatekeeper called for a stretcher. Two men came and laid Farhad on the stretcher. Hasti whispered in Hossein Ali's ear to stay in the taxi.

In the hospital foyer, behind the information desk, a girl with an ironed nurse's hat and a uniform as white as snow was talking on the phone. Above her head, there was a picture on the wall that showed a nurse with her finger to her lips. Hush.

"My darling," the talking nurse said, "I told you that I can't. I have guests tonight." Pause.

"No, swear to God, my heart does not belong to anyone else." Pause.

"Tomorrow night I am on call, too. No, swear to God, I'm not having an affair with the golden-eyed doctor. Believe me. You are so unappreciative! Bye-bye."

The talking nurse took out a piece of paper. "Name?"

The patient moaned, "Mister Hossein Ali."

"Occupation?"

"Lottery ticket . . ." He couldn't even say "Lottery ticket seller."

"Address?"

Hasti glanced at Farhad, who was wearing the same dark gray winter jacket that he had been wearing in Salim's house. He was not a big oaf any longer. She thought of giving Salim's address, but what came out of her mouth was her own address. "Valiabad . . ." What stupidity. Then she made up for that stupidity. "We don't have a telephone, and even this address is mine. I'm a social worker." She had said "social worker" a few hundred times already.

The girl guided them to Room 116 at the end of the corridor. The doctor was the same golden-eyed doctor, with eyeglasses that had golden rims. Hasti mentioned Dr. Bahari, and the golden-eyed doctor smiled and said, "Where did you find this monster? You're doing good deeds."

"You can do so as well," Hasti said.

The doctor rang a bell. An old woman came in. The doctor commanded, "Room 520 . . . He's a patient of Dr. Bahari." Then, on the phone, he ordered an X-ray . . . and that they show the image to him.

The old woman asked Hasti, "Didn't you bring any pajamas for him?" The doctor ordered her to get a patient gown from storage.

The old woman, the stretcher-bearers, and the patient all left. When Hasti sat, anxiety took over. "Would you like some tea?" the doctor asked, and he rang for some.

She had to find Dr. Bahari. She had to take Morad home. She had to bargain with the taxi driver over the fare. She wanted to pound the wall with both fists and say, "I am so worried."

The wall was all white. In front of her was a cheap painting showing a farm in the sun. Several white lambs were grazing. She counted them. Seven. As she was about to feel calm, it occurred to her that there was a wolf hiding somewhere. She couldn't see the wolf, but she could feel its presence.

The old woman returned. They had done the X-ray, and the patient had been put to bed. Hasti rose.

"Don't you want some tea?" the doctor asked.

"Why, yes!" She was so tired . . .

Waiting for the tea, she stood in front of another cheap painting by the door. Several fish had their open mouths close to one another. Did they want to kiss each other? Were they talking to each other? Suddenly, a spark flashed in Hasti's mind; if the damned worry was not there, a poem would have flown from the painting. The fish have convened a seminar on their struggle with fishermen. They are discussing different kinds of lures and traps. That big goldfish is saying, "The line of the trap looks like a straight long worm. The lure is the worm itself, or maybe it isn't. The fisherman is a monster." And that yellow fish is saying, "But the main enemy isn't the fisherman. He works hard to keep body and soul together . . ."

When they brought the tea, Hasti asked the doctor to have them take two glasses outside—one for the driver and one for the man with him.

"Three," the doctor ordered. "Take a glass of tea for the gatekeeper, too."

When they arrived back at the barren land in front of the shacks, the taxi stopped, and the driver told Hasti, "Sister, go bring your other patient."

Hasti and the real Hossein Ali arrived at Fazlollah's mother's house. A man with blue eyes was sitting by Morad's mattress. When he saw Hasti, he rose, said hello, and asked, "Did you hospitalize Hadi?"

"Yes."

"Where?"

"National Iranian Oil Company Hospital, Room 520."

"This is Morteza," Morad said.

"That's right!" Morteza added.

"Now, I must take you to my house," Hasti told Morad. "This young man will carry you on his back."

"This," Morad replied, "is a place where faith in the heavens has disappeared."

Morteza asked permission to call and inquire about Baktash's health. He said that when he finds a place, he will come pick him up.

Hossein Ali put Morad on his back, and Fazlollah's mother covered him with a blanket. In her men's shoes, she walked along with Hasti, saying, "Aqa Bak's fiancée, I hope you always live in comfort. I hope you always go to weddings. I hope you always eat good food, like meat and fava-bean rice . . ."

Hasti sat in the back seat of the taxi and put Morad's head on her lap. Fazlollah's mother removed the blanket from atop Morad. Hasti asked Hossein Ali to sit in the front. She took off her jacket and put it over Morad.

Morad was shivering. He was saying, "A warm place under a secure roof . . . My bones are cracking . . . They have crucified me . . ."

Grandmother and Teimur Khan were standing at the door. Teimur Khan put Morad on his back. All the passengers of the taxi came inside the house, and the driver, too. They laid Morad on the living room sofa. New sheets, new pillowcases, an old comforter with a new cover. Hasti took a bottle of water from the refrigerator and brought it back to the living room with a glass. The driver and Hossein Ali each had some water.

"How much do I owe you?" Hasti asked the driver.

"If I didn't have a wife and children, nothing. But you can pay whatever you can afford."

Hasti took out all the money she had in her purse and held it in front of the driver. The driver took thirty tomans and said, "If only we could be captured and taken to a different land."

Hasti put ten tomans in Hossein Ali's pocket. Hossein Ali took out the money and said, "All of us are in debt to Aqa Baktash. I am a Muslim, not an ungrateful infidel!"

"Take it, man!" Morad shouted. And the driver said that he would take Hossein Ali as far as Jaleh Square.

With Teimur Khan's help, Touran Jan gave Morad a footbath with warm water, vinegar, and mustard and put Shahin's pajama bottoms on him. His jeans had turned to oilcloth. Hadi's jacket was the same way. Teimur Khan was soaking cotton balls in medicinal alcohol and rubbing them on Morad's body beneath his sweater. He took off the sweater and put Shahin's shirt on him. Touran Jan took his temperature. It was 103 degrees. Morad's teeth were chattering. With that high fever, why was he shivering? Hasti brought Shahin's blanket and covered him. There was a damp cloth on Morad's forehead. Teimur Khan had probably put it there.

Now she had to find Dr. Bahari at whatever cost. Hasti decided to call Mr. Ganjur, but Grandmother dissuaded her from that. Instead, she called Mardan Khan. Peggy answered and said that they had guests. She added that in that caravanserai, there were always some guests. "He must have his friends around him, smoke cigarettes, then pipes, then whisky and soda . . . Right now, your mother is reading his coffee cup."

Hasti said that she had to talk to Mardan Khan urgently. Mardan Khan picked up the phone, and Hasti said hello.

"My darling . . . ," Mardan Khan said. "Come on, get a taxi and come over. Do you want me to send Bijan to pick you up?"

"I have a patient in bad condition."

"Who is it?"

"Morad Pakdel."

"The same guy who was having lunch with you in the Plan Organization cafeteria?"

"Yes."

"Cross him off. If you give me permission, I'll find you a good suitor. If Salim Farrokhi doesn't work out, to hell with him. He's so arrogant. I can trap Bijan for you."

"For God's sake," Hasti said, "stop it. For now, I just want Dr. Bahari."

"Dr. Bahari hasn't come today. He had a patient. But I have several telephone numbers for him. A paper and pencil . . . No, wait, I will find him for you myself."

"I don't want to ruin your weekend."

"There are many other weekends," Mardan Khan said. "You seem to be desperate." He wrote down Hasti's address. He already knew her telephone number.

Teimur Khan was pouring soup into Morad's mouth. Touran Jan put the tablecloth beside the sofa in the living room and started to have dinner with Hasti and Teimur Khan. She put a drumstick on the plate in front of Hasti. How hungry she was! But she couldn't stop thinking about Dr. Bahari. Mardan Khan would certainly find Dr. Bahari. In her purse she had the gold coin that was Grandmother's New Year's gift to her—a lucky charm.

Hasti was sitting by the sofa rubbing Morad's feet. Morad was saying, "Hasti, don't let me die. I want to make peace between the Persian speakers and the Turkish speakers of the slum. The Turkish speakers are from Tabriz, Miandoab, Meshkin Shahr, Ardabil . . . I will take you to Sare'in so that you can draw . . . The Persian speakers are from Khorasan, Sabzevar, Nishapur, Gonabad, Qaen, Birjand, Torbat . . . Hasti, if you still have some opium, give me a bit."

Hasti made a small ball of opium just like Haji Ma'sum had done and gave it to Morad to eat.

As Teimur Khan was taking leave, he said, "Call me when you need me."

"Water, water."

Why did Morad lose track of time and space after he drank the water?

"The Turkish speakers call them gypsies and exiles . . . From the water pump at the corner, I want . . . to draw water secretly through pipes . . . during the night . . . That day of the electricity cabling . . . how much we laughed . . . Smuggled electricity . . . smuggled water . . . smuggled life . . . Who took Hasti away? Where? Hasti, take me to your house and sing me a lullaby . . . Caress my head. I wonder what happened to the soup Fatemeh made. Did she wash the herbs? The water pump is so far away. Hasti, let's swim, let's cool down . . . 'The sea of love is a vast sea . . . ' One must go bring water over and over again. There's an argument over washing dishes. There's an argument over washing clothes. One water pump for six hundred people . . . Hasti, hold my hands and tell me the tale of *The Patient Stone* . . . until I break. I was dreaming of you. Where is my youth?"

Hasti was crying while taking the cloth from Morad's forehead, washing it with cold water, twisting it, and putting it back on his forehead. She moistened a towel and rubbed his face with it. Morad kept hallucinating.

". . . Besides, they are saying, 'Get the hell out of here . . . We'll bring a bulldozer and knock the place down over your heads . . . ' Even the cleric says, 'This is illegally occupied land, so your prayers will not be accepted.'

What benefit has city-dwelling brought them? Only disgrace. Fazlollah's mother, go see if they have brought the child. They pinch the children so that the children will cry and make people feel sorry for them . . . The rent for a child is three tomans a day . . . Diarrhea, jaundice, ulcer . . . they don't even consider these conditions diseases until they can no longer function. Then they go to Haji for opium . . ."

Morad's voice became a whisper. "We have sent several letters to the prime minister's office . . . to the queen's office . . . Several times they came and took our picture . . . We have had enough . . ."

Hasti was falling asleep when the doorbell rang. Morad opened his eyes. "I knew they would come . . . They've tracked us here."

Dr. Bahari, with his small eyes and wide, smiling mouth, entered.

"You came at last," Morad said. "I knew it. But I'm just a beginner . . . I'm unable . . . And for now, I'm so sleepy . . ."

Dr. Bahari took Morad's pulse. He raised Shahin's shirt that Morad was wearing and put the stethoscope over Morad's heart and then over his lungs. "Take a deep breath . . . ," he said. "Now exhale. Breathe again. Sit up."

Morad lacked the strength to stay upright and was flopping over repeatedly, even though Hasti was holding him. She was surprised by how thin he was, his ribs sticking out, and by his white body and sunburnt face, hands, and feet.

"I didn't know that SAVAK's torture is like this," Morad said. "They said that bright light . . . They would pull out the fingernails with pliers . . . They would hang people upside down . . . Please don't take Hasti away . . . Hasti has been wasted on me. Hasti has stress, but she doesn't have hatred. One who has hatred, Mr. Interrogator, cannot connect with people . . . I have hatred, not toward people, but toward those bastards . . ."

Dr. Bahari was not smiling anymore. He went with Hasti to Shahin's room. Hasti had the gold coin in her fist. "It's surprising," Dr. Bahari said, "that he is suffering from pneumonia this season. In his condition, we cannot hospitalize him. And as for you, girl, why would you bring someone like this to your house?"

"We were classmates in the university. We've been friends for many years . . ."

"Your mother was telling me that the son of the well-known bazaar merchant, Farrokhi, has proposed to you. What is this mess that you have created?"

Hasti gathered her courage. "I have created an even bigger mess."

Dr. Bahari took Hasti's hand in his, the same hand in which there was the gold coin, and the gold coin moved from one hand to the other. "You really do make a mess," Dr. Bahari said. "How can I take money from you, the daughter of Eshrat . . . ?" He put the coin on Shahin's blanket-less bed.

"No," Hasti said, "an even bigger mess . . . For God's sake, on the lives of your children, don't shame me." Because Dr. Bahari didn't say anything, she continued, "My bigger mess is that, using the magic of your name, I registered a patient by the name of Hossein Ali, who has a broken leg, in the National Iranian Oil Company Hospital."

"When?"

"This morning."

"Which room?"

"Room 520. But that one is experienced. He will not give himself up like this one. As soon as they put a cast on his thigh, he will . . ."

"I see . . . ," Dr. Bahari said. "Eshrat Ganjur's daughter is involved in political activities."

"No. I swear on my honor, I'm not. I am absolutely not involved in any political activities. I became involved in this due to friendship."

Dr. Bahari wrote a prescription and instructed, "Antibiotics, once every six hours, and other medications . . . Food: chicken soup, fruit compote, broth, and a lot of juice. Take his temperature every morning and every evening. If his temperature rises, call me. My telephone number . . ." He wrote several telephone numbers on top of the prescription. But then he didn't give the prescription to Hasti.

Hasti saw Dr. Bahari to his car. "You didn't give me the prescription," she said.

"I'll buy it and bring it myself. The closest pharmacy to you that is open on the weekend is the one on the corner of Dowlat Street in Qolhak."

"So, you won't shame me?

He shook hands with Hasti and said, "If you ask me, get married as soon as possible. What's wrong with Farrokhi's son?"

Grandmother stood beside Morad saying long prayers. Prayers of several different kinds. Dr. Bahari had not only brought the medication, he had also put several boxes of fruit juice on the table. There were two Lion brand pain-relief patches among the medications. The doctor took the patches to the kitchen and warmed them on the stove. Then he made Morad lie on his stomach as he stuck the warm patches on his back. He took Morad's temperature and gave Morad the antibiotic mixed with fruit juice to drink. Morad couldn't swallow. The doctor waited and tried again. Grandmother was now repeating short prayers while counting on her prayer beads.

"Do you have an electric humidifier?" the doctor asked.

"No."

"Boil water in a kettle and bring it along with a basin."

"My father told me," Morad said, "'If you wish to go, go; get lost.' My mother cried. Farzaneh took off all her clothes and said, 'Down with America!' 'Girl, shame on you,' I said. 'In my father's rooftop room?'"

Grandmother prostrated herself, cried loudly, and asked God to have mercy on the youthful Morad. She lifted her head from prostration and said hello to the doctor. "Doctor," she continued, "once my martyred son caught a cold in the harshness of winter, and I cupped his back in a few places."

The three of them bathed Morad's feet for a second time. They made him inhale the steam. They wrapped the towel around his neck and head and made him lie down. The doctor prepared a syringe and gave him a shot.

"Is the torture over?" Morad asked.

Morad's subconscious seemed to be aware of the seriousness of his condition, as he kept talking about death. "Where is death?" he asked. "Why doesn't it come to wrestle with me? There was a prophet who wrestled God . . . Jehovah . . . If I die, perhaps I'll see God. I'll ask God, 'O God . . . ' They were saying, 'O Great Lord, why did you create us . . . ?' Alas! Alas!"

While drinking some tea, the doctor asked Morad, "Which part of your body hurts?"

"A pain comes and passes through the middle of my chest, and it wants to take my life. A horsefly had come into Fatemeh's shack. It kept buzzing and buzzing. The Angel of Death must have sent it. The Angel of Death wouldn't give himself a bad name. He's all alone. One person for hundreds of thousands . . . She had collected cucumber skins from the garbage. She had found a clay pot with a bit of yogurt in the bottom of it. 'What did you eat for lunch?' I asked her. 'Yogurt and cucumber,' she said."

The doctor took the stethoscope from his pocket and put it over Morad's heart.

"What have you done to your body?"

"Mr. Interrogator, I am a new sympathizer. No, I don't have a gun . . . nor cyanide . . . I'm a trial member. A guerilla fighter is a legendary man. The maximum number of years he will live is four."

Whenever Dr. Bahari came, he would call Morad "Mr. Sympathizer." He would laugh loudly and say that he knew that Morad was hallucinating.

A man named Morteza had come and taken Mister Hossein Ali from the hospital. *That was Farhad Dorafshan*, Hasti thought. *But who was the Farzaneh that Morad had talked about one night when his fever was so high*?

That night, Dr. Bahari had come late. He connected an intravenous tube to Morad's arm. He broke different syringes and poured them into the bag. "Farzaneh," Morad said, "marriage would be an insult to you. Feelings of ownership . . . I oppose . . ." Only once did he call out, "Hasti, my whole being, where are you?"

But that night, his fever wasn't high.

At first, Morteza would call and ask how Baktash was. Then he started coming over. He would come late at night. He would ring twice and then one single ring, and Hasti would open the door. Although he was fat, he was agile. He would look around and then thrust himself in . . . His eyes were dark blue. One night, he even stayed for dinner. And he made the best cutlets! Later, Hasti heard from Salim that Morteza was Pan-Iranist at first. Then he supported the National Front; then he was Marxist without Lenin, an independent leftist in the People's Fada'i Guerrillas . . . But Salim immediately cut off his words because he didn't have a fever.

"Did he break from the People's Fada'i Guerrillas?" Hasti asked.

"Miss Nourian," Salim replied, "it's better that you not know anything. I acted irrationally when I said who is what! When one acts irrationally, everything will be ruined."

Morteza said that he had found a place—on the third floor of a house. A couple lived on the first floor. On the second floor, a Zoroastrian retired teacher whose husband had gone to the United States to see their children. But he wouldn't say where the house was. Hasti, who had been eavesdropping, as usual, had heard that their team consisted of Baktash, Morteza, and Farzaneh, and that the fake birth certificates for all three of them were done. Again, Hasti felt jealous.

"As soon as we have settled into the house and you feel a bit better, we'll come and get you."

"I have burdened Hasti enough. Farzaneh can take care of me." Once again Farzaneh, and once again Hasti's jealousy.

Hasti was organizing the agenda for the last meeting of the Council on Artistic Creation, and her secretary, with her Aleppo boil fixed on her cheek, was typing loudly. There were many requests from all over the world. Artists from many countries wanted to come to Iran, stay at the Ministry of Art and Culture's Foreign Artists' House, and study Persian artworks. Some of them had promised that they would write articles about Persian art and publish them in serious journals. Several had written that they had no money and they would be grateful if the Ministry of Art and Culture would take them to Isfahan and Shiraz for free. It was a land of opportunity, and one could guess who had informed international spongers of this.

Hasti heard a man's voice from the adjacent room saying to Fakhri, "I found its trail. No need to write a letter."

Silence and the sound of the typewriter . . .

The man's voice: "All my efforts and all the efforts of Professor Mani ended up in India."

Fakhri's voice: "How can one take such a painting out of a museum?"

"Well, someone apparently has. The new ambassador from Iran to India took it as a gift."

Hasti thought, *The poor man made the inlaid frame with twisted wires of ivory and silver. Professor Mani drew the half-naked image of Gandhi and said, "I depicted him in the clothes of the Jains . . . the light of India . . . the father of India . . . But they killed their father themselves."*

Hasti was sitting at the council table, and the acceptable requests, with pictures and details, were in a folder in front of her. Professor Isa came before anyone else. He sat in his place and started making calls.

"I'm retired, but I haven't cut ties with the faculty nor with the Ministry of Art and Culture. There's a table; there's a telephone . . . I teach four hours a week."

And then he called Daryakenar Town . . .

Professor Mani came. Dr. Zandi came, too, and right from the beginning, Hasti saw that Dr. Zandi's gaze was different. With his question, her lips started to tremble and her mouth became dry. "Miss Nourian, any news from Mr. Morad Pakdel?"

Professor Mani intervened. "He has settled down. On behalf of some foundation or other, he's gone to Kerman to build inexpensive houses for workers." Then he smiled. "A perfect job for Morad Pakdel."

Hasti was shocked, and she saw even more shock reflected in Dr. Zandi's face. Did they both know and Professor Mani was trying to cover it up?

In order to forestall any new questions, Hasti turned to Professor Mani and told him, "They have removed your painting of Gandhi from the museum, and Iran's new ambassador has taken it as a gift to the government of India."

"So much the better, dear girl. They will care for it better in India. Don't worry. Worry causes a poisonous substance to be secreted into your blood."

Everyone laughed, even Hasti.

They studied the files and accepted eighteen requests. Hasti urged that instead of a French musician, they should choose an Indian or Turkish artist. Dr. Zandi explained that the French musician was a friend of the queen. Hasti asked that instead of the artist residing in Greenwich Village, they choose an Asian artist, and Dr. Zandi intervened, saying that the shah himself had recommended the Greenwich Village artist.

"How about we make it nineteen?" Hasti said. No one voted in favor, not even Professor Mani. The friends of Persian art had to come from Europe or the United States and spend their summer vacation in Iran, and even go to Shiraz and Isfahan for free. This way two birds will be killed with one stone.

When Hasti came home, she saw Mohsen Run's minivan in front of the house. "Hasti Khanom, did I tell you that Farideh is not afraid of cheese anymore?" He had told her—on the same awful night that Hasti had argued with Salim.

There was a tray on the table in the living room, and on the tray, Touran Jan's Quran was blessing a plate of flour and some green leaves in a bowl of water. Touran Jan's lips were moving in prayer. Hasti was surprised to see Morteza in the bright light of day. Morad had put on jeans and a new blue-and-white checkered shirt. Teimur Khan was caressing his thick mustache with his fingers.

Hasti turned to Morad. "I think you have been exposed," she said. Morteza bit his lip.

Morad said, "No one is a stranger here, Morteza Jan."

Hasti recounted the story of the questioning by Dr. Zandi and Professor Mani's trying to cover it up. Yes, the Day Zero operation had been exposed, and now tomorrow, early morning, someone must go to the shantytown and . . . Grandmother was reciting her prayers.

"I can go," Teimur Khan said.

"They don't know you," Morteza said. "If Hasti Khanom goes . . ."

Grandmother said loudly, "For God's sake!"

Despite Touran Jan's warning, Hasti agreed. Since Morad had come to their house, the number of her absences from the office had gone sky high. One more day on top of that. She would call Bijan, her colleague at the Ministry of Art and Culture, and he and Fakhri would do something so that there would be no waves.

Teimur Khan, Morteza, and Morad put their fingers in the plate of flour and passed beneath the Quran, and Touran Jan threw the water with the floating leaves on the ground behind them.

The minivan turned around, moved forward, and stopped at Brigadier General's house. Asadollah Khan, Brigadier General's orderly, took Brigadier General's pillow-like legs off the stool. Teimur Khan, who had gotten out of the car, accompanied Brigadier General with his claw-footed canes toward the minivan. His orderly had put the stool in a good spot. With the help of Asadollah and Teimur, Brigadier General adjusted his legs on the stool and slid his bottom onto the front seat of the minivan.

Teimur Khan held his legs and put them inside. Asadollah took the stool to the house and closed the door. Then, with a hop and a chant, "Ya Ali!," he and Teimur Khan joined Morteza and Morad in the van.

Hasti went home and asked Touran Jan, "Who planned all that?"

"The two of them, consulting Teimur Khan—and with my meddling. But we didn't know that they had been exposed." She held the Quran in front of Hasti and said, "Face Mecca and swear. Go tomorrow, but from tomorrow on, forget about Morad."

Hasti hadn't gotten in touch with Bijan yet when someone knocked at the door. It was Teimur Khan. "Those entrusted to Grandmother's care got out at Ferdowsi Square," he said. He added that Brigadier General had again requested that they take him out for a drive . . . He had said that before his legs had become swollen, Ferdowsi's statue was sitting . . . Now it's standing!

13

The sun was gazing down on the homeless people and rental children in the shantytown, and there was no cloud in the sky to cry. Half-naked boys were playing soccer with a plastic ball on the bare ground in front of the shacks, but there was no goal post and no goalie.

By the time she reached Fazlollah's mother's shack, Hasti was soaked in sweat. A horde of women and children surrounded the trash pile. Fatemeh saw her and shouted, "Hey, Aqa Bak's fiancée, go in. I'm coming." Hasti sat on the stack of bedding. The sheet was different; a rug had been spread on the floor of the shack. Mother and son entered with a sack full of treasures: cucumber skins, eggplant peelings, mushy zucchinis, marred apples, a half-mushy melon, and a muddy bouquet of plastic roses.

Hasti addressed Fatemeh Sabzevari. "Sister, go tell Leopard Abbas to come here."

"Leopard Abbas is in Sahand's shack. Haji Maʿsum should take you there."

Haji Maʿsum entered wearing a different suit.

"My darling, Hasti Khanom, why didn't you come to my place? But today, I don't have any opium. I swear by the black stone of the Kaaba that . . ."

They set off together. "I must see a man called Puria," Hasti said. "I have a message from Aqa Bak."

"Of course. Is Aqa Bak well? Happy? What time is he coming tomorrow?"

"He can't come tomorrow." It slipped from Hasti's tongue that tomorrow's operation had been canceled, and she immediately regretted the slip.

"Why was it canceled? We've recruited so many people. The clubs are ready, gasoline tins, bricks. Leopard Abbas will pour gasoline on the cars in the street, Sahand will strike matches, and we, men and women, will pour in and smash windows and furniture. We'll shout, 'We want houses. We want bread and water.' It will be impossible to stop. We'll create a doomsday."

Leopard Abbas did not have the majesty of a leopard, nor was Sahand as grand as Sahand Mountain. Sahand said in Turkish that he didn't know Persian, but Leopard Abbas said that he would call Puria Khan.

When Puria Khan appeared, Hasti saw that he was none other than Salim Farrokhi. She was shocked.

Morad had told her to wear a scarf, and she had done so. Hasti said hello, and the sun shone in Salim's blue eyes, making them glitter and the pupils sparkle, his eyes framed by eyelashes as if adorned with black kohl.

"Who would have thought to see *you* here?" he said.

"I have a message for you from Morteza and Baktash."

Together, they went into a narrow side path where several chickens and a rooster were pecking at the dry ground.

"What is Baktash's real name?" Salim asked.

"Don't you trust me?"

Salim responded that in business of this kind, one should not trust anyone.

"Are you mad at me?" Hasti asked. "But how can one go out to a restaurant after listening to such a sad narrative and weeping . . . ?"

Salim smiled and recited a line of Parvin E'tesami's poetry, "No hard feeling remains."

"But you didn't even phone me."

"I asked, 'What is Baktash's real name?'"

"Morad Pakdel."

"How do you know him?"

Hasti explained that they were studying in the university at the same time, and that he is a friend of Shahin's, and . . .

"So, what's the message?"

"Morad and Morteza have sent a message that the Day Zero operation has been exposed. Stop tomorrow's action."

"Where are they themselves?"

"I don't know exactly; in a house in the vicinity of Ferdowsi Square."

"Let's go to the peacemaking ceremony and tell Aqa Sheikh Sa'id."

On the way to Sahand's shack, Salim explained that the three of them had been in the shantytown when one of the Persian speakers had said that Baktash's fiancée, who he thought was Farzaneh, had come and taken both Hadi, whose leg was broken, and Morad, who was sick, to the hospital . . . Probably Morad had recovered and had warned Shahin Khan . . . Hasti thought, *Who said that he had warned Shahin*?

They approached Sahand's shack, with Leopard Abbas, Sahand, and Haji Ma'sum behind them. Haji Ma'sum and Leopard Abbas knelt, sat back on their heels, and placed their hands on their knees next to several other men sitting the same way. Sahand joined other men who were sitting on the floor in the same position; young and old, strong and weak, they didn't know what to do with their hands. Aqa Sheikh Sa'id was sitting cross-legged at the end of the room, his back toward Salim and Hasti, who were standing by the door. Sahand's shack had a carpet, and a plate of candies had been left in the middle of the carpeted floor. On the white walls, several pictures of a Seyyed the likes of which Hasti had seen in Fatemeh Sabzevari's shack . . . some of them black and white and one in color.

Fazlollah entered holding the bouquet of plastic roses that had been washed, and he offered it to Salim. Salim said, "Put it next to the plate of candies." Fazlollah put down the bouquet and left.

"Allegiance to the Prophet . . . ," Aqa Sheikh Sa'id said. "God of the universe gives revelations to the prophets, and they announce them to the people . . . Shake each other's hands today, and tomorrow demolish the house of tyranny over the heads of the tyrants. God of the universe, God of genies and humans, says, 'O those who will drink the nectar of martyrdom tomorrow in order to meet God . . . '"

At Aqa Sheikh Sa'id's request, everyone said loudly, "Peace be upon the Prophet," and the men stood up. First, Leopard Abbas and Sahand shook hands. Then each put his right hand to his lips and then to his forehead in a gesture of respect. The other men and Haji Ma'sum did the same. Haji Ma'sum offered the candies to everyone. The plastic roses had been stepped on.

When the men had left, Salim whispered something in Aqa Sheikh Sa'id's ears, and he came toward Hasti. He had his head down and prayer beads in his hand. He looked fatter than he had the day of the street narration. Hasti repeated what she had told Salim.

Aqa Sheikh Sa'id responded, "The blood of the martyrs is boiling and summoning the blood of others."

"But," Salim said, "our friends' lives are in danger. If the people move tomorrow, this danger will threaten many lives, even your own."

"So be it."

"But wasn't it agreed that the clergy and the intellectuals would work hand in hand . . . ?"

"It's too late," Aqa Sheikh Sa'id said. "We'll stay here tonight, recite many prayers together, and ask Our Glorious Master to . . . We'll pass all of them under the Quran."

"If everyone prays until morning, they won't have the energy to attack on the street. It was Baktash, Morteza, and Hadi who taught them not to bend to anyone and not to lower their heads in subservience—that they are no less than anyone else."

"This is the command of God, the Magnificent, and I, the lowly servant of God, obey the orders of My Glorious Master."

"Aqa Sheikh, have you forgotten what these three people have done in the last few weeks for the people of this shantytown? They found them jobs, gave them electricity, improved their economic status . . ."

"These are worldly matters, not those of the afterlife."

"But one of them has broken his leg working for these people, and the other has become sick . . ."

Aqa Sheikh Sa'id thought and said, "If you don't want to come, don't come."

Later, when Aqa Sheikh Sa'id was executed in prison, Salim remembered him clearly, saying that in one of their conversations he had spoken about the beliefs of the masses, and how far those very beliefs had taken the barefoot Arabs! But Morad considered the strike of the textile-factory workers the turning point in the struggles of the ill-fated people of Iran. And as always, Hasti couldn't decide which one was right!

Salim told Hasti to wait at the street corner until he brought the car that he had parked by the clinic.

Before reaching the bare land in front of the shacks, Hasti heard the women shouting, “Hey, Aqa Bak’s fiancée! Hey!” The women ran and reached her, and the children followed. Hasti felt sick to her stomach. But she didn’t budge. The women had tied their chadors at their waists, crossed the ends, and knotted them behind their necks; some had clubs in their hands, and some bricks . . .

“Aqa Bak’s fiancée,” Fatemeh Sabzevari said, “is Haji Ma‘sum telling the truth?”

“What is he saying?”

“He’s saying that your fiancé has been arrested and everyone has been exposed.”

“Yes.”

“You walk ahead, and we’ll follow you. We shouldn’t waste time.”

“But the operation is tomorrow,” Hasti said. “You must listen to the cleric.”

One woman stepped out from the crowd and screamed, “Street or no street, he must tell us today what to do. We’re fed up!” It was not clear from where Aqa Sheikh Sa‘id appeared. He faced the women and said, “Tonight is the night that we pray. Tomorrow, with God Almighty’s help . . .”

Salim opened the front door of the car for Hasti. Then he sat behind the wheel and started off. As he made a U-turn, he asked, “Other than the few people we met, did anyone else see you?”

“All the women and children of the shantytown saw me, and I was so scared!”

“Of what?”

“Of the wrath of the proletariat who are not even proletarian.”

Salim bit his lip, and Hasti continued, “And of the fact that you too have gotten involved in political activity.”

“For now, I am the liaison between the clerics and the intellectuals.”

When they arrived at Jaleh Crossroads, Hasti suggested that they go have lunch together at the Plan Organization cafeteria. Salim replied that there was still a lot of time until noon.

"Then you can come to my office to have coffee and rest," Hasti said. "After that, I'll take you to show you the ministry's handicraft workshops. And now that there are no hard feelings between us, 'We will mend the garb rent by separation from the beloved.'"

Salim agreed, but he didn't seem to notice the poem that Hasti had turned into prose. "If need be," he said, "Morad can come to our place to hide."

At Hasti's office, Fakhri was introduced to Salim. Fakhri extended her hand, but Salim didn't shake it, and Fakhri pouted. She went to her own room, and the tick-ticking of the typewriter . . . The servant brought Turkish coffee. Hasti had not sat at her desk, but rather on the chair beside the armchair in which Salim was sitting. She was busy scheming: how could she fix herself in Salim's heart again? Salim stood and put the empty cup on the table. He paced the room, squeezing his reddish-brown beard in his fist. It was as though he was no longer present in Hasti's office. His eyes weren't magical anymore. Even light didn't move in his eyes because, just like his mother, he was squinting.

"Is your back aching again?" Hasti asked.

Salim ignored the question. "Tell Shahin Khan to go visit Morad. If he needs to change his place, call me and tell me, 'The button collection has arrived from India.' I'll go with Shahin Khan to pick him up."

Hasti said to herself, *Shahin Khan. Shahin Khan. Shahin who has received his BA, presented himself for his mandatory military duty . . . now at officer's training. "Forward, march! Halt! Left face. Right face. Present arms. Order arms . . ." No, he is out of it. Let him march.*

Salim sat at Hasti's desk and begged her, "Hasti Khanom, for God's sake, don't get involved."

"I heard you when you said that politics is ephemeral and that what will most likely endure is art."

"But you came today."

"Today I was a messenger. I have sworn on the Quran to step aside."

And in her heart, she said, *If only Morad lets me . . . although it's my own fault, especially now that Farzaneh has become a nightmare for me.* She was surprised that Salim paid no attention to her swearing on the Quran, no more than he had to the poem that she had turned into prose.

Salim asked permission to make a few calls. Hasti stood up and dialed zero to get an outside line. “The telephone isn’t tapped, is it?” Salim asked.

“What is a tapped telephone?”

“I mean, no one is recording the telephone calls, right?”

“No way. This is a government ministry. Also, the minister is a son-in-law of the shah, and his ministership is eternal.”

“Nothing is eternal.”

Salim dialed.

“Tell your guest to come to the phone.”

. . .

“Puria.”

. . .

Salim made the guest understand that he will pick him up at night and that it is necessary . . . What if this guest is Farhad Dorafshan? What if he reveals that Morad’s fiancée—in the eyes of the residents of the shantytown—is none other than Hasti? And that Hasti has taken him to the hospital . . . ? *Whatever will be, let it be. Is it in my hands*?

Salim dialed again.

“Taji, ask my mother to come to the phone.”

Long silence . . . *While that mountain of flesh moves.*

“Hello, Mother dear. How’s your heart?”

. . .

“Mother dear, don’t wait for me for lunch. Tell Taji to clean the fountain room and arrange a bed . . . I have a guest today.”

. . .

“Yes, that’s him.”

. . .

“Why should you be worried, Mother dear? I’ll have lunch with Hasti Khanom. Would you like to speak to Hasti Khanom?”

Hasti sent her regards. She even said, “I kiss your hand, Mrs. Farrokhi.” *How much buttering up*? she thought. *Changing the poem to prose. Offering to mend the clothes that are rent from separation from the beloved. How far can one go*?

Salim held his head in his hands, lowered it, then raised it and leaned on the arm of the chair. Then he closed his eyes, his hands on the arms of the chair.

Hasti knew that he was resorting to the "meditation" to which he had taken refuge from his back pain in Hasti's house one night. He had told Hasti, "In your view, I was spacing out."

Hasti sat at her desk and started to draw his profile. The image that had imposed itself on Hasti's mind was Salim with closed eyes and extended arms picking the one and only bergamot orange of a huge tree. The monster was also sleeping beneath the tree.

To draw Salim's hands, she tiptoed toward him. Long pink nails—she was tempted to kiss his nails. But Salim's peace with respect to the earth and the heavens would have been disturbed. When Salim came out of that state, Hasti asked, "You didn't bring me a bouquet of flowers?"

"No, bergamot girl."

Hasti sat next to Salim. "That's strange. I was just drawing the image of a bergamot orange."

"The bergamot orange on top of your heater has probably dried out."

"No, it hasn't. I let Grandmother make jam with it, so that one night when you come . . ."

"It didn't say, 'Ouch!'?" Salim thought and continued, "Hasti, I'm frightened, too."

"What are *you* afraid of?"

"I'm afraid of not understanding Iran's situation correctly."

"No one does. It seems like Iran is a soccer ball that anyone who arrives, kicks. They don't let it get close to the goal."

"And how many intellectuals are there?" Salim continued. "Five hundred thousand? A million?"

"And what's worse, most of them are no more than Don Quixotes. Don Quixotes of the Third World." Hasti didn't know from whom she had stolen this expression. From Hamid Enayat? From Simin . . . ? Or perhaps Bijan Ganjur had said it.

"And yet the government's crackdown is directed more toward the intellectuals and the leftists, who don't know where they stand with

God . . ." Again, he took his head in his hands and moaned, "They will burn this house down."

"Perhaps they will build a better house."

He paced the floor and asked, "Hasti Khanom, have you seen the processional mourning groups on Ashura—when they march in the streets chanting and mourning the martyrdom of Imam Hossein? Each group has a leader. The Turkish group, the bazaar group, the Arab neighborhood, Pachenar district . . . When the time comes, however, they will merge and stand behind each other like a roaring flood. The intellectuals are not united . . ."

He stood in front of Hasti and said, "In order to know a nation, one should see who they respect."

No, Salim was not a Don Quixote. But at what conclusion had he arrived? The conclusion that he has become part of the essence of existence.

Both were silent until Hasti couldn't take it anymore. "Isn't it dangerous that you give refuge to dissidents in your house?" she asked.

"Not really. No one has noticed that I am in Tehran. In addition, my father . . . Hasti Khanom, why should I hide it from you? After supporting Mosaddeq and being disappointed by politics, my father became nothing but a button merchant, a womanizer, and a dependent of the royal court. O God, what can I say? My heart is breaking."

On the way to the ministry's handicraft workshops, Salim poured out his heart to Hasti. It was Mr. Farrokhi who had imported from England all the beads, pearls, and women's dress ornaments for the celebration of 2,500 years of monarchy and for the coronation festivals. "I used to pursue the orders myself," he said. "I would ask, 'What are all these beads and spangles and ornaments for?' My father would tell me on the phone, 'It's none of your business.' And now he has won the bid for the royal army buttons."

"The army buttons?"

"They want to change the buttons of the officers' and soldiers' uniforms. They think everything else is perfect, and that now they have only this one thing left to fix!"

When they arrived at the inlay workshop, a tour leader in front and the tourists behind him were all coming out of the building. Old, young, beardless, bearded, women, men, with cameras around their necks, without cameras. An old woman was asking the tour leader, "How much is three thousand tomans per month in dollars?"

The tour leader didn't know.

"Four hundred something," Salim said.

The old woman was surprised. "Despite all this delicate work?"

They went to the carpet workshop. A Bahadori-design carpet was half finished. Two women wearing the regional clothes of Kermanshah and Qasemabad were sitting at the loom tying knots. The plan caller was singing out, "Two red . . . three blue . . ." Colorful balls of wool were hanging over the top of the white threads as though they were paints on the palette of an artist.

The tour leader was explaining in his peculiar version of English that Iranians weave flower gardens as carpets and cover the floors of their rooms with them. He added that the Japanese do the same thing with flower decorations. Hasti was gazing at Salim, who seemed to be deep in thought. Did it mean that he wasn't listening?

In the pottery workshop, after the tour leader pointed to the electric kiln and said that electric kilns give a uniform heat to the pots, his words attracted Salim's attention. "God created humans from dry clay like pottery clay, and the potter imitates God's work in making pots. That is, he gives the clay shape, soul, and life so that it will be a tool in the hands of someone who himself has been created from soil and who, for prostration to God, lays his forehead on the ground."

Salim added, "And the fact that Omar Khayyam spoke so much about the potters' workshop and said that in the end we will all become clay for potters is because Nishapur—Khayyam's birthplace—has been one of the most important centers of pottery."

At the mention of Khayyam's name, there were whispers in the crowd of tourists.

The tour leader said that he would take them next to the ministry's shop to buy souvenirs. He informed them that there is a 20 percent discount for tourists. After that they would go to a traditional teahouse for Iran's national dish, *chelo kebab* . . .

Hasti said to Salim, "Why don't we go eat nontraditional food?" She recited a line by Khayyam: "'The outcome of the potters' workshop is not only this,' O Salim Khan."

Look who was giving courage to whom!

The Plan Organization cafeteria was quiet. There was no sign of the head of the harem and the pretty ladies, nor of amateur singers. Hasti's eyes fell upon Mardan Khan, who was drumming with a knife on the table. The servant brought coffee and put it in front of him. If Mardan Khan came to their table, perhaps he could help. And Mardan Khan did come. But even he behaved himself in the face of Salim's distinguished bearing. As they were shaking hands, he said that he had heard good things about Mr. Farrokhi from Mrs. Ganjur.

14

Fakhri told Hasti that Bijan Ganjur had called twice and that he had even come in person one day. He had something important to discuss with her. As Hasti's hand went toward the telephone, someone knocked on the door. At Hasti's "come in," Bijan entered. He sat in the armchair and instructed Fakhri not to let anyone disturb them.

He lit a cigarette and told Hasti, who had sat on a chair next to him, that her mother was pregnant. Hasti asked why sharing this news was so important, and Bijan said that he and Hasti together could resolve the issue. Hasti responded that it wasn't such a difficult problem—that in due time her mother would give birth.

"Listen to me," Bijan said, "and don't interrupt. Your mother is thinking of getting a divorce from my father." He added that this would hurt him and Hasti, and if they counted Parviz, then three people would be hurt. And if they counted all the people around, then . . .

Hasti finished Bijan's sentence: " . . . the number would be huge." She added, "But now that she has become pregnant in her forties, why does she want to get a divorce?"

"She has told me," Bijan replied, "that she is in love with Mardan Tavassoli and that the child is his. But she hasn't told Father that yet. She plans to put her hand on the Quran and beg him to divorce her so that she can go her own way. She'll tell him that if he doesn't divorce her, she'll write a letter to the attorney general and say that he was the cause of her suicide. She'll cut her veins in the bathtub, or eat enough opium, or put her hand on a bare electric wire."

Bijan suggested that they go together to see Mardan and convince him to dissuade Mother Eshi from placing her hopes on him. Then the two of them would go and talk with Mother Eshi. What ties are knotted together in people's lives and how hard it is to undo those knots! The emotional baggage . . .

Together they went upstairs to Mardan Tavassoli's office. The stairs were sparkling, and Bijan was comforting Hasti, saying that there are only a few problems in this world that have no solution, and that if there is no solution, one must just forget about those problems.

Murray had two secretaries, each of whom was the epitome of a certain type of beauty. The dark-skinned beauty with protruding cheekbones and dark eyes had a Latin-script typewriter and a red telephone on the desk in front of her. The blonde beauty with long straight hair, an intercom machine and a Persian-script typewriter in front of her, asked Bijan if they had an appointment.

"Tell him our names; he'll see us."

"Please have a seat. He's in a meeting now."

At last, the office door of Mr. Hitti's replacement opened, and Mardan came out, along with Mr. Crossley and Sir Edward. All three greeted Bijan and Hasti, and Crossley wouldn't let go of Hasti's hand. Hasti asked Sir Edward how La'l Banu was doing. Sir Edward replied, "Come visit her one day soon. She's very lonely. I've bought her a talking parrot."

"I'll give you my German Shepherd," Crossley said.

Sir Edward complained that La'l is scared of dogs and considers them impure.

Mardan laughed loudly and said, "Edward is foreign and impure, too. He's converted to Islam, but he hasn't been circumcised. They should place him in a vat with a hole and call a penis-trimming doctor who specializes in bloodless circumcision to do it, poor him . . ."

Except for Edward, everyone laughed, even Hasti and Bijan. Hasti remembered Touran Jan's words: "If only there were a joyous circumcision party! There's nothing but funerals . . ." Hasti shifted from one foot to the other restlessly. Edward's face had turned beet red. He raised his right index finger in the air and threatened, "I won't approve your budget."

Then Crossley and Edward spoke in the same difficult language they had spoken at Hitti's farewell party. Crossley raised his voice, and Edward raised his higher, until Mardan gave up and apologized. "And if you don't approve my budget," he said, "I'll take it as a conflict of interest between British and American cousins in Iran."

A man in jeans and short sleeves came into the secretaries' room with a folder in his hand. He said hello and followed Hasti, Bijan, and Mardan into the office of the country's top educational expert. Mardan sat at his desk and asked Bijan why Ahmad hadn't come to the office for the past several days and why he had given some time off to his secretary, Hitti's former secretary, who knows all the ins and outs of their work.

The man stood by the desk. He took a passport and several plane tickets out of the folder, laid them in front of Mardan, and said that he had gotten PanAm tickets. Boeing 707, flight 143. He asked if he should telegraph Mardan's mother-in-law, and Mardan replied, "Next weekend."

"Then may I be excused, sir?" the man asked.

And Mardan replied, "Go, my man."

"So how is it," Mardan asked, "that you have come to visit humble me? Perhaps you want me to be a witness to your marriage." He added that he had considered Bijan for Hasti . . . and that, that boy—Morad Pakdel—is no good for her. He seemed like an ill-fated person to him . . . "And despite all Eshi's compliments, Salim Farrokhi acts as if everyone owes him—such a *gentleman* . . . He has frightening eyes." Mardan rang, and the servant appeared instantly.

"Turkish coffee? Tea? Nescafé?" Mardan asked.

"Nescafé."

Hasti was staring at the tickets on the desk and thinking. *Perhaps he wants to be rid of Peggy and the children.* For one moment she thought, *Maybe it is serious and he wants to marry Mother Eshi, and in that case, there would be no need for their interference.* But at the bottom of her heart, she knew that there would be no marriage and that becoming the country's top expert in educational affairs was the result of having an American wife. As Hasti was picking up the cup of Nescafé, she asked Mardan to order that no one disturb them. Pressing a button on a machine that looked like the machine in front of the blonde girl and hearing a pleasant voice that said, "Yes, sir?" he issued the order.

"Sir," Hasti said, "please leave my mother alone. You'll just have one fewer in your harem."

Mardan laughed. "Let her enjoy her life for a little while."

"Are you prepared to marry my mother?"

"What are you talking about? If I like a woman, I don't need to marry her. I like many women, so as you said, should I assemble a harem?"

"Eshrat Khanom," Bijan said, "has interpreted your liking her as love. She's waiting for you to propose to her."

"You're kidding. There were never any words of that sort between us."

Mardan opened the inlaid box on his desk, and the box started playing a happy tune. He put a cigarette between his lips and fiddled with the lighter until it gave off a flame. He took a puff. He took several puffs. He put the cigarette in the crystal ashtray so that it would smoke away, and he caressed his thin mustache.

Those unfortunate ones cut themselves off from any kind of joy, even from love. They consider a romantic relationship forbidden, even though they are only trial members . . . I shouldn't be jealous of Farzaneh . . . Sit for five hours cleaning guns. Exchange books and guns. Exercise. Climb mountains. Go to Palestine or the outskirts of Nishapur . . .

Mardan's voice brought her back. "What are you thinking about?"

"So that they can do something for these people."

"Hasti," Bijan asked, "what are you talking about?"

Hasti was startled. *That's how one comes to hallucinate, becomes stricken by nightmares . . .*

Bijan asked, "Are you feeling okay?"

"Yes, of course."

Hasti turned to Mardan and said, "My mother is pregnant and she says the child is yours."

"She knows well that it's not."

"So, you admit that you have had an affair with her?"

"Didn't you know?"

"Where did you see each other?" Bijan asked.

Mardan laughed loudly. "I'll give you the address. You can go there to have sex. A four-bedroom apartment on Vila Street. The apartment is free in the morning. Although Dr. . . ."

"Dr. Bahari?" Hasti asked.

"Hasti and I are like brother and sister," Bijan said, "and we are not into this kind of indecency."

"You mean *we* are into indecency, and you are better than us? No, my dear, you too take Pasita to Erect Hill. I saw you myself."

"Stop it!" Hasti shouted. "Stop reciting your conquests. Tell my mother. Make her understand that you don't intend to marry her. Tell her that it's not your baby. Do something!"

"Something decisive," Bijan added. "Call her now, right here in front of us."

"Who do you think you are? How dare you boss me around?"

"'A newly arrived youth from the States.'"

Hasti felt like she was about to throw up . . . *Get ahold of yourself, girl.*

Mardan pressed the button on the intercom, and the pleasant voice said, "Yes, sir?" Mardan ordered her to dial Ahmad Ganjur's number and ask for Mrs. Ganjur.

Why wasn't the phone ringing? Why was Mardan rearranging the stuff on his desk?"

The phone rang. "Eshi dear, hello! Did I wake you from a sweet afternoon nap?" He continued giving compliments and calling her darling . . .

Hasti couldn't hear what her mother was saying to know the reason for these compliments, and she waited until Mardan said, "I've heard that you're pregnant."

. . .

"Well, I have a sixth sense!"

. . .

"Stop this nonsense, Eshrat dear. You know yourself that's not true. Stay and live your life with Ahmad and give birth to his child."

. . .

Mardan was listening and sucking on his upper lip. "I never made such a promise to you. Get this thought completely out of your mind. It's impossible! I have three children from Peggy. I have no intention of ruining my life. Do you understand?"

. . .

"Seduction is two-sided: the seducer and the seduced."

. . .

"Write a letter to whomever you want, woman. To the American ambassador, even to the American president."

. . .

"Stop talking about suicide. I have taught you to enjoy your life. So enjoy it!"

. . .

"Are you crazy? I never promised anything to you. From the very beginning, I defined the extent of our relationship. When the bird is free and the arrow at hand, who wouldn't take a shot?"

. . .

"Stop crying. If you want to tell Peggy, go ahead. I have defined the extent of my relationship with her, too. Peggy will leave for America with the kids. You want to destroy two families, but you will get nowhere. Mark my words."

. . .

"Forget about me, woman. You told me from the beginning that you would not intrude on my life."

He hung up without saying good-bye. He took a cigarette from the inlaid box on the desk and fiddled with his lighter. The lighter wouldn't spark. Bijan stood up and struck a match for him.

"You two go and talk some sense into her."

Hasti stood up, hoisted her bag onto her shoulder, and said, "You are not innocent, either. But why with my mother? You have two beautiful young secretaries."

Mardan didn't answer their good-bye, and he didn't move from where he was sitting. Hasti and Bijan hurried down the stairs. Hasti's legs were shaking.

Together they went to Bijan's office. A man with salt-and-pepper hair was sitting in one of the armchairs in the middle of the room. Hasti and Bijan sat on either side of him.

"Did you read the book?" the man asked.

"I don't have time to read books. Our reviewers have reported that the book is about the Mosaddeq era and the royal court—that it has nothing to do with the Sufi sect of Hurufism and the Safavid era."

"Mr. Ganjur, the author is dead."

"But there are many living readers."

"You've gone too far. Using even ordinary words is forbidden. In your opinion, *night* means 'repression.' *Morning* means 'the dawn of the revolution.' *Forest* means 'the center of opposition.' You don't give publication permission to books that raise awareness, but you do for any nonsensical book laid in front of you . . . *The Nobles, Twist, Make Me Hot.* With this approach, this nation will never, ever attain social and political awareness."

"Actually, I agree with you. But the things that you have just said can get you imprisoned. Don't talk this way any place else."

"If you are such a democrat, why are you sitting at this desk?"

When the man had left, Hasti said, "Bijan, leave this job."

"This job is my father's wish. He says, 'If you don't do it, someone else will.'"

"But wasn't it you who said, 'Don't sell yourself to any school of thought'? Now you are defending a flawed ideology. And I wanted to get publication permission for Sa'edi's *Place of Murder*!"

"You work in the same ministry, don't you?"

Hasti had no answer to that.

"For now," Bijan continued, "let's solve the situation with your mother. Perhaps this way I can say that I have paid my dues to my father . . . Then I will think about doing something about my own life."

Hasti sat at Bijan's desk and called her home. Why wasn't Touran Jan answering? Was her leg aching? Had she gone to see Brigadier General or Teimur Khan?

Finally, Grandmother answered, and Hasti told her that she was going to her mother's house and that her mother was very ill.

Touran Jan asked, "What's wrong with her?" but it sounded like "What the hell is wrong with her?"

"I wish I knew."

Hasti was thinking that she needed to do something about her life, too.

Bijan knocked on the gate of his father's house. Again. Several times. It seemed like there was no one home. Where had all those people gone?

Parviz comes home from Tehran American School at 3:00 p.m., and they never leave him alone in the house. It was not Sunday, when Pasita spends her time off with boys from her country. What had happened? Bijan fixed his feet on the metal gate's protruding decorations and pulled himself up to the top. Hasti heard his feet as he landed after jumping down. The gate opened and Bijan brought the car in. Hasti walked in. The pool, empty; the cement wall, cracked, chipped, swollen; trees whose leaves had been burnt in many places. She was saddened by the flowerless garden.

The battlefield: Mother Eshi was sitting on the floor in a corner of the family room. Her collar was torn, there was a Quran in front of her, and she was screaming nonstop. Pasita was rubbing the back of her neck and her shoulders: "Now, now. Relax." Ahmad Ganjur was holding his head in his hands and howling. He was yelling. He was braying. He was raising his head and shouting, "All bluster and bluff!"

Parviz was sitting on the family room sofa crying. Naneh Agha was holding a glass and imploring Parviz to take a sip for sake of his brother. "It's willow extract water and rock candy." The Afghan cook and Taqi Khan were standing side by side. Both astonished. Lady was there too, holding up her tail.

Mother Eshi's eyes were on fire. Her face and bare upper chest were red. Her dress was red, too. "I said," she shouted, "'Divorce me!' If not, I'll write a letter to the minister saying that you are responsible for my suicide."

Pasita was saying, "Now take it easy. Relax."

Mother Eshi pushed Pasita away and resumed yelling. "Leave me alone!"

Hasti went toward Parviz. She hugged him and kissed his tears. "Get up and go to the garden and play with Lady."

"All of you," Bijan commanded, "except mother and father, leave and go about your work." He told Pasita, "And you, take Parviz to the garden."

Naneh Agha took the willow extract water to Ahmad Ganjur and told him to take a sip for Bijan Aqa's sake. She complained about Bijan, that he had left the master in this state and gone.

Ahmad Ganjur took the glass from Naneh Agha and drank it to the bottom.

"Shamelessness to this degree? Woman, what did you lack in life that you brought this disaster on yourself and on me?"

Mother Eshi stopped yelling. "I just felt like it."

Pasita was telling Parviz in English, "Get up, my dear."

Parviz wasn't moving. "I want to stay with Papa Ganjur."

And because Pasita was trying to pick him up, he started thrashing and kicking.

"Get up, my dear boy," Ahmad Ganjur said. "Get up and go with Pasita. I'll buy you a prettier fish than that one."

Parviz took Lady in his arms, pouted, and said, "Bad kitty. Did you eat the pretty fish? I'm not speaking with you."

When the leavers had left, Ahmad Ganjur rose, pulled up his pajama bottoms, and sat on the divan. He bent his head down and started crying. Hasti noticed that Bijan had tears in his eyes, too. Bijan sat next to his father, held his hand, and said, "Father, Mother Eshi is lying. It's not Mardan's baby."

Ahmad Ganjur raised his head. "How do you know?"

"I know. Let the four of us sit together and solve this problem without yelling and shouting and crying."

He took Mother Eshi's hand and pulled so that she would rise from the floor. Mother Eshi didn't yield. "Can't one solve problems sitting on the floor?"

Bijan began. "Hasti and I went to Mardan's office this afternoon."

"That was way out of line!" Mother Eshi shouted. The veins in her neck bulged.

Bijan seemed calm. "I'm not frightened by your shouting. On the phone, Mardan told you . . ."

Ahmad Ganjur moaned. "I caused myself to be cuckolded. O woman, I gave you free rein, and you spit in my face."

He stood up, went toward his wife, and spat at her. Eshrat wiped the spittle off her face. "The hell with you," she said.

Suddenly both had become old, angry, full of hatred, and sworn enemies of one another.

"I'll fix that Mardan," Mother Eshi said. "I'll go to Peggy and tell her that they have rented a four-bedroom apartment and . . ."

As if he hadn't made all that fuss, hadn't yelled and howled, and at the end, even spat, Ahmad Ganjur said, "Do you mean the apartment on Vila Street? I rented it for them. Their houses were far away. It's for resting . . ."

"Yeah, right . . . I bet if Peggy goes to America, she will never come back."

"Mother, why do you want to ruin the lives of two families? Settle down and live your own life."

Bijan emphasized that it should be a life without such indecency and asked why one should expose oneself to contempt.

Mother Eshi became enraged again. "You shut up! Do you think I don't know that you take Pasita to Erect Hill?"

Bijan turned red. "For now, we are not discussing the matter of *my* life. I believe you two can live together peacefully, as in the past." Then he turned to his father and continued, "And you, Father, forget what has happened."

Eshrat hit the ceiling. "There's no way I'm going to live with Ahmad! I'll give up my marriage portion for a divorce and free my soul."

"Mother, where will you go?"

"To the Hilton Hotel."

"With what money?"

"It serves Ahmad right to have to pay for it. Isn't he saying that he loves me?"

"I'm not paying a cent."

"Then I'll go to the holy shrine of Shah Abdol Azim and take refuge there. And I won't eat anything until I die. I'll go become a servant at Imam Reza Shrine. I'm not staying in this baboon's house. He's a piece of shit. Look at his ugly face."

Ahmad Ganjur jumped up without pulling up his pajama bottoms, set upon Mother Eshi, and started hitting her. Hasti made herself a shield in front of her mother, and Bijan grabbed his father's hands.

Hasti insisted on taking her mother to the bathroom. As Mother Eshi splashed water on her face she asked, "If I come to your house, will the old woman let me in?" Hasti bit her lip. Mother Eshi continued, saying that she was willing to swear that the old woman's son was a hero and that he had been killed in the path of Mosaddeq. She was willing to say anything the old woman wanted about her son . . .

"Mother, stay right here."

What sin had the old woman committed to have to live under one roof with a woman whom she had hated for a lifetime? Although Shahin's room was empty . . .

Mother Eshi pounded on her chest and said, "I'll get my revenge on Mardan, on Ahmad, on all these ogling, greedy men."

"What revenge? It was your own choice."

"He whispered in my ear so much that love is a glorious thing, that women must break the gender barrier to become fully human. He talked so much about gender equality . . . I'm going to take a shower."

Hasti went to the bedroom. Scene of combat. Moving rapidly, she started to clean up all that had been thrown. Her mind was working as fast as her hands and feet. She gathered all the cassettes and put them in the cassette case . . . *Breaking the gender barrier, not for someone who is married and committed. This wantonness does not befit us . . . In the breaking of the barrier, one must be careful not to destroy a home . . . a nest . . .* She picked up the pillows from the floor and put them in their places . . . *She has told me many times, "You are so out of date. You haven't been able to trap a weakling like Morad. You haven't been able to tame Salim."* She threw the blue velvet blanket on the bed and spread the coverlet over it. She climbed on the dressing table and tried to put the curtain back on its rod. With all those bobbles and tassels, the curtain was heavy. She changed her mind, folded the curtains, and put them in the corner of the room. Then she went toward the tape recorder . . . *I prefer dignity. Without "needs." I'll compose my poetry. I'll paint. This is a kind of transcendence. She doesn't understand. She says the human body is not without needs. What shall I do? . . .* She picked the tape recorder up off the floor. It was broken. It couldn't be fixed. She put it on the curtains. She picked up the radio. That was destroyed, too.

At the bottom of my heart, I don't want to be confined by a husband. At the right time, I'll break it off. I myself don't understand what I am doing. Perhaps I'm lying to myself, too. Must everyone get married? Suppressed complexes? Why suppressed? Harnessed. Transcended is right. I just like the word transcendence . . . She straightened her back. She felt very, very happy.

She went to the kitchen and brought a cloth to clean the dressing table. Her mother entered wearing a terrycloth bathrobe and threw the red nightgown on the bed. She sat at the dressing table and put cream on her face. She took out a double-chin straightener from the drawer and rolled it under her chin. Hasti found the sewing kit and started mending the torn collar.

So what if I feel lost? Who is not? The earth is lost. I am one of the inhabitants of earth, too. A poem . . .

Mother Eshi's voice didn't let her think about her poem. "I myself saw Ahmad in Pasita's room. I heard their laughter. Both naked. They didn't even realize that I had opened the door."

Gender equality . . . Because Ahmad was with Pasita . . . Mother followed suit . . .

"Are you listening?"

Hasti looked at her mother, who was powdering her face. Then lipstick. She pressed her lips together. She evened out the lipstick with her finger . . . *How hard should one work to break the gender barrier?*

Mother took a thin, blue cotton dress out of the closet. "I talked to Pasita. I told her that I would ask Dr. Bahari to find a midwifery job for her in the hospital."

Hasti had finished with the sewing, but the poem in her mind had remained unfinished. She searched for it and found it . . . A poem about the earth being lost. *My first poem was by three people . . . My second poem by two or three people . . . I didn't ever compose the poem about the seminar of the fish. I fell into the abyss of Morad's illness . . . I'll compose this one by myself. Helen Hitti is gone, and La'l Banu has a talking parrot. Can't I trust myself?*

Mother was brushing her hair. The hair that Farhad, Tehran's most sought-after hairdresser, had given waves and curls. A lady had even bought a sports car for Farhad; she had given Farhad the gold-chained key to the car as a New Year's gift . . .

Mother gathered her hair behind her head and bound it with a large, golden clip. She shuffled through the drawers in search of nail polish.

"That bitch Pasita looked me in the eye and said, 'I won't leave this house unless the master fires me. If I do midwifery at the hospital, I'll have to pay all my salary to rent a room and for food and clothes . . . '"

Mother Eshi was painting the nails of her right hand, and Hasti was watching her . . . She was so disgusted by her that it felt like she wasn't the one who gave birth to her, but rather a stranger. *Such emotional detachment. Morteza had talked about emotional detachment. The same night that he had stayed for dinner and made the cutlets himself. What tasty cutlets*! For the hundredth time, Touran Jan had recited her story and talked about her son's martyrdom.

"That day in front of the Parliament building," Morteza had said, "I believe two people were shot and both accidentally . . . Mosaddeq's supporters had taken Mosaddeq to an antique store near Shahabad Avenue. Someone by the name of Reza peeked out from the antique store and was shot. And there was someone by the name of Khajeh Nuri who had gone onto a rooftop to watch, and he was shot . . . It must have been another day. It was on Ekbatan Street . . ."

Mother Eshi held her hands in front of her eyes and said, "The only nail polish that goes with a blue dress is pearl white. Isn't that so, Hasti?

"Yes," slipped off Hasti's tongue.

"Mardan loves pearl white nail polish."

Morteza had said, "Mosaddeq took advantage of the conflict of interest in Iran between America and Britain; unfortunately, he failed. Now we must take advantage of the same conflict."

Hasti smiled to herself. Mardan had also talked about a quarrel between the cousins over the conflict of their interests . . .

"Thank God you smiled. You know that I will deal with both Mardan and Ahmad . . ."

"If only we could be captured and taken to a different land." Who had said this? A land without forbidden words. A land where the wantonness of mother, mother's husband, Pasita, and Mardan are not dumped on a person. A land that has no Erect Hill. If Peggy were to tell Mardan, "You jerk, I'm pregnant by another man," what would Mardan do? A land free from this and that conflict of interests . . .

Mother stood in front of her. "Do I look good?"

On their way to the family room, Mother Eshi said, "Pasita is right. Her salary is a hundred dollars a month, which Ahmad Ganjur transfers to her family in the Philippines. But her income with tips and other things comes to two hundred dollars."

In the family room, Parviz was sitting on his father's knees and had Lady on his own knees. Father and son were staring at the television, which was broadcasting commercials. A woman was dancing with a tissue in her hand and singing, "Look ladies! Look gents! *My* tissue is Silk tissue! . . ." Then a commercial for Snow laundry powder . . . And now a show. A man intoned in a sad voice, "*Days of our Lives.*" Hasti's mind was heavy with life's load, and Ahmad Ganjur said, "Days of our Lies . . ."

Hasti asked Parviz, "Which of your fish did Lady eat?"

"The black-and-red striped one."

"But the fish are in the aquarium."

Parviz was about to cry. "It wasn't feeling well. The fish doctor put it in a bowl of water. Lady caught it, took it away, and ate it."

Mother Eshi sat by the phone and dialed.

"Hello, Mehri Khanom. Is Peggy home?"

Mother Eshi asked for a time with Peggy and agreed to be there at 10:00 a.m. the next day, by telephone taxi.

. . .

"Ahmad's driver can go to hell!"

"Khanom Jan," Bijan said, "even if you do something so that Peggy doesn't return from America, Mardan said explicitly that he won't marry you. For now, the only solution for your life and my father's, in my opinion, is that you live apart for a while and try to forget the past. My father is willing to make this sacrifice. Together, you can have an honorable life . . ."

"Now you're talking out of place again. I know what's bothering you. You're scared that the disgrace of your father's life will catch up with you . . . You're afraid that they will not allow Hayedeh to marry you."

And Hasti was thinking, *No matter which part you fix, another part is broken.*

15

In any incident, all the people around feel some blame. Even Touran Jan felt at fault, however little she was in the picture. Hasti had been silent about the main disaster, nor had BBC broadcast the news, and even if it had, they didn't have a radio. Asadollah Khan, Brigadier General's orderly, would bring the radio to the front of the house, and the neighborhood council would analyze and interpret the news. Some of them would nod, saying that it is all the fault of the British, and some would set their watches by Big Ben's clock.

Hasti had told Touran Jan that her mother was hospitalized and that several doctors were watching over her. Grandmother had asked what Dr. Bahari thought. Fearing that Touran Khanom's curiosity would result in exposure of the secret, Hasti teased Grandmother, saying "Grandma dear, if I'm not mistaken, you've fallen in love with Dr. Bahari."

"At this old age? Dr. Bahari is like my son, to boot . . ."

Hasti had laughed—the first day that she was able to laugh. She had laughed and asked, "Which Grandmother was it, then, that, when Dr. Bahari was coming to visit Morad, would buy the nicest-looking, finest cucumbers from Mohsen Run and put them in front of Dr. Bahari? Who would steep the best tea in the house and serve it to him? Dr. Bahari would lay his finger on Grandmother's hand and wipe imaginary sweat from his forehead, meaning that you are embarrassing me with your kindness . . . Which Grandmother was it who wore her newest chador? And washed her face so very clean?"

"Dr. Bahari is familiar with people's suffering."

When Mother Eshi sank into the earth like a drop of water and disappeared into Tehran's population of millions, everyone was worried, and the smile disappeared from Hasti's lips. In Touran Jan's words, Hasti's face had become narrow and her color pale. It was several days that her period was late. A deeper alarm was set off in Hasti by what Naneh Agha had said on the phone.

"Where *is* this Mother Eshi that I may go and kiss her hands and feet and tell her, 'See how many people you have drawn down with yourself?' My dear Hasti Khanom, if only you knew what kind of life we are living. May neither Muslims not infidels ever experience such hardship. Master doesn't touch food. Parviz Aqa has become as thin as a rail. We held several birthday parties for him this month. Master invited all his classmates. Birthday cake, ice cream. After the kids had made a big mess, Master told Parviz, 'Open the gifts and say "Thank you. Bring better gifts next time . . ."' He opened the gifts, but said, 'Next time, bring Mother Eshi' and started to cry."

The lengthy list of Naneh Agha's heartaches had just begun, and Hasti wasn't listening, until she asked, "My dear Hasti Khanom, has she really killed herself?"

In any disaster, the first rumor is a snowball that, by the time it rolls from the mountain peak down into the valley, will have turned into an avalanche. Now everyone was distraught about Mother Eshi. *Through her suicide*, Hasti thought, *she has taken revenge on everyone, even on me, because she saw the disgust in my eyes.*

Hasti told Touran Jan, "My mother is very ill," and Touran Jan's heart also ached, so much so that she decided to make halva for those deceased who have no one to pray for them and to take it to the shrine of Imamzadeh Saleh on Thursday night, in Mohsen Run's minivan. She would ask someone to recite the stories of Her Holiness Zeinab and Her Holiness Fatemeh, enumerating their exemplary qualities and their tragic fates, so that she could weep her fill and ask for God's forgiveness. She feared that her sunset curses, when she bared her head . . . and her harsh and coarse insults had caused her former daughter-in-law to be in this position. Who knows? Perhaps when she was cursing, the bird of prayers was flying nearby and had uttered, "Amen."

Touran Jan was worried about Hasti, who couldn't sleep at night, and if she did sleep, would have nightmares and suddenly wake up. Perhaps Eshrat was on the verge of death.

"Hasti, my child, go to your Simin Khanom and stay the night there."

"What will you do all alone?"

"I'll ask Mohsen Run to come and sleep in Shahin's room."

Hasti picked up the phone. An unfamiliar voice said, "Siman Khanom's house." As soon as Hasti found out from the idle talk of her addressee that Simin was home, she kissed Touran Jan's white hair and set off. Simin opened the door herself. When she saw Hasti, she said, "I've been looking everywhere for you."

Hasti came to the living room. A fire was burning in the fireplace. The phonograph was on, and the sitar music of Ravi Shankar was playing. Simin had a cigarette between her lips. She threw a log in the fireplace and fiddled with the fire. "I'm preparing Leila's trousseau. I've seen some old armchairs and straight chairs in the haunted secondhand shop at Hasanabad Crossroads. The arms are carved. The table's carved, too. We'll repair them to your taste." She threw her cigarette in the fireplace. "I think we had better get the covers for the dining room chairs in blue silk, because her husband is in the navy. I commission you to do a painting with the sea and a ship, too."

Hasti didn't say a word. Their thoughts were so far apart! Wedding, trousseau, haunted shop, antique furniture, carving, a painting with the sea and a boat, Ravi Shankar's sitar music, and the fireplace. Why didn't Simin understand? Why did she fiddle with the fireplace so much and not even look at Hasti? Why did she stand by the fireplace, put her hand on the mantle piece, and talk about mountains?

"Have you seen the mountains?" she asked. "The white lace of a bride covers them. I love Tajrish because I can see the mountains up close. I can climb them. My feet are in touch with the rocks and pebbles. My feet are ascending. The rocks are welcoming and stable. But they seem to merge into one. Like marriage."

Hasti was thinking that Simin is getting old and has become too talkative. She wouldn't let Tajrish go, saying that it was as though the neighborhood were sleeping at the foot of the mountains. Of the bareness of the mountains in the summer, of the changing of their colors, colors that no one has given a name to . . .

Simin turned on the lights of the living room, and just then she noticed Hasti's pale face. Hasti was waiting for that sign to start crying. Simin turned off the phonograph. Naneh Fatemeh brought tea. Simin peeled a tangerine for Hasti. And Hasti explained everything, sometimes while crying and sometimes with a lump in her throat. Then Simin understood what she was dealing with.

"Get up, my dear, and sit next to the fireplace," she said. She held the box of tissues in front of Hasti, sat across from her, and said, "Look, my dear, the fact that you can cry is a good thing. It's important to know pain and suffering. Even the study of aesthetics is worthless without pain and suffering. Perhaps a day will come when we cannot cry, when we cannot laugh . . ." No, these weren't the words that would calm Hasti.

"In my experience," she said, "when everything is in shambles and one cannot bear it any longer, if one is patient and calm and uses one's energy wisely, the problems will be solved."

"If my mother has committed suicide . . ."

"Then you will face a big problem. Again, you must be patient so that the passage of time will make you forget. But from what you have said about your mother, she loves life. Such a person would not commit suicide. The threat she has made and causing herself to disappear are a kind of request for forgiveness and an attempt to make herself dearer for later. These kinds of people see life as a celebration."

Hasti was gradually becoming warm and encouraged. She took off her winter coat. She wiped her tears with a tissue and listened to Simin's voice, from which the happiness of a wedding and preparing the trousseau had disappeared. "What if they arrest Morad?" she asked. "They arrest Salim? They arrest me?"

"Well, they haven't arrested any of you yet. If they do arrest you, your minds will go to work automatically to determine what to do. And then, grace and self-control are needed." She was deep in thought. She sighed and said, "But Morad gets angry quickly, and your reactions are unpredictable." She stood up and threw more wood on the fire.

"In any case, life is not a picnic. Nor is it always a celebration. Especially if a person becomes the wife of a political activist, even more so a political activist who believes in revolutionary messianism."

Naneh Fatemeh came and drew the curtains. "Won't you eat dinner?" she asked.

"Add an extra plate," Simin said. She laughed and said to Hasti, "She's not so smart! She hasn't learned my name yet. She doesn't know how to do many things, and she doesn't *do* many things. But she is extremely kind. Tonight, you'll eat bread and kindness."

"It's the best kind of fare."

"When she wants to wake me in the morning, she comes and scratches my palm or one of my fingers. When I'm leaving the house, she entrusts me to God and recites this poem:

I'm entrusting to You my lady;
Return her to me safely.

"Do you remember Haji Ma'sumeh and what a fox she was?" Hasti did remember, but she said nothing about the present Haji Ma'sum, resident of the shantytown.

Hasti lay down on the bed in Jalal's study, the same bed in which Jalal had slept so many times. Jalal's books, the pages of which had been turned by Jalal's hand and in the margins of which he had written notes here and there throughout his short life—all are on the shelves. Photos of Jalal are on the wall opposite the bookshelves. There is also a photo of his father in clerical garb: a long black robe and a black turban. Simin had left his glasses, watch, different kinds of pens, pencils, calligraphy pens, and a Pelican ink bottle on his desk just as they were in his lifetime . . . Jalal's wedding ring was on Simin's finger; that is, Simin had two wedding rings on the ring finger of her left hand. Jalal's travel backpack with his hiking poles was in the corner of the room. The study was so filled with Jalal's belongings that it seemed as though he himself had a presence there. It seemed that until a few minutes ago he had been sitting behind his desk writing . . . His mind worked faster than his hand. He hurried when writing . . . He had gone to drink something and will be back soon.

The room was cold. In Simin's words, intensely cold, a freezer, the North Pole, Siberia. Hasti wished that she had not been shy and had taken the hot-water bottle Naneh Fatemeh had offered. She wished that she had gotten a sleeping pill from Simin, although Simin had said, "What good is sleep that has been induced by a lousy pill?"

Hasti's eyes have closed. She hears footsteps. Maybe Jalal has returned. Hasti senses that he is coming on tiptoe. He mistakes Hasti for Simin. He pulls the blanket up to her shoulders, puts his hand on her back, and sticks the blanket under her from head to toe so that there is no gap through which cold air can enter. Then it seems like Jalal kisses Hasti's forehead and her closed eyelids, but Hasti does not feel the kisses. Perhaps Simin has received the kisses herself in her bedroom. Hasti is in between dream and wakefulness. She sees Jalal standing by the bed. He looks like the portrait from his youth that is on the wall. Like he did when Hasti and Morad had seen him in Firouz Café.

"Mr. Al-e Ahmad," Hasti says, "I didn't know you were alive."

"I'm alive in this house," Jalal says. "I'm alive in your mind and that of my wife."

"And in the minds of many others," Hasti adds. Then she asks, "Is your ghost haunting this house? Is your lost spirit wandering around in this house?"

"Ghosts are a lie," Jalal says "fabricated nightmares and dreams . . ."

"Have you visited Simin?" Hasti asks.

"I'll let her go to sleep. Then I'll visit her in her dreams."

Suddenly, Hasti has an idea. "Mr. Al-e Ahmad," she says, "do you believe in revolutionary messianism?"

"At least I know that whoever believes in martyrdom is no longer lost."

Hasti feels that a body is touching her legs. What if it is actually Jalal? No, it's not Jalal. It feels like a leopard is walking on her legs, and right there it squats. Hasti screams, turns on the bedside lamp, and sits up. It's a cat. A big leopard-like cat. Its skin is a mixture of messy stripes the color of redbrick dust and dirty chalk. The cat jumps down from the bed. It extends its body and walks slowly and gently out of the study. Hasti realizes that the reason the room is so cold is that the door is open. She gets up, and, shivering, she closes the door. She hopes that her scream has not awakened Simin. No, it hasn't.

Hasti turns off the light and closes her eyes, but she cannot sleep.

It has been nearly two weeks since Jalal died. The students know that Simin will certainly come to class. The auditorium is full. There are even students sitting in the doorways. Some are standing. There are some girls in black chadors and several clerics. Simin enters dressed in black from head to toe, including a black veil on her head. Like always, she is without makeup.

She comes and stands behind the instructor's table. Morad and Hasti have put white carnations, gladioli, and tuberoses on the table. They have wound a black ribbon through the flowers, and on the ribbon, they have written in white: "In your husband's words, 'You are a flower and so is your life.'" For the seventh-day mourning ceremony for Jalal, Simin had this sentence written on the black ribbon of the flower garland that was laid on his grave. In white letters, without a signature. But everyone knows. Morad and Hasti know, too. Simin looks at the flowers and the ribbon, and then her gaze travels over all the students. Most of the boys are wearing black ties or have tied black ribbons around their arms. Most of the girls are wearing black. Hasti is in black, too.

Simin's gaze fixes on Hasti and Morad, and for a second, a short-lived smile forms on her closed lips. This smile says, "I know this is the work of you two."

Simin picks up the eraser but does not erase the board where "we hope you can bear this life without the glory of Jalal" is written. It's Morad's handwriting.

Simin turns to face the class.

"A Japanese Zen-Buddhist professor came to express her sympathy," she says. "A professor who is in Tehran. And I asked her my questions about Zen and about Chinese and Japanese art. We sat together on the veranda in silence. She stood up and searched in my small garden. She found a lone, yellow wildflower, plucked it, and brought it and gave it to me. That's all. Our silence and the lone yellow flower in my hand filled the space of any speech; it even overflowed it."

Farkhondeh is there, too. Farkhondeh hates to see Morad and Hasti. Sometimes she loves Simin, and sometimes she hates Simin so much that, in her own words, she hates her to death.

Farkhondeh raises her hand. Simin recognizes her. Farkhondeh says, "Madam . . . Isn't this calm that you are displaying a cover for the storm within you?"

Simin recites a poem by Hafez:

I wonder who resides in my weary-hearted soul,
That I am silent and they are in tumult and turmoil.

Farkhondeh says, "Your modesty, tenderness, and accessibility are also a cover for your boundless, excessive pride."

"It's possible," Simin replies.

"You have never had the problems of being a woman," Farkhondeh says.

"I have done my best to have fewer. You do your best, too."

"No, dear lady. You have had the means. I don't have such means."

"In my youth," Simin says, "I translated a story. I don't remember the name of the author. I do remember the gist of the story: if on a cold, dark, winter night, you have hidden a lit lantern under your coat, on your heart, you won't shiver from cold, nor will you be scared of the dark, nor will you fear loneliness."

This reference should have calmed down Farkhondeh, but she suddenly explodes, pounds on the desk in front of her, and shouts, "Cry, woman! Morad Pakdel and Hasti Nourian have set this stage to make you cry. Why don't you cry? Love, hope, and self-confidence have all become a tidbit, thrown in front of the dog, and the dog has devoured it." And she cries and cries.

Simin puts her hand in her bag, and Hasti hopes that she doesn't take out a cigarette and put it between her lips, although she has never seen Simin smoke in class. Simin takes her notes for the course from her bag and puts them on the table, and Hasti sighs in relief. Simin waits for Farkhondeh to pour out her tears. Facing the class, she says, "One of you, go bring Farkhondeh a glass of cold water." Then she continues, "Farkhondeh, calm down. Why do you want me to cry? Why should I teach you frailty and weakness? Keep the tears for when you are alone." She thinks a moment and adds, "You are smart; you understood well what I said. The key to the secret is this: hope, love, and self-confidence."

Simin ignores Farkhondeh, cleans the board with the eraser, and writes on the board: "Indian Art." She identifies the categories of Indian art. She clarifies what they will be studying during this semester. Then she turns to the students and says, "The main line of Indian art is a moving spiral. It is as if a tornado has come and twisted through every little thing. Such a line reflects samsara or the cyclicality of life . . . expresses the cycle and continuity of life and the belief in reincarnation, that is, previous lives, based on the system of levels or caste. Therefore, Indian art is very allegorical."

She swallows and says, "In the meditation technique of the Ramakrishna order of ascetics in India, there is an interesting allegory, and I will start this semester's Indian art course with this allegory.

"The tree of life has its roots in the unknown; that is, previous human lives. Like any other tree, this tree has a trunk, branches, leaves, and fruit. Its trunk is the human body. Its branches, leaves, and fruit are human deeds. Sitting quietly atop the tree is a bird that is the human spirit—a human's confident and dignified self. A restless sparrow keeps jumping from one branch to another, pecking on the sweet, ripe fruit and the unripe fruit of the tree as well. It even goes to other trees. It's very restless and impatient. This restless sparrow is the sinful self; it is human temptation. Hopefully, the large and calm bird that is sitting atop the tree can attract the attention of the restless sparrow so that it will fly toward it, rest in its shade, and gain peace.

"Do you know how this ancient allegory can be compared with modern psychology? Last year you studied enough art psychology."

Morad raises his hand. Simin says, "Go ahead, my dear."

"This tree," Morad says, "can be compared to human nature according to Freud, with a bit of help from Jungian psychology. The unknown world in which the tree has its roots is our subconscious—according to Jung, our tribal or human subconscious. The tree itself is the self or our consciousness. The confident bird is our superior self. The restless sparrow is our animal self. If the superior self controls the animal self and it gains power over the self—that is, our consciousness—then, as the poet Sa'di said, 'A human reaches a place where he will see none but God.'"

Farkhondeh raises her hand. Simin is waiting. Farkhondeh says, "In my opinion, a human is a wishing tree—the wishing tree in Shiraz that you described one day. You said that lost people sit under it and say, 'What shall I do?' And you said that it is well known that Sa'di planted this tree in the new mosque in Shiraz."

Simin smiles. "No, my dear. Take my word for it. A human is the tree of wakefulness, tree of enlightenment and awareness . . ." Someone taps on the auditorium door and enters. It is Mr. Ajami. He's holding a glass of water.

16

Teimur Khan could be heard quietly singing in the living room a poem by Rumi that described exactly how Hasti was feeling:

> O beloved, align your heart with mine.
> If I don't follow you, then you can whine.

She went to the kitchen. Brigadier General's new orderly was pouring tea. Hasti was hopeful. Had her mother been found? Was Touran Jan celebrating? "Who are the guests?" she asked Abedi.

"Our very own Brigadier General, a third lieutenant, and the guy with a handlebar moustache who's singing."

> With the Quran in your hand, you entered seclusion.
> I am that Quran; give up that seclusion.

She went into the living room, and Shahin rose. He put his officer's hat on his shaved head, stood up straight, and saluted. "Third Lieutenant Shahin, the long-necked, reporting!"

Brigadier General said, "At ease."

Sister and brother embraced each other and couldn't be separated. Hasti sat beside Shahin, held his hand in hers, and kissed him again and again. "It's so good that you are back, the man of our household!" Then she picked up a glass of tea and handed it to him.

"He came last night," Touran Jan said, "after you left. I prostrated myself and kissed the ground."

And then most likely she had burnt some incense.

"Why didn't you give us any news all this time?" Hasti asked.

"Well, we were in Aqdasieh barracks. Thanks to Lieutenant General Tondar and our very own first sergeant, I was sent to Aqdasieh; otherwise . . ."

He turned and said, "Brigadier General, you must forgive me. The lieutenant general had come to review the military academy. I . . . At first we were all at school . . ."

"The lieutenant general is my close cousin," Brigadier General said. Then he lay his hands on his claw-footed canes that were standing on either side of him.

"At the order of the first sergeant," Shahin continued, "I reported to the lieutenant general. He said, 'Soldier, prepare a statement.' When I took the statement to him, I said . . . I respectfully said that I am your neighbor and that we are very close. To be honest, I exaggerated as much as I could."

"Did he ask how I am?"

"Yes, he did. He asked how your legs were and said, 'This cousin of mine must have surgery.'"

"I was afraid to have the surgery in Germany . . . and here they will cripple me. Who is there to take care of me?"

Touran Jan put her hand on her chest and said, "Me."

Shahin then went on to talk about his first sergeant, saying what a rascal he was. He never thought of his soldiers. He shifted most of the work to those under his command. His room was full of opium pipes, charcoal braziers, and bottles of cognac and whisky. He didn't know which son of a bitch had reported him. The commander had come for a review, and after watching the march, he had ordered Shahin, "Soldier, come forward! Tighten your bootlaces!" The door of the first sergeant's room was locked. The commander had ordered, "Unlock the door." The first sergeant had dithered, put his hand in his pocket, but didn't find the key. The lieutenant general ordered Shahin, "Soldier, break the lock." The first sergeant found the key.

"Oh, God, what did we all see? On the mantle, there was a collection of Hafez's poetry with a Quran on top of it. There was a prayer rug spread on the floor. Imam Ali's picture on the wall. A clerical robe by the prayer rug. The first sergeant raised his hands and begged to do a divination from Hafez for the lieutenant general. The commander slipped his lash into his riding boots and entered the room. He sat by the prayer rug and asked, 'Don't you have some fine Shirazi wine?' The first sergeant swore by the life of the lieutenant general that he did not."

As Shahin told the story, after picking up the collection of Hafez's poetry, the first sergeant bored the lieutenant general with a litany of supplications to Hafez. With closed eyes, he raised his head toward the ceiling and kissed the Hafez collection. He opened it and gave it to Shahin to read. Shahin noticed that there was a bookmark in the book. He read the first sergeant's designated poem:

> Good news, O heart, that there is someone Messiah-like coming,
> From whose sweet breath, the beloved's scent is coming.

Shahin laughed and said, "What a trickster he was!" Teimur Khan and Grandmother were breathless from laughter.

"The lieutenant general said, 'What Hafez means is that my wife is having a good time in the United States, and she will come back soon.'"

His wife had gone to the States as a companion to the queen. The queen was to deliver a speech about women's rights at the United Nations . . .

"The lieutenant general's wife always wears splendid dresses . . . ," Brigadier General said.

Hasti was thinking, *The queen's speech must have been written by the prime minister's brother, or Majid, or Gholam Ali. Whoever has written it has prepared a fiery speech. Why is Shahin, whose favorite teacher was Hamid Khan, giving all these compliments and being so happy to serve in the army . . . ? If only Teimur Khan would start singing . . .* She knew why she couldn't laugh herself.

"My dear Imam Ali, my dear," he sang loudly.

Abedi passed the tray of fruit by everyone. Hasti took an orange, peeled it, and arranged the pieces like a flower on a plate for Shahin.

"The lieutenant general had gone to inspect the kitchen," Shahin said. "He asked the first sergeant, 'What do you have for lunch?' He saluted and said, 'Sir. Soup, sir.' The lieutenant general asked them to raise the covers of the pots. When the first cover was raised, he said, 'But this is lentil rice!' 'Even better, sir.'"

Sister and brother went to Shahin's room. "How long do you have off?" Hasti asked.

"One week. Until they assign us to different cities. I have chosen Shiraz or Isfahan."

"You gave so many compliments to the lieutenant general so that he would recommend you, didn't you?"

"Yes."

"Shahin, you bootlicker!"

"These two are proper cities."

He took off his military uniform and threw it on the bed. He took a new pair of pajamas from his bag and put them on. Hasti hung his uniform on a hanger and thought, *For one week we can manage to keep Mother Eshi's disappearance hidden.*

"Where's Mother Eshi?" Shahin asked. "I called three times today, but each time her husband picked up the phone and asked, 'Bijan, good news or bad news?' And I hung up."

"She's gone to visit the historical monuments of Shiraz and Isfahan with a group of Americans," Hasti said.

Shahin put his arms around his sister's neck and asked, "Why have you lost weight, Hasti? Do you remember when you were little, whenever you cried, Touran Jan would say, 'If you cry, your dimples will get mad and fly away'? Now your dimples have flown away."

"Well, I've grown old."

Shahin sighed. "Our whole life we've lived in this run-down house with the story of our father's death."

In the office, Hasti was turning the pages of the previous night's newspapers and gazing at the photos of unidentified corpses. Whenever the phone rang, her heart would sink, and when she called here and there, it seemed like her heart would leave her chest and rise up to her throat. Father and son had checked all the three-star and two-star hotels and even all the hostels. They had gone to the coroner's office and to telephone taxi agencies. They had even gone to the Shah Abdol Azim Shrine, and Ahmad Ganjur had sent Bijan to Mashhad.

When Hasti came home in the evening, she would sit and chat with Shahin. She was happy at her brother's happiness. The lieutenant general had fixed things so that he was about to be transferred to Shiraz. For dinner, they would eat chicken and pomegranate stew, meat and yellow split-pea rice, meat and green-herb stew, and chicken and red currant rice. Perhaps Fatemeh Sabzevari's wish that Hasti always eat good food had been granted, although it was meat and fava-bean rice that she had specifically mentioned. Touran Jan would send with Shahin a plate for Brigadier General and one for Teimur Khan. She would also put halva on the side of each plate. Shahin didn't know that the halva had been made as an offering for the souls of people who have no one. He didn't even notice Touran Jan's motion and Hasti's shaking her head in refusal.

As soon as they saw Shahin off in Mohsen Run's minivan, Hasti called Mardan Khan. She couldn't wait any longer. Secretly she hoped that Mardan wouldn't answer. If he didn't, it would mean that Mother Eshi was in his house. But Mardan did answer, and he asked, "Any news?" Then he added, "I'm coming to see you."

Mardan came to Hasti's office. In response to Hasti's question, whether tea or Turkish coffee, he asked only for an ashtray. When he left, the room was filled with smoke.

The morning of the appointed day her mother had gone to see Peggy. Mardan hadn't gone to work that day. Peggy had listened to what Eshrat had to say. Then she had said, "Men love variety. One cannot expect a man, even a non-Muslim man, to spend all his life with one woman. You're lying that the baby is Murray's. Murray knows what to do. I've been married to Murray for sixteen years, and I have only three children."

Then Peggy had gone to yoga, and Murray and Eshrat had been left alone.

"Poor Ahmad, he's a wreck."

"You've seen Mr. Ganjur?"

"Of course. We've sat together, gotten drunk together, and cried together. A lonely pregnant woman in a cruel city. And it's all my fault."

Her mother had gone home . . . With five suitcases, a fur coat, a fur jacket, and her box of jewelry, she had telephoned for a taxi. She had gotten five hundred tomans from Taqi Khan. When Taqi had called Ahmad at his garage at Azari Crossroads, Ahmad had said, "Damn all of you! Why didn't you get the taxi's license number?" Naneh Agha is illiterate, and the others hadn't thought of it.

Bijan was still in Mashhad, and there was still no trace of Eshrat.

"The last words that she said to me were, 'I'll give to charity whatever I have, and I'll go to Imam Reza Shrine. I'll tie my neck to the steel bars and starve myself to death. I'm sinful,' she said. 'I must suffer.'"

Hasti cried along with Mardan. But suddenly an idea flashed through her mind. "Mrs. Farrokhi! Maybe Mrs. Farrokhi has some news."

"No, she doesn't. Ahmad said that since you refused the marriage proposal of Farrokhi's son, the Farrokhis are not friendly with Eshrat."

Hasti thought, *When did Farrokhi's son officially propose to me that I could have refused*?

"Besides," Mardan continued, "Eshrat is wiser than to take this shame to the Farrokhi house."

"So we must go to the police."

"It will bring shame on all of us. To hell with me! I'm going to leave this damn country anyway. But this shame will affect many people, including you.

"Hasti," he begged, "forgive me. How much pain I have caused all of you with my carelessness, and worst of all, Ahmad, on whose shoulders I added so much weight, but he never complained. Only once he called and asked, 'Is my wife at your place, you jerk?'"

One night, Ahmad had said, "Eshrat has loved me for twenty years; I have plucked the flower of her youth. If she is found, I'm ready to send her to England with Bijan. Now that I am certain that the baby is mine, I'll do whatever she wants. The best hotels. If she wants to live separately from me for a while, I'll get the best house for her. I'll spend lavishly on her. I wish my hand had been broken, that I hadn't raised it against her . . ." That night Ahmad had been very drunk.

As soon as Mardan left, Hasti opened the window. A piercing gust rushed in. She closed the window. But another spark in her mind was still glowing . . . She would go to Bowling Center. Maybe Raya would know something, and if Raya didn't know, she would call Salim. Her mother didn't need to go to the Farrokhi house with the whole story. She could have said just that she was not speaking with her husband and was seeking refuge with Mrs. Farrokhi, couldn't she? But this whole time? Anyway, Mrs. Farrokhi, fearful as she was of Mr. Farrokhi's womanizing, would intervene so that mother and Ahmad would reconcile. Even if she couldn't reconcile them, at least everyone would be happy at mother's existence in this world.

Hasti's heart was not in her work. The days they had council meetings she would try to just get them over with. Even Professor Mani had noticed her distraction. He had asked several times, "What is it, my dear girl?"

One day, after the council meeting, Dr. Zandi had said sarcastically that Miss Nourian was worried about Morad Pakdel, and Hasti had become so angry that even she herself could hardly believe it. She had pounded on the council table and shouted at Dr. Zandi, "My private life is none of your business, Dr. . . . Do you think I don't know what you do? You well know that I do! Do you think that I can't shout everywhere at the top of my lungs that your honor has . . ."

Professor Mani had put his hand on her back and said, "You and Pakdel are like my children. I won't allow anyone to ridicule you." He had insisted that Dr. Zandi apologize, which he did. He had even wanted to kiss Hasti's hand, but she didn't let him.

One day, when everyone had gone to see the wedding exhibit that the Italian engineer had built, Hasti hadn't gone, saying that she had a headache. Besides, of the trousseau, only the inlaid table and the Bahadori-design carpet were ready.

Fakhri sympathized with Hasti and told her, "Miss Nourian, maybe your constant headache is due to eye strain." Hasti put her hands on her temples and said, "I have to go to the eye doctor." She felt like crying. Her mother had wanted to take her to her eye doctor. She had insisted that she should wear contact lenses instead of glasses and had promised her that it would be worth the trouble. Her whole life she had lived with the death of her father, and she still didn't know if he had been a hero or had been shot by accident . . . And now, the suicide of her mother, whose body couldn't be found.

Peace and quiet only came to Hasti when she was working on her poem, "The Earth's Complaint," and she put the weight of her feelings onto the planet. When the poem was finished, she read it to Fakhri. Fakhri didn't quite grasp it, but she said, "It's a sad poem." She typed four copies and took one copy for herself so that she could read it carefully and understand it.

Hasti picked up the phone and called Ahmad Ganjur's house. "It's me, Mr. Ganjur, Hasti."

"Do you have any good news, my daughter? If you do, I'll give you any reward you want."

"I think I have found a clue. A last hope. If we are disappointed, we must then inform the police."

There was silence.

"Can you hear me, Mr. Ganjur?"

"Yes, my daughter. I was thinking that I will sacrifice my honor for your sake. I didn't have much honor to lose anyway. But you will be affected, and so will Parviz, and your other brother."

"Shahin," Hasti said.

She blurted out, "Maybe Mother Eshi has gone to Mrs. Farrokhi's house."

"I called several times. Once a young woman said, 'There's no one here by that name.' The second time, an old woman said, 'I don't have any news.' I asked for Mrs. Farrokhi, and right away she asked, 'Why doesn't Eshrat come to Bowling Center anymore?'"

Hasti wouldn't give up. She hoped that maybe all of them were lying at her mother's request. Maybe her mother wanted everyone to suffer. And weren't they suffering? This time it was Ahmad Ganjur who asked, "Can you hear me?"

"Yes."

"I, too, got a bit hopeful, but there were no more phone calls."

"Who called, Mr. Ganjur?"

"One day, the phone rang three times. But when I answered, the caller didn't talk. Maybe it was Eshrat. Maybe she had missed me."

Hasti said that she would go after the clue anyway, knowing that the person who had called was Shahin.

Is life a bad dream that everyone interprets as they like? Is life a historical misunderstanding? In any case, "time" is its warp and weft. That night Simin had said that sometimes time passes like the wind, extinguishing the flame and fire of disaster. Sometimes, it is no more than a breeze, repelling only the flame. But sometimes it doesn't blow. Then, moments stop, because time has not been able to overcome emotions. Then, the flame of disaster spreads beneath the ashes of time, and its sparks burn body and soul all over again . . . But for some, like Ahmad Ganjur, this misunderstanding is mixed with optimism, and some even celebrate this very misunderstanding. Then Eshrat Ganjur couldn't have committed suicide.

Isn't life a type of poker? A type of twenty-one? But one cannot read the other player's hand, and the root of the disaster is right there. Mardan Khan had talked about the useful number. He had said, "In twenty-one, I could have twenty. In that case, my only useful number would be one." *Was Mardan's useful number my mother? Was she Ahmad Ganjur's useful number? Whose useful number was she? And now she is the useful number of all her family members and relatives, even Touran Jan. She must be found.*

Hasti kissed Fakhri and asked her to somehow provide an excuse for her absence. And life? This most precious gift given to humans. Has this gift been given to the residents of the shantytown, too? Has it been given to all the oppressed people of the world? They are fed at weddings and funerals, and they don't even know whose food they are eating. They are not seeds, but birds eat them from the surface of the desert lands. Do those birds ever think that they are not seeds to be pecked? . . .

Dr. Zandi hadn't said that Hasti misses Morad . . . He had said that Hasti is worried about Morad. Professor Mani had taken advantage of the ambiguity of the words he had used, had interpreted worry as missing, and had connected it to the private lives of Hasti and Morad . . . How much did this Dr. Zandi know? Was he also a bird that was seeking seeds named Morteza, Morad, and the like?

If only she had gone to Bowling Center sooner. "Every Friday," Raya had said, "Mrs. Ganjur comes to the spa with Mrs. Farrokhi. Mrs. Ganjur comes in a prayer chador. She doesn't take a bath or get a massage. She sits on my chair and knits baby clothes. But she makes Mrs. Farrokhi get a massage as soon as she comes out of the shower and makes her melt away her fat in the gym . . ." Raya laughed and added, "Me, I can't manage massaging her . . . Me and Soheila together . . . She keeps saying, 'Oh, it feels good.'"

Hasti called the Farrokhi house from Bowling Center. If they gave her the runaround, she would quote Raya's words. How come they hadn't asked Raya to lie? Well, maybe no one had thought of Raya. A pregnant woman wouldn't go to the sauna. Her baby would die.

Salim answered the phone, recognized Hasti's voice, and asked if she had had a good trip. Instead of responding, Hasti asked how Salim was and said that she missed her mother and Salim . . . Salim explained that the other night when his father had behaved so shamefully . . . he had come out of Mrs. Ganjur's bedroom into the corridor in pajamas, and how much Mrs. Ganjur had screamed. Now he had a backache. Hasti was too happy to feel sorry for Salim's back. She asked to talk to Mrs. Farrokhi or her mother. *Thank God that her mother was under a safe roof . . . Morad wanted to sleep under a safe roof. Will he now? . . .*

"My mother has gone to Mr. Ganjur's house," Salim said, "to sympathize about your mother's absence, but she will be back at noon."

"When did my mother leave your house?"

"It's been three or four days now."

"May I come to see you?"

"I would be honored."

Hasti was elated to know that her mother existed, but worried about where she had gone now. She had to buy a headscarf and go to the Farrokhi house by taxi. The eye doctor could wait until later. Her eyes could still see. Suddenly, she felt that she had become damp. She needed pads, too. She washed her face. Raya had Johnson's Baby Powder, which she used to rub on the bodies of women like Mrs. Farrokhi after massage, and she said that she also had a bit of lipstick in her bag.

Hasti knew the way to Salim's room. He was lying on the floor and had pulled the blanket up to his neck. The empty bed with the pillow was in its place. Hasti sat on the floor next to the mattress. She asked how Salim's backache was and said she hoped that he would feel better soon. She quoted Touran Jan, saying, "A young person's flesh is as if it were on the top shelf; he can extend his hand and pick it up." She was talking nonsense.

Salim smiled and said, "There's nothing wrong with my flesh. The vertebrae are apparently made of bone."

Hasti hadn't gone there to talk about flesh and bones. Taji cured her fatigue when she brought tea and fruit. Taji was wearing an apron and a headband. The orange was so big that Hasti thought it was a grapefruit. The knife was sharp, too. She peeled the orange and arranged the pieces in the shape of a flower on a small plate. She put one piece in Salim's mouth and remembered Niku who used to peel tangerines for Salim.

Eventually Salim told her more about the disgrace of that night . . . That night Mrs. Ganjur had screamed nonstop . . . His father had snuck into her room at 2:00 a.m. Salim had arrived just as his father was fleeing the room in his pajamas, with a pillow thrown after him . . . Salim had heard Mrs. Ganjur's voice . . . Once she was no longer screaming, she had yelled, "Do you think I am a walnut tree in the middle of the village that anyone who arrives can pick its walnuts and break its branches!?" Then Mrs. Ganjur had cried . . . Salim finished the story by saying that when Mrs. Ganjur was there, his mother felt well, and the house had some order.

Mrs. Farrokhi hadn't shown up, and Salim, with those eyes (Were they magical? Visionary? Mysterious? Scary?), assumed that Hasti was restless. "Call Mr. Ganjur's house," he said, "and ask when my mother is coming home."

It wasn't necessary; she was just happy to be with Salim. Salim smiled at this flattery, and the smile was lost in his reddish-brown beard. They didn't have anything else to talk about. Hasti took her poem from her bag and said, "Salim Khan, I have written a poem."

"You also compose poems? I thought you were a painter."

"Do you want me to read it for you?"

Salim closed his eyes.

The Earth's Complaint

In infinity you adorned me with the robe of life.
Life, the outcome of the most extraordinary accidents.
Allegorical forms of love and beauty remained in the heavens.
And you made the younger brother, Sorrow, a part of them.
They wove lies and were damned.

They found the question to be obsolete religion,
And they never found the answer.
Now, don't you hear the sound of cries?
Their first word is "Ouch, ouch,"
And the tear flower is their gift to one another.
Upside down tulip, cages with nine layers, each one inside the other.
I am turning around myself and the sun,
And there is no planet by me, so that I say,
"What good will come from this loneliness and suspense?
And from this lost sphere that is me?"

Salim opened his eyes. It seemed as though he had awakened from an otherworldly dream. "*Is* there a flower called 'tear flower'?" he asked.

"Yes, there is. Tulip buds just like two bloody tears, at the end of branches and leaves, upside down, as if they are about to fall. If one has a tear flower at home, one doesn't need to cry oneself."

"That's strange. Do you remember one night I told you that your bewilderment is a mystical bewilderment?"

Hasti did remember.

"Do you remember that you had painted me a picture on fiberboard and it was broken right on this bench?"

She remembered that, too.

Salim wanted to know what Hasti had painted on the fiberboard. Hasti wasn't too shy to say that it was a picture of a bitter orange and Salim's eyes in profile and in full face . . .

Salim closed his eyes and said, "Be nicer to me, O bitter orange girl!" He opened his eyes and said, "There's a notebook and a pen on the side table. Get them." Hasti found the notebook and the pen. Oh, my God! Perhaps the thirty-fifth notebook . . . the thirty-sixth . . . and now a literary piece or several maxims . . . or maybe he wants to write down Hasti's poem.

"We will marry ourselves," Salim said.

"What did you say?"

"We say the marriage vows ourselves. Say, '*Ankahto nafsi laka*.'" (I give myself to you.)

Like a parrot, Hasti repeated the unfamiliar Arabic words.

Salim said, "*Qabalto alnekaha lenafsi.*" (I accept you in marriage.)

"Write it down on the last two pages of the notebook," Salim said in a commanding tone. "'With the good omen, protection, and blessing of the Twelfth Imam.'"

He repeated the marriage vows, and Hasti asked, "Do you spell *ankahto* with an *h*?"

Salim smiled. "Yes, it's with an *h*."

Hasti signed both pages of the notebook. Then she gave the pen and the notebook to Salim, who put it on his chest and signed both documents. The notebook remained on Salim's chest, but no one knew where the pen had fallen. Now she could kiss Salim's pink nails, his ears, and his eyes, and Salim could kiss his wife so hard that she couldn't breathe.

Hasti put her face on Salim's beard and whispered in his ear, "O Salim, the lesson of love cannot be found in a notebook."

Salim whispered, "You're now my wife. Man and wife. You're my everyone and everything in this world. You're the oil in the lamp of my being. I will extinguish your confusion and your depression . . ."

"My love, put your hand behind me."

"As soon as my back stops aching, I'll come to your house with my father, mother, and sister to officially ask your hand in marriage. Our parents have a right to share in our happiness . . ."

Hasti heard Mrs. Farrokhi's voice asking, "Why didn't you bring her to the living room?" *This Mrs. Farrokhi, who didn't come and didn't come. What timing that she came now*!

17

"I'm not stupid! I understand. The place your mother has gone is an indecent house. I will never set foot there, dear."

Hasti looked at Mrs. Farrokhi. She had lost a lot of weight, and now her face and neck had yielded themselves to so many folds and furrows that one could call her Afsar Wrinkles. She had dyed her hair light brown. Hasti was now her daughter-in-law, whether Mrs. Farrokhi set foot in the house that her mother had gone to or not.

"I went to the hairdresser with Eshrat, dear."

The curls in her hair shouted that it was Farhad's work.

"Women come and go in see-through dresses. Men with neckties or bow ties. Of course, Eshrat is chaste. Even if she were to be among a regiment of soldiers . . ."

Hasti's gaze traveled to the armchairs that had new covers and the arms of straight chairs that had been polished with oil. The cast-iron heater that used to give out so much smoke had given way to a new, luxury heater of a brand Hasti didn't recognize. These were her mother's prints in this house. If only her mother would allow her to not worry for just one day.

"Do you understand what I'm saying? Help your mother, dear. She won't reconcile with Ganjur. He has to pay her subsistence. She asked the clerical authorities about that. But if Ganjur finds out what kind of house she is in, he can avoid paying her subsistence."

"But where *is* my mother?"

Mrs. Farrokhi put her hand in her purse, took out a piece of paper, and handed it to Hasti. Hasti read the address. "Vila Street, before the Medical Clinic, number . . ."

The four-bedroom apartment that Ganjur rents, and his wife ends up there! Hasti looked at the ceiling. The chandelier in the middle of the room was clean and shiny. But what Hasti was looking for was a solution. She got up, hit the switch, and the chandelier lit up. The clouds were pouring rain onto the garden. Perhaps the trees were joyful, and it was only Hasti's heart that was as gloomy as the clouds.

"Of course, I haven't said anything to Mr. Farrokhi. And Salim doesn't get involved in other people's business. If Mr. Farrokhi found out, he would destroy that apartment. And of course, Ganjur has been with that maid, the one with slanted eyes, for a year now . . ."

"Why didn't my mother go to a hotel?"

"Hotels are no different. All of Tehran has become a house of pleasure. Of course, Eshrat isn't poor . . ."

Didn't Hasti know that Ganjur gave her mother as much money as she wanted, and that no one was as extravagant as her mother? Hadn't she left money in Hasti's notebooks when she was a student? And in her purse? When Hasti graduated, hadn't she given a party for her in the garden of her home? How much she had flattered Professor Mani and his wife and Simin. And despite the fact that Morad made many wisecracks and ironically praised frugality, hadn't her mother calmed him down with a glass of whisky and a few caviar sandwiches? And when Farkhondeh shouted her slogans and said, "So, Hasti Nourian is of the nobility and an aristocrat, and we didn't know it," hadn't her mother sat beside her, kissed her, and peeled a cucumber for her? The Russian bear, Marusa, had prepared Hasti's blue dress on time, and that gift was enough by itself. But on top of that, her mother had hung a turquoise necklace around Hasti's neck.

"Mrs. Farrokhi," Hasti asked, "how was it that my mother decided to go to such an apartment?"

"This house was not her place anymore, dear. The other morning, right in front of me, she called the housekeeper at the apartment and asked that she prepare the end room for her. The sheets . . . everything. Then she made the housekeeper swear not to tell anyone. She kept saying, 'You mustn't tell anyone! You'll get a big tip from me.'"

Mrs. Farrokhi rang and Taji appeared. She asked Taji to prepare lunch. Hasti said she should leave. There were a thousand things waiting for her in the office.

"It's past noon. I swear on Salim's life that I won't let you go. Especially since it's raining cats and dogs."

At lunch, Mrs. Farrokhi ate salad. "Who brings food to Salim Khan?" Hasti asked.

"Nanny."

If Hasti could have food with Salim, maybe he could eat something. She could feed Salim herself and tell him that she loves him to infinity. She had a "lit lantern on her heart" under her blouse, and she knew that with that she could help her mother. She knew that these knotty problems could be solved one by one.

"She got a taxi," Mrs. Farrokhi continued. "We went to the bank together. She called it the 'problem-solving bank.' Anyway, she pawned the jewelry, silver, gold, and furs. Her receipt is with me. I've put it in the metal box by my bed. The key is around my neck."

A gold chain hung from Mrs. Farrokhi's neck under her dress. The key was probably attached to the end of that chain.

"Three empty suitcases of Eshrat's are under my bed. She has taken two suitcases. But what if I die? What if Eshrat kills herself?"

"Why do you think she might kill herself?"

"She didn't pawn that gun. That ivory-handled gun. The one a foreigner had given her for her birthday."

Hasti asked Dr. Bahari's secretary, "How much should I pay for the visit?"

"Paying for the visit is optional."

She made a file for Hasti, and, as the reason for the visit, she wrote "headache." When it was Hasti's turn, and Dr. Bahari saw her, he laughed and asked, "Have you become sick for lack of a husband?"

Dr. Bahari asked how Mr. Sympathizer was doing and said, "It was a dangerous case of pneumonia." He repeated his special joke that Hasti had heard several times before: "One can be a sympathizer and get pneumonia, too. One can be bald and be run over by a car, too." Then he thought and said, "But Hasti, I have a question. Why should the present generation suffer so that the next generation can be happy when there is no guarantee that it will be?"

Because Hasti didn't answer, Dr. Bahari asked about Hasti's headaches—whether half of her head aches or all of it and when her head aches.

"I didn't come to you for my headache. I came for a cure for my mother's problems. Why should the present generation pay for the mistakes of the previous generation?"

She told him about her mother's problems. At the end she explained that her mother was then residing in a house of pleasure a hundred steps from the medical clinic. Dr. Bahari bit his lip.

"Why did she destroy you? I doubt that Farrokhi's son will marry you with your mother's actions, although Farrokhi himself . . . Well, Afsar al-Moluk is five or six years older than Farrokhi. At the time of the oil nationalization, he spent most of his wife's money on the movement and stayed loyal to Mosaddeq until the end.

"But what can I do for you and for Eshrat?"

"Grandmother has faith in you. She says that you are familiar with suffering."

He wiped the imaginary sweat off his forehead and said, "Do you mean that I should convince Grandmother to bring Eshrat to her place? I'll take care of it. Tonight, pretend to be sick. Make her call me. When I come, I know how to play my role. Remember how well I played the roles of bathhouse owner, bath attendant, and masseur? . . . That night seems thousands of years ago."

Hasti thought, *Isn't life a series of plays, often written by novice writers, plays that might get published or might not, that have a thousand ifs and buts?*

As soon as she returned home, Hasti pretended to be sick. Grandmother had her drink rock candy dissolved in hot water and made her lie down on the sofa in the living room. She sat beside her and said that Hasti's illness was due to worry about her mother.

"Now that she is well and her illness is known, is it my turn to fall ill?"

Grandmother rose, prostrated herself, and kissed the floor. "It would have been a shame if that beautiful body had been buried."

"She doesn't want to go back to her husband's house anymore."

"If he buys her a piece of jewelry, she'll go back."

"But it's Pasita, too. Her husband and Pasita have an . . ."

"Grease Monkey, the garage owner? How dare he . . . ? Really!"

Touran Jan went back to square one. Still, Hasti kept trying. "She doesn't want to go back to her husband's house for a little while."

"She'll probably make it a condition that Grease Monkey send the maid away; then she'll go back . . . How are you feeling?"

"Terrible."

When Dr. Bahari arrived, he took Hasti's pulse. Took her blood pressure. He put the stethoscope on her heart. Checked her eyelids . . . "Your headache is due to worry and fear. And you have become anemic."

"Thank you for saying this," Touran Jan said. "I've been telling her the same thing."

"My diagnosis is the best. I was the one who, from the start, diagnosed Eshrat's pregnancy. Ganjur distracted everyone. It's because his mind is only on Pasita."

"And she's not speaking to her husband," Grandmother said.

Grandmother left and came back bringing tea for Dr. Bahari. The doctor patted Touran Jan's hand lightly in appreciation, picked up the tea, and, like someone who is continuing a conversation, asked, "What do you think about it?"

"About what, Doctor?"

"The idea," the doctor said, "that Hasti rent the furnished room above my office and take care of her mother there until I have enough time to have Pasita leave and to get Eshrat and Ganjur to reconcile."

"And leave me alone? With no one? Just go?" Touran Jan's voice was trembling.

"You're right. I wasn't thinking about you, Hajieh Khanom."

"I haven't had the honor of visiting Mecca, and I'm not a Hajieh Khanom."

"But you *are* right."

Then Dr. Bahari gave a lengthy speech about the elderly. That the children grow up and leave and the elderly stay alone . . . They lose their minds . . . That he has often convinced young people to take their old parents into their own home. "When the living conditions of the elderly change, their senility is cured. In the past, old age was not a problem. Everyone—sons, daughters, sons-in-law, daughters-in-law, grandchildren, and great grandchildren—all used to live together. Even if the house is full of enemies, it is better than being alone."

"I, too," Touran Jan said, "sometimes think I'm losing my mind. I wish God were content with me and would take me, especially since Hasti wants to rent a room and leave me for a mother who was never a mother to her." And she started crying quietly.

Dr. Bahari put his hand on Grandmother's shoulder. "But you're not old!"

"I'm seventy years old!"

Dr. Bahari was pacing and continuing to talk about the phenomenon of aging, saying that it starts when the sperm is formed, but that real old age begins at sixty-five. "In old age, the body shrinks, the brain shrinks, vertebrae collapse on top of one another. Loneliness and being excluded is the biggest pain for an old man or old woman." He stood in front of Touran Jan and said, "Do you know why I am enchanted by you? I saw you take care of a stranger, a political activist, and there was even fear of his being exposed. You took care of him as though you were his mother. A lioness like you, Mrs. Nourian, with this much knowledge, benevolence, and holiness, can postpone 50 to 60 percent of old age."

"I wish Khanomi would agree to come live with us."

"Who's Khanomi?"

"My former daughter-in-law. Eshrat. She has given me two beautiful grandchildren. She used to call me 'Sister.' Alas . . ."

"Leave it to me to convince her," Dr. Bahari said. "I'll go with Hasti to the hospital to bring her here."

"To this rundown hovel?"

Hasti came out of the state of illness, rose, put her arms around Grandmother's neck, and kissed her again and again. "This rundown hovel is more than my mother and I deserve. This is a house of piety and chastity, and you are life's blessing." Hasti noticed that Dr. Bahari, happy and content, had tears in his eyes. She was thinking, *Why did I trouble him this much*? But the doctor's presence was necessary. Hadn't her mother, in Mrs. Farrokhi's words, forbid the housekeeper of that house of pleasure to tell anyone that Mrs. Ganjur was there, and of course Dr. Bahari himself knew about the house . . .

18

Eshrat Ganjur couldn't sleep on her back. It was harmful for the innocent baby. The clock belonging to the upstairs neighbor was ticking loudly. If she turned off the light on the bedside table, she would be scared, and that dreaded thought would come again. It had come also when she was in the Farrokhi house. Somewhere, they were unloading bricks. Then they were tossing iron bars, one after the other. How could she sleep with those strange dreams! She could go to the kitchen, turn on all five gas burners, and not strike a match. But first she would have to close up all the kitchen's cracks and openings with blankets, sheets, and anything she could find. She could go to the roof and throw herself onto the street below. The first day that she had come to this house, she had gone to the edge of the roof. The herb seller opposite the building had shouted, "Sister, be careful! You might fall!"

How lonely she was. She was wasting away, and there was no one in the apartment. Even the nights that the rooms were full, she had the same sensation. She felt like having some cold watermelon juice. She got up and opened the window. Tehran was ugly at night as well as in daylight. The streetlights, like fruit on top of cement monsters, were lit, but no one was shouting, "Lights of cement fruit, lit lights, come buy them!" The opposite buildings were caves that demons had built, and the darkened windows were their mushy fruit. No one buys mushy fruit. Nor did anyone shout, "Hey, we have darkened fruit!" The shutters of all the stores had been pulled down and their doors locked. One could shout, "Hey, we sell locks!" A policeman came and checked the locks . . .

She wished she had asked Hitti how to operate the revolver. She wished that she had studied English well enough to read the instructions for the revolver, insert the bullets, put the revolver to her temple, and *bang*! But what if her hand trembled? What if she injured herself and no one came looking for her? And this Hasti, why did she abandon her mother? How long had it been? If she didn't kill herself, it was because of her children. Hasti, Shahin, Parviz, and this innocent baby. She was waiting for this one to be born. She would bring him and give him to Pasita and then . . . But she wished that this one, like the other three, would suckle at her breast and make her heart pound. She wished that the baby would make a fist of his little hands and pedal his legs and she would watch him. She wished it would be morning. She wished she could sleep on her back. She looked at her clock. Only one hour had passed. But the clock upstairs continued ticking.

She had gone to see Dr. Sa'edi. She had heard good things about him from Hasti. How far away his office was! Dr. Sa'edi had said, "I can't give you sleeping pills. It's harmful for the baby." The doctor was Turkish-speaking. He had said, "'Biology is destiny' for you women. Freud said that." Eshrat didn't know anyone by the name of Freud. Dr. Sa'edi had said, "Based on this, occupation: homemaker, wife, mother, hostess." And he had said, "Most bourgeois women get depressed doing this kind of work. Busy yourself with activity outside the house."

She heard gunshots. *Bang. Bang. Bang.* She heard the footsteps of the neighbor upstairs. Perhaps he too had heard the gunshots.

She had gone to Farhad with Afsar al-Moluk. While he was cutting her hair, Farhad asked, "Do you want to dye it?" No, she didn't. Farhad said, "You've changed. You're wearing a prayer chador. Don't you want to look beautiful like you always have?" She didn't. Eshrat said, "Farhad Jan, don't you need a manicurist and pedicurist?" Farhad asked, "Who would that be?" She had said, "Me." Farhad had said, "I don't like the idea. With this belly that is growing every day, you can't put women's feet on your lap."

Occupation: homemaker, wife, mother, partygoer, and always beautiful. Bijan hadn't held back and had bluntly said, "You don't have any talents. You don't have any skills. You can't get a divorce." No! She wouldn't go to Ganjur's house! If Hasti would rent her a room or if the old woman would let her in. The old woman had called her Khanomi and had always spoken to her respectfully. But as soon as she got married, the hurtful words began . . . That day on the phone, how many sarcastic remarks Mehrmah had made! Hasti had told her, "Mother, stay where you are."

The upstairs neighbor's bed started to creak. She wished that the sound of gunshots hadn't awakened him. How can one sleep with the creaking of the bed and the ticking of the clock?

You can call Salim a loyal child. After dinner, Farrokhi would get up and go out, and Afsar would cry. Salim would put his arms around his mother's neck and kiss her. He would kiss her hand and wipe her eyes with a Silk-brand facial tissue. One night after dinner, Eshrat had said to Salim, "Salim Khan, why don't you give Sister Dear and me lessons these few hours that you are with us after dinner?" She called Afsar "Sister Dear." In the mornings, he would walk with her in the garden. When Afsar felt like eating kebab, he would take her to Tajrish, and they would eat kebab. He would take Afsar to Farhad's hair salon, even though his own heart ached. Occupation: good-tempered and kind, but unhappy. Afsar had taken him to see a cleric. Salim brought a bunch of books—English and Persian—and put them on the table. Eshrat didn't understand a word in any of them and returned the books.

You can call Salim a loyal child, but not Hasti. As for Shahin, he had gone to the military to march in place. And Parviz loved his Papa Ganjur more. May his Papa Ganjur go to hell!

On Mother's Day, other children would write the best compositions for their mothers and read them in front of the class. But Hasti would never bring a single flower for her mother or even call her and wish her Happy Mother's Day, if only in dry and empty words. On Mother's Day, she would disappear, just like these days that she has disappeared. Hasti could have called Salim and asked him. Salim didn't know how to lie. Then she could have come to see her mother, and together they could have trapped Salim into marrying Hasti. No, not at all. There was no news from Hasti. Eshrat had to say that Hasti had gone on a trip. Occupation: homemaker, wife, mother, hostess, partygoer, always beautiful, liar.

One night, she had asked Salim, "What kind of a girl do you think Hasti is?" Salim had said, "She is beautiful, dignified, knowledgeable, and artistic." Eshrat had said in her heart, *Then why don't you marry her and solve all our problems*? But it became clear that, in Salim's opinion, Hasti herself had a problem. Eshrat asked, "What kind of problem?" Salim said, "Hasti Khanom must be honest with herself. For now, she is vacillating between art and politics, love and office work, disbelief and faith." That night, Salim had given them lessons and had answered Eshrat's questions. He said, "Hasti Khanom doesn't know what she wants. If I were her, I would choose femininity and art. Love and art are inseparable. For a female artist, the problem of being a woman is not relevant. Both men and women respect her; therefore, she is equal to men and takes up her feminine role with pride." Eshrat asked, "You mean she should quit her job?" Salim said, "Yes." Eshrat said, "Then she will be depressed." Salim said, "Hasti Khanom is already depressed." Eshrat grimaced. "I wish to be just like Hasti." Salim said, "Hasti Khanom can paint and put on exhibitions. She can read books. She can travel. With intellectuals, like Professor Mani . . ." Eshrat wanted to say, "Painting has its own place, but love . . . She would keep having babies and, like her mother, become a captive of her children." But she didn't say it.

She had gone to see the cleric. She had said, "Sir, I think of suicide." The cleric said, "That's a great sin." Eshrat said, "I have already sinned." The cleric said, "The path to repentance is open." Eshrat said, "I don't know whether to return to the house of a husband who has betrayed me or not." The cleric ordered her to perform ablutions every day, say two rounds of prayers, and after the end of the prayers ask God to put whatever path is beneficial to her in front of her. The cleric said, "God is most merciful." Why doesn't this most merciful God come to her aid?

Salim had said, "Well-to-do Iranian women don't have to do much. There is no need for a wife's income, and the maid and servants do the tiring work." Eshrat said, "Who knows whether Hasti will marry a well-to-do man." In her mind, this was a kind of marriage proposal to Salim. Salim said good night and left. Eshrat said in her heart, *You go be a mama's boy. You won't marry Hasti. You'll marry Niku who is a sheep. Like a sheep, she just puts her head down and grazes.*

What a loud noise! It sounded like they were pounding shingles onto the roof. If only she could fall asleep.

Several times she had gone in a prayer chador to Parviz's school. She would sit in the store opposite the school and wait for Parviz to get off the school bus. Her heart would fly to him, and she would want to find a way through the cars and embrace him. Once, she decided to kidnap Parviz. Poor Afsar al-Moluk didn't object. One day at 3:00 p.m., she waited in front of the school for a long time. A policeman came up to her and asked, "Sister, what are you doing here? I see that you have been standing here for a long time." He wanted to take her to the police station. Eshrat begged, "Don't ruin my reputation at work." She put a twenty toman bill in the policeman's hand and said that she had come to see her son. When Parviz came out of the school, she said, "There, he's my son," and she cried and cried. The policeman asked, "Would you like me to bring him so that you can see him?" She said, "No, he's afraid of policemen. Whenever he didn't eat, I would tell him I would call the policeman." The policeman said, "It's a dog's life, being a mother!" Then he called a taxi for her.

That night, Afsar al-Moluk cried as much as she could. Salim's affectionate words and kisses couldn't calm her. Eshrat put Afsar's head on her chest. They cried together, and Eshrat said, "We women are doomed by our children and our husbands. That's just the way it is." Salim put his hands on his mysterious eyes and said, "All the oppressed people in the world must become equal to the oppressors." He lectured a lot. His mother said, "I don't understand, dear." Eshrat didn't understand, either.

The baby kicked in her belly. If he stayed alive and she could see the pedaling of his legs, it would be so good. If Hasti would come. If Bijan would come. If only one of them would come . . . Couldn't Hasti get a separate room for her mother? If the old woman let her in, she was ready to live in the storage room next to the toilet. Then she would go study. She was in the eighth grade when she got married. She would have to take many exams. She had heard that of the thousands who take the university entrance examination, only a small percentage are accepted. Well, she would take the examination over and over until she got accepted . . . Salim had said, "We all wear masks. And you women wear several masks, one on top of the other. You appear to be happy, but your heart is full of pain . . . Our world is a masked ball . . ." Eshrat had thought, *And you want a masked wife too . . .* Occupation: seemingly happy but with heartache.

If she read the instructions of the revolver carefully, maybe she could figure out how to load it, and then *bang*! She would be released. But would she really be released? The cleric had said, "Pray to God that He protect you from satanic temptations." He had said, "Since Adam and Eve chopped up the baby Satan and ate it, a wild animal has settled inside all humans, and Satan had wanted exactly that—that a piece of his damned body be inside humans, and a human not be all godly, but rather be satanic, too . . ."

When it was morning and Hasti came, she put her arms around her mother's neck. Eshrat wanted to drive her away, push her even, but she couldn't. She wanted to cry, but tears wouldn't come. Hasti gestured to her, and she put on her prayer chador. Dr. Bahari brought the suitcases, and they all got in the car. On the way to Touran Jan's house, they made her aware of which secrets they had revealed to Grandmother and which secrets they had not.

Hasti inserted the key and opened the door. Touran Jan put her arms around her former daughter-in-law's neck. She kissed her and said, "Welcome, Khanomi. Oh, fate! All this time . . ."

Eshrat kissed Touran Jan's hand and said, "Sister, I've taken refuge with you so that you can make me a good person, like you have done with Hasti." Hasti brought tea, and only then did she notice her mother's short, salt-and-pepper hair. She was startled too by her mother's yellow, freckled face and puffy eyes.

Dr. Bahari took Hasti to her office. Hasti still had Salim's gift, the fiberboard, and she knew that she was going to draw a picture of the doctor on one of the pieces. This plan was not pie in the sky. It was real. She smiled at this thought.

"I'm happy that you're happy."

Hasti was full of energy. When she was happy, she would spin like a top. She would move rapidly in facing problems too, and life—this mixture of happiness and sadness—whirled her around. Would it whirl her until it threw her down and eternal peace and silence arrived? No, it was too soon. The only thing she wished for was peace and quiet in whatever situation she faced. She also wanted courage—the courage to be straightforward, not to lie, and not to have a mask on her face. About her mother's actions, she had told so many lies that even she herself had forgotten the truth. Will the day ever come that lies are uprooted from the earth and all words, thoughts, and deeds are good, as Zoroastrians believe?

Fakhri put a folder in front of Hasti. "Miss Nourian, you're feeling well today, aren't you?"

Hasti called Ahmad Ganjur's house, and in response to her mother's husband, who asked, "My daughter, good news or bad news?" she replied, "Very good news!"

"She's alive! Is she well? Where has she been? Where is she now?"

"She was at the Farrokhi house. Now she is at ours."

"Thank God! I have a reward . . ."

Then she called Salim. "Hello. How are you?"

"Hello. How are you yourself?"

"Great! 'Because I have you, I have everything!'"

"You are saying what my heart says."

"What are you doing? Are you lying down or sitting?"

"I'm sitting. I'm reading Hujwiri's book on mysticism. Why do you ask?"

"I want to imagine you in my mind."

"Why don't you come over?"

"We haven't told Mrs. Farrokhi yet. When we do, we will be together every day."

"This pleasure of being together . . ."

Hasti wrote a letter to the minister asking for the two months off that she was due, and she gave it to Fakhri to type. She wanted to ignore Fakhri's inquiring look, but Fakhri insisted. She explained that she would give her vote on the council to Professor Mani and that Fakhri must get ready to take her place.

"Me?"

Bijan entered Hasti's office without knocking. He put a box with a green velvet lid on the table and collapsed into the armchair. He closed his eyes and said, "The matter of Erect Hill is over."

"I don't want to hear anything about Erect Hill."

Bijan sighed. "Erect Hill does exist. It overlooks a land full of pebbles and thorn bushes and tissues that are stuck in the thorns. In the morning, shepherds bring sheep to graze there, and they gorge on the thorns and tissues."

Hasti rang the bell and when the servant came, she ordered that he bring a glass of tea for Mr. Bijan Ganjur, deputy director of the Office of Book Evaluation. Bijan opened his eyes and said, "I'm no longer deputy director of the Office of Book Evaluation. Father summoned me from the garage. He said I should leave whatever I was doing and come bring your reward. Why don't you open the box?"

Once he had his tea, his exhaustion passed. "Father is snapping his fingers and dancing around like a child," Bijan said. "He keeps saying, 'My darling is alive. My beauty is alive.' Everyone in the house is celebrating."

Hasti opened the box. A square emerald in the middle, surrounded by diamonds, set in gold plate. According to Bijan's explanation, that he had understood from his father's explanation, the emerald had no impurity. It had been the jewel on a woman's face veil; they had used it to attach together the two sides of the face veil. It would be located at the back of the head. For Hasti, it wasn't important whether the emerald was pure or impure. And it didn't matter which woman had used it as a jewel on her face veil. She was thinking, *How can the pure jewel of humanity be attained? The jewel of human worth and honor*? She worried that probably Keshvar, the dealer, had put it in trust with Ahmad Ganjur, that its owner must be dead, and that the heirs might not know where the jewel of their deceased mother or grandmother was . . . or they might not even know that such a jewel existed at all. Those worries made Hasti close the box and say, "I've found my own mother. Mr. Ganjur doesn't owe me anything."

While putting the box in his pocket, Bijan said, "Tuesday morning, Keshvar will bring Parviz to see your mother."

Was her mother no longer anyone's Eshrat or Mother Eshi? Khanomi, Sister Dear, Mother . . . a time when even names descended from the heavens have been changed by consensus . . .

As soon as Bijan left, Hasti started cleaning. She opened the drawers of the cabinets and took out her personal belongings.

When Hasti arrived home in the evening, she found the realm peaceful. Khanomi and Touran Jan were cleaning herbs in the kitchen.

“She says prayers, too,” Khanomi said. “Loudly. After prayers, she holds up her hands toward the ceiling and says, ‘O God, bless the day!’” Touran Jan laughed.

The holes in the telephone receiver connected Hasti and Salim, and setting the next day’s time increased their happiness. “Tomorrow at 10:00 . . .” Every day, half an hour before that time, Hasti would become restless and wouldn’t go far from the phone until it rang and her heart stood still. And when the letter that granted her leave was delivered to the house, she brought the telephone to her bedroom, closed the door, and waited for Salim to call her from his shop.

On Tuesday morning when Keshvar brought Parviz, Hasti hadn’t yet received her leave letter . . . When she came home from the office that evening, she noticed that her mother’s eyes and the tip of her nose were red. And Grandmother herself, as she told it, had burst into tears. Mother and young son had kissed each other repeatedly. Parviz wouldn’t let go of his mother’s skirt. He had put his head on the bump of his mother’s belly and had said, “I want a little sister. I won’t let Lady scratch her.” Navidi had come to take him, but he had thrashed and kicked and wouldn’t leave. Khanomi had said, “Let him stay today until evening.” Keshvar, the dealer, had said, “Master cannot live one minute without Parviz Khan.” Keshvar had put several bundles of large bills on the table on behalf of the master. Khanomi had held Parviz’s hand, and Parviz had gone with her, but he had run back toward Grandmother, taken refuge there, and said, “Sister Touran, isn’t this your house? Let me stay here. Isn’t it true that I am the jewel of my mother’s life? If I leave, I will break, turn into smoke, and go up in thin air. Then you’ll be sad.” Touran Jan had cried and said, “Oh, my child . . .” Then she had said, “Tell your brother or Mr. Navidi to bring you here after school every day. Okay?” Navidi had promised Parviz to take him to the zoo that afternoon. Parviz had asked, “Will you buy me hazelnut ice cream, too?”

Mother took Hasti to the eye doctor and from there to the optometrist. She drove both Hasti and the optometrist crazy searching for a pair of frames that she liked. Finally, light purple frames with dark purple temple pieces satisfied her. Then she instructed Hasti to look carefully in the mirror, and she added that with those frames, she looks nothing like a spinster with glasses; she looks even prettier than she did before.

It would take a while for the glasses to be ready. But it took no time for the people of the neighborhood to count Khanomi's presence on Valiabad Street a blessing. The "concert hall" of Teimur Khan's motorcycle and bicycle repair shop was the first place to welcome Khanomi. And Mohsen Run seemed to have fallen in love with her. Any seasonal fruit that Khanomi ordered, he would find from somewhere and bring it to the house the next day. Well, fresh almonds hadn't come out yet, but good-looking cucumbers, bell peppers . . . Khanomi paid cash for the remaining installments on Mohsen Run's minivan, and Mohsen Run, free from installments, shouted louder in his handheld loudspeaker announcing his wares to the housewives. He even brought better herbs and vegetables. Farideh hung out on the balcony of her house, and only when Khanomi indicated to Mohsen Run, "The girl is waiting for you, poor thing . . ." did he remember that Farideh was not afraid of cheese anymore. He sat her next to him in his minivan, and they went for a ride together.

Brigadier General had his orderly bring a small carpet to the front of the house so that Khanomi and Sister Touran could sit on it. He himself didn't put his legs on the pillow anymore, but from time to time he caressed his claw-footed canes. He even asked his orderly to make lemonade for them, but the orderly didn't listen. Brigadier General swore on the life of his close cousin, the lieutenant general, that whenever he goes to visit him, he puts in a good word for Shahin. Shahin's letters indicated that he had indeed put in a good word for him, though the letters were in the form of circulars, full of the joking of the honorable colonel with the lieutenant. He was comfortable in the garrison until Hasti wrote to him that their mother was living with them. Shahin called at midnight, waking everyone and telling Hasti that he was shocked . . . Hasti told him about the fight between their mother and Ahmad Ganjur and Shahin was not shocked anymore; he started to laugh out loud.

Khanomi would throw a plastic tablecloth on the bed and ask Sister to lie on it. She would massage her knees and her back with castor oil that she had warmed. It was Dr. Bahari's recommendation, and it could not be ignored. Which Grandmother was it who had requested that he examine her?

Sister Touran memorized poetry and recited it for Khanomi. "Practice for the memory," she said. But she didn't think of poor Mehrmah these days. At the request of Khanomi, she wrote the poem that Hasti liked in nice calligraphy and took it to Teimur Khan. Khanomi bought a tambour for Teimur Khan, and Teimur Khan very quickly learned how to play the tambour from one of dervishes of the Safi Alishah Sufi Center. When Teimur Khan sang a piece of the poem, without playing the tambour, Khanomi pulled Hasti to the concert hall too, quoting Attar's poem, "When the bewildered man reaches this status . . ."

Once again, bewilderment of a nonmystical kind was forced upon Hasti's mind.

Why didn't Salim propose to her family? Didn't he say that others have the right to share in their happiness?

Until one day Mrs. Farrokhi called and set a date to come visit Sister Dear. Hasti reluctantly revealed that she thought they were coming to ask for her hand in marriage, and Khanomi started to plan. She ordered fruit from Mohsen Run. He shouldn't forget the grapefruit. She took Hasti to the Russian bear, Marusa, and from her boutique she bought Hasti a red and white polka-dot dress, a dark blue overdress, and a white silk headscarf. The scarf was hemmed all around with gold thread.

They went to see Farhad. Farhad gave them a Western magazine of hairstyle models, and Mother started to flip through it. The hair salon looked like a laboratory, and when Hasti ascended the hairdresser's chair, she felt that the salon was like an operating room. Farhad was wearing a purple velvet suit; he had tied a purple ribbon on his forehead; and his hair came to his shoulders. Was he a Native American? Was he a Gypsy? The female assistant held up the white lab coat, and Farhad put it on. Now he looked like a doctor. He examined Hasti's hair and said, "It's wild; it doesn't have any shine."

Mother suggested nigella-seed juice and chamomile tea.

"I don't agree. That's an old wives' tale."

On a revolving table, all kinds of scissors, combs, tweezers, electric razors, and many solutions and tools that Hasti didn't recognize—even though she was wearing her glasses—were all set out in an orderly manner. Farhad said, “Comb!” and the “nurse” put it in his hand. “Lotion, scissors, razor, hairbrush . . .” And the woman didn’t make a single mistake! When the “brushing” was over, Hasti took a breath in relief, although she didn’t recognize herself in the mirror.

Mrs. Farrokhi came. Alone. And the representatives of three generations—Grandmother, Mother, and Hasti—pursed their lips. Hasti removed her scarf.

“You’re wearing glasses, dear?” Mrs. Farrokhi commented.

Hasti helped Mrs. Farrokhi take off her overcoat. As Mrs. Farrokhi was shaking Grandmother’s hand, she said, “Farrokhi!” She kissed Eshrat. When she noticed the table in the middle of the living room, she asked, “Sister Dear, have you married the prime minster?” And Hasti thought of the chocolate cake that was waiting in the refrigerator.

After having tea with a simple, citrus-flavored cake, Mrs. Farrokhi started the discussion. “Sister Dear, why don’t you go back to your own home and your own life?”

“This is my home, too. I have taken refuge with Sister Touran so that she can make me a good person like she did Hasti.”

Mrs. Farrokhi looked Hasti up and down. “You look prettier with glasses, dear.”

Then she turned to Khanomi and said,“Ahmad Ganjur has called many times.” He had asked her to mediate and reconcile them. He was willing to sacrifice a sheep in front of his wife’s feet as soon as she returns home . . . to fire that maid with slanted eyes. “Get up, Sister Dear,” she ordered, “and call Bijan or Navidi to come pick you up.” Ahmad had begged her.

Khanomi thought and said, “You know, Sister Dear, Sister Touran has been a teacher for years. I’ve come here so that she can guide me. After the baby is born, I’ll go study. Sister Touran has done the same.”

“How can someone love her husband for twenty years and all of a sudden ruin it all? What are you planning to do? Ahmad is willing to register the house and everything in your name.”

“We have arrived in this world naked, and we will leave it naked. We’ll take with us only a nine-meter-long white shroud, which also decays.”

"What can I say? How can one leave all that luxury and those maids and servants and come . . . ? That slant-eyed maid will take everything for herself."

Khanomi said that she didn't want to hear anything more about Pasita and Ahmad.

Mrs. Farrokhi picked up a good-looking, fresh cucumber and started to peel it. The knife was dull. Touran Jan asked her how Salim was. Hasti knew better. She knew that he had finished Hujwiri's book and was now reading Attar's *Memorial of the Saints* for a second time and taking notes. Mrs. Farrokhi would only see Salim at dinnertime. When Mr. Farrokhi dressed up and left the house, Salim would calm her. Nevertheless, Afsar al-Moluk believed that having a bad husband is better than having no husband.

"Why didn't Salim come?" Touran Jan asked. "I've made jam for him with the bergamot that he gave us."

Afsar al-Moluk's eyes sparkled, and she said that she had heard so much about Mrs. Nourian's jams from Salim. "When I left home, Salim hadn't come back from the shop yet, and he is still waiting for Qodsi to come from Isfahan."

Khanomi gave a bitter smile, saying, "And perhaps Qodsi is waiting for Niku to come together."

"Perhaps."

Hasti thought that they were all wasting their time. She was Salim's wife. Though when the marriage vow could be done by the couple, the divorce vow could be, too.

When Mrs. Farrokhi left, Touran Jan said, "Khanomi, invite Dr. Bahari and his wife and children for tomorrow, late afternoon. Parviz will be here, too."

They were bringing Parviz late afternoons as Touran Jan had suggested. After he finished his dinner, Sister Touran would tell him a story. And one night, Hasti told him the story of the bitter orange and bergamot girl. Khanomi would put him to sleep. Navidi would carry him, place him on the back seat of the car, and cover him with a blanket. Khanomi would ask Navidi to drive slowly, lest her child fall from the back seat, and Navidi would reply that no such incident had ever happened.

Hasti asked, "Can't you invite them for the day after tomorrow?"

"Why the day after tomorrow?" Mother asked. "The chocolate cake will go bad."

"I'd like to draw a picture of Dr. Bahari. But that's okay. I'll draw it tomorrow."

Khanomi laughed and said, "Dr. Bahari is going to come and see how much better Sister Touran is feeling." She put her arms around Sister and kissed her.

At Hasti's request, Touran Jan woke her up very early in the morning. From the bed, Hasti watched Grandmother say only one short, morning prayer. She got up, sat, and saw that there was no sign of the picture album and the letters from her martyred son on Grandmother's prayer rug. She remembered that in recent days, Grandmother hadn't mentioned anything about Hasti's father.

Hasti drew several pictures. Profile, front view, three-quarter view. Mother and Grandmother liked the drawing that showed the doctor in a lab coat, with a stethoscope around his neck, and behind him, a sign on the wall: "Paying for the visit is optional." But the picture didn't look much like Dr. Bahari. Grandmother instructed her to draw his eyes smaller. Mother suggested that she make him smile. Hasti was altering the drawing when the telephone rang. She had forgotten about Salim's call, yet she flew toward the messenger of the beloved.

"Hello!"

"I've heard you look prettier with glasses. I'd like to see you with glasses. Would you like to have dinner together tonight?"

"We have guests in the afternoon. Dr. Bahari with his clan, Teimur Khan and his clan. You come, too; then we can leave together."

"Together we can go to the end of the world."

"So, you're coming?"

"Certainly. I want to have some of the bergamot orange jam, too."

"You mean my heart that you have taken away and haven't given back?"

19

Where had Touran Jan and Mother gone? Why didn't they leave her a note? "Is anyone home?" Hasti shouted.

She went to the bedroom and turned on the light. Grandmother's housedress was thrown on the bed. Her prayer rug was spread on the floor. Why hadn't she put her prayer rug away? Wouldn't Satan, as she always said, pray on it if it were left open? A blue plastic bucket was by the prayer rug. She sensed that someone, somewhere, was breathing. Whoever it was, the person was hiding in the wardrobe. The door of the wardrobe was locked. But they never locked *any* door. Water was dripping from below the wardrobe door onto the rug.

"Is someone in there?" Hasti shouted.

"Hasti, are you alone?" It was Morad's voice.

"Morad, what are you doing in there?"

Morad began sobbing. He hit his head on the wardrobe door and said loudly, "They killed him. He spun around three times. That most precious one . . ."

"Who did they kill? Why did they lock you in the wardrobe?"

"When I heard doors opening, I threw the latch on the wardrobe door myself. I was helpless. I couldn't close those eyes . . . Aagh!"

"Well, open the latch and come out."

"I can't. It's stuck."

Hasti put her back on the wardrobe door and pushed. "How about now?"

Morad was crying loudly and hitting his head on the wardrobe wall. "No, no." It was clear that they had been exposed. Who was killed? Morteza? Now Morad was whimpering.

"Pull yourself together, man!"

"How was it possible? I was helpless! Why him? They will bury him and throw dust on those eyes. He was the most insightful . . ."

Hasti went to find Teimur Khan. She asked him to bring whatever tools he had to try to take the hinges off the wardrobe door. She and Morad hadn't been able to open it, as much as they had tried. The latch was rusted inside the wardrobe. Morad had used all the curses he knew, shed all the tears he had, and let out all the screams he could. Hasti was fed up. She shouted at him to be quiet. *Why does he get involved in something that he can't bear*?

She learned that Morteza had his coat on his shoulders and a bag full of books on his arm. A policeman had asked him to stop, but he had started running instead, weaving through the traffic. The policeman had blown his whistle. Morteza had turned around, pulled out his gun, and shot. Other policemen had come—what a big crowd had gathered. And the bitch who lived on the first floor of the team's house was standing on Iranshahr Street with her hands on her hips, watching them . . . and the noble blood of Morteza . . . And that loser, the husband of the bitch, had tied Morteza's hands with a rope. As if Morteza had killed his father! Morad was a bystander . . . Nothing, nothing he could do.

When Teimur Khan came, he asked for a nutcracker and hit the end of the hinge. The hinge didn't move. He asked for machine oil, which they didn't have. Okay, how about warmed vegetable oil? When Hasti brought the oil, Morad was crying as Teimur Khan was urging, "Patience, patience, patience." Angered, she yelled at Morad, "Let us concentrate, man!"

After applying oil and using a file, a screwdriver, and a hammer, one hinge finally came off. When Morad's restlessness reached its maximum, Hasti shouted, "Stop this madness, Morad!"

Crying, Morad said, "I'm going to throw up any minute now."

Teimur Khan released the door of the wardrobe with one hinge, and Morad crawled out on his hands and knees. One hand over his mouth, he ran toward the toilet. Hasti peered at the bottom of the wardrobe where some water had accumulated.

Morad returned, muddy, soaked sleeves and trouser legs rolled up, dirty . . . with a big, bushy black beard. He was rolling on the floor, crying, speaking in broken fragments. "I was shouting, 'Pool draining!' The pool drainer hasn't had lunch today . . . That turnip soup had turned cold . . . I had gone to buy cigarettes and a magazine after lunch . . ."

"Is the water hot for a bath?" Teimur Khan asked Hasti.

It was hot.

"Is there herbal tea and rock candy in the house?"

There was.

"Is there an electric razor in the bathroom?"

There was.

"Shahin Khan's clothes?"

They were in the storage room.

And only then did Teimur Khan and Hasti think to ask, "Where have Grandmother and Mother gone?"

Morad said that they had gone to Salsabil Street, to Akhtar Iran's house, to seek shelter for him. They had gone by telephone taxi and they would return by the same taxi. Teimur Khan picked up Morad in one scoop. He didn't even say, "Ya Ali," and he took him to the shower. Hasti was standing there confused. Should she first go to the storage room in the courtyard and find some clothing for Morad? Or should she go make some herbal tea? Or should she dry the water on the bottom of the wardrobe? How could she wash and purify the wardrobe that had become so dirty and polluted? The family photo albums, Father's letters, and the issues of *Education and Socialization* that contained Hossein Nourian's poems were under the suitcase on the bottom of the wardrobe. Grandmother's treasures were all damp.

She remembered Salim's words: "Our friends' lives are in danger." He had also said that if Morad's location was unsafe, he could hide him in his house. She telephoned Salim, and the first problem was solved. She had known for a while that problems will not remain unsolved forever.

Salim answered the phone himself.

"Why are you calling? Didn't we just talk in the park after lunch today?"

"Do you remember Baktash M.?"

"Of course!"

"He's here. Can you come over?"

"Of course!"

Next, she had to clean the bottom of the wardrobe. A big sponge, the plastic bucket beside the prayer rug, and a pair of gloves were enough. But how could she dry Grandmother's only keepsakes from her son? She would take them to the storage room at the end of the courtyard and put them on the windowsill.

Hasti guessed that after Morteza was killed, Morad had wandered around the streets with the plastic bucket, pretending to be a pool drainer, and got himself to their house by that means. He had been delayed at one house by actually draining the water of their pool . . . He had eaten turnip soup that had turned cold . . . But where did he get the plastic bucket? He couldn't have bought it. The bucket was old.

She put the herbal tea and rock candy in Grandmother's kettle, filled it with water, and placed it on the stove. She was about to go find clothes for Morad when she heard Salim's car horn. She ran out. Salim was locking the door of his car when she reached him.

"I don't want you to get in trouble, too," she said. "Get back in the car, turn right, and then right again. I'll open the courtyard gate for you." She was still holding the keepsakes from Father.

She opened the gate and Salim drove in. When he heard the news, he was shocked. "That's terrible," he said. "It's horrible!"

"You go to the kitchen. I'll go to the storage room to find some clothes for Morad."

"Has Morad been shot too?

"No, dear, thankfully not."

A complete set of clothes was prepared . . . The keepsakes from Father were placed on the sill. But the herbal tea had boiled over and extinguished the flame, and Salim was cleaning the stove. Hasti took the clothes to the bathroom and knocked.

Morad had changed. His beard had been shaved. Shahin's clothes were too big on him. But the look that he cast on Hasti with his lips pressed together was one that Hasti knew she would never forget for as long as she lived. That look was saying, "Why didn't you wipe my tears?" All these years of love and friendship. Why didn't you caress my head and say, "Calm down, my friend"? Why did you shout at me? Why did you snap at me? Oh, Hasti, you haven't seen a friend's death . . . It hits like a bolt of lightning, like the collapse of a roof, like an earthquake. One is totally overwhelmed by powerlessness in the face of such a disaster. Why don't you understand?

Teimur Khan was putting the wardrobe door hinges back in place. Salim entered the bedroom carrying a tray holding four glasses of herbal tea from which the vapor of calmness was rising. Morad was sitting on his knees in front of Grandmother's prayer rug and putting his head on the prayer stone. Hasti was sitting on the bed, in shock. She had just realized the depth of the disaster reflected in Morad's traumatized look.

Salim put the tray on the bed next to Hasti's overdress and pulled up Hasti's scarf, which had slipped off the back of her head. He went to Morad and placed his hand on his shoulder. Morad rose. They embraced each other. Morad leaned his head on Salim's heart, and Salim's tears fell on Morad's hair.

Was Hasti's heart made of stone that her tears had lost their way? Once Salim had told her, "Sometimes I think that you are a merciless woman." But was she really merciless? Why didn't her tears come? Why was she jealous of their male friendship? Why was comprehending male friendship beyond her?

"Let's go to the living room," Salim said. "There's too much noise in here."

Hasti picked up the tray and followed them as they went, hand in hand, to the living room. Salim picked up one of the glasses and encouraged Morad to drink. "It is what it is, brother . . . ," he said. "What can you do?"

"They will throw dust on those eyes . . . ," Morad said, "those eyes that were the most insightful . . ."

Hasti put her head on the arm of the sofa and realized that she was about to cry, too. Salim raised Hasti's head. With a glass in his hand, he said, "Drink, Khanom."

Teimur Khan came to the living room and sat on the sofa. Morad said, "Thank you, brother."

"You're welcome. May Imam Ali be your protector."

From Salim's questions and Morad's answers, Hasti was reminded that the team house was on the third floor, Mrs. Vikki Shokouhi lived on the second floor, and the bitch and her husband lived on the first floor. She learned that Farzaneh had gone to the university gate, as agreed. Morteza had gone to get books from the office.

Suddenly, from within the crowd, Morad sees Mrs. Shokouhi's Peugeot on Shah Reza Avenue. Mrs. Shokouhi honks, and at her direction, Morad hops into the car and sits next to her. Vikki Shokouhi turns from Lalezar on to Manouchehri Street and stops at the gate of Jeanne d'Arc School. She gives Morad an old pullover of her husband's; she thinks his long coat will get in the way. Having given Morad the blue plastic bucket, she asks him, "Where is the nearest house where you can take refuge?"

Pretending that he was a pool drainer was Mrs. Shokouhi's idea . . . What a woman! She had promised that she would get Farzaneh out, too. She had witnessed the incident from beginning to end . . . She was hanging sheets to dry on the rooftop clothesline when she heard the voice of the first-floor woman, who yelled toward the police car, "There he is . . . That's one of them!" However much she shook the sheets, Morteza didn't notice it. How kind she was to them . . . She brought them cutlets, omelets, and soup. She gave them ice. She had promised that she would walk calmly to the university on the pretext of taking her husband's coat to the dry cleaners. Her husband had gone to the States to see their children. And she herself was a high school principal . . . She is from Shiraz and a Zoroastrian. What a brave woman! She kept her cool.

Morad turned to Teimur Khan and said, "Brother, can you bring the phone here?" Morad dialed a number and listened, and when it was answered, a smile formed on that sad face. He hung up and said, "It was Mrs. Shokouhi's voice. She has arrived home safely. Hasti, you call and say, 'I have just come from the States. Your husband said that your daughter should have arrived by now. Has she?'"

Morad swallowed and said, "Mrs. Shokouhi liked Farzaneh. She used to say, 'You remind me of my daughter. And Baktash reminds me of my son.' Morteza would ask, 'How about me?' She would say, 'You are not like anyone. You are one of a kind.'"

Morad put his hand on his forehead, and crying, said, “She knew who she was dealing with. That loftiest . . .” Still crying, he turned to Hasti and asked, “Are you going to call?”

Salim rose and said, “Absolutely not! I won’t allow Hasti Khanom to do any such thing. I’ll call myself. Phone number?”

Teimur Khan rose and said, “None of you. I will call.”

“This is a stupid thing for any of us to do,” Salim said. “Most likely the telephones in that building are being tapped. They might trace us.”

They heard the door open and close and then several footsteps. Grandmother and Mother entered the room. Khanomi was smiling. “How amusing all these things are,” she said. “You might think that you’re acting in a play.”

Yes, Akhtar Iran and her husband had agreed that Baktash could stay at their house for a few days. “He’s welcome here,” they said.

“Why did you call yourself Baktash?” Khanomi asked. “Of course, it’s a nice name. If my baby is a boy, I’ll call him Baktash.”

“Mrs. Ganjur,” Salim said, “you didn’t see anyone around the house, did you?”

“No.”

“I’ll take Morad to our house. Late at night.”

Khanomi turned to Teimur Khan and said, “Teimur Khan, go get your tambour and sing for us the song that Hasti likes.”

When Teimur Khan had left, Khanomi said, “Now we have to think of something for your dinner tonight. But Mr. Pakdel, you really looked ridiculous. Was your beard fake? Why did you pretend to be a pool drainer? I didn’t recognize you. When Sister Touran came and recognized you, I was surprised that she didn’t burst into laughter. After you threw yourself into Grandmother’s arms and both of you started crying, I understood that you had fled from your enemies. I have a revolver . . .”

Teimur Khan returned with his tambour.

“Before leaving,” Khanomi said, “I called Navidi and told him to bring Parviz for dinner. I’ll call him and ask him to get dinner for us on his way.”

“Someone must go to Akhtar Iran’s house,” Touran Jan said, “and tell her not to wait for Baktash tonight.”

"Don't worry!" Khanomi said. "I'll send Navidi. As soon as he brings Parviz, I'll ask him to go to Salsabil Street. Those alleys and small lanes will be good for his big stomach!"

Morad dialed and waited for a long time with the receiver in his hand. There was no answer. He looked calm.

Was it Mother who had calmed the atmosphere? Did Morad sense that Mother hadn't figured out much . . . and that it was better if she remained in the dark?

Teimur Khan caressed the tambour. He closed his eyes. He started playing softly and slowly . . .

"Excuse me, Teimur Khan," Salim said, "are you studying with Dervish Maftoun?"

Teimur Khan stopped playing and said, "You know Dervish Maftoun?"

"Yes, I've visited all the Sufi centers."

Teimur Khan twisted his mustache and said, "All Sufi centers won't do. A man of God must be loyal to only one master. Young man, do what your heart tells you to do."

Salim bit his lip and said nothing.

Teimur Khan resumed playing. Soon he began playing and singing Attar's poem:

When the bewildered man reaches this status,
    Confused, and his way lost,
Whatever God determines for his life,
    Shall be lost to him, even loss itself.
If they ask you whether you are drunk,
    You don't exist to say whether you are or not;
Whether you are in the circle or outside the circle;
    Whether you are at the side, or hidden, or visible;
Whether you are ephemeral, or eternal, or both;
    Whether you are neither here nor there.
He will say, "I don't know anything at all;
    I don't even know that I don't know.
I am in love, but with whom? That I don't know.
    I am neither a Muslim nor a pagan, so what am I?"

As Teimur Khan got up to leave, Mother said, "I won't let you go without having dinner. Tonight you played and sang in such a way that it made me feel anxious. What if Navidi has had an accident?"

After dinner, Parviz lay down on the sofa, put his head on Hasti's lap, and asked her to tell him the story she had told him the other night . . . the story of the girl that came out of a grapefruit.

"Tonight," Hasti said, "I will tell you the story of Babak Khorramdin."

"Like always," she began, "there was a time, once upon a time. I wasn't there myself. I have heard it from my professors. No one must leave the room and no one must enter. Parviz, you might not understand everything, but don't ask.

"Once upon a time, there was a man called Babak Khorramdin, and he had a horse called Qareqashqa. Babak was a head taller than other people of his time, and he had big dreams. He knew that people with power always exist and that most of them are cruel. Nevertheless, a person must start from somewhere and create courage out of fear, hope out of despair, bravery out of failure, freedom out of captivity. And if he scatters this seed . . ."

From Parviz's orderly breathing, Hasti knew that he had fallen asleep. "The rest for another night," she said. Scheherazade stopped talking.

"Oh, Scheherazade, the storyteller," Salim said, "finish the story tonight."

Morad said, "Hasti, continue."

At Mother's signal, Navidi came to pick up Parviz. "At the beginning of the story," he complained, "Hasti Khanom said, 'No one should leave . . . '"

"Mind your own business," Mother responded.

Hasti continued the story. "Babak wished that he could free his people who were captives of the oppressive caliph of Baghdad. The caliph's heart was filled with hatred for Babak, and he said to himself, 'I will do something so that no one in my territory will ever crave freedom.' They brought Babak to the court of the caliphate. The caliph was enraged and commanded that they cut him up limb by limb. First, they cut off one of his hands. Babak held his other hand under the flowing blood and rubbed it on his face so that he would not look yellow and frightened in front of the enemy. Babak was killed. His murderer, Josaq, got on Qareqashqa in Samarra. The horse galloped and galloped and carried him to Sabalan Mountain. It dropped Josaq against Sabalan Mountain so hard that he broke into pieces. But listen to what happened to Qareqashqa. He cried so much in sorrow for Babak that Atgoli Lake was filled with tears, and Qareqashqa drowned himself in his own tears. The people of Tabriz still gather round that lake on Friday nights in hopes that the horse might be resurrected with Babak riding upon it."

Morad sighed. "Morteza was Babak's brother."

Touran Jan recited:

My aged tree is a hundred thousand years old;
    My heart does not fear heat and cold.
This separation hit my soul with an ax,
    But the tree does not die as long as its roots last.

Teimur Khan caressed the tambour and said, "My dear Imam Ali, my dear."

20

Eshrat hung up the phone and started snapping her fingers in joy. Hasti and Touran Jan stared at her.

"If my belly hadn't grown so large," Eshrat said, "I would dance the Baba Karam right now . . ." It took her a long time to say what had happened. She kept pacing in the living room and rubbing her hands together.

Bijan Ganjur and Hayedeh's wedding didn't call for *that* much excitement. Early in the morning, Keshvar had left on the living room table three wedding cards, one each for Hasti, Touran Jan, and Eshrat Ganjur, along with several packets of large bills. There seemed to be more packets of currency than on previous occasions. Bijan had added a note: "Mother Eshi, my wedding without you would be no fun; forget the past. You have been kinder to me than my own mother. And Hasti is my sister." And there were Keshvar's tempting suggestions—that they could go together to the States, that they could even take Shahin and Grandmother, and a thousand other thats. As soon as Mother had stepped out of the house, the ring of the telephone had drawn her back to the living room. Hasti had thought that when Mother came back to the room without saying a proper good-bye, it was a way of avoiding giving a straight answer to Keshvar.

Mother finally revealed that Afsar al-Moluk had said, "Tomorrow night, Sister Dear and Mrs. Nourian, together with Hasti, are cordially invited—for dinner." She added that when the cleric tells them the best time for the wedding, they are going to bring bread and cheese, following tradition, and take their daughter-in-law. So what if Qodsi hasn't come from Isfahan. They can still come to ask for Hasti's hand in marriage and hold the wedding. If she, Afsar al-Moluk, is holding the engagement party in her own humble abode, it's not because of snobbery; it's because they have a guest who, she suspects, is afraid of the secret police. When they arrested Mosaddeq, Farrokhi went to Haj Aqa Givechi to hide, and tomorrow night the guest will go somewhere that Salim has found for him. The guest wants to see Hasti before he leaves, and Salim has agreed. Salim will pick them up at 5:00 p.m. sharp. Touran Jan prostrated herself and kissed the floor, and of course she burned some incense.

At the Farrokhi house, Mr. Farrokhi and Afsar al-Moluk came out to welcome them, and Mr. Farrokhi opened the car door for them. Afsar al-Moluk hugged Hasti tightly and said, "My beautiful daughter-in-law!" Mr. Farrokhi, with salt-and-pepper hair, was taller than Salim, but his eyes were exactly like Salim's. He was wearing a dark blue suit and a blue tie. And he didn't have a beard. Facing Touran Jan, he put his hand on his chest and said, "It's a great honor. I am privileged to meet you!" Then he turned to Mother Eshi, bowed, and said, "At your service!" Then he said to Hasti, "My lovely daughter-in-law."

Salim left the women and his father to discuss the marriage portion, rings, wedding dress, and tea, fruit, and sweets, and he sat next to Hasti at the end of the living room.

"Morad is going to Professor Mani's house tonight," he whispered. "He doesn't know it's our engagement night . . . He's more honest than I am. He revealed to me the secret of his years-long love for you. I didn't want to break his heart . . ."

Hasti was busy arranging the peeled orange on a plate and listening to Salim. "Only my mother knows that we have married ourselves, and her religious guide . . ."

Eshrat's voice didn't let Hasti hear the end of Salim's sentence. "Where are you going to buy them an apartment, Mr. Farrokhi?

"Mother," Hasti said, "Mr. Salim Farrokhi and I are the ones who are getting married! I will stay right here, with Mrs. Farrokhi."

"Why? Isn't it easier to take care of a small apartment?"

"Mrs. Farrokhi," Hasti said, "has given me the dearest person she has in this world, so I will stay with her and not separate her from her son."

Afsar al-Moluk's eyes sparkled, and she looked proudly at her husband. "Well done!" Mr. Farrokhi said. "There's no doubt that you have found a wise daughter-in-law."

Afsar al-Moluk walked the whole length of the room, sat beside Hasti, and put Hasti's and Salim's hands together. She was so happy that she didn't know what to say. Everyone clapped and congratulated them and then had some sweets, even Nanny and Taji, who were standing with crossed arms just outside the living room door.

When Morad saw Hasti, he said, "Your mother has misled you, too? Why have you made yourself up like this? Headscarf . . . glasses . . ."

Hasti didn't reply. She was about to walk toward the middle platform in the fountain room when Morad said, "Oh, I forgot to tell you to take off your shoes at the door. You are now in the holy land of Salim's residence! I've forgotten the Arabic phrase for it."

Hasti looked at the rows of shoes and slippers at the door of the fountain room, including a pair of light brown women's slippers.

"Morad," she asked, "what are all these shoes and slippers for?"

Morad laughed and said, "The women's slippers for you, your ladyship, and the leather shoes for me. They were bought just yesterday. Each of the others has a purpose: one for going to the bathroom, one for the serving pantry, one for dining room, one for the street, and you can continue . . . Again, I've forgotten the Arabic phrase for it!"

Hasti took off her shoes and put on the women's slippers. Was seeing her the reason that Morad was this happy and cheerful?

"You'd better practice from this moment," Morad said. "You cannot walk on Salim's felt carpet in the shoes you use to go to the bathroom."

Hasti sat on the reddish-brown felt carpet decorated with designs of flowers and bushes in different colors. One could travel to the heavens at the sight of all those colors! The fountains in the middle of the trapezoid-shaped blue tile pool were on. The clear water was kissing the edge of the pool until it passed through a narrow channel over blue tiles toward the garden where it kissed the feet of the trees, too. The platforms on the other two sides of the pool were decorated with different kinds of felt carpets with beige and brown backgrounds, with flowers and without. On the right-hand platform, Hasti noticed bedding leaning against the wall. *Perhaps Morad slept right there.*

Hasti was thinking how strong the hands must have been that had pounded the felt carpets and how much they must have asked God for help . . . And later, when the time came to do the drawing and designs, they must have been relieved. On one of the bookcase shelves, many cassettes were carefully arranged. A tape recorder—with speakers at the four corners of the platform—lay beside the platform on which Hasti and Morad were sitting face-to-face.

"He has all the cassettes of Ali Shariati," Morad said.

Hasti's gaze left the tape recorder and focused on Morad. He had gained some weight. He was wearing jade green trousers and a gray knitted wool turtleneck. He was no longer the Morad that had rolled up his trousers and shouted, "Pool draining!"

"What are you thinking about?" Morad asked. "Salim?" He had a cunning look. "If he didn't rely so much on religion, he would make a good husband for you." He swallowed and asked, "Do you want me to encourage him to marry you?"

Hasti didn't say anything until Morad lit a cigarette. Then Hasti asked, "On that dark night in our house, didn't you say to Teimur Khan, 'Cigarettes won't heal the pain of losing a friend'?"

Morad took a puff from his cigarette and said, "Most of his books are on religion: *Mafatih al-Jinan* (Keys to the Heavens), *Hilyat al-Muttaqin* (Adornment of the Pious), *Zad al-Ma'ad* (Provisions for the Hereafter). If you marry him, you'll have to read all of them."

Hasti defended her absent beloved. "Salim is a mystic who is, to some extent, religious."

Morad laughed. "Religious, ascetic, and Muslim. And you want to make a mystic in love out of him."

"Did you want to see me for this kind of talk?"

Salim entered with a big tray. He put the tray on the floor and took a bigger tray from someone out of their view. He put that one down too and said, "You can go."

The enticing aroma of nut-laced rice reminded Hasti of Fatemeh Sabzevari, who had told her, "I wish you always go to weddings. I wish you always eat good food, like meat and fava-bean rice . . ."

Salim took off his shoes and put on slippers. Morad rose, jumped down from the platform, and helped Salim spread the cloth for dinner. "Three old, close friends!" Salim said.

During dinner, Salim explained that Morad was the architect of the fountain and the channel, and that Morad is an engineer who is also an artist. Even the lighting of the fountain room was Morad's work. It was Morad's idea that the source of the light not be visible.

When the dinner cloth was removed, Morad lit a cigarette.

Hasti turned to Morad and said, "Mrs. Farrokhi said that you want to talk to me."

"You are the only one who can help us. No one will be suspicious of you, especially with this look that you have created for yourself—making yourself the very model of a bourgeois young lady. Of course, they haven't come to arrest Salim yet, and I hope they won't. But they have arrested Aqa Sheikh Sa'id, Fazlollah and his mother, and several others from the shantytown. Luckily, they all know Salim by the name of Puria."

"Have they arrested Haji Ma'sum, too?" Hasti asked.

"No."

"So, what should I do?

Her heart trembled; she had promised not to be Morad's puppet anymore. Get married like all the other women of her day and have children. She had promised Salim that she would have nothing to do with politics. But she saw that it was politics that wouldn't let go of her. *If only everyone, whether teacher, or doctor, or engineer, would leave politics to politicians. But wasn't it those same politicians who were causing so much harm*?

"Do you want me to go to the shantytown again?" she asked.

"No. Don't set foot there! It's a hornet's nest. Do me a favor and go to the house of Morteza and Farzaneh and me. Ring the second-floor doorbell two times in a row and say on the intercom that you want to talk to Mrs. Vikki Shokouhi. If your mother goes with you, that would be even better. A bourgeois young lady and a pregnant woman cannot be gunmen. Your mother is brave, and she likes adventure. It's better if she pretends that she is Mrs. Shokouhi's cousin and says that she has come from Shiraz to Tehran to give birth."

"Do you think it's the right thing to do?" Hasti asked Salim.

"If your mother goes with you, I don't think it will be dangerous."

"What if Mrs. Shokouhi won't let us in?" Hasti asked.

"That's impossible," Morad responded. "She's a smart and kind woman. She'll take you in. She'll bring juice and sweets, too. If she thinks that the snitch on the first floor is suspicious, she'll know how to fool her."

Morad lit a cigarette and talked about Mrs. Shokouhi, saying that when she retired, the schoolgirls went on strike and called out, "Long live Mrs. Shokouhi!" They wanted to pour into the streets; they didn't let the new principal enter until Mrs. Shokouhi convinced them to. "Mrs. Shokouhi had said that a great person had said, 'When you get old, hand over the work to the young . . . ' One of the girls had asked, 'Who was that great person?' Mrs. Shokouhi had said, 'It was me, dear!' The girls laughed and started going back to their classes. She kissed the new principal in front of the girls."

Why was Morad dragging it on so long? Why wouldn't he stop talking about Mrs. Shokouhi?

"One day the father of one of the teachers had died. Mrs. Shokouhi got a phone call about it in the morning. When that teacher comes back from her class . . . while she is drinking tea, Mrs. Shokouhi says, 'Early this morning, the father of one of the teachers has sort of died.' That teacher asks, 'It wasn't my father, was it? Because my father has had a stroke.' Mrs. Shokouhi says, 'It's better to die than be a weak invalid and impose on one's family until the end of one's life.' That teacher asks, 'So, it is my father?' Mrs. Shokouhi says, 'You said it yourself, dear.' And she takes the teacher whose father has died and her friends in her own car to that teacher's house."

Hasti was bored. "So, what message should I give Mrs. Shokouhi?"

"Ask her, 'That day when Morteza was killed and you gave the blue plastic bucket to Baktash . . . ' You know that my alias is Baktash."

He was silent and put a cigarette between his lips.

"So, you were saying?"

"Ask if their roommate, a young girl named Farzaneh, has come home or not and if she has been arrested or not."

"Isn't it better if I call first and make an appointment?"

Salim answered Hasti saying that for sure the telephone in that house has been tapped.

Morad gave the address and said, "Whatever news you get from Mrs. Shokouhi, call Salim and somehow inform him. If she is not arrested, say she has gone on a trip."

"What if Mrs. Shokouhi has no news?"

"Then there will be more work for you. Pack a small bag with pajamas, a towel, and soap and begin with Qasr Prison. Say it is for Farzaneh Azizi . . ."

Salim didn't let Morad finish his sentence. "I don't agree at all."

Morad was smoking one cigarette after another. "I don't know why I want to involve Hasti in the struggle."

Hasti smiled and said, "Do you remember that Simin used to say in class that one can fight to change the current situation by means of writing and painting? The same way that it can be done with words and songs?"

"It's possible to raise awareness in intellectuals, but how about the masses? They neither see, nor read, nor hear, and even if they do see, read, and hear, they don't understand. For now, the only way to fight is with arms."

"Why is Farzaneh's arrest that important?"

"She knows so much. Fortunately, you know very little."

"I know nothing."

Hasti turned to Salim in order to end this conversation about Farzaneh.

"Are you reading *Zad al-Ma'ad*, *Mafatih al-Jinan*, and *Hilyat al-Muttaqin*? Grandmother recites the *Jawshan Kabir* (Great Armor) prayer and the *Wa In Yakad* (The Verse of Evil Eye) from memory. *Ayat al-Kursi* (The Throne Verse) is the prayer she recites every night. She won't fall asleep until she recites it for the house and its inhabitants."

Morad laughed and said, "Touran Khanom has written in calligraphy on stiff paper, 'This house and its furniture and its inhabitants belong to Imam Musa Kazem,' and she's posted the sign on the wall above the house entrance."

"Absolute faith," Salim said, "is a gift that God has bestowed on humans." Then he turned to Hasti and said, "I have read these books. Why do you ask?"

"No reason. I was just wondering."

"I've collected these books so that I can choose the most beautiful prayers and translate them. A committee in England is seeking the most beautiful prayers of all religions and plans to publish them together."

The ashtray in front of Morad was full of cigarette butts and extinguished matches. Hasti picked up the ashtray, rose, and asked Salim, "Where should I empty this?"

When Hasti returned, Salim said, "Tonight is as holy as Laylat al-Qadr, the night when the first verses of the Quran were revealed to the Prophet. It's the last night that Morad is here. I've prepared for an unforgettable night."

"It's late," Hasti said. "I have to go."

"You can fill my empty place tonight," Morad said. "Sleep in Mrs. Farrokhi's bedroom. When the guests leave, Mr. Farrokhi leaves, too." Then he turned to Salim and said, "Brother, I've caused you so much trouble. And in the end, I made you throw a party as a cover-up." He swallowed and wailed like someone whose mother has just died.

"Salim, marry Hasti and free her from me."

Hasti was about to throw herself into Morad's arms, but it was Salim who put his arms around Morad's neck. Both men were crying, and Hasti was thinking, *The tears of one of them are from excitement and the tears of the other one are from letting go. And the root of both is sacrifice.*

Salim went toward the tape recorder and pressed a button. The sound of music rose from all corners of the fountain room and echoed under the ceiling. Salim explained that the instrument was a tambour, that Darvish Maftoun was playing, and that soon he would sing. Morad leaned his head on the wall of the platform and said, "Salim, I haven't heard this cassette before."

"Hush!" Hasti said. And she let herself be carried away by the music.

"Is it the Last Supper that you prepared?" Morad asked.

"Who knows?" Salim said. "Maybe we'll have many more dinners together."

The sound of the tambour reached a peak. The sound of weeping came from the cassette. It seemed like several people were crying, and the tambour, perhaps because of their crying, grew faster and faster and louder and louder. Suddenly, the sound dropped, and Hasti sensed that she was falling from the mountain peak down into the valley. What a feeling! The tambour was quiet. It sounded like someone weeping from the pain of separation.

Hasti was listening to the music and had become enthralled and mesmerized. Darvish Maftoun was singing a poem by Hafez:

Any direction I traveled, my bewilderment grew.
Alas, this desert, this endless path.

Salim had closed his eyes and was swaying from side to side, and Hasti was picturing the audience present at the Sufi invocation session. She thought that perhaps they had been in a state similar to the one Salim was in now. Then she imagined Darvish Maftoun: long hair . . . and she was imagining that he too had closed his eyes. Perhaps he was swaying . . . He was playing the tambour with the side of his palm and capturing the hearts of the audience just like he had captured Hasti's heart. Suddenly she felt that she was swaying, too. From left to right, to left to right.

The song rose to a peak, and an enchanted and intoxicated voice shouted in Arabic, "*Ya dalil al-mutahayyarin zidni tahayyuran*!" (Oh, proof of those who are bewildered, increase my bewilderment!) The song and the music seemed to be coming out of the fountains of the trapezoid-shaped pool, which were also reaching their peak, and Hasti's heart was soaring, too. Sounds from the speakers assaulted her, engulfed her, and traversed through her. Darvish Maftoun was singing, "Sitting intoxicated and bewildered on the ground." They were not sitting on the ground. They were sitting on felt carpets covered with images and designs. But it seemed like the three of them *were* intoxicated and bewildered, and Hasti was thinking, *If only we were on the ground, on the earth, over the earth, and of the earth.*

The song and the music were tearing at Hasti's heart. A voice at the last minute shouted in Arabic, "*Liman al-mulk al-yawm*?" (To whom does kingship belong on this day?) Hasti sensed that Salim had shouted this or even she herself, although she didn't know what it meant. The first section of the cassette was over, and Hasti awakened from a dream in an unknown world. They were talking about bewilderment, but she had found herself again in a safe land. She felt that the fountain room had recorded the song and the music under its roof.

But Morad's voice shattered it all. "So what?"

Salim rose and took several volumes from his bookcase. Slips of white paper marked pages of the books. He opened one and said, "The sixth of seven stages of love in Attar's *The Conference of the Birds* is the valley of bewilderment. Forouzanfar has written . . ." And now from the cassette player, there came the sound of a single lute.

Salim read, "The path one must traverse is long and arduous, but, despite all the bewilderment, one must take it because the Beloved is essential. In this valley, the lot of the seeker is pain and remorse. With every breath, a thorn pierces his side, and sighs and regret follow. His sigh is accompanied by pain and suffering. Neither is his day, a day, nor his night, a night. Disappointment and devastation go together . . . In this stage or valley, the seeker is beyond negating and proving. Even the one who is not worthy of the state of annihilation, his existence is apparent, as he is gone, and in the state of bewilderment, no trace or news of him can be found. And he cannot control himself at all. According to Attar, in this valley, heart and home are invisible. People have no perception of them except in their imagination. Complaining here is saying thanks, blasphemy is faith, and faith is blasphemy."

"It doesn't matter," Morad said, "if Forouzanfar or Attar has written it; if a person gets to this state, he's on the verge of madness."

"I didn't understand," Hasti said. "It's over my head."

"The spiritual system of mysticism," Salim said, "cannot be comprehended through words. Spiritual and mental experiences cannot be linked. We imagine that we can transfer concepts . . ."

Morad completed Salim's sentence, "But we don't."

"The realm of mysticism," Salim said, "is the realm of personal states and . . ."

Morad lit a cigarette and asked, "So why do they speak and write?"

"Because some emotional states are awakened by words and sentences. The important thing is the state, not the words—states that cannot be juxtaposed on words."

"In any case," Hasti said, "read!"

Salim picked up another book and said, "This is Attar of Nishapur's *Muslim Saints and Mystics.* He has described Dawud Tai's condition in the valley of bewilderment this way: 'Which face and hair was it that has not been shed on the earth? And which eye is it that has not shed tears on the earth? A great pain from this sense fell upon him (Dawud Tai) and he lost patience. He was bewildered, and in that state, he went to Imam Abu Hanifa's teaching session. The imam saw him in that state and asked, "What has happened?" He told what had happened. "My heart has turned cold to the world. Something has emerged inside me that I don't know how to access. I cannot find what it means in any book, and it does not appear in any religious decree."'"

He took a third book and said, "This is Hujwiri's *Revelation of the Veiled.*" He read, "When the intention cannot be expressed in words and a person has no solution for it, other than perpetual bewilderment, what other choice is left for him?"

"These words," Hasti said, "whirl one around in the air and let go, so that one falls somewhere. Perhaps then a spark will light in one's mind."

"It is similar to a car's spark plug," Salim said. "When you ignite it, it turns the car on." He continued reading: "Whoever is closer, his bewilderment is greater and so is his humility. The mystic has no doubt in his existence, and the mind has no chance to grasp his quality . . ."

Morad extinguished his cigarette in the ashtray full of half-smoked cigarettes and said, "I almost understood. When the seeker gets as close as possible to God, he falls into bewilderment. But I doubt the basic premise."

"You understood well," Salim said. "Bewilderment is the final stage of science, and the highest level of knowing. The Sufi, in his seeking, reaches a place where there is only a single hair-width between himself and God, and that is where he gets lost. If this veil that is as thin as a single hair is removed, he will reach God—that is, he will reach the collective whole."

"The result of such words," Morad said, "is to bring people down as low as a felt carpet. Like the felt carpet under our feet. No matter how much you beat it, you will only manage to remove the dirt and dust. You will not be able to save humans from being bewildered. Instead, you will encourage them to be even more bewildered."

"So," Salim said, "in your opinion, what is the path to deliverance?"

"Getting out from under the subjugation of the West." Morad sighed and continued, "And this is the essence of the words of our ancestors. This corner of the world has always been an island of bewilderment."

Hasti closed her eyes and remembered Mr. Crossley's words. "Did you say 'island of bewilderment'?" she asked. "The Island of Bewilderment does exist."

After Morad left, Salim and Hasti, the present Adam and Eve, looked at each other with wonder. They were not in La-la Land. Nor were they on the Island of Bewilderment. They were in the fountain room in Salim's house. The fountains of the pool at their peak, the sound of the tambour echoing . . .

"I plucked the bergamot orange," Salim said. "It didn't say, 'Ouch!' God smiles on us, angels come dancing to welcome us, and we receive our share from eternity."

Hasti was dreaming. She is walking on a road, neither the beginning nor the end of which can be seen. The road is level, and along its shoulders, there are cypress trees. She asks the trees, "Whose beloved are you? Are you the grandchildren of the cypress of Kashmar?"

She arrives at Atgoli Lake. The people waiting are transparent and she herself is so transparent that it is as though light is flowing through her body. Suddenly, the water in the lake parts. The horse Qareqashqa comes out of the water. It stands beside Hasti and says, "Get on. You will arrive." Hasti says, "It's too late!" Qareqashqa says, "It's never too late. Don't be afraid."

A large golden key is in Hasti's hand. Qareqashqa says, "Now come out. This key fits all locks." Hasti is in flight like a bird in the cloudless sky. She sees a large *X* that has been drawn on the allegorical face of the younger brother, Sorrow. "What has been crossed out?" she asks. Qareqashqa responds, "Sorrow left and tears left. May you and I survive!" Now, it's Teimur Khan who is singing. "So the answer to the question is love?" she asks. But it's Qareqashqa who answers. "One dimension of it is love."

Hasti flies and flies and goes beyond the earth's atmosphere. She is completely weightless. She sees the earth going around the sun. She praises the sun and says, "I adore you. Everything of mine is from you." A voice pledges to the sun, "To the sun and its light." She asks herself, "Who has said this to whom, 'I adore you?'" She remembers that it was Touran Jan who had said that to Morad . . . The sound of monotonous drumming is coming. Teimur Khan is pounding on the hinges of the wardrobe in which Morad is stuck.

Hasti opened her eyes. She saw Salim sitting in his pajamas near the boiling samovar. He was mixing something with a spoon in a big mug. He added milk to the mug and mixed again. Mug in hand, he came to Hasti's side and said, "Drink, sweetheart. It's egg yolk, milk, and honey."

Hasti said, "The first hello is for you!"

Salim kissed her and said, "I was watching you. You were talking in your sleep."

"What was I saying? From now on, let's not hide anything from each other."

"You were saying. 'Salim has called me the bitter orange girl.' You were saying, 'I'm imprisoned in the seven-locked room. Captive in the nine-layered cage.'"

"What else was I saying?"

"Not all your words were clear. You were talking about a golden key. You were saying, 'So it is the key to the secret of freedom and deliverance. For everyone.' Who were you addressing?"

"The horse Qareqashqa."

"You recited a poem, too, 'When in chains, they shall break the chains.'"

"It was for you. From now on, every poem I compose will be for you. You are my poem, the only source of my joy in this world."

"You're not in pain, are you?"

"My cure is with you!"

"May my soul suffer all your pain!"

Appendix ~ *Glossary*

APPENDIX

Characters and Persons Mentioned*

Characters (in alphabetical order)

Abedi: Brigadier General's new orderly.
A'lam al-Dowleh: An acquaintance of Professor Mani and a Qajar descendant.
Abd al-Reza: A member of the Farrokhi household.
Ajami: Male servant at Tehran University's Faculty of Fine Arts.
Akhtar Iran: One of Grandmother's cousins.
Amir Shahin: Son of Akhtar Iran and Karim Aqa.
Aqa Sheikh Sa'id: Dissident religious leader.
Arzani: One of Simin's neighbors.
Asadollah Khan: Brigadier General's orderly.
Baktash, Aqa Bak: Fellow activist of Farhad Dorafshan.
Bijan: Ahmad Ganjur's son, recently returned from prolonged studies in the United States.
Brigadier General: Neighbor and friend of Grandmother.
Cheragh Maznian: Colleague of Farhad Dorafshan.
Dr. Bahari: Medical doctor and friend of the Ganjur family.
Dr. Ovanesian: Grandmother's Armenian-Iranian medical doctor.
Dr. Sa'edi: Medical doctor visited by Eshrat Ganjur.
Dr. Zandi: Member of the Council on Artistic Creation.
Emad: Adult son of Brigadier General.
Fakhri: Hasti's secretary.
Farhad: Highly sought-after male hairdresser and beautician.
Farhad Dorafshan, Hadi: A friend of Salim.
Farideh: Mohsen's neighbor's daughter.

* Real person

Faridi: A Tudeh Party member and former student of Simin.

Farkhondeh Dorafshan: Former classmate of Hasti and sister of Farhad and Firuz Dorafshan.

Farrokh A'zam: A female friend of Mrs. Farrokhi.

Farzaneh: Fellow activist of Morad.

Fatemeh Sabzevari: Shantytown resident.

Fazlollah: Fatemeh Sabzevari's teenaged son.

Firuz Dorafshan: Brother of Farhad Dorafshan.

Firuzeh: Acquaintance of Mother Eshi and customer of Farhad, the beautician.

Ganjur, Ahmad Ganjur: Hasti's stepfather, garage owner, and employee of American advisers at the Ministry of Education.

Gholami Ali: Possible writer of Queen Farah's speech.

Grandmother, Touran Nourian, Madam: Hasti's paternal grandmother, who raised Hasti and her brother; retired teacher.

Hayedeh: Potential wife for Bijan.

Haj Aqa Givechi: Friend of Salim's father.

Haji Ma'sumeh, Haji Ma'sum: Simin's hermaphrodite servant.

Hasti Nourian: Twenty-six-year-old, single, college-educated woman employed by the Ministry of Art and Culture.

Helen Hitti: Young adult daughter of Mr. Hitti.

Hossein Ali: Shantytown resident.

Hossein Nourian: Hasti and Shahin's long-deceased father.

Ja'far Aqa: Mechanic in Ahmad Ganjur's garage.

Jalal Al-e Ahmad* (1923–1969): Novelist, short-story writer, translator, ethnographer, social critic, and political activist whose best-known work is *Gharbzadegi* (Weststruckness); Simin Daneshvar's husband, recently deceased at the time of this story.

Jamshid Khan: One of Simin's neighbors.

Jeffery, Ja'far: Haji Ma'sumeh's brother.

Karim Aqa: Akhtar Iran's husband.

Keshvar: Dealer in jewelry and friend of the Ganjur family.

La'l Beigom, La'l Banu: Pakistani wife of Sir Edward.

Leila*: Leila Riyahi, Simin's niece and adopted daughter.

Leopard Abbas: Shantytown resident.

Lieutenant General Tondar: Nephew of Brigadier General.

Majid: Possible writer of Queen Farah's speech.

Marami: A Tehran University employee.

Mardan Khan, Murray, Mr. Tavassoli: Friend and colleague of Ahmad Ganjur.

Marshal Naneh: Servant of one of Simin's neighbors.

Maryam: Teimur Khan's wife, mother of Mohsen, and Grandmother's former student.

Marzieh: Alias of Farkhondeh Dorafshan.

Mehrmah: One of Grandmother's cousins, now deceased.

Mina: Mrs. Farrokhi's daughter-in-law.

Mo'addel al-Saltaneh: Hayedeh's father; member of the former aristocracy.

Mohammad Aqa: A neighborhood grocer.

Mohsen, Mohsen Run, Run: Teimur Khan's son; fruit and vegetable peddler.

Morad, Morad Pakdel: Hasti's former classmate and close male friend, with whom Hasti is in love.

Morteza: Fellow activist of Farhad Dorafshan.

Mother Eshi, Eshrat: Hasti's mother.

Mr. Crossley: American archeologist and friend of Mr. Hitti.

Mr. Hitti: American serving as a teaching expert at Iran's Ministry of Education.

Mrs. Farrokhi: Wealthy friend of Mother Eshi and mother of Salim.

Mrs. Hakimi: Seller of homemade sweets.

Mrs. Hitti: American wife of Mr. Hitti.

Mrs. Mani: Professor Mani's wife, originally from Czechoslovakia.

Naneh Agha: Servant in the Ganjur household.

Naneh Fatemeh: Simin's new servant.

Nanny: Female servant in the Farrokhi household.

Navidi: Driver in the Ganjur household.

Ne'mat: Fellow activist of Farhad Dorafshan.

Niku: Qodsi's husband's niece and potential wife for Salim.

Parviz: Elementary school–age son of Ahmad Ganjur and Mother Eshi.

Pasita: Filipina maid in the Ganjur household.

Peggy: Mardan Khan's American wife.

Professor Isa: Member of the Council on Artistic Creation.

Professor Mani: One of Hasti's former professors, now retired.

Puria: Fellow activist of Farhad Dorafshan.

Qodsi: Salim's sister.

Qoli: Afghan cook in the Ganjur household.

Raya: Masseuse at Mother Eshi's spa.

Sahand: Turkish-speaking shantytown resident.

Salim, Salim Farrokhi: Young man recently returned from studies in England, a suitor of Hasti.

Shahin: Hasti's college-aged brother.

Simin, Simin Daneshvar* (1921–2012): The author appearing as herself in the novel; university professor, writer, and, in this story, mentor and friend of Hasti.

Sir Edward: British expat working in an Iranian government office.

Sohrab: Member of the Council on Artistic Creation.

Taji: Female servant in the Farrokhi household.

Taqi Khan: Male servant in the Ganjur household.

Teimur Khan: Neighbor and tenant of Grandmother, cycle repairman, musician.

Vikki Shokouhi: Neighbor of Baktash, Farzaneh, and Morteza; retired school principal.

Za'far: King of the genies, character in a play.

Zebarjad: Villager, character in a play.

Other Persons Mentioned (in alphabetical order)

Abolfazl, Ali Abbas*: 'Abbas ibn 'Ali (647–80): Half-brother of Imam Hossein, known as a great warrior and revered by Shi'a Muslims for his loyalty to Imam Hossein.

Abu Hanifa* (699–767): Muslim theologian of Persian ethnicity who established the Hanafi school of Sunni jurisprudence, which is still widely followed in India, Pakistan, Central Asia, Turkey, and Arab countries.

Ahmad Shah* (1898–1930): Ruler of Iran from 1909 to 1925, when he was deposed; last ruling member of the Qajar dynasty.

Ali Akbar*: 'Ali al-Akbar ibn al-Hossein (662–80): Son of Imam Hossein, killed at the age of eighteen at the Battle of Karbala.

Ali Asghar*: Abdullah 'Ali al-Asghar ibn al-Hossein: Infant son of Imam Hossein, killed at the Battle of Karbala in AD 680.

Amir Arsalan: Title character of a popular folk tale that has been told on the stage and screen, as well as in print and orally.

Anushirvan*: Khosrow I (ca. 512–79): Sasanian King of Kings, AD 531–579, featured prominently in Ferdowsi's *Shahnameh* (The Book of Kings).

Ardeshir Zahedi* (1928–): Foreign minister of Iran (1966–71) and ambassador to the United States from 1960 to 1962 and again from 1973 to 1979; married for a time to Shahnaz Pahlavi.

Aref*: 'Aref 'Arefkia (1941–): Singer of popular music who introduced Western melodies and romantic lyrics to Iranian music, a pop idol of the 1960s and 1970s.

Attar*: Farid al-Din 'Attar (ca. 1145–1221): Mystic poet whose best-known work is the long, allegorical poem *The Conference of the Birds*.

Ayub Khan*: Mohammad Ayub Khan (1907–74): President of Pakistan from 1958 to 1969.

Azod al-Dowleh Daylami* (936–83): Emir at the height of the Buyid dynasty, ruling over most of what is now Iran and Iraq.

Babak Khorramdin* (ca. 795–838): Azeri-Iranian revolutionary leader who fought the Abbasid Caliphate for local control.

Bhagavan: One of the names of Buddha, meaning "the blessed one"; commonly used as a title.

Bijan Mofid* (1935–84): Playwright, songwriter, and stage director whose best-known work is the musical play *Shahr-e Qesseh* (Story Town).

Bozorgmehr*: Sixth-century minister and military commander under Anushirvan and other Sasanian kings, featured prominently in Ferdowsi's *Shahnameh* (The Book of Kings).

Chief Nassiri*: Ne'matollah Nassiri (1911–79): Head of SAVAK, Iran's secret police, from 1965 to 1978.

Darvish Maftoun: Sufi musician.

Dawud Tai*: Abu Sulaiman Dawud ibn Nusair al-Tai (d. ca. 777): Islamic scholar and Sufi mystic, student of Abu Hanifa.

Denis Papin* (1647–1713): French physicist, mathematician, and inventor.

Dowlatshah*: Mohammad 'Ali Mirza Dowlatshah (1789–1821): Qajar prince, patron of the arts, and poet.

Dr. Farahvashi*: Bahram Farahvashi (1925–92): Iranian linguist and scholar of the ancient languages and cultures of Iran.

Dr. Shariati, Ali Shariati* (1933–77): French-educated sociologist of religion and Islamist philosopher, prolific writer, and popular speaker who promoted a return to true, revolutionary Shi'ism.

Entezami*: 'Ezzatolah Entezami (1924–2018): Award-winning stage and screen actor.

Fath Ali Shah* (1772–1834): Second shah of the Qajar dynasty who ruled from 1797 to 1834.

Ferdowsi*: Abul-Qasem Ferdowsi Tusi (ca. 935–1019): Revered poet and author of *Shahnameh* (The Book of Kings), the national epic of Greater Iran (with over fifty thousand verses, the longest versified prose work ever written).

Foruzanfar*: Badi'ozzaman Foruzanfar (1904–70): Persian literary scholar and critic, distinguished professor of literature at Tehran University.

Hafez*: Shams al-Din Mohammad Hafez (ca. 1325–90): Lyric poet of Shiraz, Iran, whose works continue to be read, recited, and much loved throughout the Persian-speaking world and beyond.

Hamid Khan, Hamid Enayat* (1932–82): Political scientist, translator, and professor at Tehran University; in this story, Shahin's favorite professor.

Her Holiness Fatemeh*: Fatimah bint Mohammad (ca. 605–32): Daughter of the Prophet Mohammad, wife of Imam 'Ali, and mother of Imam Hassan, Imam Hossein, and Her Holiness Zeinab; known for her piety.

Her Holiness Zeinab*: Zeinab bint 'Ali (626–82): Sister of Imam Hossein who protected the ailing Zayn al-Abedin at the Battle of Karbala and afterward.

Hujwiri*: Shaykh 'Ali al-Hujwiri (ca. 1009–72): Mystic, theologian, and preacher credited with contributing to the spread of Islam in South Asia; author of *Revelation of the Veiled.*

Imam Ali*: 'Ali ibn Abi Taleb (ca. 600–661): Cousin and son-in-law of the Prophet Mohammad, fourth caliph (656–61), considered by Shi'a Muslims to be the rightful successor to Mohammad and the first imam.

Imam Hossein*: Hossein ibn 'Ali ibn Abi Taleb (626–80): Also known as Aba Abdollah al-Hossein, grandson of the Prophet Mohammad and son of Imam Ali; martyred at the Battle of Karbala; third Shi'a imam.

Imam Musa Kazem*: Musa ibn Ja'far al-Kazem (745–99): Seventh Shi'a imam.

Imam Reza*: 'Ali ibn Musa al-Reza (766–818): Descendant of the Prophet Mohammad, eighth imam recognized by Shi'a Muslims; buried in Mashhad, Iran.

Iraj Mirza* (1874–1926): Major poet and satirist of the late Qajar period.

Jabir ibn Abdullah Ansari* (ca. 607–97): Prominent companion of the Prophet Mohammad.

Josaq: Reputed to be the executioner of Babak Khorramdin.

Kasravi*: Ahmad Kasravi (1890–1947): Prominent Iranian intellectual, historian, and nationalist, known for his anticlerical views.

Khalil Maleki* (1901–69): Leading Iranian intellectual, Marxist theoretician, socialist, and political activist affiliated with the National Front, which supported Mosaddeq.

Khayyam*: 'Omar Khayyam (1048–1131): Mathematician, astronomer, philosopher, and poet from Nishapur, Iran, made famous in the West by Edward FitzGerald's 1859 translation of a selection of his quatrains, *The Rubaiyat of Omar Khayyam.*

Le Corbusier*: Charles-Edouard Jeanneret (1887–1965): Swiss-French architect, a pioneer of modern architecture.

Maharishi Yogi* (1918–2008): Indian guru who developed transcendental meditation.

Marrat Qeis: Character in stories surrounding Imam 'Ali.

Mehdi Akhavan-Sales* (1929–90): Poet and a pioneer of free verse or new poetry in Iran.

Modabber*: Mohammad Modabber (1890–1966): Painter who produced canvases illustrating religious stories and traditions meant to be used to accompany narrations.

Mohtasham Kashani* (1500–1588): Poet best known for his Shi'a religious poetry, especially poems about Imam Hossein's martyrdom.

Monajjemi: Engineer and friend of Jalal Al-e Ahmad.

Mosaddeq*, Mohammad Mosaddeq (1882–1967): Prime minister of Iran from 1951 to 1953 who supported the nationalize Iranian oil, was in conflict with Mohammad Reza Shah, and was ousted in a 1953 coup d'etat instigated by the British MI6 and joined by the American CIA.

Moshfeq Kazemi*: Seyyed Morteza Moshfeq Kazemi (1904–78): Poet, playwright, and novelist; author of *Tehran makhuf* (Horrible Tehran) (1922), considered Iran's first social novel.

Mr. Shoghal: A poet.

Naser al-Din Shah* (1831–96): Ruler of Iran from 1848 to 1896, when he was assassinated.

Nima*: Nima Yushij (1897–1960): Considered the father of modern Iranian poetry.

Obeyd Zakani* (ca. 1319–70): Poet and satirist whose most famous work is *Mouse and Cat*, a political satire; known for his bawdy writings.

Omid*: M. Omid, pen name of Mehdi Akhavan-Sales.

Parvin E'tesami* (1907–41): Well-known female poet who composed in the classic style.

Pourdavoud*: Ebrahim Pourdavoud (1886–1958): Scholar of ancient languages and history and translator of the Avesta into modern Persian.

Qamar Vazir: Character in the tale of Amir Arsalan.

Qollar Aqasi*: Hossein Qollar Aqasi (1902–66): Painter who specialized in vivid and colorful canvas murals illustrating religious traditions and stories from *Shahnameh*.

Queen Fanar: Mispronunciation of Queen Farah.

Queen Farah*: Farah Pahlavi (1938–): Third wife and now widow of Mohammad Reza Shah; mother of the crown prince and three other children; supporter of charitable causes and the arts.

Raj Kapoor* (1924–88): Indian film actor, producer, and director.

Rostam, Rostam Farrokhzad*: Seventh-century military leader and key figure in Ferdowsi's *Shahnameh* (The Book of Kings).

Rumi*: Jalal al-Din Mohammad Rumi (1207–73): Sufi mystic and poet, originally from Balkh (now part of Afghanistan), settled in Konya (now part of Turkey), whose works continue to be read worldwide; now counted as the best-selling poet in the United States, due largely to the work of poet Coleman Barks.

Sa'di*: Sa'di Shirazi (1213–91): World-renowned poet and prose writer of Shiraz, Iran, whose best-known works are *Bustan* (The Orchard) and *Golestan* (The Rose Garden).

Sa'edi*: Gholam-Hossein Sa'edi (1936–85): Playwright, novelist, and short-story writer.

Sabiheh*: Khalil Maleki's wife.

Safi Ali Shah* (1835–99): Founder of the Ne'matollahi Safi 'Alishah Sufi Order.

Sakkaki*: Yusuf ibn 'Abi Bakr Sakkaki (1160–1229): Muslim scholar known for his work on language and rhetoric.

Sathya Sai Baba* (1926–2011): Indian guru with millions of followers and hundreds of Sathya Sai Centers throughout the world.

Sediqeh Dowlatabadi* (1882–1961): Early Iranian feminist, promoter of modern education for women, publisher, and supporter of Reza Shah's reforms on behalf of women; in the late 1930s, director of the Women's Center, a Pahlavi-endorsed organization.

Sha'ban Ja'fari* (1921–2006): Practitioner of Iranian traditional wrestling, supporter of Mohammad Reza Shah; considered instrumental in the overthrow of Mosaddeq.

Shahab al-Din Sohravardi* (1154–91): Philosopher and founder of the Illuminationist school of philosophy; executed for heresy.

Shahnaz Pahlavi* (1940–): Daughter of Mohammad Reza Shah and his first wife, Princess Fawzia Fuad of Egypt.

Shahriar*: Mohammad-Hossein Shahriar (1906–88): Azeri-Iranian poet who wrote in both Azeri and Persian.

Shams*: Shams Pahlavi (1917–96): Eldest sister of Mohammad Reza Shah.

Shamshiri*: Mohammad Hassan Shamshiri (1897–1961): Known as Haj Hassan Shamshiri; bazaar merchant, restaurateur, philanthropist, and political activist who provided financial support for Mosaddeq's cause.

Shams Vazir: Character in the tale of Amir Arsalan.

Sheikh San'an: Character in a folk story first made famous by the twelfth-century poet Attar.

Sohrab Sepehri* (1928–80): Prominent modernist poet and painter.

Takhti*: Gholamreza Takhti (1930–68): Popular wrestler who won three Olympic medals (1952, 1956, 1960); known and loved as well for his chivalrous behavior.

Taqizadeh*: Seyyed Hassan Taqizadeh (1878–1970): Iranian statesman, constitutionalist, and scholar.

Vali*: Ja'far Vali (1933–2016): Theater director, playwright, and actor.

Zayn al-Abedin*: 'Ali ibn Hossein Zayn al-'Abedin (659–713): Known as Imam Sajjad, son of Imam Hossein; fourth Shi'a imam.

Zoroaster*: Zarathustra (ca. 628–551 BCE): Iranian prophet regarded as the founder of Zoroastrianism, the pre-Islamic religion of Iran that influenced the development of Judaism, Christianity, and Islam and that is still practiced in a few communities in Iran, India, and elsewhere.

Glossary

Agha: A term of respect for a woman.

Ahmadabad: A village north of Tehran in which Mohammad Mosaddeq owned property, to which he was exiled after being ousted as prime minister of Iran in 1953, and where he is buried.

Aqa: A term of respect for a man.

Aqdasieh: A district of northeastern Tehran.

Ardabil: City and province in northwestern Iran.

Ashkanian Dynasty: Parthian dynasty, which ruled Iran in the third century BCE.

Ashura: The tenth day of the month of Muharram, the day that Imam Hossein was martyred in the battle of Karbala, marked by Shi'a Muslims with mourning rituals, marches, public lamentation, and, by some, self-flagellation.

Atgoli Lake: A small lake in Ardabil Province.

Baba Karam: A lively and playful dance that mostly mimics stereotypical behavior of the lower class.

Banu: A term of respect for a woman, used after a first name; also means "lady."

Beigom: A term of respect for a woman, used after a first name.

Birjand: City in Khorasan, now capital of South Khorasan Province.

The Bitter Orange and Bergamot Orange Girl: Popular Persian tale in which a girl comes out of a fruit that is a cross between a bitter orange and a bergamot orange and marries the prince.

Celebration of 2,500 Years of Monarchy: A series of lavish festivities put on by Mohammad Reza Shah Pahlavi in October 1971 in Persepolis, outside Shiraz, to celebrate the founding of the Persian Empire by the Achaemenid, Cyrus the Great, in 550 BCE; attended by royalty and heads of state from all over the world.

chador: A semicircular piece of cloth worn by women over their clothes to cover their hair and body, leaving the face uncovered; usually held closed under the chin.

Chehel Sotoun: A pavilion built by Shah Abbas II in the seventeenth century as part of his palace complex in Isfahan.

***chelo kebab*:** Grilled meat served over rice; a popular Iranian dish.

***The Conference of the Birds*:** Long, allegorical poem by Farid al-Din Attar, the twelfth-century poet of Nishapur, Iran.

Cypress of Kashmar: A mythical cypress tree celebrated in Ferdowsi's epic poem *Shahnameh*; sacred to Zoroastrians.

Darband: Formerly a village in the foothills north of Tehran from which a popular hiking trail to the peak of Tochal begins; now incorporated into Tehran.

Daryakenar Town: A beach town on the Caspian Sea in Mazandaran Province.

Fada'i Guerillas: Organization of Iranian People's Fada'i Guerillas, a Marxist-Leninist organization that preached and practiced armed struggle against the Pahlavi regime in the 1970s.

Ferdowsi Square: Major intersection and traffic circle in central Tehran, characterized by a statue of Abul-Qasem Ferdowsi, author of Iran's national epic poem, *Shahnameh*.

flower-bird china: China dishes decorated with flower and bird images, based on traditional Chinese flower-bird painting.

Franklin Publishing Organization: Franklin Book Program, a US-based non-profit organization dedicated to promoting and supporting book publishing in developing countries. Active from 1952 to 1977, it fostered both the translation of books into local languages and the publishing of original works.

Gavmish Goli: Hot springs located in Sare'in, Ardabil Province.

Gonabad: City in Khorasan Province (now Razavi Khorasan Province) in eastern Iran.

Haji: A title of respect, originally for someone who has made the pilgrimage to Mecca; used before a name.

Hosseinieh Ershad: A modernist Islamic, religious institution in northern Tehran that hosted numerous speakers, most notably Dr. Ali Shariati, whose lectures in the late 1960s and early 1970s attracted thousands.

Hurufism: Sufi doctrine that associates numbers with letters of the alphabet as a means to mystical knowledge; popular in western Iran in the fourteenth and fifteen centuries.

Imam Reza Shrine: A complex of buildings in Mashhad, Iran, which contains the mausoleum of Imam Reza, the eighth Shi'a imam.

Imamzadeh Saleh Shrine: A mosque in Tajrish Square, Shemiran, Tehran, in which the tomb of Imamzadeh Saleh, son of the seventh Shi'a imam, is located.

Isfahan: Capital of Isfahan Province in central Iran; capital of Iran in the sixteenth and seventeenth centuries under the Safavids.

Isfahani block-print cotton: Cotton fabric hand printed using carved wooden blocks, a handicraft long associated with the Iranian city of Isfahan.

Jan: A term of endearment added most often to first names.

Karbala: City in Iraq, sixty miles southwest of Baghdad, site of the shrine of Imam Hossein; also refers to the site outside Karbala where a battle was fought in AD 680 between the army of the Umayyad caliph Yazid and Imam Hossein and a small group of followers, resulting in the death of Imam Hossein, a number of other descendants of the Prophet Mohammad, and other leading Shi'a Muslims.

Kerman: Capital of Kerman Province in southeastern Iran.

Kermanshah: Capital of Kermanshah Province in western Iran.

Khan: A title of respect for a man, used after a first name.

Khanom: A title of respect for a woman, used after a first name or before a last name.

Khorasan: A province in northeastern Iran.

Kourosh Store: Large, fancy department store in Tehran, now the name of a shopping mall.

Mashhad: City in northeastern Iran and major Shi'a pilgrimage site, where Imam Reza, the eighth Shi'a imam, is buried.

***Memorial of the Saints*:** A book-length collection of biographies of thirty-nine Muslim saints by Farid al-Din Attar.

Meshkin Shahr: City in Ardabil Province.

Miandoab: City in West Azerbaijan Province.

Naneh: Term for an older woman, usually used before the first name.

National Front: An umbrella organization founded by Mohammad Mosaddeq in 1949 in support of democratic principles; outlawed after the 1953 ouster of Mosaddeq but later partially reorganized under several guises.

Nishapur: City in Khorasan Province (now Razavi Khorasan Province) in eastern Iran, home of Omar Khayyam and Farid al-Din Attar.

Pachenar: A district in southern Tehran.

Pan Iranist: Adherent of a political ideology that advocates reunification of Iranian peoples and/or member of the Pan Iranist Party, a nationalist anti-communist party that sometimes supported Mosaddeq's National Front.

Pishdadian Dynasty: Legendary pre-Iranian dynasty mentioned in *Shahnameh*, the epic tenth-century poem by Abul-Qasem Ferdowsi.

Plan Organization: Government agency responsible for economic and development planning and budgeting; later called the Plan and Budget Organization.

Point Four Program: US program of technical assistance and economic aid to underdeveloped countries initiated in 1949 by President Truman and active in the early 1950s; came to focus primarily on agriculture, public health, and education.

***Provisions for the Hereafter*:** Book by Ibn al-Qayyem (1292–1350) about the Prophet Mohammad's life and the early period of Islam.

Qajar: Dynasty ruling Iran from 1796 to 1925.

Qasemabad: Name of several villages in northern Iran.

Qolhak: A neighborhood in northern Tehran.

***Revelation of the Veiled*:** Eleventh-century book on Sufism by Shaykh ʿAli al-Hujwiri.

Saʿi Park: A large park in northern Tehran.

Sabalan Mountain: The third highest mountain in Iran, located near Ardabil.

Sabzevar: City in Khorasan Province (now Razavi Khorasan Province) in eastern Iran.

Sahand Mountain: One of the highest mountains in Iranian Azerbaijan.

Sareʿin: City in Ardabil Province in northwestern Iran, known for its hot springs.

SAVAK: Iran's secret police and intelligence service from 1957 to 1979, the official name of which was Sāzemān-e Ettelāʾāt va Amniyat-e Keshvar (Intelligence and Security Organization of the Country).

Saveh: A small city sixty miles southwest of Tehran.

Seyyed: A title indicating descent from the Prophet, used before a first name.

Shah Abdol Azim Shrine: Shrine and mausoleum complex located in Ray, an ancient city just south of Tehran now incorporated into Tehran; popular pilgrimage site for Shiʿa Muslims.

Shemiran: A neighborhood in northern Tehran, situated at the foot of the Alborz Mountains; fresh air and pleasant climate helped to make it a choice home for well-to-do Iranians.

Shiraz: City in southwestern Iran and capital of Fars Province; major center of poetry, literature, and the arts in the thirteenth century and capital of Iran in the late eighteenth century.

16 Azar: Annual commemoration of December 7, 1953, when three students were killed by Tehran police as they were protesting the resumption of ties with Great Britain subsequent to the coup d'etat that ousted Mosaddeq and reinstated Mohammad Reza Shah in power.

Sizdah Bedar: Thirteenth day of the year in the Iranian calendar, marking the end of the New Year holiday. Typically spent picnicking in nature.

Sufism: The mystical dimension of Islam, the adherents of which attempt through various practices to come closer to and to experience God.

Tabriz: City in western Iran, capital of East Azerbaijan.

Tajrish: A neighborhood in northern Tehran.

toman: Ten rials (the official unit of currency); worth about fourteen cents in the 1970s.

Torbat: Partial name of more than one city in Khorasan Province.

Tudeh Party: Communist Party of Iran, founded in 1941; at first opposed to Mosaddeq, the party later played a part in mobilizing support for him in 1952 and 1953 and suffered mass arrests and the execution of many top leaders in the aftermath of the 1953 coup d'etat that ousted Mosaddeq.

Valiabad: Street and neighborhood in central Tehran.

***The Wonders of Creation*:** Book by Zakariya al-Qazwini (1203–83), geographer and natural historian.

***Ya Ali*:** A phrase invoking Imam Ali's help; commonly used at the start of a strenuous task.

Simin Daneshvar was born in Shiraz, Iran, in 1921, and educated at a bilingual English-Persian school. She completed her education at Tehran University, from which she received a PhD in 1949. She is the author of three published novels and five collections of short stories. Her first novel, *Savushun*, published in 1969, soon became the all-time best-selling novel in Iran and has been translated into English and a dozen other languages. Many of her short stories have also been translated into English. In addition to writing, Daneshvar taught art history at Tehran University from 1959 to 1979. While many writers of her generation left Iran after the establishment of the Islamic Republic, Daneshvar continued to live, write, and publish in Tehran until her death in 2012.

Patricia J. Higgins studied anthropology at the University of California, Berkeley, from which she received a BA, MA, and PhD. She conducted eighteen months of dissertation research in Tehran and later spent ten months as a Fulbright Lecturer at Tehran University. Her work has been published in several journals, as chapters in edited volumes, and as contributions to encyclopedias. She is the co-translator of Ali Shabani's *The Thousand Families* (2018) and Iraj Pezeshkzad's *Hafez in Love* (2021), and a co-editor of *The Routledge Handbook of Persian Literary Translation* (2022). At SUNY Plattsburgh, she rose through the ranks as a faculty member to university distinguished service professor of anthropology and served as associate vice president and then interim provost and vice president for academic affairs.

Pouneh Shabani-Jadidi is an instructional professor of Persian at the University of Chicago. She received a PhD in linguistics from the University of Ottawa in 2012 and a PhD in applied linguistics with a focus on translation from Tehran Azad University in 2004. She has published books, book chapters, and articles on linguistics as well as translation and Persian language pedagogy. She is also the co-translator of Ali Shabani's *The Thousand Families* (2018), Iraj Pezeshkzad's *Hafez in Love* (2021), and Sohrab Sepehri's *The Eight Books: A Complete English Translation* (2021). She is the editor of The *Routledge Handbook of Second Language Acquisition and Pedagogy of Persian* (2020) and co-editor of *The Oxford Handbook of Persian Linguistics* (2018) and *The Routledge Handbook of Persian Literary Translation* (2022).